Praise for *Someo...*

'Mara . . . lays out the pie... diabolical wit, some good suspense and an unexpected note of sentimentality.' *New York Times*

'This heart-thumpingly tense thriller may give you nightmares.' *Sun*

'Someone is getting inside your house . . . It's a chilling premise, and Andrea Mara executes it brilliantly. This one is an absolute page turner!' **Shari Lapena**

'A gripping story, beautifully told. Andrea Mara is masterful.' **Patricia Cornwell**

'Does for bathtubs what *Psycho* did for showers. A thriller honed to a fine point, sharp and keen and piercing; it's darkly comic, too, and uncommonly observant. This is suspense you can feel good about.' **A. J. Finn**

'This is Andrea Mara at her heart-stopping best. *Someone in the Attic* is a dark, creepy, twisty thriller full of clever misdirection that would make Hitchcock proud, but it's also a moving and thought-provoking tale of regret and letting go of the past. A brilliant book.' **Claire Douglas**

'Fast-paced and chilling, you won't want to sleep alone after reading it.' *Woman & Home*

'A super-creepy, addictive thriller, which layers mystery upon mystery. Not one to read late at night!' *Good Housekeeping*

Andrea Mara is a No.1 *Sunday Times, Irish Times* and Kindle best-selling author. Her books have sold more than 500,000 copies worldwide, and four of them have been shortlisted for Irish Crime Novel of the Year. She is also the author of *No One Saw a Thing*, which was a Richard and Judy Book Club Pick, sold more than 100,000 copies in thirteen weeks, and was No.1 in the UK, Irish and Kindle charts. She lives in Dublin, Ireland, with her husband and three children. You can find Andrea on Twitter/X @AndreaMaraBooks and Instagram @andreamaraauthor

Also by Andrea Mara

The Other Side of the Wall
One Click
The Sleeper Lies
All Her Fault
Hide and Seek
No One Saw a Thing

SOMEONE IN THE ATTIC

Andrea Mara

PENGUIN BOOKS

TRANSWORLD PUBLISHERS

Penguin Random House, One Embassy Gardens,
8 Viaduct Gardens, London SW11 7BW
www.penguin.co.uk

Transworld is part of the Penguin Random House group of companies
whose addresses can be found at global.penguinrandomhouse.com

First published in Great Britain in 2024 by Bantam
an imprint of Transworld Publishers
Penguin paperback edition published 2025

A CIP catalogue record for this book
is available from the British Library.

ISBN
9781804990797

Typeset in ITC Giovanni by Jouve (UK), Milton Keynes.
Printed and bound in Great Britain by Clays Ltd, Elcograf S.p.A.

The authorized representative in the EEA is Penguin Random House Ireland,
Morrison Chambers, 32 Nassau Street, Dublin D02 YH68.

Penguin Random House is committed to a sustainable future
for our business, our readers and our planet. This book is made
from Forest Stewardship Council® certified paper.

For Dee, with love

1

THREE MINUTES BEFORE IT happens, Anya takes a deep swallow of white wine, sets the glass on the shelf, and slides further down in the bath. The water is at her chin, tepid now and cooling fast. She should have closed the bathroom door. Chris is always moaning about steam and mildew, and he *always* leaves the door open. Now, she does so too, on autopilot. And to stop him nagging. But Chris isn't here tonight. He's thousands of miles away in LA and Anya is blissfully alone. He won't know if she closes the bathroom door. She's just not sure she has the energy to get out and do it. Three large glasses of wine and a long day at the office will do that.

That's the other nice thing about Chris being away. Nobody judging her for opening a bottle of wine on a Wednesday night. Or finishing a bottle of wine on a Wednesday night. It sits on the tiled surface at the end of the bath, coated in condensation. Just half a glass left, she notices now. She's had more than she thought.

Beside the wine, her phone buzzes to life, startling her. She leans forward to see who it is but doesn't pick up. Chris. It's nine in Dublin, so lunchtime in LA. He'll be slipping away from his colleagues, calling to say how much he misses her. That he's got a big surprise when he comes home. It's a ring. She knows this because she saw his search history. She shakes her head, wet strands grazing her shoulders. The buzzing stops and she picks up the phone to text.

> Sorry, can't talk. Up to my eyes, working late. Going to be same right the way through week so no point trying to get me on phone, see you Friday when you're back x

Chris is going to have to go.

He is very good-looking and very nice. He's also bland and boring and far too particular about the mind-numbing minutiae of everyday life. Like bathroom condensation.

And sooner or later, he'll figure out who she's really seeing when she says she's working late. His sister, not as innocent as Chris, is definitely starting to smell a rat. Though she couldn't know who it is, Anya reckons. She smiles when she thinks about him; Chris's opposite in every way. Yeah, Chris is going to have to go. Although, technically, since it's his house, *she* is going to have to go.

A faint rustle from above draws her attention to the ceiling. The mice are still there. *Dammit*. So much for Chris and his humane traps. They should have got a cat. Chris said they couldn't because of the dog. *Get rid of the dog, then*, she wanted to say. Dogs are no use with mice. As though reading her thoughts, Ziggy barks downstairs. He's been barking all evening, and Anya has a sneaking suspicion the dog-walker didn't come today while she was at work. Anyway, that's Chris's problem. If he wants to pay someone fifteen euro an hour to walk his dog – or not walk his dog – so be it.

Two minutes before it happens, Anya slides up and takes another sip of her Pinot Grigio, then one more before slipping back down. Her eyelids droop and she decides against finishing the wine. She has an early start tomorrow, then drinks with Eleanor on Friday night. God, why had she agreed to that? Eleanor will talk non-stop about her kids, just as she always does. There is literally no reason to stay in touch, but Eleanor is like a tenacious puppy. It's as if she sees Anya as a project. Or perhaps it's the duty of time. Thirty years of friendship isn't easy to shake. Anya knows. She's tried. Good god, she's tried.

And now Julia is back in Ireland too. Saint Julia. Although – Anya smiles to herself – she's also Divorcée Julia. That the marriage between her friend and her ex-boyfriend didn't work out has given her no end of quiet pleasure over the last decade. And now Eleanor is so excited to have the three of them reunited. As though they're some kind of friend group. As though it hasn't been five years since Anya last saw Julia in person. As though they didn't have the mother of all arguments when they last spoke by phone. As though Anya has forgiven Julia for almost destroying her business. Why did she say yes to this? Because Eleanor is like glue, really annoying glue, and doesn't take no for an answer.

Julia will be insufferable, of course. And she'll somehow drop it into conversation that she sold her business for a seven-figure sum. Anya will nod and murmur congratulations and she will not admit she already read this in the *Sunday Independent*. Julia's never been the same since the night— Anya stops the thought before it takes off. She doesn't like to think about the night Donna died. It's not guilt, because why would it be guilt when it wasn't her fault? But Julia – though she's never said as much – thinks it's Anya's fault.

One minute before it happens, Anya takes a final sip of wine, and slips further down in the bath. A moth flits around the light. Steam melts from the mirror as the room temperature cools. Through the open door, the landing is in darkness. The only sound is the whirr of the inadequate fan and the rustle of mice in the attic.

Louder, she thinks, half asleep, than the kind of noise you'd expect from tiny mice.

Now a creak, one she barely registers.

Another creak.

And a scratch. But her ears are below the water and the sound is muffled.

Another creak. One she hears in her mind retrospectively, when the attic hatch begins to move.

The attic hatch is opening. Swinging loose now, like a slow pendulum.

Opening all by itself.

Not all by itself.

There is someone in the attic. Chris is thousands of miles away in LA and there is nobody else in the house.

Except there is.

There's someone in the attic.

Her breath is stuck inside her throat and her body is immobile under water as a dark shape emerges through the opening and drops to the landing floor. A figure all in black. A face behind a mask. There is someone in the attic. And they're—

Thirty seconds later, it's over. Anya is dead.

2

THE VIDEO IS SHORT and noisy and easy to ignore, because really, it's just another video – like all the other short and noisy videos on her daughter's phone. Which is why, at first, Julia pays no attention at all. Julia is busy. Julia, if she's honest, is also quite stressed. And while she's used to admitting the former, she never admits the latter. Firms don't hire people like Julia to do the job she does if she's likely to get stressed over something as ordinary as ordering pizza and moving continent. But right now, she's at home with her kids, where no one can see her, and she lets out a tiny sigh as Isla asks her once again to look at the video. This Friday night, the video is the least of her worries.

Her worries, in order of priority, are as follows:

1. Settle the kids in their new schools.
2. Settle the kids in their new home.
3. Encourage the kids to accept the new babysitter.
4. Figure out why the garbage disposal isn't working.
5. Let the pizza guy in through the outer gate.
6. Find cash to tip the pizza guy.
7. Make the incessant buzzing stop (see 5 and 6 above).
8. Stay calm when Isla shouts and Luca cries, and hope the eggshells she's treading on eventually become more solid.

'Isla, have you seen my purse?'

'No, but, Mom, you seriously need to look at this video.' Isla is sitting at the island, holding up her phone.

'What I *need* is to let the pizza guy in, but first I have to find cash for a tip.'

'How will you tip him?' Luca asks, without lifting his eyes from his Nintendo Switch. 'They don't even have dollar bills here.' Contempt drips from every word. *What kind of dumbass country doesn't have dollar bills?*

He has a point, though. Do people tip with coins? It's twenty years since Julia last ordered takeout in Ireland. Does she *have* any coins? In the four weeks since they moved here, she's been paying by tapping with her phone in what feels like an almost cashless society. A long way from her days fumbling for change to take the 46A to college.

'Can't you use the money you left for the babysitter?' Luca nods towards a drawer in the island.

'That's for Pauline, in case she needs cash when I'm at work. And she's not a babysitter, she's a housekeeper.' This is for Isla's benefit; Isla, who, at thirteen, is disgusted that Julia would hire someone to keep an eye on them while she's at work. Isla is, of course, disgusted at everything right now – the move from San Diego, the new house, her new life here, the life she left behind, life in general, her dad, and, mostly, Julia. Evil witch Julia who ruined everything. *If only she knew the truth.*

'Isn't she babysitting tonight when you meet your friend?' Luca asks.

Touché.

'That's just for this evening because your dad has plans too.'

Luca shrugs and goes back to his game.

'What friend are you meeting?' Isla asks.

'Eleanor. My old school pal.'

'Oh. I didn't know you were still friends with her. Is she the one you had that big fight with?'

'Nope, that was Anya. She's joining us too.' *Unfortunately.* 'Eleanor and I are good.' Are they though? Julia wonders. They've seen one another a handful of times in the last ten years and they seem to have less and less in common. The sooner she can get tonight over with, the better. She takes a five-euro note from the drawer and picks up the receiver to buzz the pizza guy through the main gate to the complex.

'OK, Mom, as soon as you get the pizza, you *have* to look at this video.' Isla holds up her phone again. 'It's so weird. I can't figure out how they did it, but it looks like it was filmed inside our house.'

'What is it – the letting agent's website?'

'No, I told you already!' Impatient. Snappy. 'It's TikTok.'

Julia bites her lip. *Hello, eggshells.*

'OK, let me grab the pizza, then I'm all yours.'

Julia sighs again, louder now, as she walks through the long hallway towards the front door, her heels echoing on the white-and-gold marble floor. Low evening sun filters through the glass panels on either side of the door but she reaches for the Louis Poulsen standing lamp anyway, switching it on with a touch. Light fills the hall and she glances at her reflection in the mirror above the narrow table – the sunburst mirror she'd had shipped all the way from San Diego in a bid to make this mausoleum of a house feel like home. She smooths down her hair. Still in the suit she'd worn to work that day, she looks distinctly over-dressed for takeout pizza. She doesn't even like takeout pizza, but going for drinks with Eleanor and Anya on an empty stomach is a bad idea. Especially Anya. Still Queen Bee, all these years later.

Eleanor means well, but why she invited Anya is beyond Julia. Of course, maybe she's mellowed since they last spoke. Or maybe she's the same narcissist she always was. Julia knows where she'd lay her money.

Now, she stands in the doorway, looking at the orange-and-purple sky. The longer, brighter evenings are just one of the many things about which her kids complain – *why can't it be dark already like it is at home?* They'll get used to it, and eventually they'll love that August evenings are longer and brighter. But for now, everything is other and different and strange, and they still can't understand why she uprooted them, and she still can't tell them the truth. So she's bribing them with pizza. Pizza that is, of course, at least according to her kids, inferior to pizza back home. There are a lot of things Julia misses about San Diego, but the pizza that tastes the same here as it does there is not one of them. She misses her yoga sessions with Milena, the instructor who became her friend. She misses the moms from the school: never true confidantes – and she couldn't tell them the truth about Isla – but good company all the same. She misses the smell of the ocean. Brentwood, she realizes as she sniffs the air now, smells of nothing, not even cut grass. She misses the San Diego weather. *God*, she misses the weather. She shakes herself. No time for wallowing.

The delivery guy is making his way past the townhouses, and on to the wider, greener part of Brentwood, the luxury gated community in which she and Isla and Luca live in a spacious, double-fronted house with a sweeping gravel driveway and somewhat pretentious white columns holding up the porch. Having grown up in a mid-century, slightly faded home with tricky electrics and creaky floors, adult Julia has always favoured new-build houses. But there's something about Brentwood, for all its high-end newness. Something soulless. And at this time of the evening, it's almost eerie.

The delivery driver pulls in outside their gate and hops out with the pizzas. Feeling guilty about how long the driveway is, Julia walks down to meet him.

'Number twenty-six Brentwood? Two margheritas?'

'That's me. Now if only they were drinks instead of pizzas,' Julia says, reaching to take the boxes and passing the man the tip.

'Cheers.' He pockets the money without responding to her quip. Her kids are right, she's not funny. 'Never been in here before,' he says. 'Those huge gates and all that security is something else. It's bigger than I thought – you wouldn't think we were in the middle of Foxrock.'

'Yes. It used to be a convent, but they razed the whole thing to the ground about ten years ago.'

'So, from one gated community to another, eh,' he says, as he turns to walk away.

And nodding quiet agreement, Julia goes back up the driveway with her two margheritas-not-margaritas.

'OK, can I please have your attention?' Isla says, on Julia's return. The kitchen is shadowy now, losing light more quickly than the rest of the house, despite the huge glass wall that looks out on the back garden. As Julia moves towards the island, something brushes against her ankle and she jumps, forgetting yet again about Basil, Luca's new pet rabbit. The result of more bribes, Basil is cute and fluffy and exactly what you'd want from a rabbit, except for the whole unexpected-encounters-with-small-live-animal moments that Julia is still getting used to.

Isla holds up her phone. On-screen, Julia can see what looks like a plain white ceiling and an attic hatch. As she watches, the hatch drops open, and a black-clad figure lowers himself through the opening, then drops the last few feet to the floor. The person's face is covered by a balaclava, with two barely visible slits for eyes, and Julia finds herself instinctively stepping back as the masked face looms close. The figure reaches forward and seems to remove the camera, because the next thing she can see is the stairs carpet, as the man – or woman? – descends.

'See – that's *our* stairs!'

'Isla, it's a beige carpet. We viewed four houses here in Brentwood before choosing this one, all with the exact same carpet. Every other house in Ireland has beige carpet.'

'Wait, you'll see.'

As she watches, the camera sweeps across a white-and-gold marble hallway, taking in a front door with glass panels, a Louis Poulsen lamp, and a narrow side table beneath a sunburst mirror. *Her* sunburst mirror, shipped all the way from San Diego.

'What is this, Isla?'

'That's what I'm trying to tell you – someone's made a video inside our house. It looks like it's part of this viral video thing for *The Loft*.'

'*The Loft*?'

An exasperated sigh at Julia's lack of cultural knowledge. 'The TV series. They have this, like, PR campaign? Where they put up a creepy video of a guy hiding in an attic in someone's house. He lets himself out when the people aren't there, and creeps around their home. At first people thought it was real, and it went totally viral.'

'Right . . .' Julia is still staring at the phone, where the video is playing on a loop.

'And then they revealed that it was all staged to promote this TV show, *The Loft*. And they put up more videos, and other people started to copy them, and somehow, we've ended up there. I'm guessing you didn't let someone in to film?'

'No . . .'

They turn towards Luca, who's eating a slice of pizza, his face lit by his Nintendo Switch. He looks up.

'What?'

'Do you know anything about this video?'

'I'm not even allowed on TikTok. How would I know anything?'

A fair point, Julia acknowledges. Luca is also only nine and never in the house without an adult. Even at thirteen, Isla is rarely home alone. So how on earth did someone get into their house?

Luca puts on his headset, cutting his mother and sister out of his world. Julia wants to ask him to take it off while he's eating but finds she doesn't have the energy. Instead, she watches the video again.

'Could we ask the people who look after the account? The *Loft* TV people?'

'This one isn't on their account. It's a repost.'

'Wait, so it has nothing to do with the TV show?'

Isla sighs. 'I just *said*, people started to make their own videos. Letting themselves out of hiding spaces, pretending there's a stranger living in their attics. The TV people had to put up a disclaimer saying that they weren't responsible for copycats. But people keep doing it.'

'So this is a copycat?'

'Yes.'

'Only we didn't film it.'

'Exactly.'

Julia tilts her head, looking at the ceiling. The kitchen is silent, her children wholly absorbed in their screens. With timing that would have been comical in other circumstances, there's a sudden creak from above, as though someone has stepped on a floorboard. As though there's someone up there. And of course there's nobody there, she knows that, it's just the noise the house makes when it's quiet, but in spite of herself, a cold chill settles across her skin.

3

JULIA WATCHES THE VIDEO again, this time in the hall. There's no doubt. It's her house. These are her things. She steps out of her heels and walks slowly up the stairs, her feet sinking into deep pile carpet. Beige. Just like everywhere. Just like in the video. At the top, the wide, bright landing stretches ahead. Six doors. And – she looks up – a hatch to the attic. She hasn't been up there yet, there's been no need. Half of their belongings are still being shipped – the winter clothes, the Christmas decorations, the ski gear. The attic is, as far as she knows, completely empty.

She stands still, listening. From downstairs, the low hum of the TV wafts up, but otherwise there's nothing. No creak, no scuffle, nothing to suggest there's someone up there. She shakes herself. It's some kind of online prank. To see her reaction, maybe. Is that it? A hidden camera? She looks around, above the doors, at the light fitting – an over-the-top suspended crystal sphere. It wouldn't be hard to hide a tiny camera in the middle of all those crystals . . . Then again, the clip seemed to have been filmed from floor level . . . But that's silly. There are no hidden cameras on her landing and there is nobody hiding in her attic.

She goes back down to the hall and finds Isla standing in the kitchen doorway.

'Did your dad say anything during his days here? Could it be something to do with him?' Julia asks.

Isla snorts. 'Dad barely knows how to use his phone. I don't think he made the video.'

'No, but if the clip wasn't filmed when I was here, it must have been when your dad was here. Nobody else has been in the house.'

'Except Pauline.'

'Well, yes.' Somehow Julia can't imagine their no-nonsense housekeeper filming videos for social media. 'I'll phone your dad anyway. You go finish your pizza.'

Gabe picks up after one ring.

'All OK?' He sounds on edge, and has done for months, but it's been more pronounced, she realizes now, in recent weeks.

'Yeah . . . Are *you* OK?'

'I'm fine. What's up?'

'Do you know anything about a video made in the house?'

'Huh?'

'I guessed not, but I wanted to check. Was there anyone inside the house when you were here?'

'The alarm guy. The alarm should be working now. I stuck his card on the whiteboard. And the letting agent called with the missing key for the balcony door in your bedroom. Why?'

'Were you home when they were here?'

'Alarm man, yes. Good guy, supports Liverpool.' In all his years living in San Diego, Gabe never stopped following his beloved Liverpool, and instinctively likes anyone else who supports them. 'I was here when the letting agent called too. Same gobshite who gave me the keys when we were moving in.' Julia smiles into the phone. This could mean anything. Gabe has a low tolerance for people who talk too much, people who talk too little, people who think they're smarter than he is, and people who aren't terribly sharp. 'Gobshite' covered a multitude in Gabe-speak.

'Anyone else?'

'A neighbour called to welcome you. I suspect he was surprised when I answered the door.' Julia can hear the grin, and this is more like the Gabe she's used to. 'Tony is his name. Well groomed, sixties, preppy polo shirt, golf-course tan, quite pleased with himself. I told him I'm your husband.'

'You're not my husband.'

'I know. But I couldn't resist. When I opened the door, his face was a picture. He'd clearly spotted you here with the kids and decided to connect with what he believed to be an attractive single mother.'

'Are you saying I'm not an attractive single mother?'

'You are, but he's not your type. I was protecting you from the local lothario.'

This is very Gabe, still meddling nine years after they'd split. Sometimes it's sweet, sometimes intrusive. 'I'll decide what my type is, thank you. But back to the video – I take it this guy Tony wasn't inside the house?'

'Nope. What's all this about?'

'Someone made a video of a guy letting himself out of an attic and creeping around a house, and it's our house. Isla spotted it on TikTok.'

'On what?'

'You *know* what TikTok is – social media where people share videos they make themselves.'

Silence for a moment. 'That's weird.' The wariness is back.

'Well, if it wasn't you and it wasn't me, I'm guessing it's some kind of Photoshopping. Don't worry about it. Anyway, OK to stick to Monday for switch-over?'

He is, he says, and they disconnect. She puts her phone on the hall table, thinking suddenly of the old rotary phone in her childhood hallway and the hours she spent on it, talking to

Eleanor and Anya. And Donna, of course. She pushes down a lurch of sadness.

In the kitchen, cold pizza congeals in the two boxes. Luca has gone to the den and Basil is in the small tepee they set up under the whiteboard. Isla looks up from her phone.

'I was thinking, we should ask the person who reposted the video where they got the original.'

'Oh, good idea!' Julia says, with far more enthusiasm than the suggestion warrants. But any chance to connect with Isla is welcome, so yes, she has become *that* mother. She's rewarded with a mildly disdainful look, but no snappish retort, and she's counting her blessings.

As Isla scrolls, Julia moves across the shadowy kitchen to the whiteboard. The card for the alarm guy is there, alongside a leaflet about gardening. She picks up a whiteboard marker and writes 'Phone gardener' on the 'To Do' column, beneath 'Check school uniforms' and 'Pay for Luca's tennis'. As she replaces the cap on the marker, she knocks against a magnet and a greeting card skates to the floor. Julia picks it up and opens it to read it again.

Dear Julia, Gabe, Isla and Luca,

I can't explain how gorgeous it is that you're back home with us in Ireland!

Looking forward to showing you the ropes. Have put your names on the waiting list for our tennis and golf clubs. We'll bring you as guests until you can join. CANNOT WAIT to catch up!

Lots of love, Eleanor, Ian and kids x
PS Juju, message me SOON for drinks xxxxx

Julia checks the time – said drinks are happening in ninety minutes and she's still in her work suit. She sticks the card back on the whiteboard, then turns to watch Isla, who is typing something, her thumbs flying at dizzying speed.

'What did you write?'

'I asked where he found the clip. I said it was our house and we didn't film it.'

Julia bites her lip. She wouldn't have told this person it was their house. But then she should have typed the message herself.

'Actually,' Isla is saying, 'it made me think of this other thing I saw . . .'

She searches as Julia watches.

'Got it. OK, so it's a true story about these college kids back home. They discovered this guy secretly living in their basement – he'd been there for months and they had no idea. Imagine, some stranger actually living in your house, sneaking up at night to roam around when you're asleep. He could literally stand in their bedrooms, staring at them.' Her eyes gleam. 'Imagine you woke up and there was someone at the end of your bed watching you.'

'Then I'm glad we don't have a basement to worry about too.' Julia clears the pizza boxes off the island, extracting a leftover crust and eyeing up the garbage disposal. It's been acting up for days, and maybe the crust would be pushing it.

'Oh wow, there's a whole bunch of linked articles,' Isla is saying. 'Jeez, this guy found a man living in his attic. Literally climbed up through the hatch and came face-to-face with a stranger. And here's one about a kid who looked up at a vent above his bed and saw eyes looking back at him.'

Julia throws her a look.

'Wow, nobody believed him until they found a dead body up there months later. Oh my god, maggots fell through the vent. That's how they knew.'

'OK, enough! Did the TikTok person reply?' Julia nods towards the phone as a notification pings.

Isla checks. 'Yeah. He says he found it on the hashtag #TheLoft and reposted it along with heaps of others. He doesn't know anything about the person who made the video, though. Just the profile name, Lepus123.'

'So can we check the profile for this Lepus123?'

'Sure, but most people don't put information about themselves in their TikTok profiles. Uh . . . nope. Nothing. Just Lepus123. No followers – a blank avatar.'

'We could message them to ask how they made the video?' And *why*, she thinks.

Isla begins to type.

'Wait, I'll do it.' Julia reaches for the phone.

'Why?'

'I don't like the idea of a thirteen-year-old messaging strangers on the internet.'

'But if you do it, it's just you typing the same words. It's still my account.'

'True . . . But I'd feel better.'

Isla passes the phone, muttering under her breath. Julia thinks for a moment, then types:

Hi. Could you please tell me where you got this video?

She hands the phone back to Isla.

'Wow, Mom. Hardcore. You should have been a CIA interrogator.'

'Hey, stop teasing!' Julia says, meaning *please keep teasing*, because it's infinitely better than subdued silence. 'Can you send it? I didn't want to press the wrong button.'

Isla frowns. 'It won't send.' She looks up. 'I just refreshed it, and the account has disappeared. Whoever posted the video deleted their profile.'

Julia takes the phone again. The Lepus123 account is gone. The video is gone. The repost on the other account is gone. She clicks into #TheLoft, but there's no sign of the video of their house. Many other clips, yes: black-clad figures letting themselves down from attics and prowling around houses. Some are clownish, some look eerily real. But it's just a social media trend, she reminds herself. Somehow someone got ahold of a video of their house and Photoshopped in the masked figure.

That gives her an idea. She clicks through to Isla's profile on TikTok.

'Mom, don't go into my videos,' Isla says, reaching for her phone.

'Hang on, I just want to see if there are any of this house.'

There are many of this house, Julia sees now. Isla's bedroom: lit by laser lights, adorned with posters of Dua Lipa; clothes and crystals scattered across the thick beige carpet. The kitchen makes a number of appearances – the camera sweeping around stark white walls punctuated with Gabe's paintings, family photos and Julia's ancient Monet print. Another clip shows the inside of the fridge, catching bottles of white wine and rosé in among the shelves of organic vegetables and expensive cheese. Julia glances at her daughter.

'Do you really have to film *inside* our fridge? And' – she looks down at the screen – 'my to-do list on the whiteboard?'

'Urgh, you just don't get it.' Isla holds out her hand. 'I need my phone.'

'One sec . . .'

On-screen, there's a clip of the landing and stairs as Isla descends. The video moves on to sweep through the hall, with text that says 'When the lamp in your hallway costs more than your yearly allowance.'

Julia looks up. Isla shrugs. 'It's true, right?'

'I'm not sure it's something to put online. But either way, I guess it's possible that whoever made the video used this one? Look here, the camera moves across the front door, then on to the lamp and the mirror. Like the one we saw?'

'I guess . . .'

Julia is looking at the phone again. In the next clip, Isla is sitting on her bed, her face in close-up, and she's crying.

In real life, she's trying to grab the phone.

'Hey, hang on. Can we talk about this?'

Isla slumps against the island.

Julia hands her the phone. 'What's with the video?'

'It's nothing.'

'Is it about moving here?' she asks carefully.

'Obviously.' Taciturn Isla is back.

'You'll settle in, sweetheart.' *Oh, platitudes, how weak you sound.*

'Really?' Isla's not slumping any more. Hands on hips, eyes flashing. 'You pull us out of our schools and move us halfway around the world and won't even tell us why.'

'You know why. We always said we'd move back here eventually, and if you don't go to secondary school and do the Irish Leaving Cert, college is too expensive and we—'

'Stop! It's bull, and you know it. You sold your business for millions. You're rich. And you're too mean to pay for college or just goddamn let us stay in California.'

Julia feels herself bristle and tries to dampen it down. 'That's not fair. And things weren't exactly going brilliantly before we left.'

'What are you talking about?'

'The whole thing with Riley.'

'Oh, for god's sake, Mom. Riley was a bitch, but she was just one person.' Isla throws out the word 'bitch' so casually, but a sideways glance at Julia gives her away. Boundary-testing is in full swing. 'And anyway, she wasn't even in school for the last month.'

I know she wasn't, and I know why.

'What?' Isla must see something in her face. Julia scrambles to rearrange her features. She can't have Isla find out what really happened to Riley, not when they've made it this far.

'Nothing. Back to the original point – I imagine someone could have taken the video from your account and used it to create the attic one – Photoshopping in the masked man? Taking him from another video on the *Loft* hashtag?'

Isla looks thoughtful. 'I guess . . . I wouldn't know how to do it, but other people might. There are some cool video-editing apps out there . . .'

Julia lets out a silent breath. *Subject successfully changed.*

'So that's it, then. Someone pranked us – maybe one of your friends back home or some rando who follows you, which is just a *bit* creepy. But either way' – she lifts her hands – 'it's gone.'

And just like that, it's over. Isla takes her phone to her bedroom. Luca plays *Mario* in the den. And Julia, getting ready for her night out, in her expensive new dressing room, in her expensive new home, goes back to thinking about the other things on her to-do list, and forgets all about the video on her daughter's phone.

4

DARK POLISHED WOOD AND gleaming high tables greet Julia when she pushes through the door of Capitol Bar later that same evening. It's busy with Friday-night revellers, and it takes her a few minutes to find an empty booth. She's early, having jumped in a cab as soon as Pauline showed up to mind the kids, and is deep in work emails when Eleanor arrives, descending on her like a tornado.

'Juju! My god! So good to see you!'

Julia inches out of the booth and Eleanor pulls her into a hug.

'You too,' Julia says, standing back to take in her friend. Like Julia, Eleanor is short and favours heels, but that's where the similarities end. Where Julia is ash-blonde and fair, Eleanor is dark – dark hair and Bambi eyes, with a ski-slope nose, full pink lips and an always-on smile. She hasn't changed much from the twelve-year-old girl Julia met all those years ago at school; not in appearance and not in personality. Eleanor is opinionated and dramatic and bossy and loud, as though making up with presence for what she lacks in stature. However – Julia reminds herself – she's also loyal and kind and good. Her my-way-or-the-highway take on life can get a bit much, but Julia – mostly – understands that it's not that Eleanor thinks her opinions are superior to those of others, it's just that she's blinkered; she thinks everyone experiences life the same way she does. This is not at all the case. Eleanor lives in a 4,000-square-foot townhouse on Dublin's wealthy Morehampton Road and her life is nothing like that of 99 per cent of the population. Tonight, in her pink silk midi-dress with gold hoop earrings, she looks every inch a model. Though of course she's not – she's Eleanor Jordan-Keogh, one-time PR, now stay-at-home mum of three and, to Julia's irritation, world expert on parenting teens, although her eldest child is six.

'So how *are* you? My god, I can't believe you actually left the bright lights of California for Dublin!'

Julia laughs. 'Says the woman who wouldn't leave Dublin 4 in a fit.'

'Sure, but you've always been the high-flyer. I mean, your *business*! I read about it in the *Sunday Indo*.' Her eyes are wide. 'Did you really get that much when you sold?'

'Well, I don't know how much was mentioned, but yeah, it was a good decision.'

'You're a millionaire! Wait' – she glances side to side with exaggerated care and lowers her voice – 'a *billionaire*?'

'No! But I'll buy the drinks tonight.'

This is a figure of speech, of course. Julia won't need to buy the drinks. Eleanor sold her own business, a PR firm, some years earlier, and her husband's job in hedge funds means no mortgage on the cottage in West Cork, the villa in Peschiera or the townhouse in Dublin 4.

A waiter arrives and Julia orders a bottle of Veuve Clicquot.

'Oh, three glasses, please!' Eleanor calls after him. She looks at her watch. 'Anya will be late, as always.' She rolls her eyes and Julia wonders for the hundredth time why Anya has to be there at all.

Eleanor leans in. 'By the way, she nearly choked when I told her you'd be living in Brentwood.'

'Really?'

'Yeah, I phoned her last month and mentioned you were here viewing houses. She's been dreaming of living there since they knocked down the convent and laid that first brick.'

'Oh. I didn't realize.' Julia chews her lip. 'I hope it won't look like I'm trying to rub her nose in it . . . Gabe was really fixated on Brentwood because all the houses come with a garden lodge, and he needs a studio to paint.'

'Ah – I assumed it was because it's just across the road from Kerrybrook. That you wanted to be close to home.'

Julia dips her head non-commitally. That hadn't been part of the decision. Her parents had moved to the west of Ireland five years earlier, selling the family home in Kerrybrook, so there was no practical reason to live near by. No nostalgic reason either. Julia'd had a pretty happy childhood, but she wasn't sentimentally attached to where she'd grown up. And of course, Donna had grown up there too. That made it . . . strange.

A sudden memory flashes through her mind. Julia and Donna aged ten, cycling endlessly around the green in Kerrybrook, for no purpose other than summer and time. Before starting secondary school, before meeting Anya and Eleanor. Before discovering make-up and cider and boys. Simple innocent pleasures that Anya later laughed at. Julia remembers going back to Donna's house to watch MTV, their shared love of Madonna and Bon Jovi, belting out the lyrics to 'Like A Prayer'. Julia's mother standing at her front door, calling across the green for her to come home at teatime. Julia curling up on an armchair to watch *The Fall Guy* and *The A-Team* while her younger brother and sister bickered over space on the couch. Her bedroom with its *Smash Hits* posters on purple walls. Would the new owners have painted her room, now that her parents had sold? She shakes herself. Nostalgia isn't her thing.

'Nah, that was just chance, really,' she tells Eleanor.

'Your mum and dad must be *thrilled* to have you back.'

Julia shifts on her seat. They've visited her parents exactly once in the month they've been home and other than that they've relied on weekly video calls, just like they did from San Diego. 'Yeah, they're delighted.' In her head, she adds 'visit Mum and Dad' to her to-do list. 'But no, renting in Brentwood has nothing to do with Kerrybrook: the garden studio was the main draw – that and the security of a gated complex.'

'For crime-ridden Foxrock? All the bankers and CEOs out joy-riding?' Eleanor smirks and Julia rolls her eyes.

'Yeah, yeah, I know. I guess it's because it's what we had in San Diego and we're used to it.'

'So, have you caught up with anyone else? I hope not – I'd better be first,' Eleanor says with mock seriousness.

'Of course you're first. I've lost touch with most people from school and college.'

A beat passes as they both remember why, and an image of Donna flashes through Julia's mind for the second time in minutes. In the States, she could go months without thinking about her. Gentle, quiet, unassuming Donna. Anya used to say she was boring, and sometimes Julia believed it because it was a little bit true. Donna didn't have Eleanor's charisma or charm. She didn't have Anya's spiky magnetism. But she was good and kind, with a wry sense of humour that most people missed. And they didn't appreciate her until she was gone. *God, being home is hard.*

'Well, I'm all you need,' Eleanor says. 'I drink champagne, I love shopping, and I can even be dragged to the gym as long as there's lunch after. I've got some new Lululemon bits I'm dying to try out.'

Julia smiles. Eleanor had read once that Victoria Beckham never wore sportswear outside the home. *If Victoria doesn't do casual, then neither do I*, she'd announced, and had stuck to this rule rigidly since.

'I won't have time for the gym,' Julia says. 'I'm still sorting the kids and the house, and I've taken on a new work contract.'

'So you're still sacking people, even after selling your sacking-people business?'

A group of women around their own age files into the booth behind them, loud with excitement on their night out. Julia raises her voice above the din.

'Yep! Only twenty hours a week, so I can focus on the kids. I'll take on more hours in October.'

'Do you like it?'

'Ish . . . It's weird having a boss again, but I don't miss all the admin. You're probably the same?'

Eleanor nods. She had worked in PR all over the world before setting up her own agency in Ireland, only to realize she was stuck doing all the things she hated – admin, HR, accounts – while missing out on what she loved. She'd sold the business with – *expensive* – help from Anya, who ran Hase Accounting, a successful mid-size accountancy firm. Not that Eleanor had a choice about using them – Anya's business model was to put pressure on everyone she knew to use her services.

'Yeah, I'll go back to it someday, but I'm in no rush. And Gabe? How's he doing? Any sign of getting a proper job? Or is he still trading off making twinkly eyes at people and getting them to buy his art?'

Julia laughs. 'He's good. Laid-back as ever.' As she says it, she's conscious that it's not true at the moment. 'And his eyes are still twinkly, even if his hair has disappeared.'

'The smartest man I know. He could have had his pick of anyone in our class in college – guys or girls – and he ends up with the one who finances his art career. He didn't actually seem that smart in college, to be honest.' She leans closer. 'Do you reckon Gabe ever resents having to rely on you financially?'

'God, no. In fairness, he's not into buying "stuff". And he earns enough to pay for the things he *does* like – meals out, gig tickets, endless T-shirts – just not enough to pay for less fun things like rent or bills, which suits him fine.'

'Now *that* I can relate to, though for me it's not so much gig tickets as Zadig & Voltaire with a dash of Moët.' Eleanor looks around. 'Speaking of which, where's he gone with our champers? Are you in the mood for some tapas?'

'Go for it.'

'OK, let's get patatas bravas and prawn pil pil. Anya won't eat anyway, she never does. So how're the kids? It must be hard for them . . . I was reading some research the other day that said the absolute *worst* time for upheaval in a child's life is—' She stops herself, perhaps noticing Julia's expression.

'They're OK,' Julia says carefully as the waiter arrives with the bottle of champagne and three flutes. 'Luca's missing his old life, but we got him a pet rabbit and that's helping. Isla – well, she needed a fresh start. She was struggling, problems with one particular girl.'

'Oh no, poor Isla. At her old school?' She turns to the waiter, who has finished pouring champagne, and orders the food.

'Yes, and then Riley, that's the girl, joined her soccer team too. Soccer was her escape, so that was hard.'

'Awful. Why are kids so mean? I'm dreading mine getting to that age.' Eleanor's kids are still tiny – Julia is the outlier among their wider group of friends, the first one to have a baby. The fix-the-marriage baby followed by the second fix-the-marriage baby followed by the split. Eleanor, on the other hand, had spent her twenties and thirties travelling, and had married and divorced a tennis coach in Cairns before coming home to settle down at thirty-seven with her childhood sweet-heart, Ian Keogh.

'Yeah, it was difficult.' She takes a careful sip of champagne. 'Long story. Too long for tonight, especially if Anya's going to descend any minute.'

Eleanor looks at her watch again. 'Jeez, this is late, even for Anya.'

'She always valued her time more than anyone else's.'

'Ah now, she's not the worst.'

She literally is the worst. Julia casts her mind back to the fight two years earlier. Anya's out-of-the-blue email asking for advice on an employee 'issue'. No reference to the fact that she was asking Julia to provide for free a service that usually cost four hundred dollars an hour. Just a clipped request for advice. Julia had given it. What else could she do? She wasn't going to charge a friend – even someone she hadn't been close with in almost twenty years. And it was pretty straightforward. Anya had caught one of her employees offering accountancy services off the books to existing clients at a discounted rate. It meant no fee for Hase Accounting, only for Vincent Gale, the employee. What Vincent didn't realize was that one of the customers he'd offered his services to was Anya's friend, Anya explained to Julia, though she didn't say who it was. If she had, Julia might have asked for follow-up details and spared herself some drama. Anya wanted to fire Vincent Gale. Julia had explained that she needed to suspend him on full pay first and carry out an investigation. But ultimately, if he'd definitely been stealing clients, yes, she could eventually fire him.

And then all hell broke loose.

Vincent Gale did not go down easy. He was, Julia later realized, someone exactly like Anya: self-delusional and believing himself always in the right. When Julia first heard he'd sued for unfair dismissal, she was bemused. He'd been caught – he didn't have a leg to stand on. But there was more to it than that, she soon discovered. Anya hadn't suspended him on full pay. She hadn't carried out an investigation. Like the best narcissists, she didn't *really* think the rules applied to her. Why should she pay him when she knew he'd been stealing? she said. So she fired him outright. And of course Vincent Gale won his case for unfair dismissal. Anya had to pay out and suffer a humiliating PR mess. She blamed Julia, claimed Julia hadn't explained things properly, lashing out like an aggrieved toddler who didn't like being in trouble. And that was the last time they spoke.

Eleanor picks up her phone. 'I'll try ringing.'

'Or just leave it?' Julia says lightly. 'If she's coming, she'll turn up, and if she's not, she's not.' *Here's hoping.*

Eleanor purses her lips. 'Isn't it time you two buried the hatchet?'

Julia bristles. 'What do you mean?'

'You know what I mean.' Eleanor's voice softens. 'It was twenty years ago.'

Ah.

'And Donna would have hated that we fell out over it.'

Julia can't help thinking Donna would have hated that she was dead more than any subsequent falling-out.

'If she turns up, I'll be civil. Now, enough about Anya. How are you?'

A half hour slips by as Eleanor fills Julia in on life in the Jordan-Keogh house: three under six, and *so much* joy and fulfilment, but no sleep and no time. Julia smiles to herself. Eleanor might have three under six, but she also has a full-time nanny and a cleaner twice a week. The average busy parent would have to dig deep to find sympathy. The waiter returns with golden patatas bravas smothered in sauce and a sizzling prawn pil pil. As they eat, Julia tells Eleanor about the attic video.

Eleanor's eyes widen. She puts down her fork and picks up her phone. 'Is it still up? Can I see it?'

'No, it's gone.'

'Ah, OK.' Now Eleanor's pulling down her notifications and efficiently swiping them away. She stops, frowning. 'Who's tagging me on Facebook? I haven't done anything remotely Facebookable in ages.' She clicks in and her mouth drops open.

'Oh my god . . .'

'What is it?'

'Jesus Christ. It's Anya.'

'What's she done now?'

'She hasn't done anything. She's dead.'

5

JULIA STARES. HOW CAN Anya be dead? Isn't she supposed to breeze in the door any second? Busy and arrogant and annoying and alive? She waits for more, but Eleanor has lost the ability to speak and is sliding her phone across the table.

Julia swivels the phone. On-screen, there's a photo of Anya. It's the professional headshot she uses for LinkedIn: her dark hair shiny, her eyes fixed on the camera, her mouth closed in a knowing smile. The photo's been shared by Chris, her partner. Julia begins to read.

> It is with great sadness and shock I announce the sudden death of Anya Hase, my partner, my future wife. I'm heartbroken, as are her parents, Dieter and Margot, her aunts, uncles and cousins, and her adored grandmother, Birgit. Funeral arrangements to be announced. Please share the news with those not on Facebook. We ask for privacy at this time.
> Chris

'Is this real?' As soon as the words are out, Julia wonders why she said them. How could it not be real? Nobody posts fake death announcements on Facebook.

'I . . . I . . .' Eleanor is floundering. 'It looks real . . . it's Chris's account and there are dozens of comments. My god. What do you think happened?'

Julia shakes her head. 'I have no idea. Who tagged you?'

Eleanor checks her phone. 'A guy she uses for marketing. We met a few times when I did work for Anya.'

'Do you know him well enough to PM him?'

Eleanor nods and begins to type. Within moments, a ding signals a reply.

'Oh my god.'

'What?'

Eleanor passes the phone so Julia can read it herself:

Anya was taking a bath. She was on her own in the house. Chris was in LA for work. She'd had some wine. Quite a bit, it seems. And she slipped under the water and drowned. Do pass to other friends, but only if they're close. She wouldn't want it known publicly.

Eleanor's eyes glisten.

Julia feels sick. 'Oh Jesus.'

'My god, poor Chris.' Eleanor's tears spill over now. 'I'd better message him.'

Julia doesn't envy her. What do you even say? But Julia's never met Chris, so maybe it's OK to leave this kind of thing to Eleanor.

Eleanor is reading again. 'Chris found her, apparently. But not until this morning . . .' Her voice tapers off to a whisper.

'Fuck.'

'Police reckon she'd been there since Wednesday night.'

'Oh no. That's horrific.' There's a wobble in her voice and Julia works to control it. Jesus, she didn't even like Anya. It's hypocritical if she cries now. And yet. A one-time childhood friend is gone. A real, live human is dead. *Imagine slipping under the water, a whole life snuffed out, just like that.*

Trance-like, Eleanor picks up the third champagne flute.

'We're sitting here waiting for her, complaining that she's late, and of course she's late because she's dead.' Her eyes meet Julia's, a tear slipping down her cheek. 'That's two out of four of us gone.'

Julia nods, her throat tight.

'And in a way, kind of similar? Both accidents, both avoidable. Like some kind of weird karma or curse or, I don't know. Like that film, *Final Destination*. Where people are supposed to die and they don't and then they die anyway, and maybe it's going to happen to us too and—'

Julia shakes her head. 'It's not karma and it's not the same.' On autopilot, her fingers wrap around her glass. The champagne, so crisp and cold just moments earlier, tastes warm and sickly now. 'This time it was nobody's fault. Anya just slipped under.'

6

LUCA STARTS AWAKE. EYES wide. A whirring in his ears. What woke him? Is his mom here? He remembers now. His mom went out and Pauline was babysitting. What if Pauline's gone and his mom's not back? He needs to check. He climbs down the ladder of his bunk and pads across the bedroom floor. Pushes the handle and pulls the door. The landing is dark, at least at first, but then something moves. Something on the wall. Luca holds his breath, frozen. There it is again. It takes a moment to understand, but then he does. It's outside – a tree, he thinks, moving in the wind, making a shadow through the window at the top of the stairs.

Across the landing, his mom's door is a little bit open. He nudges it and slips in. *Please let her be there.* He moves further into the room, eyes adjusting to the dark. And lets out a breath. The outline that fixes everything. She's home. He's safe.

Back in his own bed, he burrows under his duvet and tries to think about other things. Other things that are not night noises or new houses. And as sleep takes hold, he hears a sound. A creak. A creak that's like an attic hatch.

Now he's wide awake again.

His body is tingling and he's listening for more noises but keeping his head deep under the covers, and everything is muffled now by the duvet and the loudest sound is his own breathing. He holds his breath, trying to hear.

Footsteps. Coming from the landing. Right outside his room. Is that his door opening? Could it be his mom checking on him? He's afraid to look. He keeps his eyes clamped shut. There's another noise now. Breathing. It doesn't sound like his mom. And a smell. A smell that reminds him of when he's sick. The oil his mom puts on his pillow. He can't remember the name. Why is that smell in his room? Is he sick? Maybe this is a dream. Maybe if he tries really hard to ignore them, the smell and the noise will disappear. Maybe it really is a dream. Dreams can have smells and sounds. That's what it is. A million hours later, sleep takes hold.

7

WHEN THE DOORBELL RINGS at nine the following morning, Julia is in the kitchen hunched over a coffee, feeling hollow and sick. She and Eleanor had come back here after Capitol Bar and had stayed up talking until three. Reminiscing about school days and college days and pulling out old photos, but, mostly, going around in circles. How can Anya be dead? Repeating themselves over and over. The *I can't believe it* and the *how easily it could happen* and the *it could have been anyone.* 'People die every day,' Eleanor had said as her taxi pulled up outside, 'so I can't understand why it's so hard to take this in, but it is.' With one final hug, she was gone.

Julia had crawled into bed, without drinking water or removing her make-up, and now, on Saturday morning, two empty wine bottles on the kitchen counter mock her. The doorbell chimes a second time and she peers out to the hall. Through the glass panel at the side of the front door, she can see the figure of a man, finger poised, about to ring the bell a third time. Alastair O'Ryan, she thinks, a neighbour from one of the townhouses near the main gate. She'd only met him once, when she was coming home from work one evening, and he'd kept her talking for twenty minutes, despite her key-jangling and foot-shifting hints. *Great*, this is the last thing she needs. But politeness kicks in and she walks out to answer.

Alastair is hovering close to her doorway – so close that Julia has to take a step back after opening the door, to avoid breathing her unwashed, wine-soaked morning breath on him. Alastair's in his late forties, she reckons, a few years older than her, with dark eyes and heavy brows matching the dark curly hair that's currently peeping out from under a black cycling helmet. She spots his bicycle – old-fashioned, sturdy-looking – resting against the front wall of her house.

Alastair's wearing a black baggy jumper with navy corduroy trousers, just as he was the last time she met him, but, she realizes now, he's actually not bad-looking beneath all the hair and the helmet and the oversized clothes. His jumper is dotted with dog hairs and bits of yellow fluff, and she has a sudden urge to grab a lint roller.

'Hey, Julia, I wasn't sure if you'd be up yet. Just letting you know I brought in your bins.' He nods towards the side of the house. 'You forgot to. It's one of the by-laws – you must bring them in on the same day they go out. It's for aesthetics, apparently.' He rolls his eyes. 'The management company are sticklers.'

'Oh, thank you. I didn't realize.' She's sweating despite the morning chill, and she's *never* drinking again.

'Sure. If you need anything at all to help you settle in, just ask. I'm here every day – I work from home.'

'Brilliant, thanks so much.' What Julia needs is toast and ibuprofen, and she starts to close the door, but Alastair seems in no rush.

He inclines his head.

'I like what you've done with the place.'

'Oh. We haven't done much. We're only renting.'

'The table and the mirror are nice,' he says, still looking in. 'Is the waste disposal working? If not, let me know and I'll get you a phone number. Hillman's management company are slow at dealing with problems. You're better off getting it fixed yourself and sending them the bill.'

Julia nods. Hillman is the development company that built the houses and owns about half of them, renting them out through Raycroft Estates letting agency and managing them through a rather inept management company. None of her dealings with Hillman, Raycroft or the management company have left her feeling in any way confident about their competence, and even who to contact for any given problem is unclear.

'Oh, thank you. Wait, how did you know the waste disposal's not working?'

'It's always been a bit glitchy. The previous tenant had problems with it.'

'Yeah, it's a pain.' She sighs. 'Sometimes the more advanced the technology, the less reliable it is. The "smart" alarm is the same. And the super-fancy built-in coffee machine too, although thankfully it's working this morning.' She gives him a wry grin, certain now that her hangover is a visible aura around her. 'So, the previous tenant came to you about fixing the garbage disposal?'

Alastair laughs. 'God, no. I wouldn't have a clue. He and I were pals, though, and that waste disposal used to drive him mad. Here, I'll give you my number' – he stretches out a hand – 'pass me your phone and I'll pop it in.'

With rare perfect timing, Luca's voice rings out. 'Mom! Where are you?'

'Oh, I haven't got my phone on me, and I'd better go before my son . . .' She throws up her hands as if to say, *Who knows what he'll do?* 'Thanks for bringing in the bins.'

'No probs.' He fixes an earbud in his ear, taking time to adjust it, and pulls his bicycle away from the wall. 'Audiobook,' he says, tapping his ear. 'I'm at a really good part.' He glances at his bike, then back at Julia, a slightly guilty look on his face. 'Don't worry, I'm just using one AirPod, I can still hear the traffic.'

She smiles at his need to explain – assessing cyclist safety isn't top of her to-do list. Alastair is . . . interesting.

He salutes and turns to wheel his bike down the driveway, slowing as he passes her car, appearing to glance in through the driver's-side window, though she's not quite sure. He continues on towards the gate and Julia closes the door.

Julia's bleary Saturday morning morphs into a blurred afternoon. She tells the kids about Anya, or a diluted version of what happened. They're shocked, they check Julia's OK, then move on relatively quickly. With Gabe, it's a different story.

Julia had broken the news to him last night, phoning him from Capitol Bar, and now she calls him to give him the full account. Gabe is stunned and, like her, surprised at how much it's affecting him.

'It's complicated, I know,' she says, rubbing her tired face with her free hand.

Complicated. *An understatement*, she acknowledges to herself, taking the phone through to the living room to continue the conversation from a horizontal position on the couch.

Gabe and Anya had dated when they were all in college together. *Dated*. The word makes Julia smile. Nobody called it that in Ireland, not back then anyway. Gabe and Anya had been seeing one another for a month before Anya dumped him for someone – *anyone* – with better prospects than 'starving artist', as she explained to her friends. They'd stayed pals over the years, though, throughout Julia and Gabe's marriage, and even more so after the divorce. But when Anya threatened to sue Julia two years ago, Gabe picked a side, so to speak, supporting Julia when she needed a shoulder to cry on. Well, he picked a side privately at least – Julia was never sure if Anya was aware, not least since he still commented on Anya's Facebook posts and wished her happy birthday. Gabe was good at that – staying on friendly terms, keeping everyone happy. Not in a deliberate, cynical way – more an innate habit, because it was easier to stay friends than to fall out, and Gabe, like a river running downhill, always took the path of least resistance.

'Had you seen her since we moved back?' he asks.

'No. She was supposed to come for drinks last night but . . .' *But she was dead.*

Silence.

'Why, had *you* seen her?' she asks.

She can almost hear him shaking his head into the phone.

'I've been a bit distracted . . . I should have texted her,' he says. 'Now it's too late.'

Eleanor calls by at four, and it's strange seeing her again so soon after so much time apart. They sit together over coffee, laughing and crying, eulogizing Anya-with-a-y – she had started secondary school as 'Anna' – remembering how she'd re-imagined her name, claiming it was part of her German heritage. They'd heard all about this heritage on the first day, when they were put together for icebreaker games. Anya was still Anna at that point but was at great pains to explain her German lineage and the correct pronunciation of her surname – Ha-za – as well as the myriad exotic places she'd lived as a small child. Her mother was Spanish, she said, hence her own dark hair and eyes, and her father was descended from Bismarck. They'd lived in Moscow, Milan and Madrid, travelling constantly because of her mother's fashion work, Anya had explained. It was years later that Julia discovered Anya had never lived anywhere other than Bray in North Wicklow and her father was the son of a steelworker from Düsseldorf. Mrs Hase née Kelly was a seamstress from Kenmare. Neither of Anya's parents were, for better or for worse, related to Bismarck at all.

Julia and Eleanor reminisced about the good bits and the bad bits. Anya surprising them with tickets to see Robbie Williams. Anya breaking into the teacher's desk to see the science paper but not showing anyone else. Anya bringing Donna shopping for a Debs dress, because Donna didn't know where to start. Anya telling Julia's mother that Julia was on the pill, to deflect attention from the cigarette in her own hand. Julia had not forgotten that one. Anya inviting them to her parents' holiday home in Tenerife. The time she 'accidentally' spilt red wine on Eleanor, when they both turned up in the same dress. The time she bought two pairs of new Doc boots – one for her and one for the other three to share. The time she lied about Donna.

'And then there were two,' Eleanor says as she heads for home, leaving Julia feeling cold to her bones.

On Saturday night, before going to bed, Julia checks on her children in their new bedrooms. Luca is buried beneath his duvet, the stuffed dog he denies by day tucked safely under his arm. Basil the rabbit is curled up in his nesting box under Luca's desk. In her room, Isla is lying on her back, prone, with no audible sounds of breathing.

'I know you're faking. Keep working on it,' Julia whispers as she kisses her forehead.

On the floor beside the bed, Isla's iPhone charges, still lighting up with silent notifications. Julia quietly unplugs it. Outside on the landing, she plugs it in again. The no-phones-in-bedrooms rule is being stretched to its outermost limits, but moving continent does that.

Above her, the ridiculous crystal light fixture sparkles. She flicks the switch, extinguishing it, and stands for a moment, staring at the attic hatch. Remembering the video that seems so long ago but was only last night. Julia is not given to fanciful notions. She is practical, sensible, efficient. No superstitions, no mountains out of molehills. And yet. Looking at the attic now, she can't help picturing it. Someone on the other side of the hatch. Crouched down. Listening. Waiting to come out. She shakes it away and walks into her bedroom. Within minutes, she's lying down, ready for the sleep she's been craving all day. But now her mind is wide awake, skittering over images from the last twenty-four hours. Anya slipping under the water. The empty champagne flute in Capitol Bar. The late-night drinks with Eleanor. Alastair standing at her door. The video on Isla's phone. The attic hatch. The man in black. On a loop, her mind goes over all of it, refusing to succumb to sleep. And something is nagging at her. Something about Anya? No, it's something about Alastair, she realizes. And finally, as she tries to work out what it is, sleep takes over.

8

THE ARRANGEMENT IS QUITE simple, as Julia has explained many times to many people. There's the main house: in San Diego, it was a ranch-style home in an expansive gated community, and here in Dublin it's a luxurious five-bed in Brentwood. Then there's the smaller home. In San Diego, it was a city-centre condo, and in Dublin it's a fifth-floor apartment a two-minute walk from the outer gates of Brentwood. The first reaction – always – is a raised eyebrow at how much this living arrangement must cost. But to Julia, it's logical. Any long-term relationship break-up means going from one home to two. And paying for two. This way, instead of two family homes, and moving the kids from one to the other, there's the main house and the apartment. And so far, through nine years and one continent move, it's working.

Usually, they spend five nights at a time in each home, then switch over. If switch day is on a weekday, Julia wakes in one home and returns from work to the other, and she and Gabe don't see one another during the crossover.

Today is switch day and, ordinarily, Julia would go to the apartment. But it's also a big day – Isla and Luca have started at their new schools, so she wants to be at the house to see them. She also has an instinctive urge to see Gabe to talk about Anya, and as soon as she arrives he's in the hall, pulling her into a hug that smells of clean laundry and oil paints. They stand like that for a moment without speaking.

'You OK?' he asks finally, pulling back, his brown eyes concerned and sad.

'Yeah. Ish. You?'

'Kind of. I can't stop thinking about it.'

'Same.'

'How can she be there and then gone?' He rubs the stubble on his chin. 'I just can't take it in.' His eyes glisten. 'It's like when—'

He stops. She knows. *It's like when Donna died.* But he won't say it. Gabe never talks about Donna.

'How are the kids?' Julia asks.

'Subdued.'

'OK, let's rally the troops and order the food.'

An hour later, the takeaway arrives.

'Isla, take out those air buds or ear pods or whatever they're called and come to the table.'

A sigh. 'AirPods, Mom. Oh my god. I've told you that, like, a hundred times.'

Julia knows they're AirPods. But she's become a person who makes deliberate mistakes to engage with her daughter.

Luca, dutiful as ever, is taking his lunchbox from his schoolbag to empty his crusts and apple core.

'Don't use the garbage disposal,' Julia reminds him. 'It's still not working.'

He stares at her. 'I'm *never* going to use that.'

'Oh, why?'

'It can kill you.'

Gabe laughs. 'I don't think so, buddy.'

Luca nods vehemently. 'I saw it on a TV show. A woman's

44

scarf got caught in her garbage disposal and choked her to death. She couldn't get free. Both ends were sucked in and it strangled her.'

'Oh my god, Luca, what show was that?' Julia makes a mental note to keep a closer eye on his screen time.

'*Orphan Black*. Dad knew. Don't be a fun sponge, Mom, it was really good.'

'Gabe, you have to check what they're watching.'

He does his trademark get-out-of-trouble sheepish look. When they first got together it was cute. By the time Julia found herself managing everything – the baby, the mortgage, the long days at work – it wasn't quite so cute. But the split had mellowed everything again and now her displays of exasperation are performative as often as they are genuine; acting on autopilot in the role she's fallen into.

'I thought it was about little orphan kids . . . like in *Oliver Twist*.'

Julia's not buying it for a second but says nothing else. Gabe is Gabe. And sometimes – though she'll never admit it – it suits her that he lets the kids get away with more. He says yes, and she doesn't have to.

Gabe starts dishing out food as Isla flops into a chair, tugging at her stiff skirt. She's right, Julia thinks, the uniform is hideous, especially for someone used to wearing jeans to school. A below-the-knee skirt, a scratchy jumper, a starched shirt and knee-high socks. The socks had confused Isla more than any other part of the uniform. *If they want to cover our legs with a long skirt and knee-high socks, why not let us wear jeans?* Fair point.

'So, how was day one?' she asks now. Beneath the table, something brushes past her foot and she flinches before remembering that it's just the rabbit.

Isla scowls. 'I don't want to talk about it.'

'Did something happen?'

Isla meets her eyes. *'Yes, something happened.* My mother moved me from my home and my friends and dumped me in this . . . this *place* in the middle of nowhere.'

Gabe clears his throat, but Julia doesn't look at him.

'OK. I'm sorry, but we've been through this. It was always the plan and—'

'Yeah, whatever.'

'Did you chat with any of the girls in your class?' *Urgh.* She'd have hated these questions at Isla's age.

'Nope. They had a visit to the school in June to do some icebreaker games, but obviously we didn't live here, so . . .' A shrug.

'It'll take a few days to settle in . . . What did you do during lunch break?' Julia asks, making it sound casual.

'Everyone ate their packed lunches at the hockey pitch, so I did the same.'

'Oh, that's nice! So you got talking to some girls?'

'No – they all sat in groups. Lots of them seemed to know each other from their old schools.'

'And where did you sit?' *Why,* Julia wonders, is she putting herself through the torture of asking this?

'By myself.'

Julia nods and smiles and wonders if someone had told her thirteen years ago that this is what it's like – having your heart broken for your children time and again – would she have run off to a cabin in the woods to home-school them for ever and inoculate them from the world?

She reaches across the table to squeeze Isla's hand, but she pulls it away.

'They were talking about *The Loft,* by the way, and the videos.'

'Who were?'

'The group of girls at the hockey pitch. We're not supposed to switch on phones at school, but everyone does, and they were all scrolling through the videos.' For the first time, the sullen tone dims. Julia nods but doesn't interrupt. 'I was about to tell them my house is in one of them, but the video is gone so they might think I'm making it up.' She chews her lip. 'Nobody wants to be the weird girl pretending she was in a viral video so she can make friends.'

Gabe pauses halfway through dishing rice on to his plate. 'The video's gone?'

'Yeah, the account was deleted on Friday night.' Julia pours herself a glass of wine and holds the bottle towards Gabe, but, as expected, he declines. He hasn't officially given up alcohol, but he seems to have quietly stopped drinking in recent months. 'I'd still love to know who made it and why. Anyway' – she turns to Luca – 'how was your day?'

'Weird.' Luca sighs. 'First of all, the whole class is just boys. Why don't they have girls in the school? A whole bunch of boys, all dressed the same.'

Julia smiles. 'It'll seem strange for a while. We did try to get you into a school that's more like your old one, but it was full. This was the only place with a spot available.'

Luca hangs his head. 'I miss my old school.'

'I know you do, love,' Julia says, 'and it'll take a while to settle, but we'll get there.'

'Why did we have to move?' His eyes are huge and sad.

'Sweetheart, you know why.'

'It's because of Isla.'

Silence. Gabe is busy with his beef randang. Isla's mouth is open, but Julia jumps in before her daughter has a chance to speak.

'It's because we needed to get here before Isla started secondary school. If you were older, we'd have moved home in time for *you* to start secondary school. Now, eat up, then we'll play a

game of chess and you can have some extra screen time to cele-
brate day one.'

This does the trick, and nobody calls her out on the fib. And
anyway, if you say something often enough, Julia knows, the lie
becomes the truth.

9

'I SHOULD GET GOING to the apartment,' Julia says as Gabe leans to top up her glass.

'Oh, stay a few more minutes.'

She doesn't answer, but doesn't stop him pouring. For the first time since they moved in, the sitting room feels *lived* in. The high ceilings and polished floors and empty grate that seem cool and soulless much of the time are less austere tonight. Maybe it's the wine. Maybe it's the adult company.

'Do you want to talk more about Anya?' he asks tentatively, and she's touched. Normally, Gabe likes things to be simple – safe topics, low drama, fun chats. When they were twenty, she loved that about him – how laid-back he was. When she was working twelve-hour days trying to make ends meet in their early years in San Diego, it drove her crazy. She wanted someone who'd share the burden, the emotional labour, the decision-making. And that was never Gabe. The very early days, before mortgages and babies, had been good. Great, even. They'd grown close in the months following Donna's death, bonding in their grief, and when running off to the US seemed like a perfect escape for Julia, Gabe had been happy to follow. That summed him up – happy to follow. But after a while, she wanted someone who'd occasionally take the lead.

'It's just so sad,' she says now. 'Although I haven't seen her in years and we'd grown apart and we'd fought . . .'

'I know.' He puts a hand on hers. 'How's Eleanor doing?'

'She's OK. She rang me at work. She's spoken to Chris, Anya's partner. He was going to propose. Anya probably never knew.' She looks at Gabe. 'Kinda makes me feel like we have to grab the moments when we can, you know?'

He nods. Then opens his mouth as though about to say something.

'What is it?' she asks after a moment of silence.

'What is what?'

'You were about to say something?'

'No.' A casual shrug.

She's known Gabe half her life, and he's definitely gearing himself up to admit something. Sometimes waiting works – staying quiet, letting him fill the silence – but not this time. This time, he just shakes his head, wide-eyed and faux mystified.

She gives in. 'Right. On another note, I was thinking during dinner, when we were talking about the video – could it have something to do with Riley? Or her mom?'

'I doubt it. What would it achieve? Oh, I meant to ask' – he stretches – 'are you OK to stay here the weekend after next? I might need to take a short trip, spilling over to Monday the ninth.'

'Should be fine. Where are you off to?'

He looks away. 'Back to the States to sort some work stuff.'

'Grand.' She sees Gabe reach for the bottle to top up her wine again and puts her hand over the glass. 'No, thanks. I'd really better go now.' She gets up and slips on her shoes.

'I'll call you a cab,' he says.

'God, no, I'll walk.'

'It's dark out.'

'And it's only a two-minute walk.'

'It's at least five.'

'I'll be fine.'

Isla has AirPods in and doesn't raise her eyes from her phone when Julia leans to kiss her forehead. On-screen, a video hashtagged #TheLoft is playing, showing a family sitting down to dinner, seemingly oblivious to being filmed. As Julia watches, the family turns suddenly to face the camera, each one wearing a clown mask. She flinches and takes a step back, stumbling slightly over Isla's hair straightener. Julia picks it up and puts it on the dresser, reminding Isla to make sure it's always unplugged. This earns her an eye-roll, because it's already unplugged, and why, Isla asks, is she finding fault for no reason? Julia concedes with a nod and leaves for Luca's room. He's reading in his bunk bed and she has to climb up the ladder to reach him. Silently, he hands her his book and inclines his head for a kiss as she clicks off his reading light. Luca points at the wall above his head, at the air vent.

'Can he see me through that?'

'Who?'

'The man in the attic. I close my door at night, but I think he can look in through the vent. And Isla told me a story about a boy who—'

'Sweetheart, there's no man. You know that, right?'

Lit by the light from the landing, his eyes look huge and dark. 'There is. He was in my room and he smells funny, like the oil you put on my pillow when I'm sick.'

'Oh, honey. That's just the smell that's been there since the last time you were ill. It probably seeped through to your mattress. Look' – she kisses him again – 'I gotta go, but call me from Dad's phone if you need me, OK?'

Another nod. Julia climbs down. 'Will I leave the door open so Basil can come in?'

'No, it's better if it's closed. That way I'll hear the man if he opens it.'

Outside, the sky is tar black and starless, and the Brentwood streetlights – Victorian-style lamps – emit an amber glow that is designed to be soft and atmospheric but doesn't really illuminate the path. Julia pulls her coat collar up as a late-August chill catches her off-guard. The houses she passes are all in darkness. Ahead, the outer gates of Brentwood loom high against the night sky. There's no sound. No crickets, no traffic, no late-night walkers. She glances at her watch. Almost eleven on a Monday night. Of course anyone with sense is tucked up indoors. She yawns as she approaches the pedestrian gate. All around there is heavy silence.

And then a snap.

10

THE SNAP IS QUIET but distinct in the black night air. Her head jerks up. Listening now. Another sound. Like someone walking through grass. Her eyes swivel to the open space between the townhouses and the gates. A wooded area fronted by a green. Green by day, but black now, impossible to see. The swishing sound is slow and deliberate and getting closer. Should she go back to the house? That's ridiculous. It's probably just someone out for a night-time walk. But in the woods? In the grass? She needs to go, one way or another. She picks up speed, moving quickly to the gate, and feels around for the exit button. Why is there no light? How is anyone supposed to find the buzzer in the dark? Behind her, there's another snap, another swish. Her hands move frantically over the surface of the gate, settling finally on bulbous familiarity. Relief washes over her as the gate buzzes to life, clicking to unlock, then swinging slowly – so, so slowly – open. The swishing sound is very near now and it's clearly one of her new neighbours out walking, but she doesn't want to meet them or look back, and as soon as the gate is wide enough to slip through she does just that. And then she's gone, walking fast, almost running, down the Stillorgan Road.

Inside the apartment, she begins to breathe more easily. Slipping off her shoes in the hallway, she double-locks the door and pads across the thick-carpeted living room to sink on to the couch. The leather is cool against her skin and her breathing slows. She shakes her head, laughing quietly now. What on earth would anyone think if they saw her – running in heels at eleven o'clock at night? And over what? A noise. Julia Birch is not given to flights of fancy. She doesn't watch horror movies – not because she's afraid, but because she doesn't get the appeal. She's not melodramatic. So how had she been so spooked? Wine, maybe. The lateness of the hour. Walking instead of driving. And perhaps the video. On her phone, she searches under the hashtag #TheLoft. The first video shows a hatch very much like the one in her house. A figure dressed in black climbs down a ladder and stands in the middle of the landing. Suddenly, he swoops, his face coming right to the camera and, just like the first time, Julia jumps. This isn't funny.

The apartment feels eerily quiet and, for comfort, she turns on the TV and hunts through her bag for her book. It's not there, and she has a rare moment of annoyance at this two-home set-up. If she lived in one place all the time, she could get her book now from her night stand. Actually, it's in the car, she remembers, sitting on the passenger seat since Friday evening. Jackson Brodie's investigation would have to wait.

Usually, although she will admit it to nobody, she relishes the time in the apartment. A few days each week when she can focus on work, catch up on reading, practise yoga, knowing the kids are safe with their dad. Tonight, though, being alone is unsettling, and she wishes she could walk into the kids' bedrooms to kiss them goodnight again. It's all just so new, she reminds herself, getting up to rummage through the kitchen cupboards for snacks. Gabe has bought a six-pack of King Crisps and she grabs a packet, savouring the salty crunch as she flops back on the couch. The taste brings her back twenty-five years, to nights out in the Long Stone and the Stag's Head and, closer to home, in the Playwright and the Wishing Well. Pints of lager, long before Dublin discovered craft beers and she discovered good wine. Getting ready with Eleanor and Anya and Donna. Deciding what to wear. Jeans and a nice top, always. The giddiness on the way to Café en Seine. The queue in Eddie Rockets on the way home. The craic and the laughs and the tears. She finishes the crisps and crumples the bag. Twenty years in San Diego is a long time. Ireland has changed. *She* has changed. The kids will settle. She'll settle. And if she buries her head deep enough, her problems will disappear.

11

GOING TO THE FUNERAL feels hypocritical and uncomfortable and all kinds of wrong after all the things she's said and thought about Anya in the last two years. But of course there's no question – of course she's here, standing beside Eleanor, halfway down the right-hand side of the church. It's a week exactly since the news broke, and in that time a clearer picture has taken shape. Anya had left work at six on Wednesday, 21 August, declining an invitation to join her employees in a nearby pub. She never joined them, apparently – didn't like to mix business with pleasure. *Unless for her own benefit,* Julia thought, when she heard this.

Anya had driven home to Blackrock, parked in the garage and let herself into the house she shared with Chris. Chris was in LA, so Anya was home alone, apart from Chris's dog, Ziggy. As far as Chris could tell, Anya had opened a bottle of wine and carried it upstairs to the bathroom. She'd taken a bath and drunk most of the bottle. Nobody could say for sure what happened, but the presumption seemed to be that a combination of heat, alcohol and tiredness had caused her to fall asleep and slip under the water, never to emerge again.

On Thursday, as Anya lay dead in the bath, the dog-walker, Eric, had arrived and let himself in, to be greeted by a frantic Ziggy. Eric assumed Anya had gone to work without letting Ziggy out (not the first time, apparently) and had taken the dog for a long walk. He'd put food in the dog's bowl on their return, and left, not realizing Anya's body lay upstairs.

On Friday morning, Chris had come home to the grim discovery. For the first hour, he hadn't noticed a thing, Eleanor told Julia. It was only when he needed a fresh tube of toothpaste that he'd gone into the main bathroom.

And there she was.

Chris called an ambulance, even though he knew there was no hope. This was according to his sister, Lynn, who had taken on the role as chief disseminator of gory details. *And if only she'd left the door open*, the sister said, *like Chris kept telling her to*. Maybe the bathroom wouldn't have overheated. Maybe the air would have kept her awake. And maybe she wouldn't have stayed asleep when she went under.

Chris had been staying at his parents' house – he couldn't bring himself to be in the home he shared with Anya, although the police had said it was fine to go back. There'd be an inquest, of course, but for now, the gardaí said it looked like a tragic accident. The empty wine bottle on the shelf at the end of the bath. The used wine glass, stamped with Anya's lip gloss. Her phone. A magazine, open on a feature about Caribbean holidays on one page and 'eating for fertility' on the other. And holding the page flat, a small green paperweight in the shape of a rabbit.

After the funeral, mourners were invited back to Haddington House Hotel for drinks and food. Julia didn't want to go, but Eleanor had insisted, and now they're here, seated at a table with Chris's sister, Lynn, and her husband, Glyn ('Lynn and Glyn – we *had* to get together, it was *too* hilarious,' Lynn told them), eating salmon and drinking wine. Lynn has been talking for thirty minutes solid, very much enjoying her role, it seems to Julia, in the inner circle of the funeral party. Anya couldn't stand Lynn, Eleanor had said in the taxi on the way to the hotel and, as far as she was aware, the feeling had been mutual. Indeed, Lynn's sentiments are being confirmed now, in the form of posthumous passive-aggressive digs.

'Poor, poor Anya,' Lynn says, putting down her fork and shaking her head. 'Glyn and I just can't get our heads around it. A woman in the prime of life. Gone.' A pause. 'Of course, the drinking in the bath wasn't ideal.' A head tilt. 'Not that that would stop Anya.' A little laugh. 'We know she loved her wine.'

'Don't we all,' Eleanor says loyally, nodding at the bottle of Albariño that sits between them. On the far side of the table, one of Lynn's twin toddlers knocks over a glass of milk, and Glyn, a thin-faced man with thick hair and an impatient look on his face, begins mopping it up with a crisp linen napkin.

Lynn glances at the wine. 'Oh, don't get me wrong, I'm not judging.' She smiles brightly. 'But drinking alone? And on a Wednesday night? Kinda suggests a little *problem*.' She mouths the last word.

Julia, despite all her conflicted feelings about Anya, bristles.

Lynn keeps talking as a waiter begins clearing their plates. 'What do you reckon about the magazine? Eating for fertility?'

Julia shakes her head. 'One thing Anya was adamant about – she never wanted kids.' She turns to Eleanor for confirmation.

'Mmm . . . I'm not sure. A couple of things made me wonder recently. She was talking about big changes and life decisions and a move.'

'Really!' Lynn's eyes are gleaming at the gossip. Then she seems to remember they're talking about her brother's deceased girlfriend. 'I mean, god. That's so *sad*.'

Julia's not convinced. 'I don't know. It's just a random page in a magazine . . .'

Lynn gives a tinkly laugh. 'I *adore* your accent. It sounds *so*

American.' She manages to make it sound as though it's an affectation on Julia's part.

'Well, she did live there for twenty years,' Eleanor says, and although Julia is in no way offended by Lynn, she is touched by Eleanor's defence.

She smiles and shrugs. 'My friends in the US thought I sounded Irish and my friends here think I sound American.'

'Meanwhile,' Eleanor says, reaching for the water jug, 'Gabe, her ex-husband, still sounds like he's straight out of Oatlands College in Stillorgan.'

'Oh, Gabe is *your* husband! Yes, Anya mentioned him. *Interesting*.' There's something in the way Lynn says it that prods at Julia. 'He's the painter?'

'Artist. Yep.'

'I think I've seen his paintings. Very . . . modern.' It's not an insult by any stretch, yet somehow – Lynn's tone or expression – that's exactly how it sounds. Julia is about to ask her where she's seen Gabe's paintings – it seems unlikely, he's not well known – but Lynn is still talking. 'Anyway, about the fertility article – the paperweight was holding it *down*,' she says. 'That *must* mean something. And' – her eyes widen as she leans in to impart new information – 'it was slightly odd, because Chris said he hadn't seen it before. The paperweight, I mean. A rabbit made of some kind of green stone.'

'Ah now, I'm sure Anya owned all sorts of things Chris had never seen,' Eleanor says. 'Did you see the Manolos she bought in blue velvet? She went back and bought them in pink the next day. She's unreal.' A pause. 'God. For a second I forgot.' She swallows and takes a sip of water. 'But seriously, I'm not surprised Chris didn't recognize a paperweight.'

Julia can think of dozens of possessions Gabe would never be able to identify as hers. But something else is niggling.

'Why would anyone need a paperweight to keep a magazine page open in a steam-filled bathroom?' she asks. 'I mean, do people even use paperweights any more?'

Lynn purses her lips. 'I don't think it's about what was holding the page open; it's about what was *on* the page and—'

She stops abruptly as her brother arrives at the table, and the conversation changes.

Julia sips her wine, still thinking about the green stone paperweight. Visualizing it, conjuring it up from Lynn's description. There's something about it that sets her on edge. But right now, she can't put her finger on it.

12

After dessert, Glyn, tired of wrangling his children, it seems, tells Lynn it's her turn and that the kids could do with some air. Lynn reluctantly vacates her seat, and Glyn takes her place between Julia and Eleanor. Once the kids leave, each holding one of Lynn's hands, he takes a huge swallow of his untouched pint and visibly relaxes. His harried frown dissolves, his eyes soften and a dimple shows when he smiles.

'God, I needed that.' He looks from Julia to Eleanor. 'You guys have kids?'

They nod. They get it.

'You're Anya's friends from school, right?'

'Yeah. Thirty-three years since we met in Ms O'Dwyer's German class.' Eleanor laughs. 'God, Anya was so cheeky back then.'

'Was she?' Glyn settles back on the chair and crosses one ankle over his knee. 'I feel like I need to hear more.'

'Oh, normal teen stuff really, but she was the first to smoke and the first to drink. She used to bring a naggin of vodka and a pack of Silk Cut Purple to every sleepover from the age of, like, fourteen. She was always generous, though.'

Generous, Julia thinks. That's one way of putting it. She flashes back to a sleepover in Donna's house. Anya standing in the centre of the living room, hand on hip. Pink pyjamas. Hair tossed back as she swigged from a bottle of Smirnoff, before offering it to Donna. A knowing look on her face. Donna, cross-legged on a sleeping bag, shaking her head. Anya, teasing her. 'Donna, it's a bit of vodka. It's not like you're going to be drunk on one sip.' Donna shaking her head again. That was the great thing about Donna, Julia thinks. She was quiet and shy, but she could say no when she wanted to, even to Anya. And very few people said no to Queen Anya.

'So she was the ringleader?' Glyn asks.

'Definitely. If ever we got in trouble, it was usually because of Anya, yet somehow she'd avoid getting caught.'

'She was smart like that,' Julia agrees. *And self-absorbed and manipulative*. Things you don't say at a funeral.

Eleanor lifts her wine glass. 'Unlike me. I tumbled headlong into whatever was going on – sneaking out at night, having parties when my parents were away – and only ever stopped to wonder if it was a good idea when it was too late.'

Julia clinks her glass to Eleanor's. 'That's true. You were always the impulsive one.' *Impulsive to the point that it drove the rest of us mad*, she thinks. She remembers Eleanor falling in love with someone new every few weeks, then crying desperately when it didn't work out. Staying off school because she couldn't bear to face the world, like a Victorian heroine taking to her bed. Arguing with other girls in their year and dragging the rest of them into her dramas. Forgiving and forgetting as quick as a flash. She was loud and dramatic and lacked self-awareness. But, Julia realizes, thinking back in a way she hasn't done until recently, Eleanor was loyal and trustworthy. That counted for a lot.

'And Anya didn't get in trouble with her parents?' Glyn asks. He's very interested in Anya, Julia thinks. Or perhaps he's just glad to be free of his kids and at one with his pint.

'No. Hers were pretty easy-going,' Eleanor says. 'I remember one time when my parents searched our bags at a sleepover, she switched with me so that my cans were found in her bag. My mum told her parents, but they were OK with it. God, I was so relieved.'

Julia had forgotten about that. Maybe she's forgotten all of the good stories about Anya, blotted by the bust-up two years earlier.

'The only fly in Anya's ointment was that they lived in Bray, so she had to rely on staying in Donna's on nights out.' Eleanor flicks a glance at Julia. This is close to the bone. 'Anya was the social butterfly.'

'Popular, then?'

'Oh my god, *super* popular.'

But not necessarily *nice* popular, Julia thinks. At times it was more mean-girl popular.

'And full of energy,' Eleanor continues. 'Spurring the rest of us on.'

Impatient, Julia thinks.

'And always so confident.'

Arrogant. Julia sips her wine.

Eleanor sighs. 'We were lucky to know her.'

Maybe Eleanor is being kind because it's Anya's funeral and this is what well-mannered people do. Or maybe they're both remembering what they want to remember. The Anya Julia recalls was unpredictable and spiky. You never knew where you stood with her. One minute she was your best friend, linking arms, whispering in your ear. The next minute you were out in the cold. Ignored. Not knowing why. And then she'd be back. Reeling you in with one benevolent smile. And they all let her. Because it was easier to be on her good side. And also because she was fun. That part was accurate. When she was in the right mood, when it wasn't at someone else's expense, Anya was really fun.

'She had a great laugh,' Julia says now, partly from a need to contribute something positive but also because it was true. 'She would throw back her head and give this deep, throaty laugh that was infectious.'

Glyn nods and suddenly looks desperately sad.

Eleanor squeezes his arm. 'This must be such a shock for your whole extended family. I'm so sorry,' she says, her eyes full of concern.

Glyn pats her hand, nodding gratefully.

And Julia sips her wine, marvelling at Eleanor's ability to draw people in. That's Eleanor's superpower, she supposes. Her warmth. And maybe over the time away, the years since Donna, the fight with Anya, the drifting from Eleanor, Julia's forgotten the things that brought them together in the first place.

13

On Saturday afternoon, when Julia arrives back in Brentwood, there is someone doing stretches just beyond her front gate. A woman with sweat-slicked skin whose dark, glossy hair matches her all-black running gear. When she sees Julia approach, she straightens and removes her earbuds.

'Hi, you must be Julia! I'm Shirin. I live next door.' She's panting a little. 'Just back from a run.'

'Lovely to meet you,' Julia says, wondering how Shirin knows who she is.

'My husband, Tony, told me your name,' Shirin says, reading her mind. 'I've just returned from Sicily, otherwise I'd have called by sooner. How are you settling in? There are four of you, is that right? You have kids?'

'Yes, a boy and a girl.'

'Fantastic! Looking forward to meeting you all properly – a barbecue, maybe? We'll get something in the diary. Properly introduce the husbands?'

'Ah, so, the thing is, Gabe and I are divorced and we live here at different times of the week.' Julia waits for the usual reaction: surprise, curiosity – disappointment, maybe, that the envisaged double dates won't materialize. Shirin's eyes widen and her mouth forms an O but, just as quickly, she blinks and settles her face into a more neutral expression.

'I'm sure we can still do something to help you both settle in. Does Gabe play golf? Tony is surgically attached to his golf club. There are worse things he could be doing, I suppose,' she adds with a brittle laugh, and something in her tone gives Julia the impression that Tony is indeed doing these worse things, whatever they might be.

'Gabe doesn't play, but, actually, he's been talking about taking it up.'

'Tony can bring him to the club as a guest. You'll love it here. It's so quiet and safe, none of that antisocial behaviour you read about in other places. An oasis of calm, and wonderful neighbours.' Shirin is a walking, talking brochure for Brentwood. 'Anyway, I'd better get out of these things.' She gestures at her running gear. 'Lovely to meet you!'

Inside, the house is quiet. Leaving her handbag on the hall table, Julia goes through to the kitchen, where Gabe and the kids are huddled at the island, with Basil the rabbit cradled in Luca's arms. Their heads are together, watching something on Isla's phone. Gabe, Julia notices, is wearing a crisp white shirt and navy blazer – the kind of outfit he keeps for dates, not so much Saturday afternoons with the kids. Could he be going on a date? He's hardly seeing someone after just a month back in Ireland. Then again, Gabe being Gabe . . .

On the hob, a pot of hot oil bubbles. Gabe's making his signature dish – homemade chips the old-fashioned way, like his mum used to cook in the eighties. Julia secretly hates the chip pan – thoughts of fires and boiling oil and spills and burns, and it drives her crazy that Gabe never remembers to dispose of the oil – but the chips are admittedly divine.

'Mom!' Isla has spotted her. 'The video's back up!'

Julia squeezes between her children to see Isla's phone.

The clip is mid-loop, just as it reaches the marble floor at the bottom of the stairs.

'Is it the same account?' Julia asks.

'Kind of. It's Lepus456 instead of Lepus123 but must be the same person.'

'What does Lepus mean?' Gabe asks. 'Is it Latin?'

Luca holds up Basil. 'It means this guy – rabbit!'

Gabe fluffs his son's hair. 'Is there anything you don't know?'

They keep watching as the camera sweeps across the front door, capturing the light coming through the glass panels, then on to the lamp, the sunburst mirror and the narrow hall table.

'Bizarre,' Gabe says, and Julia remembers he didn't see it the first time around.

Isla presses Play again, and Julia makes herself watch, though she doesn't like the part where the figure comes out of the attic. Even though it's not real. And even though she's seen it before, she still jumps when the balaclava-covered face looms towards the camera.

'Maybe we can contact the Lepus account holder this time, if he doesn't delete it again?' she says.

'I'll do that.' Isla presses Stop on the video.

That's when it registers. Julia's skin goes cold. She puts her hand on her daughter's arm. 'Hang on, I've just noticed something.'

14

Silently, Julia takes the phone from Isla's hand and presses Play. Four heads lean in to watch. The camera pans down the hall to the mirror.

'There!' Julia says, and presses Pause.

In the mirror, at the edge, so fleeting she'd almost missed it, is a reflection. A shadowy figure, all in black. *Could there have been someone in the house?* It doesn't make sense. No more so than the monsters she'd imagined under her childhood bed.

'Jesus,' Gabe says, under his breath.

Isla leans closer. 'Someone was here. Someone was in the attic.'

Julia shakes her head, pushing down a creep of unease. 'No. How would they get in? It's like Fort Knox with the gates and the codes and the alarms. But it has to be someone who really knows their way around video editing. Which doesn't exactly narrow it down, I guess. Lots of people do, these days. It could even be a kid . . .'

She glances at Isla before she can stop herself.

Isla's eyes widen. 'You're thinking Riley?'

'No . . .'

'Riley's gone, Mom. She never came back to school after spring break. She went to live with her dad.'

If only that were true. Julia and Gabe exchange a glance.

Isla keeps going. 'I'm guessing she's moved on to tormenting someone else and forgotten about me – she's not making videos of my house halfway across the world.' A pause, a smirk. 'Apart from anything else, she's not smart enough.'

Julia winces and Gabe turns away.

Isla sighs. 'I know you guys think our generation are super tech whizzes, but honestly, I don't know anyone my age who could make a video like that. Don't you think it's possible someone's been inside the house? I read this story online about this kid who was sure there was someone hiding in the attic, but nobody would believe him. And then' – she pauses for dramatic effect – 'they eventually searched the attic and found a *body*.'

Luca's mouth drops open. 'A *dead* body?'

'Isla,' Julia warns. 'Enough. Luca, honey, there's no dead body or live body in our attic.'

'Can you check?'

Julia blows air into her cheeks. 'Sure. After dinner?'

'No, now. *Please*, Mom.' Luca is pale and tense.

She looks at Gabe, and he gestures at his white shirt and leather loafers. 'Me? In this? Sorry, it'll have to be you.' He grins.

'Where are you off to, all dressed up, anyway?'

'Meeting some of the old gang in town. Turns out we don't wear band T-shirts and ripped jeans any more.'

Julia sighs.

'Right, if I'm doing this, you're all coming to wait on the landing.'

Julia uses a pole to push the hatch up, then hooks one end into the built-in ladder to pull it down. She climbs up, feeling around as she reaches the hatch, looking for a light switch. It's fixed to a beam, just inside the opening, and when she presses it, low yellow light illuminates the centre of the attic. The far corners are still in darkness. Julia climbs the last step of the ladder and crawls her way awkwardly into the attic. It's cooler up here and suddenly eerily quiet and, in spite of herself, a chill crawls across the back of her neck. She shakes it off. It's just an attic, and she's doing this to show Luca that there's nobody here. *Because there is nobody here.*

There are bits of yellow insulation dotted around the floor but, overall, it's not as dusty as she expected. She moves from her knees to her feet, still crouched low. The attic is empty. As it should be, she reminds herself, since they haven't been up here with any of their stuff. She stands up straight and looks around.

'No dead bodies,' she calls down, her voice echoing in the empty space. The far corners are dark, but in the distance she can see something sitting on one of the beams. Something small and light in colour. She steps forward gingerly, not trusting the flooring. The light is low now and she uses her phone's flashlight to guide her way. The flooring comes to an end and she puts one foot on the beam, testing. It's firm. She steps forward, wondering why she's doing this for what appears to be a piece of plastic. She can't hear anything from below now, which is maybe because they've all gone quiet or maybe because she's too far into the attic. She takes another step and reaches to pick it up. It's a wireless earbud; an Apple AirPod or generic brand replica. Could it be Isla's? But Isla hasn't been up here. Maybe the previous tenant dropped it, or even a builder, back when the house was first built. Either way, there is no man hiding in the attic, and there is no dead body. Luca will be relieved. And Isla too, for all her sarcasm. Julia stuffs the earbud into her pocket and makes her way through the shadowy attic back to the hatch. With one foot on the top step of the ladder, she glances down. Three faces stare back. The floor, she realizes, isn't all that far away. If the ladder wasn't here, she could lower herself down and jump the last few feet. Like the man in the video. She shakes her head.

There is no man.

The video is fake.

The attic is empty.

Everything is fine.

Back in the kitchen, she asks Isla if the AirPod is hers (it's not; of course it's not) then asks her to go to the video again so she can message whoever's behind the account. Gabe and Luca are still upstairs, Luca having convinced his dad to climb on his bunk bed to check the vent to make sure there's nobody behind it.

'He does know the vent just leads out to the landing, right?' Isla mutters as she searches on her phone.

'He's anxious. It's no harm to reassure him. Did you find it?'

Isla frowns. 'Uh-oh.'

'What's wrong?'

'It's gone again. Lepus456.'

Julia exhales in frustration. 'Dammit. I should have messaged before going up to the attic. OK, maybe that's the end of it, but to be safe I think you should stop posting and also delete any videos you've put up.'

'No way.'

'Someone is using your clips, and I don't want to give them more material, but apart from all that I hate the idea that some creepy weirdo is watching you on the internet. At the very least, delete what's up there and stop posting from inside the house?'

'God, Mom, you don't get it. That's just how it is now. People share videos. If there are weirdos out there, that's their problem.'

'Except,' Julia says, pushing down a note of irritation, 'now it's our problem.'

'Oh, so you're saying it's my fault? That's victim-blaming.'

'Of course not. But until we work out who's doing this, I think it's wise to remove the . . . raw material?'

Isla shakes her head. 'Whoever's doing this probably has all the videos they need. All they had to do was save them from my account. Deleting them doesn't help.'

'I see, but—'

'Mom, if I had any actual friends – if I hadn't been pulled out of my school and my whole life, maybe I wouldn't have to spend so much time online. So if it's anyone's fault, it's *yours*.'

Isla stalks out of the kitchen, slamming the door behind her, just as Gabe comes in.

'You know, we could just tell her why we moved,' he says softly. 'You don't have to take the blame.'

'We can't, Gabe. It would do so much damage to her.'

'You don't know that.'

'I do. I've been there, remember? I was older than her when Donna died, but it never goes away.'

And he nods. He knows. Because he was there too when Donna died. The last one to see her alive.

15

On Sunday morning, the doorbell chimes at the ungodly hour of ten o'clock. Julia is still in pyjamas and midway through a third unsuccessful attempt to make waffles. The newly purchased waffle maker is not compatible with her batter, it seems. Leaving Luca in charge of the fourth waffle attempt, Julia walks out to answer the door, and finds Alastair O'Ryan on her doorstep.

'Morning!' he says cheerily. 'I thought you might like this.' He hands her a book. 'I know you read the Jackson Brodie series and I've finished this one.'

Julia takes the book. *Big Sky* by Kate Atkinson.

'Oh, thank you. I love this series – how did you guess?'

'Saw it in your car.' He thumbs behind him, where the new Range Rover gleams under early September sunshine. 'When I called last Saturday, it was on the seat. Made a note.' He taps his temple. 'We have similar tastes – detective fiction's my favourite too.'

'Well, thank you, that's very kind.'

'No problem.' Alastair is peering past her, into the hall. 'Making breakfast? French toast?'

'Waffles, and I'd better make sure they're not burning.' She holds up the book in one hand, beginning to close the door with the other. 'Thanks for this. I'll return it when I'm done.'

'No need, pay it forward. People in the Brentwood WhatsApp group often give away books. How's the waste disposal, by the way?'

'A plumber came during the week, and it seems OK.'

'Be sure to send the bill to the management company, and report them to Raycroft Estates if they don't pay promptly.' He rolls his eyes. 'Not that Raycroft are much use. Whatever you do, avoid a guy there called Clive Gannet – he's who I dealt with when I was moving in, and, excuse my language, but he's one of the most inept people I've ever met.'

'Duly noted.' Julia hides a smile, wondering if 'inept' is the bad language Alastair meant or if he just forgot to swear.

'Right, well, if you need anything else, just give me a shout.'

Julia thanks him again, and closes the door.

In the kitchen, Luca is perched on a stool at the island, with his chess set ready and a plate of maple syrup with one tiny waffle-chunk floating on top.

'I got a bit of it off the waffle maker,' he says. 'The rest of it is still stuck there. Can we play chess?'

Julia nods. 'I'd love to.'

She wouldn't love to. What she really wants is to lie on the couch and scroll on her phone. But guilt won't let her. *You only see them half the time*, she reminds herself, over and over. And at this stage, only 50 per cent of her children actually want to spend time with her. Chess used to be a Julia-and-Isla thing. They'd started playing during lockdown. Back then, Julia had done all of it – Wordle, baking, Yoga with Adriene. Buying things on the internet was a particularly appealing hobby to while away the long evenings at home. She'd bought the chess set on Etsy – handmade, personalized, expensive – and taught Isla to play. It was a way to spend time together, and for a while at least they had both loved it.

Then bit by bit, all of the hobbies drifted away. Julia lost her Wordle streak, she stopped baking, she went back to her in-person yoga class with Milena, and Isla stopped playing chess. But Luca learned and, knowing none of this lasts for ever, now Julia can't say no. So she scrapes batter off the waffle maker and sits beside her son.

'I like this,' Luca says.

'Playing chess?'

'Daytime. He stays in the attic in the daytime.'

On Sunday evening, Julia takes the kids out for burritos, and it's later than expected when they drive back into Brentwood. The soft click of the electronic gate behind them should make Julia feel safe and secure, but tonight it's unnerving. As though it's locking them in with something malevolent. *Woah, where did that come from?* she wonders, driving past shadowy, quiet houses. Brentwood is an early-to-bed kind of place, she thinks, noting dark windows in each home they pass.

'It's like the houses have eyes,' Luca whispers from the back seat.

The car crunches on the gravel driveway, the noise jarring in the stillness. It's dark now, and Julia calls for the kids to hurry as she unlocks the front door. Inside feels cool, and it strikes her yet again that for all its luxury, the house is cold and imper-sonal, and at night it's almost ghostly. That's when she notices the absence. There's no buzz to tell her the alarm needs a code. Did she forget to put it on? As the kids come in, Julia moves through the house, switching on lights and checking the back door. Or doors, as is the case. The entire back wall of the kitchen is made up of bi-folding glass doors: nice on a sunny afternoon, but less so after dark, with an unsettling goldfish-bowl effect once the lights are on. They should ask Raycroft for blinds, she thinks, making a mental note to tell Gabe – he looks after all the dealings with the letting agent. She stares out now, into the black back garden, hugging herself against the sudden notion that someone is outside looking in.

The patio doors are locked, and so are the back door in the utility room and the balcony door in her bedroom. She either forgot to put on the alarm or it's glitching again. Filling the kettle, she phones Gabe.

'Hey, about the alarm – the guy said it should work now?'

'Uh, yeah – he said it was fine. Why?'

'I thought I put it on when I went out, but it wasn't on when I got back. I guess I didn't set it.' She takes out a mug and a camomile teabag, waiting for the kettle to boil. From upstairs comes a thump. Luca jumping off his bunk, despite being told a hundred times not to do it. 'I'd better go check on the kids.'

'Sure. Just one thing – Isla hasn't heard anything from Riley, has she?'

'No, why?'

'No reason, it just popped into my head. OK, I'll let you go – say hi to the kids.'

Before she can take a first sip of tea, Luca arrives in the kitchen, an anxious look on his face. Basil is missing, he tells her. A twenty-minute search ensues and Luca eventually locates the rabbit inside Julia's wardrobe. She goes to the kitchen to pour her cold tea down the sink, then back upstairs to check in on Isla.

Isla is on her bed with her iPad, reading a Wikipedia page about a murder in an attic.

'Hey, maybe close the iPad and stop reading creepy stuff,' Julia says. 'You won't be able to sleep.'

A head tilt, a look of disdain.

'Isla, maybe you're not scared, but Luca is, so give it a rest, eh?'

She leans to kiss her daughter's head and pretends not to notice when Isla pulls away so that all she kisses is the briefest surface of hair.

Two hours later, the kids are asleep, Isla's PE gear is washed and dried, and Julia is in bed, going over notes for her Monday meeting. The sudden creak of a floorboard snatches her attention. She sits up straight, listening, staring at the ceiling. One of the kids? But she can't help feeling it came from above. Almost like a footstep . . . *It's just the house settling. There's nobody in the attic. But isn't that an old-house thing? Do new houses make noises at night?* She shakes the thought away. They're safe inside their new house, the doors are locked. There is nobody here but them.

16

LUCA WAKES TO SILENCE and lets out a breath of relief. The man isn't in his room. Switching on his night-light, he leans over the side of the bunk to check on Basil. But Basil's not in his nesting box, which is weird because Basil doesn't really move once he goes to sleep. Luca swings his legs towards the ladder and slips down to the floor to peer under his desk. No Basil. His bedroom door isn't quite closed and he sees now that Basil must have slipped through. The nesting box under his desk is Basil's favourite place to sleep. Why would he go downstairs? Then again, he's a rabbit and Luca doesn't know why rabbits do what they do. He moves quietly to the landing. It's in darkness but, if he turns on the light, his mom might wake. Feeling his way along the wall, he moves towards the stairs, quietly calling Basil's name, even though he's pretty sure Basil doesn't really know his name. The hall floor is cold under his bare feet and the shadows on the walls give him a shivery feeling. Maybe this isn't such a good idea. A sudden noise from the kitchen stops him in his tracks. Not a rabbit noise. A person noise. Like soft footsteps. Maybe his mom is still up? But there's no light under the door. Something moves in the corner of the hall now and Luca thinks he might die. His breath is stuck in his throat and he can't move. But his eyes adjust and now he sees the rabbit. Right there, beside the kitchen door. He has to get Basil. But what if someone opens the kitchen door and grabs him when he does? He whispers Basil's name, but the rabbit doesn't come. Luca takes one tiny step forward, eyes on the kitchen door. Then another. From the kitchen comes a creak. Someone is in there. Two more steps, and he reaches to grab Basil, then turns and runs silently back up the stairs. In his room, he shoulders his bedroom door shut and leans against it, panting, Basil safely in his arms. He sinks to the floor, holding the rabbit close, rubbing the velvety fur. There's something caught in it and he pulls it out, but he can't see in the dim glow of his night-lamp. Standing, he switches on his light to examine what's in his hand. It's some kind of yellow fluff. How did it get caught in Basil's fur? He has no idea, but something about it feels very, very wrong.

17

THE BEDROOM IS STILL in darkness when Julia starts awake and it takes her a moment to get her bearings. She's in Brentwood. It's September. It's Monday. It's morning. At least, according to the rim of grey light around the blackout blind, it's morning. Her Alexa confirms it's 6.16 a.m. Too early. But she's wide awake now, staring at the ceiling, scrambled thoughts racing through her mind. The videos. Anya's death. Isla's mood. This house. This huge, luxurious house that should be their fresh start. This huge, soulless house, with its enormous attic; hanging over her, literally and figuratively. Like cold air, breathing on her neck. Her eyes roam across the ceiling and down to the balcony door opposite the bed. Isla's words come back to her. *Imagine you woke up and there was someone at the end of your bed watching you.* Still bleary-eyed, she feels around on her nightstand for her phone, but it isn't where it usually is, lying neatly on her book, and she sits up now, confused. It's always plugged in at the socket behind her bedside table, charging overnight. Did she forget? She checks the floor and spots it on the other side of the room, by the balcony door. How did it get there? She clambers out of bed to grab it, annoyed at herself for not charging it. There are two new messages. One from Isla – a link to an article, sent at midnight. Julia begins typing a reply:

No phone in your bedroom at night, you know the rules, and what were you doing online so late?

She deletes it and types again:

Sounds creepy, thanks for sending, I think . . . 👀

The story is about a woman who found her ex-boyfriend, a just-released prisoner, living secretly in her attic. He had set up a mattress beside a vent that looked into her bedroom. Julia's eyes go to the ceiling. No vent. Just one in the wall. Could someone see through it? She slips out of bed to take a closer look. The vent is up high, so she pulls the stool from under her dressing table and climbs on. It would be hard to see through unless someone was right up close . . . Suddenly, she imagines eyes on the other side and pulls back so quickly she almost falls off the stool.

She climbs back into bed to read the other message. It's from Eleanor, checking in on her. She's awake early, too. On impulse, Julia texts to ask if she can call her. When did this happen, she wonders, this asking if it's OK to phone? Sometime in her early years in the States, she supposes, when time zones and life changes pulled them apart. Back when they were in school and college they phoned one another all the time. Dragging the landline into the study off the hall. In trouble with her dad for the phone bill. In trouble with her mum for tying up the line. But speaking was *imperative*. Despite spending all day in school together, they needed to dissect and debrief at home. Which boy they loved. Which boy they kind of liked. What they'd wear to the disco on Friday. Jeans, Docs and a paisley shirt, the uniform of her teens, long before fake tan and hair straighteners and dresses from Shein. Julia can't decide which was better – there was less pressure back then, for sure, but, then again, she could have done with access to more than her mother's pan-stick foundation. Her phone starts to ring. It's Eleanor.

'Hey, all OK?' Eleanor asks when Julia answers.

'Fine, just awake early and saw you were too. How're you doing?'

'You mean about Anya? Still weird. But picturing her slipping under the water isn't taking up every waking moment now, so that's progress.' Her voice cracks slightly, belying her words. 'You?'

'Yeah, she's still on my mind, though obviously we weren't close like you guys . . . and there was a second attic video on Saturday. Everything's a bit strange,' she says. And it feels good to talk, she realizes. 'Hey, um, would you like to come over some evening this week?'

'I'd love to! I can't wait to see this fabulous house of yours. Even if it'll put my ancient old place to shame, with all its cracks and knotholes.'

Eleanor's 'ancient old place' is a listed building worth two million euro, but aside from that, at this moment, Julia would swap all her clean-line luxury for a few cracks and knotholes if it meant no attic videos and better sleep. They agree that Eleanor will come over Wednesday evening and say goodbye, just as Julia's alarm goes off and Luca arrives in her room, rubbing his eyes.

'Mom, I think the man brought Basil up to the attic last night.'

She pulls him into a hug. 'There is no man, and isn't Basil in his box in your room?'

'He is now, but he wasn't last night. And I found yellow fluff in his fur and it's like that stuff in attics . . . Insulation?'

She nods to confirm he has the right word, then immediately shakes her head. 'That could be anything. I promise you Basil wasn't in the attic. It could be from carpet or clothes, or who knows—' She stops. Something tugs at her memory but slips away just as quickly.

'What is it, Mom?'

'Nothing. Now, go get ready for school.' She kisses him and shoos him out the door, feeling guilty for dismissing his fears but certain she doesn't want to indulge them and make everything worse. *Where is the parenting manual on this one?* she wonders, as she gets ready to face Monday morning.

When she arrives home after work, Pauline is on a step-stool, dusting the smoke alarm on the hall ceiling. Pauline is a find. In her early sixties, with adult children, she's happy to do as many or as few hours as they need and, crucially, lives in Kerrybrook, just across the road from Brentwood, one neat residential street over from where Julia grew up. Pauline loves tea and talking and true-crime podcasts. She wears the same type of outfit every day – a dark jumper with sensible black trousers. She leaves her trainers in the hall when she arrives, padding around in slippers all day. She's a terrible cook, she says herself, but a dab hand at defrosting Gabe's batch-cooked meals. She has a sweet tooth and quietly disobeys Julia's 'no treats midweek' policy, much to Luca's satisfaction. He's teaching her how to play *Mario* on his Switch and has talked her into putting *Among Us* on her phone. Luca is definitely warming to her. Isla, not so much.

Julia greets the housekeeper and they move together to the kitchen.

'They've both eaten, and Luca's watching TV in the den with the rabbit.' Pauline wrinkles her nose. She is not Basil's biggest fan. 'Isla's doing homework upstairs. Although I wonder how much she might be getting done with the phone in the room, you know?'

Julia nods but doesn't bite. 'Pauline, on another note, there hasn't been anyone inside the house, has there?'

Pauline's eyes widen. 'How do you mean?'

'While I'm at work – nobody was in, were they? Tradespeople, neighbours?'

'Neighbours? No, I don't know any of your neighbours and wouldn't invite them in.' Pauline folds her arms, her face set with a tinge of defensiveness.

Julia pushes on. 'Tradespeople?'

'There was a man looking at the burglar alarm, but I told Gabe. I checked before letting the man in.' Full-on defensiveness now.

'Nobody else?'

'No.'

Julia realizes now how much she was hoping Pauline would answer yes – yes, she'd let someone in for some obscure reason and they'd filmed the clips. Because although it would make no sense, it would also explain everything.

'Is there something wrong?' Pauline waits, eyebrows up.

'It's going to sound bizarre, but there's a video clip on the internet that shows a person creeping around our house. Letting himself out of the attic. And—'

'Ah, the *Loft* thing?' Pauline reaches for the button on the kettle. 'For the TV show?'

Julia tries to hide her surprise.

Pauline catches it. 'I might not be TikTokking away with the rest of them, but I do have a son in college, so I'm not oblivious,' she says, the corner of her mouth twitching upwards. 'He even tried to make a video himself. Six years of medical school, and there he is, like a big eejit, getting his brother to film him climbing out of the attic. His brother's worse, egging him on.'

'Is he in college too?'

'No! That's just it. He's a grown adult with a job. Works in property, makes a fortune selling houses like this' – she sweeps her hand around – 'goes to all these important meetings with clients, and there he is filming his brother jumping out of an attic.'

'Are you serious?' Julia is laughing now because it's funny, but it's also because it's a relief. Knowing that normal, regular people like Pauline's sons are creating these videos makes it less sinister.

'Oh god, yes. Bored. That's the problem. Too much free time.' She clicks her tongue and takes down two mugs, holding one up in an offer of tea. Julia nods.

'But you surely don't mean someone came into your house,' Pauline continues as she pours boiling water into a teapot, 'since you've been living here?'

Julia explains what's been happening, and Pauline hands her a mug of tea. 'Look, it must be somebody faking the clips. Maybe – now, don't take this the wrong way – don't put any more videos on the internet?'

'Don't worry. Isla's been warned.'

Pauline is nodding towards the doorway now, mouthing something that looks like 'little ears'. Julia turns to see Luca, standing, listening.

'What has Isla been warned about?' he asks.

'Luca! I didn't see you!' Julia crosses the kitchen to hug him, but he's stiff and unyielding in her arms. 'Are you OK?'

'It doesn't matter about Isla's videos, Mom. It's too late. The man is already living in our attic and watching us while we sleep.'

18

TUESDAY MORNING IS A blur of exhaustion. Luca had slept in Julia's bed, starfishing and tossing and turning, while she'd lain awake trying unsuccessfully to block out the imagined sound of footsteps. Now, she's on her way back from the school run, walking through Brentwood's gates, jittery from too much coffee and not enough sleep. Her phone beeps with a notification she hasn't seen before – the joint bank account has fallen below the €2,000 threshold she'd set when they moved back. The account is used for rent and household expenses and she rarely looks at it – payments flow in from her personal account, payments flow out to pay various bills. Gabe does most of the cooking, most of the shopping, most of the household spending, and Julia never pays much attention. She does now, though, spotting immediately a payment of €3,124 going to something or someone called 'SB'. She messages Gabe to ask what it is, then looks up to see a familiar figure approaching from the opposite direction. He lifts a hand in greeting and her mind runs through her internal Rolodex of names. Something like . . . Daryl? Drew? That's it. Drew, the personal trainer. She'd met him on her way back from work one evening, and once or twice since. He'd just moved into one of the townhouses, he'd said, after years in a small apartment. Julia isn't sure how much personal trainers earn, but clearly enough to rent or buy one of the eye-wateringly expensive

Brentwood townhouses. Like Alastair, Drew is a few years older than she is, and outgoing and talkative, but unlike Alastair, he's always rushing somewhere or other – stopping to chat but with the sense that he's permanently eager to leave, like a greyhound straining at the traps. Not rude, just busy. Julia understands this well. She is also not rude, just busy.

'Morning,' he calls as he approaches, keys jangling in his hand. She notices the red 'R'-shaped key ring, just like her own. So Drew must rent from Raycroft Estates, like she does. 'Just finished a sesh with Shirin. If you ever need a personal trainer, I can do mates' rates?' Beads of sweat on his forehead dissolve as he runs his hand through his close-cropped fair hair. His eyes are bright blue, in stark contrast to his flushed skin and carefully manicured stubble. He reminds her of a PE teacher from her old school, except her teacher, as far as she remembers, wasn't wearing a Hugo Boss tracksuit. Nor did he have a tattoo of angel wings on the back of his neck, as Drew does. He rolls up his sleeves and she sees now that he also has a leaf-entwined sword on his right forearm, and the letter 'D' with a bird flying above it on his left.

'Oh, that's very kind.' She smiles politely.

'Impressive lady, Shirin. Very fit for her age. Tony will have to watch out or she'll be gone with a younger model.'

'I'm sure Shirin has all sorts of reasons for staying fit,' Julia says dryly.

'Ah, I'm only joshing. She's a good-looking woman, though. Iranian, originally, I think?'

Julia isn't sure if this is a real question or an odd kind of small talk. It hadn't dawned on her to wonder about Shirin's ethnicity, and after twenty years in multicultural San Diego this feels like a strange conversation. Then again, so far, Brentwood appears to be extraordinarily white.

'Anyway,' Drew goes on, 'if anyone's likely to stray, it's Tony, at least from what I hear on the grapevine.' A wink.

What exactly is she supposed to say to that? 'Right . . . I'd better get in, I'll be late for work.'

'Do you work near by?' he asks.

'No, I'm in the city centre at the moment.' She digs into her bag to pull out her keys.

'At the moment? Are you leaving?'

'It's contract work, so in a few months I'll take on something new.'

'Ah, yeah. Alastair, my neighbour' – he points over towards the townhouses – 'he does contract work too. Crikey, he can talk for Ireland. I'm only here a few weeks but I feel like I know his whole life story.' A grin. 'Have you met him?'

'Yes, he called by.'

'Grand guy.' Drew tilts his head just like Anya always did when she was about to say something mean disguised as something nice. 'Potentially a bit . . . *much*?' He injects a lot into that one innocuous word.

'He was very nice, actually. Offered to help if we need anything else fixed.'

'Yeah, he has a lot of time on his hands.' Drew leans closer and she can smell the toothpaste from his breath and the sweat from his workout. 'His fiancée dumped him last year, apparently, right before their wedding. Not quite jilted at the altar, but close. Their daughter lives with the ex now. He'd had money problems; she didn't take it well. He's still pretty cut up about it. Keeps the engagement ring on a shelf in his living room, like maybe she'll come back.'

Julia stiffens as his words conjure up a sudden image of Anya. Anya, who had never known she was about to become engaged. The ring still in a box, unseen and unworn. And the dark cloud that's been hovering over her for days clings a little tighter.

'That must be hard,' Julia finds herself saying, suddenly feeling sorry for Alastair.

'Ah yeah, I'm sure it is. Right, I'll let you go. See you around. And remember, mates' rates.' With a wave, he's gone.

It's Pauline who has the honour of letting her know about the third video. She comes out to greet Julia in the hall when she returns from work on Tuesday evening, stage-whispering the news.

'Isla found it.' She says it solemnly. 'They're in there looking at it now. Maybe I should have stopped them. I was going to ring you.'

'Gosh, no need to ring me over something like that,' Julia says, in an instinctive bid to dilute things. 'I'm sure it's just someone Photoshopping.'

Pauline shakes her head. 'It looks very real to me. Could someone be getting in during the day before I get here?'

'I . . . No, I don't think so. The doors were locked and, besides Gabe and me, you're the only person with a key.'

'Well, have a look and see what you think.' Pauline beckons her through to the kitchen, where Isla and Luca are bent over Isla's phone.

Isla straightens, holds up the phone and presses Play.

19

AT FIRST, THE VIDEO is exactly like the other two, but where the previous ones stopped in the hall, this goes on to show the kitchen, panning across Gabe's painting of Mission Beach, the family photo they'd had taken last year, and Julia's small Monet print – the one Eleanor brought back from France all those years ago. Identical prints for each of them – Julia, Anya, Donna and Eleanor herself. The camera moves on to the whiteboard, hovering over Julia's to-do list, and a pang of unease lurches. Eleanor's 'welcome home' card is in view, but the camera is still moving, and now it's on the fridge, then Luca's school bag and tennis racket by the door, and then the screen goes black. *It looks so real.* Julia feels a crawl of fear deep in the pit of her stomach. God, whoever's making these videos is good at what they're doing.

'Mom, it might get deleted now we've seen it – the account holder will be able to tell it's had at least one view and might guess it's us, so—'

'I know,' Julia mutters, typing quickly, aware that, on some level, she's grateful for this tiny bit of cooperation – the shared drama that's bringing old Isla back to her.

I don't know what you're trying to do, but you can expect a solicitor's letter or the police if you don't stop posting these videos.

Isla is reaching for the phone.

'It's OK, I got it sent,' Julia says. 'Obviously we can't really send a solicitor's letter without—'

'No, that's not it – give me the phone so I can save the video,' Isla says, grabbing again. 'At least then we can watch it back even if they delete the account.'

'Oh.' Julia hands her the phone. Isla presses something and then something else.

She scowls.

'What's wrong?'

'It's gone. The account's been deleted. Great, Mom. You just have to do everything *your* way.'

'Oh,' Julia says again. 'Sorry, I didn't think of that. But look, we know it's from your videos.'

Isla eyes her.

'What?'

'I think it's real. Someone's been in the house.'

'Don't be silly.' Even as she says it, even as she plays her part as the adult in the room, a chill runs across her skin. *What if it's real?*

Luca nods, his eyes wide and unblinking. 'He's up there.'

'Stop!' Julia says, and it's sharper than she intended. 'Guys, I went up to the attic – remember? A bit of dust. Nothing else.'

Luca looks like he's going to cry. 'Oh, honey, I'm sorry. I didn't mean to snap. But I promise you, there's nobody here except us.'

Pauline is beside them now, pressing a biscuit into Luca's hand. 'There, pet, that'll make you feel better, won't it? Would you like me to stay on a bit?' she asks, looking at her watch.

'No, you go on, thanks, Pauline. We'll see you tomorrow.' Julia follows Pauline out, waiting while she changes into her trainers.

'It's a big adjustment for them,' Pauline says, opening the

front door. 'It'll get easier.' She stops for a moment, examining Julia, then puts a hand on her arm. 'Do you have anyone around to lean on? Your siblings?'

'Oh. They live abroad.'

'And your parents are in Westport, I think?'

'You know my parents?'

'Not well, but I remember them when I was growing up. I was in college when you were all small.' She rubs Julia's arm. 'I remember your poor friend Donna. Horrific what happened to her. One of the saddest funerals I've ever been to.'

Pauline's eyes dampen, and tears prick the back of Julia's eyes too. She nods, unable to find words.

Pauline gives her a small squeeze. 'Right, lovey, see you tomorrow.'

Swallowing against the tightness in her throat, Julia closes the door and, staying in the hall, phones Gabe to fill him in on the new video.

'That's so weird and creepy,' he says when she finishes. 'Do you want me to come over? Are the kids OK?'

'We're fine. Though I got a bit snappy and Luca was upset. I'd better go check on him . . . Oh, one more thing – you didn't reply to my message about the payment to "SB"?'

'Which message?'

This sounds like stalling.

'How many texts did you get today asking about money going to "SB"?'

'Oh, that. It's just residual fees for the school in San Diego. We weren't up to date before we left.'

'OK, I've topped up the account. But let me know if there's something big like that again so the balance doesn't dip below two thousand.'

Silence. Too late she realizes she sounds like a boss speaking to an employee. She hadn't meant it like that.

'Yes, Julia.'

They say goodbye and she hangs up. The hall is quiet and the marble floor is cool under her feet. She stands for a moment, absorbing the silence, her hand still resting on the phone.

She pads up the stairs, shrugging off her blazer as she goes through to her bedroom and over to her walk-in wardrobe. But as she reaches to turn the handle, there's a noise. A creak. From inside. As though someone is standing in there, waiting. *For goodness' sake.* She yanks open the wardrobe door, marches inside and hangs up the blazer. She's back outside and closing the door within seconds, letting out a long breath, laughing at herself. But it's a shaky, silent, not-quite-convinced kind of laugh and her heart is beating faster than usual. She pulls out her phone, sits on the bed and types 'How to tell if video is real fake AI' into Google.

The answer, it seems, is that you can and you can't. There are elements to look out for – lighting or shadows that look strange, movement that doesn't make sense, proportions out of sync. But no definitive way to know, and even with the most sophisticated software only 80 per cent of fake videos are detectable. Which isn't much use to Julia, who has zero sophisticated software at her disposal. She also has no video clip to examine for lighting or shadows to show to the gardaí. However, maybe it's time to give herself peace of mind.

She goes downstairs to phone the police.

The garda who answers her call says she can either come in to make a report or they can send a car. The latter sounds very dramatic so she says she'll call in. He doesn't note any details over the phone so she has no idea yet how seriously they'll take her report, and she isn't sure if she can get to the station until Thursday evening, but still, it feels good to have done something.

The doorbell rings and Julia opens it to find Shirin on her doorstep.

'Julia, delighted I caught you! I wanted to invite you guys over for a barbie one evening – say Friday week?'

'Oh, thank you.'

'Both of you, of course, and the kids. But only if – maybe you don't do things together? Have I put my foot in it?'

'Not at all, that would be lovely. I'll mention it to Gabe, and if he's free he'd love to come, I'm sure. He'll be here anyway, it's his turn.'

'Marvellous! You'll meet Tony, and we can properly welcome you. It's nice to have someone next door again.'

'Oh, I thought the previous tenant only moved out a few weeks before we moved in?'

'Yes, he did.' She looks at her hands. 'It's just that it was awkward. Tony never liked Hugo – that's the previous resident. So we didn't invite him over.' She stops. There's definitely more to this story, but Shirin doesn't elaborate. 'Anyway, this is going to work out much better! So, see you Friday thirteenth at seven.'

They say goodbye and Julia closes the door. Suddenly exhausted, she trudges upstairs to take a shower.

Minutes later, hot water thunders down on her shoulders, easing the strains of the day, and she stands beneath the showerhead far longer than usual, emptying her mind.

Below her, downstairs, her children watch their screens. And above her, in the attic? Despite the hot water, she shivers.

20

IT'S LATER THAN USUAL when Julia walks through the gate to Brentwood on Wednesday evening, her hands aching from over-filled shopping bags. Antipasti and cheese and crackers do not weigh much, but vermouth and cava do. Turning her wrist awkwardly, she checks her watch. Almost seven, and Eleanor is coming at seven thirty. She hopes Pauline will have fed the kids and nobody will need help with homework.

'Hey, Julia, how are you?'

She turns to see who's speaking and finds Alastair trotting behind her, with a smile on his face and a dog on a lead.

'Oh, hi. Cute pup, what's its name?' she asks, nodding towards the dog – one of those tiny breeds everyone in Ireland seems to have now.

'This is Mavis.'

She splutters a laugh. 'Mavis! I love it. Luca wants a dog, but we need to get used to the rabbit first.'

'If you decide to go ahead, I can give you some pointers. Is he an outdoorsy kid?' He taps a finger to his lip, as though assessing Luca's suitability. 'Good at walking a dog?'

'Hmm. You couldn't call him outdoorsy, no. Video games, reading and chess are his thing, with a bit of tennis to tick the "sports" box.'

'Ah, a young man with excellent hobbies, especially the chess. Great game.'

'You play?'

'Any chance I get. I used to play with my daughter.'

Drew's words come back to Julia – Alastair's ex and their daughter. 'Oh, how old is she?' Julia asks, hoping he won't guess she's been listening to gossip.

'Eight now. But . . .' He looks down. 'Well, her mother and I aren't together and I don't get to see her.'

'I'm so sorry.'

He waves it away. Not, Julia thinks, because it doesn't matter, but because he's teetering on the brink of upset. 'I didn't mean to bring it up – it was just when you mentioned chess. She was a dab hand at it for a little kid. Do you play yourself?'

'Yep. I'm not brilliant, but it's a great way to wind down after work.'

'It sure is.' Alastair exhales. 'As long as you have someone to play with. Maybe I'll pop over to give you a game some evening!' He nods at her shopping bags. 'Party?'

'Just a friend coming for drinks in the garden.'

Another wistful sigh. 'Lovely gardens for parties. And dogs.' He points back towards the townhouses. 'They got a bit stingy with the space by the time they were building those.'

'The townhouses are gorgeous all the same,' Julia says politely.

'I'm only renting, though.' He holds up his keys and Julia sees the familiar red 'R' key ring. 'Same as yourselves. They're well built but small. Barely two parking spaces each,' Alastair continues. 'Then again, I don't have a car so I don't need parking.' Julia can hear the tinge of pride. 'I cycle everywhere. So, how's the book?'

'Oh, I haven't started it yet, but thanks again for dropping it in.'

'I can give you this one when I'm done,' he says, pulling a paperback from a deep coat pocket.

'That's so kind, but take your time. I have plenty of books to keep me going. I'd better head off.' She raises the bags of groceries. 'Good to see you.' She walks on before he can say anything else. He's just being nice, she reminds herself, and his fiancée left him and he doesn't see his child and he's probably lonely. But all the same, it's cloying.

At twenty past seven, the doorbell rings and Eleanor whirlwinds into the house.

'I couldn't wait any longer. I've actually been sitting in the car outside your house for ten minutes.'

'What?'

'Juju.' She shakes her head in mock sadness. 'You don't remember bedtime with small kids, do you? I told Ian I had to be here at five and diverted to Dundrum for a trip around Brown Thomas. *Anything* to get out of bedtime. Am I OK to leave my car? I'll get a cab home and pick it up tomorrow.'

'Of course! Wait, how did you know the code to get through the gate?'

'One of your neighbours let me through once I explained I was visiting you. *And* once he had, held me there for a good five minutes chatting. Like, literally a gatekeeper. Guy with a small dog? Kinda cute in a nerdy way?'

'That's Alastair. Loves a good interrogation . . . But anyway, you're here – come through!'

While Eleanor oohs and aahs over the kitchen, Julia pulls out two heavy tumblers and a shot glass for measuring.

'Oh, Juju.'

Julia looks up. Eleanor is standing at the shelves by the glass doors to the living room, head tilted, staring at the photo of the four of them at their Debs ball. Julia in fuchsia, because her mother insisted that blondes should wear pink. Anya in slinky red. Donna in biscuit-coloured satin. And Eleanor in jade taffeta. Their pale faces smiling happily under inexpertly applied make-up. Arms linked. Eyes shining with future prospects and the camera flash. A happy night.

'I haven't seen this before.' Eleanor's tone is hushed. 'We thought we were hideous back then, but we were beautiful.'

'Would you like it? I can make you a copy.'

'I'd love that. Actually' – she lifts her phone – 'I might snap a pic. Do you think it's OK if I put it on Facebook and say something about Anya? I haven't done anything yet and I feel like I should.'

Julia nods. 'I think that would be lovely.'

Julia finishes mixing pink negronis and Eleanor lifts her glass to taste.

'Oh wow, perfection. We've come a long way since nicking vodka from our parents' drinks cabinets and mixing it with Cadet Cola. Remember?'

Julia smiles as they move out to the patio and sit side by side on the rattan sofa so that they're both facing the evening sun.

Eleanor sips her drink. 'I actually can't believe the things we did and how we survived.' She stops, and her eyes bloom with tears. 'God. Shit. How did I just say that? It's still hard to take in that she's dead—'

She's interrupted by Isla, who sticks her head out from behind the patio door. 'Mom! I can't find my stupid Home Ec book and I need it tomorrow.'

'OK. Where did you have it last?'

'If I knew that, I'd know where it is.' She turns and flounces off.

Eleanor's eyes widen.

Julia grimaces. 'It's all ahead of you. Or not – maybe you'll get easy teens.' A flicker of defensiveness now. 'She's gone through a lot, and she hasn't settled in yet.'

'Is she in touch with friends from San Diego still? That'll really help with the transition.'

'She has two good friends, and she's online with them a lot.'

'Everything's online now, I suppose.' A rueful headshake. 'Remember when kids used to play outside? We used to be out from dawn till dusk, only coming home for tea.'

Julia bites back an eye-roll. Eleanor, who spent every chance she got horizontal in front of the television, had never in her life been out from dawn till dusk.

'It's the only way Isla can stay in touch. Her friends are literally thousands of miles away.'

'Can't they write letters? We used to write letters.'

'I can't wait till you have teens of your own. You'll see just how many letters they write.'

Eleanor holds up her hands in mock surrender. 'Fine, you're the expert.'

A door slams inside.

Julia shakes her head. 'Let's open a bottle of rosé and talk about nice things.'

Just as she's about to fetch the wine, Isla bursts through the patio door.

'Mom! Another video! And this time I got it.'

21

'WHAT DO YOU MEAN, you got it?' Julia's on her feet now.

'I saved the video, so it doesn't matter if he deletes the account this time!' Her eyes dance, and Julia, in spite of her discomfort, is oddly happy too, because this Isla – engaged and enthusiastic – is much easier than door-slamming Isla.

'*So* glad you're getting such fulfilment from our predicament,' she says, smiling at Isla and taking the phone. She sits, leaning towards Eleanor so they can both see.

Again, the video starts with the hatch, but as Julia sits in her garden with Eleanor beside her, it doesn't seem quite so chilling, even when the masked face looms towards the camera. Eleanor jumps.

'Holy shit!' She glances at Isla and covers her mouth. 'Sorry. But this is so freaky. Isn't there a chance it's real?'

Julia frowns a warning at Eleanor. 'No, it has to be fake.' She doesn't add that she's going to the garda station tomorrow to ask that very question. If the gardaí can categorically confirm they're fake, then the only concerns are who and why. That Google has already told her a categorical answer is impossible is a worry for later.

The video is still playing, the screen showing the living room now, taking in the huge, high-ceilinged expanse, the cream couches, the grey wing chair, the glass coffee table. The stove with its pristine glass door. The heavy poker, unsullied by use. 'OK, so here we go across the living-room shelves,' Julia narrates. 'Family photo, graduation photo . . . coffee table, the book Alastair loaned me, a folder of work notes—' She stops abruptly.

'Isla, you'd know not to catch any of my work notes in shot, wouldn't you?'

Isla nods. 'Uh-huh . . .'

'OK, you know my notes are *highly* confidential. I mean, we're talking names of people who're going to lose their jobs, *before* they find out they're going to lose their jobs.'

'I've never filmed your work stuff. No offence – it's really boring.'

'Yes, but if you're making a video and my folder is visible, you might not notice?'

A shrug. 'Nobody would be able to read your notes.'

'They would if they screenshot and zoomed in . . .'

'I guess . . .'

'Isla, this is serious. It absolutely cannot be the case that someone finds out they're losing their job through TikTok!'

'I didn't film your notes.' She points at the phone screen. 'The notebook is closed.'

'Sure, but what about other clips you made? Can I look at them again?'

'You made me delete them, remember?'

'I made you remove the videos from TikTok, but don't you still have the originals?'

'No. I filmed them directly in the app. So once you take them down, they're gone.'

'For goodness' sake.'

Isla's hands are on her hips now. 'You cannot blame me for you not understanding how TikTok works.' She's not quite shouting but her voice is raised.

Julia exhales, conscious that Eleanor is sitting quietly, wondering, no doubt, why she's not telling Isla off.

'I'm not blaming you, I'm just worried about work.' She keeps her tone calm. 'And realizing that, if all your videos are gone, we have nothing with which to compare this.'

'But at least you can bring it to the police?' Isla's voice is back to normal, mirroring her mother's, and Julia marvels again at how quickly her daughter flits from rage to calm.

'True.'

'And, Mom, thinking about your work notes . . . could the videos have something to do with your job? Someone you fired?'

'I don't *fire* people, I put plans in place so that employers can—'

'Yeah, yeah, but from the point of view of the person who lost their job, you're the bad guy, right?'

'OK,' Julia concedes. 'But they don't know who I am. There's no way a disgruntled employee would know to find videos made by you and put all this together. Can you message the latest clip to me? I'll go to the guards after work tomorrow.' She shakes her head. 'The whole thing is getting ridiculous. Enough is enough.'

'Now *that's* the Juju I know,' Eleanor says, raising her glass. 'The Unbreakable Julia Birch.'

It's almost midnight when Julia closes her laptop and picks up her book. But negronis and the late hour are conspiring against her and the words blur. Moments later, she's staring into space as jumbled thoughts roam through her mind. Her work notes. The payment to SB. Anya slipping under the water. The masked man. The attic hatch. Tonight's video. Who is doing it, and why? Could it have something to do with San Diego – with what Isla did to Riley? Could Riley edit the videos? *What if it's not editing?* says a voice in her head, a voice that's had too much to drink. *What if there's really someone in the attic?*

She slides down in the bed, staring at the ceiling. She's been up there; she's checked. She closes her eyes, feeling for the lamp switch. As she slips into light sleep, she hears it. A tiny scrape. Barely audible. Her eyes snap open. Heart racing, she listens for more. Another scrape. From the wardrobe? Or the landing? Jesus Christ, this is ridiculous. The sound of a door handle now. She sits up, blood thundering in her ears. Is it her door? Or one of the kids' doors? She swings her legs out of bed and yanks open her bedroom door. A shadowy figure on the landing, almost invisible in the darkness. She presses the light switch. Luca.

'Mom?' He looks scared.

She pulls him into a hug. 'What are you doing up?'

'I can't stop thinking about him. I don't want to close my eyes in case I open them and he's right there beside me.'

'Come on into my bed. You can sleep here tonight and I'll mind you, OK?'

'OK.' He clambers in.

'And it's all right to be scared. When I was your age, I was afraid to be alone in the dark too.'

'I'm not afraid of being alone in the dark,' Luca whispers. 'I'm afraid that I'm not alone.'

22

ON THURSDAY EVENING AFTER work, Julia takes a detour to her local Garda station. It's actually an old house, she realizes, converted to a police station, and only the familiar blue Garda Síochána sign outside gives an indication that it's anything other than someone's home. She pushes the door and finds herself in a narrow, dark entryway with peeling yellow paint on the walls and a red tiled floor. On her right is a hatch with shutters, now closed, and a sign that says, 'Knock once and wait patiently for an answer.' The instruction to wait patiently makes her smile. Surely even police can't dictate whether or not she feels patient while she waits.

On the wall behind, there's a mishmash of posters and phone numbers; some fresh, some with yellowing, curling corners. One shows an elderly woman, missing for three weeks. Another a much younger woman, missing twenty-five years. Julia remembers her. Remembers that she disappeared after a night out back when Julia was the same age and having similar nights out. Beers and shots and no food, because who had time for food? Walking home together but often alone. Waking up on the night bus when the driver reached the terminal, six long stops after her own. They all did it. All the time. Until the night Donna didn't come home.

The noise of the shutters draws Julia's attention back to the hatch. A young officer is asking how he can help. She tries her best to explain her predicament. He looks confused but says he'll call one of the detectives on duty, and the shutters are unceremoniously shut. Julia waits again, thinking about the girl in the poster and trying not to think about the girl in her memory.

A door to her left is opened, and she's greeted by a middle-aged man with close-cropped greying hair and a businesslike smile.

'Detective Dan Connell,' he says, beckoning.

Julia follows him through to the dim interior, down a hallway to an office with a desk. She tries to keep the look of surprise off her face, but this is not what she was expecting. On TV, police interview rooms are often grey and clinical, but this is a whole other level of depressing. The walls are a yellow-orange colour with streaks of what looks like water damage, and peeling plaster. Filing cabinets with overflowing drawers litter the room in no kind of order. The desk is distressed, but not in a shabby-chic way; it really does seem to be a hundred years old. Detective Connell gestures for her to take a seat on an orange plastic chair – a single nod to modernity – and he sits down behind the desk.

He starts by taking her details, writing in an A4 hardback notebook.

'So, the lads out front were saying you're having a problem with someone impersonating you?'

She shakes her head. 'No, that's not it. Someone seems to have taken videos that my daughter posted from inside our house and used them to create these clips you might have seen online about *The Loft*?'

'The attic ones?'

'Exactly.'

'Aren't they all a PR thing, though?'

'Yes, but this person is using videos of my house and editing them.' She pauses. 'My son is getting very anxious.' That sounds better than I'*m getting very anxious.* 'It's an invasion of privacy.'

'But your daughter posted the videos in the first place?'

'Yes . . .'

'On a public account?'

'Yes. And I wish she hadn't, and she's taken them down now. But I felt we'd reached a point where we should at least file a report.'

'Has the person threatened you or your daughter?'

'No. I mean, it feels quite threatening to see someone in a mask purporting to break into your house and wander around when you're not there . . .'

'But they haven't overtly threatened to break in?'

'No.'

He puts down his pen. 'The problem is, Ms Birch, unless they threaten you, it's not a criminal act. It would be a civil matter.'

'Oh.'

'If he's using videos you shared yourself and doctoring them for some kind of prank, you'd probably have to pursue it via a solicitor to get him to take them down.'

'The thing is, they *have* been taken down – whoever it is keeps deleting the account. We did manage to save one video.' She fishes out her phone, clicks into the clip and slides it across the desk.

'Is this the TikTok account the person used?'

'No, this is just a copy of the video, saved by my daughter. And I . . . I'm pretty certain it's fake, but I wondered if you could tell by looking at it or using some kind of software?'

Detective Connell watches the clip, eyes narrowed. He plays it again, then hands back the phone.

'Hmm, I can see why you're unnerved . . . Look, I can get one of our tech guys to examine it to see if it's real or fake. It's not an exact science, though. They'd be able to tell if it was stitched together, but if it was done without stitching, they have to use geometric analysis.'

'What's that?'

'Looking at light, perspective, measurements – like if something should create a shadow but doesn't.' He sighs. 'Now, if you're telling me you're feeling threatened, that might stretch to harassment legislation, or if you think there's any possibility that the person *has* been inside your house, that's potentially burglary, and that would be grounds to get the IP address.'

'For which you'd need the TikTok account, except they've all been deleted.'

'Yes.'

'I guessed as much,' she acknowledges. 'But I still felt it would be best to report it, so, if it escalates, there's something on record. And to have the clip examined.'

'Absolutely. I have all your details now' – he raps his fingers on the notebook – 'and if there's anything that could be construed as a threat, or if the person leaves one of the videos up so we can at least *potentially* request the IP address, come back to me?' He hands her a card. 'Details on there.'

She stands, deflated but unsurprised. Realistically, civil or criminal semantics aside, if the TikTok accounts have been deleted, what can the police or anyone else do?

Back in the apartment, as she stir-fries prawns with one hand, Julia scrolls through her work emails with the other, including one from the US office asking her to travel for a meeting in February. She checks her phone calendar, then the giant twenty-four-month wall planner that hangs on the back of the kitchen door. She flips to February and is greeted by an almost completely blank page, apart from the 24th, on which Gabe has marked an X. She checks her phone again. Her work trip is earlier in the month, so whatever he has on the 24th won't be impacted. Fleetingly, she wonders what it is. He generally includes plenty of detail – they both do.

The pen that usually hangs beside the wall planner is missing and she rummages now in the drawer below the hob for a replacement. If this was Brentwood, there would be pens and pencils and Sharpies everywhere. For a moment, she misses it – the noise, the detritus, the company. But there's something comforting about the apartment too. Not least, she thinks, as she removes an A4 folder from the drawer, because there's no attic. Beneath the folder, there's an array of chewed pens, a ball of string, two plugs, an earbud, a tealight and a lone spoon. She chooses the least battered ballpoint and replaces the A4 folder, stooping to retrieve a sheet of paper that's drifted to the floor. She turns it over. It's an invoice from someone called Gallagher and Jonas, marked 'Received with thanks.' As far as Julia knows, they're a law firm in San Diego. What is Gabe doing with a law firm? Gabe is usually an open book. He tells her everything. Too much information sometimes, when he's dating someone new. And of course they discuss everything and anything that relates to the kids. She has no idea why he needs the services of a lawyer – maybe she'll drop it casually into conversation the next time she sees him? Though he's going away tomorrow, to New York, to wrap up some work with a gallery there . . . Curiosity gets the better of her and she picks up her phone.

Gabe answers and, after some small talk, she tells him straight out – she's spotted an invoice from a law firm and is wondering if everything is OK.

There's silence on the other end of the line and at first she thinks the call has disconnected.

'Gabe?'

'It's just work stuff. A client who owes me money.'

'Can I help in any way?'

She hears the intake of breath. She feels it – the sense that he's about to say something. That he desperately wants to say something.

'No, it's fine.' He sounds resigned. And almost . . . sad.

23

'MOM, WHERE'S MY PHONE?' Isla calls from upstairs.

'On the landing. No phones overnight, remember?' Julia can hear the eye-roll in the silence that follows. 'Come down, I'm making pancakes.' Gabe is usually the pancake guy, but Gabe is in New York and Julia is here and it's Sunday, so pancakes it is.

Isla enters the kitchen, rubbing her freckled face, her eyes bleary from sleep.

Julia pours batter in the pan and looks up.

'It wasn't on the landing. You left it on the side of the bath.'

Julia knows she didn't. But Isla has a tendency to forget where she leaves things, then blames everyone else, and this is not worth the argument.

'OK. Don't forget to bring me your PE gear to wash. You need it tomorrow, right?' She walks over to kiss the top of Isla's head.

Isla is scrolling on her phone and shrugs away from her mother.

'Can you check the *Loft* hashtag again, to see if there's anything new?' Julia asks as she flips the first pancake.

Isla nods.

'Wow, there are hundreds of clips. Jeez. All these people taking the time to climb out of attics. It's insane.' She pauses. 'Though it kinda looks like fun . . .'

'Don't even think about it.'

'Joke, Mom. *God*.'

'And remember, no videos from inside the house.'

Julia makes a mental note to say this to Gabe, too. He's the cliché – the dad who lets the kids get away with far more than she ever does; not because he's 'more fun', as their children claim, but because it doesn't dawn on him to say no. Gabe the artist, the creative one, the rules-are-made-to-be-broken guy. The money's-no-object parent, because he doesn't earn any of the money. She bites her lip. Now she's just being mean. He's a good dad, and during their last few months in San Diego he went above and beyond for all of them. So if he forgets to implement the rules every now and then, she can forgive it.

Julia's attention is drawn back to Isla, who is staring at her phone, her forehead crinkled.

'What is it?' Julia asks.

Isla holds up her phone. 'Is that what I think it is . . .?'

Julia stares at the screen, not quite believing what she's seeing.

24

THE PAINTING IS ONE Julia knows well. A seascape of blurred colour.
A loose interpretation of Dún Laoghaire pier. Gabe had painted it
back when they first moved to San Diego and it had hung in their
hall for years, until, one day, it was gone. Replaced with a painting
of Mission Beach. And now here it is, on Isla's phone. In a video
clip. On someone's wall. Hashtagged #TheLoft.

Isla presses Play, and a familiar scene unfolds. An attic hatch
opens and a black-clad figure climbs out.

'Isn't that our painting? From when I was small?' Isla is asking.

'Yeah . . . your dad painted it.'

'So where is it now?'

'I have no idea.' *Is all of this somehow targeted at Gabe?*

'What's the account name?'

Isla's face changes. 'Oh. Lepus321.'

Of course it is.

'But how did this person get hold of the painting?' Isla looks
perplexed. 'I'll phone Dad.'

As Isla waits for Gabe to answer, Julia goes to TikTok on her
own phone and searches for Lepus321. The video is still there.
Actually, it's three weeks old. Carefully, without clicking anything to alert the account holder, she takes it in. #TheLoft, but
no other text of any kind. The black-clad figure. Is it the same
person? It's impossible to say. Next is the stairs – thick beige

carpet; and the hallway – shiny walnut floors and a huge gilt-edged mirror. It's not a house Julia knows, but then again, it looks like a million other hallways and a million other stairs. The camera turns towards a doorway to the kitchen. Through the open door, Julia can see a large island, three high stools, a bag perched on one. A dark pink Kate Spade tote that looks somewhat familiar. The camera pans down to a pair of pink high-heel shoes. Like the bag, they ring a distant bell. They're not hers, that's for sure. This is not her house and maybe it has nothing to do with her at all, but why is Gabe's painting there?

Isla disconnects her unanswered call to her dad. 'Probably asleep. What time is it in New York?'

Julia glances at the clock. 'Only seven.'

Isla is rewatching the video. 'Did Dad sell that painting?'

'Maybe . . . but either way, if it's this Lepus person posting, it's not a coincidence.'

'Are you going to message Lepus?'

'No. He'll just delete the account like he did before. Let's screen-record and copy-paste the link so, if he does, we have something for the guards.' *Even if they can't do anything.* 'Detective Connell gave me a card with his email address on it. I'll send him the link anyway.'

'It's creepy. I wonder why he's doing it?'

Julia fixes a smile. 'Someone having a bit of fun at our expense.' She nudges her daughter and, in what feels like a desperate attempt to bond, adds: 'Probably one of your dad's girlfriends back in San Diego.'

Isla makes a face. 'Gross. God, Dad's so sketchy.'

'Harsh!' Julia says, and they're both laughing. Julia feels mean laughing with Isla at her ex-husband's expense, but this is worth any guilt. Unsure if it's a good idea or not, she decides to capitalize. 'So, how are you feeling about school? Any easier now?'

'No.' Isla's face closes up.

Not a good idea, then.

'I still can't believe I have to wear that gross uniform.'

'It *is* pretty horrendous. It's just how it is over here; you'll get used to it.' Exactly the kind of thing she hated her own mother saying. But what else is she supposed to do?

'My friends back home would disown me if they saw it.'

'Well, stop posting everything online and maybe they'll never see!' Julia says, and immediately wonders why she said it. She rushes to a new topic. 'Did you look at the leaflet for the soccer club?' She nods towards the whiteboard, where she's pinned a leaflet for Granada FC. 'They have really strong girls' teams, apparently.'

'No.'

'Does your school have a soccer team?' she tries.

'Yeah, but I'm not joining.'

'Give it some thought . . . A good way to get to know new people?'

'Mom, stop micromanaging. You always do this. You always—' The impending rant is interrupted by Isla's phone.

'It's Dad.' She answers and explains to Gabe why they're calling, her tone excited, her anger gone just as swiftly as it appeared. Isla's eyes widen now and she looks over at her mother.

'Oh my god.'

'What is it?' Julia indicates for her daughter to give her the phone.

'Dad, I'm passing you over to Mom.' She looks up. 'You are not going to believe who had the painting.'

25

A FLUTTER OF FEAR takes hold as Julia reaches for Isla's phone. Suddenly, somehow – the shoes? the bag? – she already knows what Gabe is going to say. But even so, when the words come, there's a shock wave.

'Julia? Um, if it's the one I'm thinking of, I gave that painting to Anya.'

Of course. The shoes, the bag – not those ones in particular, but the scores of other shoes and bags Anya owned that looked just like them. Pink Manolos and blue Louboutins to contrast with her severe black dresses. Her brand. Her girl-boss look, as she liked to call it. And she was *never* not on brand.

Julia searches her memory. Had she known that Gabe gave Anya the painting?

'When did you give it to her?'

'A few years ago. Remember, we took it down and it was just sitting in the spare room, and Anya always liked it because . . .'

'Because?'

'It was our place. We used to go to Dún Laoghaire pier when we were broke and couldn't afford to go on proper dates.'

'Right. But how did you end up giving the painting to her?'

'She'd seen it on your Instagram, and then she saw the new one, the Mission Beach painting, hanging in the hall, and she messaged me to ask where the Dún Laoghaire one had gone.'

Julia steps through to the living room as his words prickle on her skin. Gabe and Anya had been messaging each other? Then again, why not? They'd known one another a long time. They'd dated. Anya was Julia's friend. That made her Gabe's friend too. Even if she and Anya had fallen out and Gabe had – apparently – been on her side . . .

'So,' Gabe continues, 'I brought it back with me the next time we came home and dropped it to her.'

'Oh.'

'That's OK, right? You didn't want it any more?' Gabe asks, missing the point entirely.

'No, that's fine, I just didn't realize.'

'It was after your fight. I guess I didn't want to mention the war.'

'So much for taking her side.' She gives herself a shake. Gabe was perfectly entitled to stay friends with Anya. In fact, that had always been his superpower – a chameleon who bonded with everyone and kept them all on his side.

'And Isla said it's shown up in some video?' Gabe is saying. 'This attic stuff?'

It dawns on Julia. The video is of Anya's house. And now, Anya is dead.

26

Then

IN ANYA'S HOUSE, FOUR girls get ready for a night out.

Julia, Anya, Donna and Eleanor – or JADE, as they liked to say when they were younger.

This is Anya's parents' house in Tenerife, newly purchased in a recently built complex. It's all marble and mahogany, a tasteful mix of traditional and contemporary with a sun terrace running the length of the villa. A canopy covers a patio to the side, and that's where they sit now, on the built-in benches at the mosaic table, sipping their drinks in the evening sun.

The girls are at that perfect time of life – twenty-two, first jobs, first money, free to do whatever they want. Of course, like most twenty-two-year-olds, they don't know that this is that perfect time. They're worrying about all the normal things anyone worries about.

Julia is worrying about her sunburn. Day one of the holiday, and she's lobster pink. Anya's been doing that thing she does. *Wow, your shoulders look kind of . . . red? They must be really sore?* Which is passive-aggressive for *oh my god, you're burnt to a crisp*. Anya, to Julia's annoyance, despite being pale as milk all year round, has

117

a golden glow already. And they only got off the plane this morning. Julia's stuck wearing a pink kimono-style dress she doesn't love, because it's the only one that hides her burn.

Eleanor is worrying about her top. It's a handkerchief top that looked amazing in the changing room in A|Wear but looks ridiculous in Tenerife. Like she'd taken her nan's scarf and sewn straps on it. She should go inside and change. But she's tipsy and mellow here on the terrace in Anya's parents' villa, vodka and Coke in hand. And after two more drinks, she won't care how she looks in the top.

Donna is worrying about make-up. She didn't bring any. This was a huge mistake, but also inevitable, since she doesn't own any make-up. The others look stunning. Bronzer and highlighter and oil with gold flecks – Donna doesn't know how to apply any of these things. Eleanor looks beautiful in a handkerchief top, something Donna can't imagine picking off a hanger. Julia's pink kimono is like a dress from a perfume ad. And Anya, well, Anya looks perfect in everything.

Anya is worrying about everything. If they don't adore the holiday, it's on her. Her house, her idea, her fault. Nobody knows yet that the swimming pool in the newly built complex hasn't been finished. Or that the so-called twenty-minute walk to town only takes them to the far outskirts. Or that she just found a cockroach in the bathroom. But as Anya knows, you put your best face on and fake it till you make it. If she doesn't mention the cockroach, it never existed.

Anya raises her glass to toast their friendship. They raise theirs, and toast her, for getting them here. They'll leave in an hour, they decide, and walk down to get dinner. Eleanor had heard the stag party on the plane talking about a club called Tropicana. Should they try that? Julia teases her about chasing boys, and Eleanor reminds her with an arched brow that they're all single. Except Anya. Will she miss Gabe? Eleanor asks. Anya tells them then that she's breaking up with him as soon as they get home, so she already considers herself single. Eleanor digs her in the ribs and tells her she's a terrible person. She doesn't mean it. It's more fun if all four of them are single on the trip, Anya knows that. She's more interested in the response from Julia. She couldn't help notice a light go on at the news. Does Julia like Gabe? Maybe Anya shouldn't dump him after all. Then again, cute though he is, she's fed up paying for everything, having 'dates' on Dún Laoghaire pier. It's getting dull and it's time to play the field. She glances over at Donna, who has barely touched her drink and looks a little glum. Maybe it's the talk of going on the pull. That's really not her scene. And it doesn't help that she looks like a freshly scrubbed schoolgirl on her way to English class. Bare-faced and pink. Actually . . . she probably hasn't brought any make-up, Anya realizes now. She sighs, then nudges Donna. Come on inside, she says, and I'll lash a bit of foundation on you.

And soon, all made up, four girls go out for dinner, with all and none of the cares in the world.

27

DETECTIVE CONNELL'S SCEPTICISM IS written all over his face, and Julia can't blame him. It sounds insane. And she's not even sure what she's suggesting. That the person targeting Julia with doctored videos also targeted Anya? Only Anya more than likely never knew; she probably wasn't on TikTok. But what did it even mean, if someone was targeting both of them? The whole thing is probably a prank . . .

But still.

Someone has taken aim at both of them, for whatever reason, and Anya is dead.

Detective Connell, to his credit, tries to tease it out.

'So you think there's some link between the videos?'

'Definitely. The account name is almost identical. And now I'm worrying that . . .' Julia twists the ring on her finger. *What? What is she worrying about?*

Detective Connell waits, pen poised.

'What if Anya's death wasn't an accident?' she says eventually.

'Ah. No, I looked it up before you came in, and although the inquest is yet to come, there's no indication of foul play. It seems she fell asleep and slipped under the water. She wouldn't have known a thing,' he adds with a kindness that brings a lump to her throat.

Julia swallows. 'But let's say for a second someone held her under. Would it be obvious? I imagine it wouldn't take much, if she's already lying flat and she's had a few drinks and it was unexpected . . .'

A brutal image flashes into her mind: Anya in the water, eyes closed. Sudden inexplicable horror: hands on her head, pressing down. Anya, unable to push up, unable to breathe. Anya understanding she won't make it. Anya going limp. Anya gone. *Jesus.*

'There was no sign of a break-in, nothing disturbed in the bathroom or anywhere else in the house, the only fingerprints anywhere were hers and her partner's, and her partner was away, that's verified, so . . .'

'Yeah.' *But what if there was someone in the attic?* She bites it back.

'Regarding the videos,' Detective Connell says, 'in light of the fact that this is the fifth one and we can reasonably assume it's meant to make you feel under some kind of threat, I think harassment legislation might cover it. I'll send it on anyway to my superintendent to see if she's happy to forward it to Security and Intelligence to get the IP address. Don't get your hopes up that we'll be able to identify whoever's doing this, but we'll try.'

'Oh, thank you.' Relief makes her well up, and she blinks it back. 'How long will that take?'

'It'll take time, and if they're using a VPN to mask their location, we won't be able to get it at all. But we can contact TikTok for a preservation order too, so that even if the person deletes this new account, TikTok will still have the data. Unfortunately, getting that data can take a while.'

She nods. 'And any luck with the clip I showed you on Thursday – with verifying that it's fake?'

'Geometrically, it looks very real, in terms of light and shadow and so on, though there's some stitching together of clips.'

'So it's fake!' Her relief almost overwhelms her.

He chews his pen. 'Or the person who made it did some editing after filming it for whatever reason. It's not definitive.'

Julia's shoulders drop.

'But we'll have a look at this new one and we might find something more concrete. Now, you said it was your ex-husband's painting that tipped you off, made you realize it was Ms Hase's house?'

'Yes. My daughter spotted it.'

'So Anya and your ex-husband were friends?'

Her cheeks flush at the unasked part of the question.

'Yes, they've known one another a long time. They had a brief relationship before he and I got together.'

'I see.' He writes something in the notebook, then glances up. 'I'm looking for commonalities, reasons the person might target both of you.'

'Well, yes. Gabe is a link for sure, but I can't see how or why it would cause someone to target us.'

'If you think of anything, give me a call, and same if there are any more videos. And in the meantime, to feel a bit safer, maybe change the locks and consider a bolt on the attic hatch.'

That, Julia thinks, as she pushes back her chair, is precisely what they will do. She thanks the detective and heads for the house in Brentwood, conscious that at eleven thirty on a Monday morning, there'll be nobody there but her. Luca's words echo in her mind. *I'm not afraid of being alone in the dark, I'm afraid that I'm not alone.* For the first time in a long time, she finds herself wishing Gabe was there too.

28

On Friday evening, Julia pops into the house in Brentwood, so she can go to Shirin's barbecue with Gabe and the kids. A small stack of post sits on the hall table and she picks it up now to flick through while Gabe shouts up the stairs for Isla and Luca to hurry. All the post comes here rather than to the apartment, and it's usually for her – share statements, bank correspondence, credit card bills. But at the bottom of the small pile there's a handwritten envelope addressed to Gabe. Julia holds it out to him, noticing the US postmark.

'You missed this – it's for you.'

He takes it, frowning. Then a dawning realization crawls across his face. He darts a look at her, and moves into the kitchen, nudging the door closed just as Isla comes down the stairs.

'Don't forget the dessert, Mom,' she says. 'Dad made tiramisu.'

'OK, I'll grab it.' Julia walks towards the kitchen, her flat sandals slapping on the marble floor. She opens the door to find Gabe staring at something in his hand. A photo? The envelope she just gave him is in his other hand. He looks up, startled, and immediately shoves the photo into a drawer in the island.

'Are you OK?'

'Yep. Just grabbing the tiramisu,' he says, waving her back out to the hall with the envelope he's still holding. 'Let's go.'

*

Shirin's barbecue is blessed by the weather gods – the evening is warm, with strands of yellow sunlight slanting across the huge patio as Julia and Gabe take seats on the cushioned rattan furniture. Isla and Luca hover behind, unsure. Shirin asks if they'd like to sit with the adults or have a go on the trampoline and Luca is halfway across the garden when Julia turns to look, discarding his trainers as he goes. Isla, regular user of the trampoline in San Diego, is now too old or too cool or too cross, and perches on the edge of a garden chair, phone in hand.

Tonight, Shirin is in a long black halter-neck dress and chunky gold bracelets that gleam against her tan. Her dark hair is loose around her perfectly made-up face and Julia is glad she opted for a wrap dress and sandals instead of the much more casual jeans and top she'd first considered.

Shirin is joined now by a wiry man with a sun-tanned face whose crisp white shirt matches his silver-white hair.

'Julia, this is my husband, Tony.'

Julia stands to shake his hand. He holds it just a touch longer than is customary, his blue eyes taking her in.

'Julia. Glad to have someone next door again.'

'And this is Gabe.'

Gabe reaches to shake Tony's hand. 'We met before,' he says, and Tony nods.

'Indeed we did. I hadn't realized your set-up, at the time. So you two aren't married any more?'

Gabe grins. 'Both young, free and single.'

Julia senses rather than sees Isla's eye-roll, and she can't blame her.

'Really.' Tony's response hits an odd note. His tone is . . . sceptical? Does he think they're lying about being divorced?

'Yep, nine years now,' Gabe says.

Tony tilts his head. 'And neither of you remarried? No other children? Long-term partners?'

Julia frowns. This feels like a cross-examination.

Gabe narrows his eyes. 'No.' The grin is gone.

'How's Siegler-Barrows, by the way?'

Gabe stares at him.

Tony is smirking now. 'A mutual friend, I believe?'

'I don't think so.' Gabe's tone is icy.

Shirin jumps in. 'Well, you're very welcome to Brentwood. Tony and I are off to Sicily from October until Christmas, but plenty of time before then to get to know you.'

'How lovely to have a house in Sicily,' Julia says politely. 'What part?'

'San Vito Lo Capo. We love it there, don't we, darling?'

Tony nods. 'Got somewhere yourselves?' he asks, as though owning a holiday home is the norm. Maybe for Brentwood residents it is.

'Nope,' Gabe says. 'Apart from occasional use of my parents' mobile home in Wicklow.'

Tony makes a face. 'Grim. I have a colleague with a mobile home in Skerries. Went there once for a poker night. Big mistake. *Utterly* bleak. Give me a villa in Sicily any time.'

Well, yes. Julia can't help feeling sorry for Gabe's parents and Tony's colleague, and perhaps for all of them here tonight if this is how Tony will be for the evening.

Tony pulls a card from his wallet and hands it to Gabe. 'If you want to invest, let me know. I've got some other properties out there too, near Palermo.'

'Oh, thanks.' Gabe takes the card, looking bemused. He earns about enough money to keep himself in beer. He definitely won't be buying a Sicilian villa any time soon.

Shirin jumps in. 'What can I get you – G and T to start? Wine? Bubbly? Beer?'

Julia opts for a gin and tonic and Gabe asks for sparkling water, and their hosts bustle about – Shirin laying out platters of antipasti and Tony fetching drinks. The doorbell chimes and Shirin goes to answer, arriving back moments later with Alastair in tow. He's wearing his customary baggy jumper and dark corduroy trousers, complete with bicycle clips, though he hardly cycled the short journey from the townhouses to here, Julia thinks. Perhaps he never takes them off. Again, his jumper is covered in fluff and dog hairs, and again Julia has a compulsion to get at him with a lint roller.

Alastair greets Gabe and Julia and looks around. 'Just us, is it?'

'No, the couple next door are coming, and the family two doors up, with their kids.' Shirin pauses. 'Oh, and of course Drew Redking too, and his girlfriend. I'm not sure of her name.'

Alastair takes a seat beside Julia, and Tony points him towards a silver ice bucket filled with beers.

Alastair grabs a bottle and raises it. 'Well, cheers, everyone.' He clinks with Julia's glass. 'Did your friend who came over have a nice time? Eleanor?'

'Oh. Yes, lovely. Thank you for letting her in.'

'No problem.' His eyes flick to Tony and Shirin, then back to Julia. 'I checked who she was, obviously. No point in the gates if we hold them open for strangers.' He takes a swig of beer, then turns to Gabe. 'So, how are you settling in – you're an artist, I believe?'

'Yep, for my sins. Finding it hard to get back in the flow of things since we moved here, though.' He smiles that crooked, self-deprecating smile Julia knows so well. 'Little bit of artist's block.'

'I'll bet,' Tony says with a smirk.

'Sorry?' Gabe bristles.

'Bit distracted?' Tony says, still smirking.

Julia looks at him, puzzled. There's a strong sense of innuendo to his tone but none of the rest of them seem to be in on the joke. She glances at her ex-husband now, noting a wariness in his expression. Does *he* know what Tony's talking about?

Shirin cuts in. 'Tony, would you mind checking the burgers? I'm famished. I'm sure our guests are too.'

Tony snakes an arm around her and gives her waist a light pinch. 'Will do, but don't be going mad on the burgers, honey, or you'll be regretting it in Sicily.'

Shirin colours.

She slips from her husband's arm and flashes Gabe a smile. 'Anyway, I'll bet you're fabulous at painting – you'll be back to full flow in no time.'

Gabe nods and gives her what looks like a forced grin, but he's distracted, staring at Tony's retreating back.

The doorbell chimes again and they're soon introduced to two more families. The noise level increases, Tony declares the burgers ready, and, when everyone is busy helping themselves, Julia mouths to Gabe that she wants to talk to him.

Isla is deep inside the world on her phone and doesn't seem to pay attention when Julia and Gabe push back their chairs and move to the far corner of the patio.

'Hey, what was that about – what Tony said about a mutual friend called Siegler something? You seemed annoyed.'

Gabe sips his water, and she can't help feeling it's to hide his expression or to buy him time.

A shrug. 'I'm not annoyed. He's obviously mixing something up.' He raises the glass to his lips again.

'Gabe, you haven't been yourself the last few weeks, months, even – is everything OK?'

A weary sigh. 'Apart from worrying about Riley's mother giving Isla's name to the police, and Luca terrified that there's someone in our attic, you mean?'

'I'm worried about those things too, but is there something else?'

'Nope.' His eyes dart away.

What is going on with him?

'Was there something worrying in the letter from the States?'

'No, just, like, art stuff. Oh, I spoke to Raycroft about the locks,' he says, changing the subject. 'They said no problem as long as we pay for it and give them a set of keys. Now I just need to find a locksmith.'

'And what about a bolt on the attic hatch?'

'They were a bit iffy about that, said they'll have to come back to me. They said yes to blinds for the kitchen, so I'll look into getting that done.'

He smiles and clinks his water against her wine, doing a perfect impression of his usual self. But Julia's known him twenty years, and this is all an act. Why? She has no idea.

29

JULIA BALANCES HER PLATE in one hand as she takes another long swallow of wine. She's been standing with Alastair for ten minutes, answering questions about her job and her house and her kids. He's sweet. But kind of pushy too. Or maybe it just feels that way because she doesn't want to talk. She takes another gulp of wine, conscious she's drinking too fast, and out of the corner of her eye she sees that Drew has arrived, with a red-haired woman in a long white dress. They make a striking couple with their matching Instagram smiles and gym-honed bodies. Drew hands a bottle of whiskey to Tony, picks up what appears to be two waters – one for him and one for his girlfriend. You don't get to look like they do by drinking white wine, Julia supposes, raising her glass to her lips again, as Luca, taking a break from trampolining, rushes over and hugs her. She kisses the top of his head and wonders if he's been talking to any of the other kids. Luca keeps to himself so, realistically, probably not . . . That's OK, she thinks. It'll take time. One foot in front of the other. They can't all be outgoing, chatty, sociable, resilient, confident kids. *I mean, one of those things would be nice*, she can't help thinking, then immediately feels guilty.

Drew joins them and takes up the small-talk gauntlet. 'How's work, Alastair?' he asks, then holds a finger up. 'IT, right? Cos my laptop's acting up – you might be able to take a gander?'

Alastair shakes his head, somewhat flustered. 'Oh. No, I wouldn't be— Work's very busy.'

'It'd only take a minute, but OK.' He shrugs, makes a face at Julia and turns to Luca. 'What about you? Do you like computers?'

Luca nods, pressing his head against Julia's side.

'Video games, I betcha?' Drew continues, undeterred by Luca's limited response.

Another nod.

'What kind? *Mario*? *Fortnite*?'

Julia rubs Luca's shoulder. 'You like *Mario*, don't you?'

A small shrug. '*Mario* and *Roblox* and *Among Us*.'

'I used to play *Sonic the Hedgehog*. Have you heard of that?'

But Luca's had enough of socializing.

'Can I play *Roblox* on your phone?' he asks Julia.

'I don't have *Roblox* on my phone.'

Now he smiles. 'You do, I put it there.'

With a faux sigh and a grin, she passes him her phone, and he makes his way to a bench at the far end of the patio.

The conversation moves on to Brentwood's management company (useless), Alastair's dog (smart) and Drew's family (something big in whiskey, hence the bottle he brought for Tony), before Julia, feeling slightly dizzy from too much wine and not enough food, excuses herself to find the bathroom.

Shirin is in the kitchen, standing at the sink, staring out of the window. She jumps when she notices Julia.

'Oh! Sorry, Julia. Can I get you anything?'

'I was looking for the bathroom?'

'Of course – the downstairs one is occupied just now, but the main bathroom is on the right when you go upstairs.' A laugh. More of a hiccuppy giggle, really. Julia is not the only one feeling the effects of the good white wine. 'I forgot, your layout is exactly the same – of course you know where the bathroom is! Anyway, if there's someone in there, just use the en suite in my bedroom.'

Julia thanks her and walks up the wide stairs with their thick beige carpet, just like hers next door. She holds the banister, more unsteady than she anticipated, and resolves to switch to sparkling water. The bathroom door is closed and the sound of running water from inside tells her it's occupied. She waits, taking in her surroundings. The walls are white, and the look is spartan, with black-and-white prints hanging between each doorway. From inside the bathroom, the sound of running water continues. It feels a little intrusive to go into her host's bedroom, but then again, she'd hardly have offered it if she didn't mean it. Julia pushes the door of the bedroom. She was expecting cushions and throws because Shirin seems like a cushion and throw kind of person, but the room is oddly muted. Dark grey walls, a burgundy cover on the bed, and more black-and-white prints. Other than that, no personal touches at all. Julia crosses the bedroom towards the en-suite bathroom and locks the door behind her. A surge of nausea rises up out of nowhere and she puts her hands on the washbasin to steady herself. *Jesus*. She's at a neighbourhood barbecue with her *kids* and has managed to drink enough white wine to feel sick. The feeling passes, but she stands for another moment, leaning on the sink, focusing on the old-fashioned razor and shaving brush that sit in the space between the taps. She stands up straight now, her eyes travelling around the bathroom, to the rainforest shower in the huge glass box, to the single bottle of shower gel that sits on the shower floor. Behind her, hanging on a hook on the back of the door, is a black-and-burgundy-striped robe. It is then that she realizes her mistake.

Flustered and embarrassed, she puts her hand on the door

handle. But before she can turn the lock, she hears a voice. Someone has come into the bedroom, someone who is talking on the phone, she thinks. Tony. She steps back from the door. *Oh god, this is awkward.* She leans quietly against the sink, waiting. If he tries the door, she'll have to own up. *Sorry, your wife told me to use her en suite and I didn't realize you have separate bedrooms.* Scratch that. That's not good. Dammit, why did she drink so much wine? Tony's voice carries through the door: he's still on the phone. Silence now as the person on the other end of the line is talking, she assumes. Then the sound of a creaking mattress. He's sitting on the bed. Maybe she can wait it out and sneak back down when he's gone. She stays stock-still, as Tony begins to speak.

'No, he's not on the scene. They've split.'

A gap as the other person speaks and Julia wonders, skin prickling, if he's talking about her. But that's silly. Tony's only just met her.

'Of *course* I'm sure. You know what I saw on the footage.'

Footage? Julia leans closer to the bathroom door.

'No, the camera's still there.'

Now Julia can hear the faint, tinny sound of a voice on the other end of the line, though the words are indistinct.

'She hasn't a clue. That's the card I've been holding in my back pocket, so to speak.'

Another gap, shorter this time as the person – a woman? – replies.

'I know, sweetheart,' Tony says next. 'I know it's been hard for you. It's hard for me too. Shirin's not the easiest.'

Oh no. Julia holds her breath.

'Sweetheart, I've told you a million times. We're separated. We have separate bedrooms, separate lives. We haven't slept together since I met you.'

Oh god.

'If she'd let me go, I'd be gone in the morning. But she won't.'

Poor Shirin.

'I can't. We're having this barbecue thing. It's to welcome new neighbours. I'm the host.'

Julia scrunches her eyes shut as though this will make it less likely that Tony will find her when his call is over. Should she start running water and coughing to make him hang up and scurry out? But what if he doesn't? The point is moot. Her limbs are frozen by alcohol and deep embarrassment.

'Soon. I promise. I'll call you tomorrow. I love you.'

Please, please go back downstairs, Julia wills him. If he tries the locked door, will she speak up, admit who she is? Or say nothing and hope he gives up? The creak of the mattress tells her he's standing up. She listens for footsteps but the carpet's too deep, swallowing sound. Holding her breath, she watches the door handle. And then, to her relief, she hears the click of another door. Opening and closing. Tony is gone.

30

THE SKY HAS TURNED pink, laced with orange, and the guests are silhouettes now against the falling dusk. Julia can see Gabe on a curved wooden bench at the far corner of the patio, flanked on either side by Isla and Luca. Gabe is doing a magic trick for Luca while some of the other neighbours look on. *He's so good with the kids*, Shirin had said earlier, watching Gabe kick a football with Luca. Julia had nodded, swallowing a small swell of irritation. If parenting was as simple as football and magic tricks, Gabe would be the best dad in the world. Her gaze flicks to Isla, who looks bored, hugging her bare arms around her. Drew's girlfriend, to her credit, had tried chatting to Isla, finding a shared interest in collecting crystals, but Isla had been monosyllabic to the point of rudeness. It's time they went home. On cue, Gabe spots her and taps his watch, eyebrows raised.

She nods and holds up a hand, fingers splayed. *Five minutes*. She needs to thank their hosts.

In the kitchen, Tony is standing by the fridge, arm outstretched, leaning against the wall, talking to Drew's girlfriend. Tony is tilted towards her, his face close to hers, and Julia wonders if she needs an escape route. She steps closer, debating. Secret phone calls and public flirting. His poor wife.

Just then, Shirin comes into the kitchen carrying empty

glasses. Her eyes go straight to Tony, who doesn't so much sprint back as slide, in what looks to Julia like a practised art. Shirin's cheeks redden and she looks away.

'I keep losing that corkscrew!' she says brightly. 'I told Alastair ten minutes ago I'd get him a wine, and now I've lost both of them. The corkscrew *and* Alastair.'

'I'll find it.' Tony moves towards her, takes the empty glasses from her hand and smiles. 'You'd lose your head if it wasn't screwed on.'

She smiles back, but it's brittle, forced.

'Thank you, darling. If you wouldn't mind pouring the wine and bringing it to Alastair, wherever he is.'

'Of course.' A quick glance at Drew's girlfriend, who is studying her phone. 'You go on out, I'll take care of it.'

Without acknowledging his suggestion, Shirin turns to the sink and fills a glass of water. The ensuing silence feels to Julia like some kind of awkward stand-off. Tony looks like he's waiting for his wife to leave, and Shirin, eyes unnaturally bright as she drinks her water, seems unsure what to do next. Julia jumps in.

'I love your kitchen – it's beautifully designed.' It's exactly the same as Julia's kitchen, but needs must during awkward silences.

'Thank you.' Shirin's voice is hoarse.

'Have you seen this?' Tony draws Julia's attention to a gleaming coffee machine that sits proudly on the counter. 'Want a coffee? It does everything. Mocha, latte, cappuccino?'

'It's a bit late in the evening for me. Lovely machine, though.'

'I got it for Shirin for her recent big birthday. Set me back a fair few bob.' A grin. 'Nothing but the best for my wife, though.' He cuffs her chin lightly. 'Even if she is getting on a bit.'

'Indeed.' Shirin's voice is tight. 'I still think there's something wrong with it, the way smoke comes out. We should get it looked at.'

'It's not smoke, it's steam, that's how they work. Shirin, bless her, is not the most technically minded woman you'll ever meet.' Tony directs this last comment to Julia with a supercilious smile.

Julia winces. It's definitely time to go. 'Well, thank you, both, it's been lovely, but we need to make a move. Time to get the kids home.'

'Already? Oh, do stay,' Shirin implores. 'You only need to go next door, and it's Saturday tomorrow!'

'I'm in the apartment tonight, and I don't want to leave it too late to walk home.'

'Ah, of course. Gosh, seeing you here together tonight, I'd forgotten you're separated.' She touches Julia's arm. 'You've really made it work. One of my good friends separated from her husband last year and it's been horrendous.' She shudders.

Julia squirms, Tony's words ringing in her ears. *I'll tell her soon. I love you too.* As she tries to think of a response, she spots Gabe and the kids hovering at the patio doors. Gabe is rubbing his arms, looking confused. Julia waves them inside.

'I was just telling Shirin and Tony that we're heading off.'

'Yeah, I don't know where I left my hoodie,' Gabe says.

Shirin is immediately on the case, glad perhaps to have something to do that doesn't involve her husband. She goes outside to check the patio, while Tony, off the hook, meanders back to Drew's girlfriend. Julia shakes her head. *Fucker.*

Isla and Luca huddle beside Gabe, cold in their T-shirts. Luca is in socks.

'Where are your shoes?' Julia asks him.

'I left them by the trampoline, but then I couldn't find them and it's dark down there now . . .'

She turns to Gabe. 'You could go on in next door and I'll stay to look for your hoodie and his trainers?'

Before Gabe can answer, Alastair arrives, brandishing the hoodie and an envelope. Drew is behind him, with Shirin following.

'There you go,' Alastair says. 'The envelope was on the ground beside the hoodie. Maybe it fell out of your pocket.' Alastair squints at it. 'Yeah, it's addressed to you.'

Gabe takes the envelope and sticks it in his jeans pocket, thanks Alastair and pulls on the hoodie. He walks over to kiss Shirin on both cheeks and, even though it's a perfectly normal gesture, Julia can't help thinking he's deliberately needling Tony after the earlier interaction.

'Actually, it's pretty dark out there. I'll look for Luca's shoes tomorrow. He's fine to go home in socks, it's only next door,' Julia says. 'I'll go with you now and grab a sweater for my walk home.'

Gabe frowns. 'Just call a taxi.'

'For a five-minute journey?'

Drew rattles his keys. 'I'll drop you. I haven't been drinking.'

Julia and Gabe turn to look at him.

'You're very kind to offer, but it's absolutely fine. I—'

Drew cuts Julia off with a wave of his hand. 'It's no bother. Sure, look, something could happen as easily inside Brentwood as it could anywhere.' He arches his eyebrows. A glance at Isla and Luca. 'Then again, I'm new,' he adds hurriedly. 'What do I know?'

'It's true, Mom.' Everyone turns to look at Luca. 'The big gates didn't stop the man getting in.'

'The man?' Shirin's puzzled tone echoes the expression on each and every face.

'There's a man living in our attic.' Luca says it solemnly.

Julia hunkers down and takes his hand. 'There's no one in the attic. I promise.' No response, just an unblinking stare.

Alastair clears his throat, and Julia looks up. He mouths, *I've got this*. She has absolutely no idea what's coming as he steps forward and ruffles Luca's hair.

'When I was your age, you know what I used to do?'

Luca shakes his head doubtfully.

'I had seven brothers and sisters. Imagine!' Alastair crouches down, closer to Luca's level. 'And a very small, very noisy house. So when it all got too much, I used to go up to our attic and sit up there on my own, for peace and quiet.'

Luca's eyes widen. Julia's too.

Alastair nods. 'And you know, it wasn't one bit scary. It was calm. A break. And sometimes, guess what else I used to do?'

Luca waits, his full attention on Alastair. Julia can't decide if she should intervene, if this is a terrible idea or if it's actually going to help.

'I used to take a sleeping bag and sneak up there when my parents were watching TV. I shared a bedroom with my three brothers and, god, they were annoying. So I'd sleep in the attic.'

Julia and Gabe swap bemused glances. Luca looks awed.

'Then I'd come down when they'd all stopped squabbling,' Alastair continues, 'and the only sound was snoring, and the house was a much nicer place to be.'

'In the middle of the night?' Luca asks.

'Honestly, that was the best time. So you see, attics aren't scary places, that's only in books and films. And I'm certain there's no man in your attic, it's just a place your parents store their suitcases. Nothing more. Now' – he leans in conspiratorially – 'I've heard you're a superstar at chess. Will we play a game sometime?'

To Julia's surprise, this does the trick. Luca's face lights up and he nods.

Julia takes his hand and smiles thanks at Alastair. She can't quite imagine inviting him over to play chess with Luca, but right now, she's grateful. If Alastair or the other barbecue guests are curious as to why Luca thinks there's a man in their attic, they don't say.

Gabe clears his throat. 'Apropos of nothing' – a self-effacing grin – 'would anyone be able to recommend a locksmith?'

Alastair stands up straight. 'Yep, I have a number – I'll text it to Julia.'

Gabe nods thanks. 'No need to send it to Julia. I'll key it into my phone now if you have it handy?'

Alastair looks a little disappointed but pulls up the number and calls it out to Gabe.

'Right,' Julia says to Luca. 'I'll walk home with you guys, pick up a sweater, and come back here to take the lift from Drew.' She turns to Drew. 'If you're sure?'

He raises his glass of water. 'Absolutely.'

Ten minutes later, Julia pops her head around Isla's door to say goodnight. Something draws her attention to the hair straightener on the floor and, sure enough, it's plugged in and switched on.

'Isla! You left it on?' Julia unplugs it, relieved it was sitting on the heatproof base. 'I've warned you so often how dangerous that is!'

Isla's head jerks up from her iPad. 'What? No! I definitely unplugged it before we left.'

'Except you didn't. If you don't take more care, you can't have it in your room.'

'Mom, you can't just accuse me like that – I unplugged it!'

'It was literally sitting there plugged in.' Julia softens, reluctant to leave on a fight. 'Just be more careful next time.'

She leans in to kiss her daughter goodnight, but Isla ducks away, and her daughter is still protesting her innocence as Julia leaves the room.

In Luca's bedroom, she finds him in pyjamas already, huddled under his duvet with a book.

'What are you reading?' Julia asks, from halfway up his bunk ladder.

'A Goosebumps one. It's about a ventriloquist's dummy that comes to life.'

'Luca, that's terrifying! Aren't you scared?'

Big eyes stare at her. 'No, it's a book. It's not real.'

'Fair point.'

'The man in the attic is real.'

So much for Alastair's pep talk. 'Oh, sweetheart, maybe this book isn't the best idea . . .'

'It's not the book.' He shakes his head. 'That's a made-up story. But the video on Isla's phone is real.' He's whispering now, eyes darting around the room. 'And the man in the attic is real.'

'I promise, there's no one there,' she whispers. 'Wait, why are we whispering?' She laughs and rubs his cheek. He doesn't laugh. His eyes go to the vent above his bed.

'We're whispering so the man can't hear us.'

31

GABE IS WAITING FOR her in the hallway. 'You going back?'

'Yep. Before I go, there was—' She's about to tell him about the overheard phone call, but he interrupts.

'Don't stay long.'

'Excuse me?' She takes a step back and stares at him. In all their time together – when they thought they were in love, when they realized they weren't, when they split up – Gabe has never told her what to do.

'I just mean . . . steer clear of Tony.'

Curiosity replaces indignation. 'Why?'

Gabe's face darkens. 'He seems like a creep.'

'Uh, I'm a big girl, Gabe. I'm not worried about Tony.'

The journey back down her driveway and up Shirin and Tony's strikes Julia as ridiculously long now – though maybe it's the wine. They should make a hole in the dividing hedge, she thinks, if barbecues are to become a regular thing. Then again, if Tony is about to leave Shirin . . . The thought sobers her up as she walks towards their porch. The door opens and Drew bustles out, shrugging on his jacket. He pulls the door behind him and grimaces at Julia.

'Bit of a disagreement breaking out there between Shirin and Tony . . .'

'Oh dear. Your girlfriend . . .?'

Drew misunderstands. 'She's gone on home ahead of me, so it's just us.'

'Poor Shirin,' Julia says instinctively as they walk down the drive.

'Or poor Tony – who knows? Shirin had something in her hand and that seems to have triggered everything.'

'And has Alastair left too?' Julia asks as they go out on to the street.

'He went home, yeah. Work to catch up on, he said.' Drew shakes his head. 'I can't believe he wouldn't take a look at my laptop.'

'Maybe he really is just up to his eyes.'

'Nah, there was something weird about the way he said it. Like he was, I dunno, flustered.'

Julia doesn't reply. Alastair might have his own reasons for refusing, but, no matter what, providing free professional services to friends can end in disaster, as she and Anya discovered.

They pick up the car at Drew's house and begin the short drive to Julia's apartment.

'That was nice,' Julia says, 'and the weather held. Great to meet so many neighbours.' Then she laughs. 'I'm entering the Small Talk Olympics, clearly.'

Drew grins. 'Well, the less polite alternative might be "Tony's a letch, Alastair's odd, and Shirin's got the patience of a saint."'

'They're probably saying something similar about us. About me, anyway. "Julia's a bit cold, isn't she? And that set-up with her ex is weird."'

' "And Drew's a bit old to be a gym bunny, don't you think?"'

Now Julia laughs properly. Drew is growing on her.

'It's what you're thinking, isn't it?'

'Not at all!'

'Look, this – the personal trainer stuff, the gym bod – is all fairly new,' he says, indicating to take the turn into Grayson Apartments. 'If you saw a photo of me five years ago, you wouldn't recognize me.'

'Witness protection?'

He snorts. 'Ha, it could be. Five years ago, I'd never been inside a gym. Gaming was my thing, and I did it morning, noon and night. Never left my couch, except when the pizza guy rang.'

'Really?'

'Yup. Gaming was everything. Much to my parents' horror – they wanted me to join the family business. Then I had an epiphany, got fit, changed my whole lifestyle, and here we are.'

'So a whole career change followed?'

'That's right.' He pulls up at the main door to her apartment block. 'And other changes, too.' The interior light comes on as she opens the passenger door. 'For example, far more interest from the women.' He winks.

Julia gets out of the car and says goodbye. Drew is no longer growing on her.

He drives off, beeping his horn, and she presses the keypad to open the door. Drew the occasional creep, with flashes of charm. Tony the would-be charmer, with huge flashes of creep. And Alastair? She's not quite sure what to make of Alastair.

Half an hour later, as she closes her eyes, it's Tony's voice she can hear in her mind. *No, he's not on the scene. They've split . . . you know what I saw on the footage.*

32

'HE'S GONE.' SHIRIN'S FACE is a chalk-white mask when she opens the door to Julia on Saturday afternoon.

Julia is confused. She's here to pick up Luca's shoes and to thank Shirin properly for last night.

'Who's gone?'

'Tony.' She turns and walks slowly to the kitchen, leaving the front door open. Julia hesitates, then steps inside.

In the enormous, light-filled room, with its white cupboards and bleached-oak dining table, Shirin is a single dark ink-stain; curled on a chair, arms wrapped around herself. Julia moves tentatively towards her and takes a seat.

'What happened?'

Shirin looks at her, as though confused for a moment as to who she is.

'I confronted him.' She sounds surprisingly dispassionate. 'He told me he's met someone.' For a moment Julia feels sick. Did Tony know she'd heard his conversation? Has she somehow triggered this?

'What . . . what pushed you to confront him?'

'Something he dropped and I found.' She swallows. 'An ultrasound. A baby scan.'

'Oh, Shirin.'

A grimace. 'What a joke. He's sixty-bloody-two. The child will

144

be wheeling him around a nursing home. What am I going to tell people?'

'You don't have to tell anyone until you're ready. And he might come back?'

Shirin grits her teeth. 'Somehow I don't think he will, this time.'

'This time?'

'There were other . . . affairs. But never a pregnancy.'

'Do you know the woman?'

'He said her name is Molly. It doesn't sound like someone who's seducing your husband, does it?' A grim smile.

'When did it happen? The confrontation?'

'Late last night when Drew was leaving. I found the baby scan and . . .'

'So you confronted him there and then?'

A nod. 'First he tried to grab the scan out of my hand. Then he denied it. No baby, no girlfriend, all a misunderstanding. And I almost believed him. The scan could have belonged to someone else; I might have got it all wrong. But something about the way he denied it made me doubt him. So I grabbed his phone and ran into the downstairs loo and locked the door. I read his messages.'

'Ah.'

'She's in his phone as just "M", but in one or two of the texts he calls her by name.' Another bleak smile. 'He was horrified! We're not the grab-your-spouse's-phone kind of couple. He couldn't believe I wouldn't unlock the door.'

Julia nods, quietly enjoying the image of the meticulously groomed Tony banging on the bathroom door. A certain poetic justice perhaps, now that she thinks about what she heard when she was in *his* bathroom.

'And did he admit it?'

'Yes. I came out eventually and handed back his phone. I didn't need to say anything – the messages were all there. He told me he met her through work, that they've been together two years.' A harsh laugh now. 'I wonder what she'd think of him leering over Drew's girlfriend. Anyway, that's her problem now.'

'I'm so sorry.'

She stretches her arms, examines her hands. 'And look, I'm not a saint – after years of his cheating, I caved as well.' Her eyes meet Julia's. 'But only once. And he's gone. And now Tony's gone too.'

'He left late last night? Just like that?' Julia wants to ask about the not-saint bit, but she can't.

'Just like that.'

'And where did he go?'

'To Molly, I suppose.' Shirin seems to shake herself then. 'My goodness, this is the last thing you need, your new neighbour moaning on your shoulder. And I haven't even made you a tea.' Her voice goes up a notch. 'I'd make you a coffee, only he took the bloody machine!' She points at the empty space on the counter.

'He took the present he bought for *you*?' Julia realizes belatedly that she sounds more incensed by this than by the affair.

'Ha.' Shirin gives a bitter laugh. 'Some present.' Her eyes flash. 'Julia, I don't even *drink* fucking coffee, I stopped five years ago. Excuse my language, but I think that sums him up to a tee.' She shakes her head. 'Gosh, sorry, this is all a bit TMI when you were only calling for Luca's trainers.'

Julia tells her the shoes don't matter, but Shirin insists – they're in a bag already, waiting by the front door. They part ways, with Julia stressing again that Shirin should call her any time she needs to talk and Shirin promising Julia she'll be fine.

She can't be fine, Julia reckons – she's probably still in shock. Thirty years of marriage snuffed out in one night. Tony, no doubt delighted to be with his girlfriend, and Shirin all alone in her beautiful, empty house.

Drizzle mists on Julia's face, soaking her light T-shirt as she walks through Shirin's gate. The large green opposite the house is grey and murky and miserable in the rain. It strikes her now that, even on sunny days, there are never any children playing there. It seems such a waste. The nuns who once lived here had acres of land, and the developers landscaped it beautifully for residents. Now here it sits, empty. Is it a twenty-first-century thing or a Brentwood thing? The latter, she thinks. There's something dispiriting and almost . . . lifeless about Brentwood, for all its glossy luxury. She turns for home, jumping when Alastair materializes in front of her.

'Hey, Juju, how're things?'

'Oh! You gave me a fright.' Why is he calling her Juju, like they're lifelong pals? She stops herself. She's not being fair. He's just being nice.

'Out for my walk, but the weather's not playing ball.' Alastair points at the sky. Better equipped for the rain than she is, he's wearing a long, black, hooded coat that sweeps almost to the ground. 'Were you checking in on Shirin?' he asks.

'Yes . . .' She's not sure how much he knows.

'I heard the news,' he confirms. 'Not surprising.'

'Really?'

'You could say I have a sense for these things, having been there myself, though we didn't make it as far as the wedding.' A grimace. 'Not that I saw it coming in my own case. Poor old Shirin.' He glances up the driveway. 'Maybe I should call in to her.'

'I'd say leave it for now; it's all still very raw.'

His face falls.

'It's kind of you, though,' Julia adds. 'Shirin's lucky to have you as a friend.'

'And she has you now too, of course,' Alastair says. 'Nice for her to have you right next door. Hey, you could do a girls' drinks night, like with your friend Eleanor. A bottle of vermouth and you're all set, isn't that the way it goes? I envy women sometimes. It's easier for you to do things like that.'

'I guess . . . Right, I'd better get in. We're both getting soaked. Take care.'

She lets herself through the gate and walks up the drive, feeling his eyes on her every step of the way.

In the kitchen, Julia passes the trainers to Gabe and accepts an offer of coffee.

'How's all next door?' Gabe asks.

'Well, long story short, Shirin found out last night that Tony is having an affair. His girlfriend is pregnant, and Tony has moved out.'

'No way!' Gabe looks positively gleeful. And something else too, though she can't put her finger on it. 'I knew I didn't like the look of that guy. Too flashy. Too tanned. Something overgroomed about him.'

'Yeah. For me it's more the whole running-off-with-a-mistress thing that I wasn't mad on?'

He grins. 'That too. But you know what I mean. He just seemed so pleased with himself.'

She tilts her head, examining his expression. It comes to her then. Gabe looks relieved.

'She's probably better off without him,' he adds. 'Maybe they'll end up like us – happily divorced, sharing a coffee on a Saturday evening.' He passes her a mug.

'Speaking of happily divorced,' Julia says carefully. 'I can't help feeling there's something up with you and—'

But she's cut off, as Isla whirlwinds into the kitchen, phone aloft.

'Mom, look.'

She doesn't need to say anything else. Julia holds her hand out for the phone.

'Have you saved it and copied the link?' Julia asks as they watch the familiar opening shot.

'Of course. Keep watching.'

The camera moves to the open fridge, scanning shelves, then stops on a bottle of wine and a bottle of vermouth, before sweeping to the glass doors at the back of the kitchen. Something snags at Julia's memory, but she can't catch hold of it.

'Wasn't Luca's backpack leaning against the doors in the last clip?' she asks Isla.

Isla nods. 'Yes, this is different. And watch, it keeps going.'

The clip continues out to the hall and across to the den. Luca's iPad is lying on the couch, and the camera swoops low, right in on the screen. It's lit up with a game that looks familiar.

'It's among us,' Isla says.

A jolt. 'What do you mean?'

'The game. *Among Us.* The one about imposters – killers who hide among us.'

Julia feels a creep of unease slide through her.

'What is it?' comes a smaller voice. 'Why are you talking about *Among Us*?'

Luca.

Julia hadn't noticed him coming in. Now he's pulled the phone from her hand and is staring at the screen. She opens her mouth to tell him it's not real, but she's momentarily out of steam. The video is playing again. Julia watches, leaning over Luca's shoulder, still trying to work out what she's missing. It's not Luca's backpack. It's something else that doesn't make sense. And suddenly, she knows.

33

Julia stabs at the phone screen. 'There.'

Gabe leans in. 'What?'

'The bottle of vermouth in the fridge.'

'What about it?'

'Alastair mentioned it just now. He said something like "all you need is a bottle of vermouth". How did he know what's in my fridge?'

Gabe's eyebrows go up. 'Meaning what – you think he made the videos?'

She stops, trying to get it straight in her head. 'I . . .' *That doesn't make any sense.* 'I don't know what I think. But he knows what books I like and he knows what drinks I drink and he knew the garbage disposal was broken. He seems to know a lot for someone we only met a month ago. And there was that stuff he said last night, about going up to his attic as a kid. That was weird.'

'But why would he sneak into our house?'

'I don't know . . .'

'Could it be about your job?' Isla says. 'Like we were saying when Eleanor was here and the video showed your work notes? Could Alastair be someone who lost his job because of one of your redundancy things?'

'I . . . God, I don't know. Drew said he had money problems and his fiancée cancelled his wedding . . .'

'But wouldn't you have recognized him?' Gabe asks.

Julia shakes her head. 'No. I never meet the employees directly. My job is always in the background.' She pauses to consider. 'How did he know about the vermouth unless he literally saw inside my fridge?'

'Maybe he saw this video.'

'But the video only went up a few minutes ago. He couldn't have. At least . . .' She tries to work it out – how long ago had she seen Alastair? Twenty minutes, maybe? She casts her mind back to the encounter, to everything Alastair said, and suddenly, it dawns on her.

'Gabe, he called me Juju just now. Only my closest friends ever call me that.' *And two of them are dead.* 'People who knew me in school and college. How could he know that name?'

'But hold on, even if he did sneak into the house, that doesn't explain how he'd know your nickname. It's not like it's written on the walls.'

She strides over to the whiteboard and takes down the card Eleanor sent. She opens it and shows him. 'There. You can't see what's written inside the card in the video, but if someone was here in the house and took it off the whiteboard, they'd see it. Juju.'

This time, Gabe has no response.

She grabs her phone and house key from the island. 'I'm going over to ask him.'

Gabe looks startled. 'Really? OK, then I'm coming with you.'

Luca tugs at Gabe's sleeve. 'No, Dad. I don't want to be on my own here.'

'Isla's here.'

'No, I need you. I'm scared.' Luca starts to cry now, and Gabe looks helplessly at Julia.

'We could wait until school on Monday and go together then?'

'No, you stay with Luca,' Julia says, already in the hall. 'I just need to get this done.'

And before Gabe can respond, she's pulling the front door behind her.

The rain has stopped and dusk has closed in, casting Brentwood's footpaths into slick darkness. Julia is half running as she makes her way towards the townhouses, slowing when she realizes she's not sure which is Alastair's. There are eight narrow three-storey homes in two terraces of four, each with car spaces instead of front gardens. She knows which one is Drew's – the first in the row. His Jeep is parked out front, and through the living-room window, a Saturday-night game show plays on a giant TV. The house next to Drew's also has lights on, and two cars out front. Actually, all but one of the houses has at least one car parked outside. And Alastair said he doesn't drive. Julia homes in on the last house, the one without a car. It's in darkness – maybe Alastair's not back from his walk – but Julia presses the bell anyway. No answer. She tries it a second time, but still nothing. Dammit. If she goes home now, she'll lose her nerve. She needs to get this out of her system while she's fired up.

She steps to the side and peers through the living-room window. As her eyes adjust to the darkness, she can make out two sofas, a very small coffee table and a fireplace.

A light goes on suddenly, somewhere out back. A kitchen light, maybe, or a sensor? She moves around to the side of the house and finds a gate that swings open to her touch, creaking loudly in the night-time silence. The side passage is empty and dark, but she can see light ahead in the back garden. As she creeps around the corner, she hears the sound of a door closing – next door, she thinks – and then the light goes out and she realizes it was a neighbour's sensor, not Alastair's at all. She stands in his back garden, wondering now what possessed her to do this. The garden is somewhat overgrown, with grass that looks like it hasn't been cut in weeks, whereas the front of the house is well maintained. The wildness out back gives it an eerie feeling as she stands in deep darkness, starting to feel cold. What the hell is she doing? This is madness. She doesn't even know for sure this is the right house. And what is she going to say to Alastair anyway? She takes a step towards the side passage, and that's when she hears the creak of the gate.

34

SLOW FOOTSTEPS MAKE THEIR way around the side of the house and Julia is an animal caught in a trap. *This was a mistake*. She's trespassing on his property in the pitch dark, all alone, with no clear idea of how she's going to explain it. Could she hide? With a surge of panic, she scans the garden behind her. It's dark, dark enough to conceal her, but it's also too late. Because the footsteps are here now. Alastair is here, standing, looking at her.

Her throat is dry as she works her jaw, trying to come up with the right words.

'Julia.'

'I . . . Sorry, I was looking for you. I thought I saw a light . . . that you were out here, maybe.'

He shakes his head. 'No, I'm just back from my walk. I saw someone go around the side of the house. What are you doing?' He takes a step closer and she spots something in his hand. A crowbar.

She moves back, and in that moment the last piece of the puzzle clicks into place. The nagging thought that kept her awake the night Alastair called – the yellow fluff on his jumper. Attic insulation.

'Alastair, I should go. I . . .' She looks at the crowbar again, and he looks at it too.

'I thought you were an intruder.'

A nervous laugh bubbles up. 'Definitely not. I'll go. We can chat another time.'

'I think, whatever it is, we can chat now? You've piqued my curiosity.'

He's blocking her way, and he's not tall or particularly well built, but he has an iron bar in his hand and she's not taking a chance. *Fuck*. Frozen to her spot, all fight-or-flight instincts desert her. Blood pounds in her ears.

'Julia.' A softer tone now. Convivial even. 'We're friends. What is it?' He sets the crowbar against the wall and, although it's still within arm's reach, it's all she needs to get her legs moving again. She inches forward and skirts around him, moving carefully past, towards the side passage, all the while keeping her back to the hedge and her eyes on him.

He swivels, watching. 'Come on. I won't sleep tonight if you don't tell me.'

Now that she's closer, she can see a single earbud in his ear, exactly like the one she found in the attic. Christ. Why did she decide to confront him? Why didn't she go straight to the police?

She glances behind her. The side passage is clear, and she's a good ten feet from him now. He's only inches from the crowbar, but if he picks it up again she can run. She takes a few more steps back so she's into the side passage. Alastair moves too, but in the opposite direction, hands aloft, putting distance between them. He tilts his head, waiting for her to explain. It's now or never. *Deep breath*.

'OK. There's some stuff that's been . . . confusing me.' She swallows. 'You knew that I had vermouth in my fridge and that my nickname is Juju and what books I like to read and that our garbage disposal wasn't working, and I just need to understand how you know all that and . . . and . . . if you've been inside our house.' There. *Fuck*. She takes another step back, feeling like she might throw up.

Alastair doesn't move. 'Why would I be inside your house?' The neighbour's back light comes on again and she can see his face more clearly now. He looks genuinely confused.

'There are these videos online and they're of our house and it's making me crazy and I just need to know for once and for all, was it you? Otherwise I don't get it – how could you know all those things?'

'That's what you wanted to ask me?'

'Just tell me, how did you know? The vermouth, the nickname, all of it?'

'Julia, I knew you had vermouth because it was in your bag – remember? When you were on your way in with your shopping, the night your friend came over? You held up your bag when you were saying goodbye. You had vermouth in it.'

'Oh . . . yeah. But . . . but the rest? My nickname?'

'Your friend Eleanor said it, when I opened the gate for her that night. I don't just let people in, I had to make sure she was visiting a resident. I'm pretty sure I told you this, last night at the barbecue? And I know sometimes people say I ask too many questions but' – he shrugs – 'what's the point of a gated complex if we just hold the gates open for anyone who comes by?'

'OK. OK, but what about your AirPod – you only have one in and' – it comes to her now – 'it was the same when you called to my house after you brought in the bins. I found one in my attic, exactly like yours.' She points to his ear.

Now he looks truly bewildered. He reaches into his pocket and pulls something out. In his palm is a second AirPod. 'It's safer to just use one when I'm cycling or walking at night, so I can hear cars.' He holds it up. 'You found one like this in your attic?'

'Yeah . . .' *One like this, and like every other pair on the market.* Shit.

'What else was there?' Alastair sounds baffled, and something else . . . Hurt?

'You knew Luca played chess. You said it at the barbecue last night.'

'But you told me that, you said it was your lockdown hobby?'

'OK, but then there was all that stuff about going up to your attic when you were a kid. Like . . . like you have some weird fixation with attics.'

Now he looks wounded. And through her fear and confusion comes a new emotion. Guilt. What is she doing, taunting someone about their childhood idiosyncrasies?

He lifts his hands. 'Yeah, I'm glad the bullies in my class didn't know about the attic thing. I didn't think you'd be the kind of person who'd—' He sucks air through his teeth. 'Anyway. What else was there?'

'You . . . you knew what books I like, you gave me a book . . .' Her heart isn't in it now.

'I saw it in your car. I thought it would be nice to gift you a book by the same author. And what was the other thing – the garbage disposal? I told you already, I knew the previous tenant.'

She nods in the darkness, her face burning. 'You did.' Shit. What is she doing?

'God, Julia, I was trying to help.'

A whisper. 'I'm sorry.'

'It's fine.'

It doesn't sound fine. He's definitely stung.

'Alastair, I'm really sorry.'

He's standing with his hands by his sides, his shoulders low, a miserable look on his face.

'Don't worry.' A heavy sigh. 'Look, I know I don't have Drew's charisma or Tony's confidence. I know I'm never going to be the popular guy at the party. So I try to do nice things for people. Ask them questions about themselves. Make them feel welcome. Maybe sometimes I'm too much. My fiancée used to tell me that. But I don't mean any harm.'

'Alastair, I'm really, really sorry. This whole thing with the videos has freaked me out and I wasn't thinking straight.'

'Can I help in any way?' He holds up his hands. 'Sorry, sorry. I need to back off and stop trying to get involved in everyone else's business.'

'No, not at all! It's very kind of you. I might need your help. You work in IT, right?'

'Yeah . . .'

'The gardaí haven't been able to say if the videos are real or fake, and they say getting the IP address is going to take time – maybe you can take a look?'

'Maybe . . . I'll be honest, that kind of thing isn't my forte, I'm in programming, and I don't think regular people can request IP addresses – but I'll happily give it a go.' A grin. 'And I'll back off with all other offers of help.'

'Alastair, you don't have to. I got it wrong. I freaked out. I'm an idiot.'

'It's fine. I know I'm OTT sometimes. But I'm more than happy to try if you show me where the video is, or maybe some of my colleagues can help. OK?'

'Thanks, Alastair. The person keeps deleting their accounts, but there's one video still up, one supposedly filmed at an old friend's house. I'll send you the link. I don't know how soon he'll realize he hasn't deleted it or if he's left it there on purpose, but . . . it's worth a try. Anyway, I'd better go. Sorry again.'

He waves it away and heads towards the back door as she makes her way through the side passage and out the front, feeling foolish but relieved, too, that Alastair hasn't been inexplicably sneaking into her house. She quickly realizes, however, that this means she's back to square one – no closer to finding out who's making the videos. And no closer to finding out why.

Back at the house, Julia tells Gabe about her confrontation with Alastair.

'Oh god, Julia.' He's trying not to laugh when she gets to the end of the story. 'Sorry, it's not funny, but when I picture you there, saying all that stuff . . . it kind of is?'

'It was awful. He was hurt, I think. He's been so welcoming, and then I turn up in his garden, accusing him . . . God.' She puts her face in her hands.

'He's an adult, he'll get over it. Don't overthink.' His tone is firm but gentle. Ever her protector.

She lets out an exasperated sigh. He's right, annoyingly, but who can just switch off worry? Easy for Gabe to say when he never has to overthink anything. Although looking at his face now as he clears the table, there's still something not quite right. Dark shadows under his eyes and a look that's almost . . . haunted?

35

THE CALL TAKES JULIA by surprise, coming as it does close to midnight on Sunday. Apart from Gabe, nobody ever phones her, and certainly not at this time of night, but when Eleanor's name flashes up on-screen she answers right away.

'Juju, it's happening.' Eleanor sounds breathless.

Julia sits up straight on the couch. 'What is?'

'The attic.'

Julia freezes. 'A video?'

'No. I mean noises. There's someone up there.' Eleanor has a tendency towards the dramatic, but right now she sounds genuinely scared.

'Where's Ian?'

'London. I'm freaking out.'

'OK, relax. What exactly happened?'

'I was in my bedroom. Trying to read. But I kept looking at those TikTok videos.' The words are coming in whispered, staccato gasps. 'I turned out the light and was dozing off and then something woke me, but I didn't know what. I was just jolted awake. You know what I mean?'

'Yeah . . .' Julia wants to tell her she might sleep better if she didn't watch creepy videos in bed, but she holds it in.

'And then a minute later, I heard a creak from right above me.'

'OK. It could be the house settling? Normal night noises?'

'I don't know. But I'm too scared to sleep in my room. I told the kids we were having a sleepover and brought them down to the den. They think I'm a fucking lunatic. They're in there now, asleep again.'

'Where are you?'

'The kitchen. Juju, is it your turn with the kids – are you in Brentwood?'

'No, Gabe wanted extra time with them after his trip to New York, why?'

'Could you . . .?'

'Come over?'

Oh god. At midnight on a Sunday when she's just about to go to bed.

But there's only one answer. Julia is never going to say no, never going to leave anyone alone, never going to leave anyone behind. Not after what happened the last time.

36

Then

FOUR GIRLS GET READY for a night out.
Tonight is no different to any other night.
At least at first.

Anya is checking the time, impatient to get to the club. Eleanor is checking her lipstick, admiring herself in the oval mirror above the fireplace. Julia is pouring vodka into four tall glasses on a small coffee table. And Donna is wondering if it's too late to back out.

Donna doesn't really like Club 92, with its Red Bull-soaked carpets and rugby-boy dance floor. If she says she's not going, Anya will berate her and Eleanor will plead and Julia will arch one eyebrow, because, after all, it's Donna's house. She can hardly have them all over for pre-club drinks and not go to the club. It will make them feel guilty. And usually, because she is compliant and nonconfrontational and likes to please everyone, she'd say yes. But tonight, once they're getting ready to leave, she'll feign a headache and stay home.

And if Donna had stuck to that plan, she might be alive today.

*

Anya eyes up the glasses and asks Julia why one has less vodka than the others. Because Donna doesn't want to drink much, Julia says. Anya rolls her eyes. She looks at Donna now, in her Dunnes Stores jeans and buttoned-up shirt. Who wears a shirt to a nightclub? If she even goes. She'll probably fake a headache when it's time to leave. Which would be fine, except that Anya is hoping to crash at Donna's after. Donna's house – well, Donna's parents' house – is walking distance from Club 92 and Anya'd much rather spend her cash on vodka and WKD than a taxi fare home to Bray.

Eleanor picks up her vodka and adds some Coke, just enough to watercolour the drink. Her lipstick leaves an imprint on the rim, a bright red shade she's trying. Her Nokia beeps with a text from Ian Keogh and she lets out an audible sigh. Julia asks what's wrong, and she shows the girls the text. Ian Keogh is very nice, and that's the problem. Too nice. Too sweet. He's been texting for months now and she can't bring herself to shut it down. But it's *never* going to happen. She needs someone with a bit of spark, and Ian Keogh is not that guy.

Donna also thinks Ian is too sweet, but what would she know? She's never been kissed, never been asked out. She wouldn't mind if someone was texting *her* on a regular basis. Specifically, she wouldn't mind if Gabe was texting her. But Gabe is Anya's ex. They'd only gone out for a month, and it finished three years ago, but that still makes him off limits. She thinks now about his twinkly blue eyes, his permanent stubble, his crinkly smile. His art. His beautiful art. Gabe had graduated from UCD along with the rest of them, but now, while they're all busy with their sensible office jobs, Gabe is making his way as an artist. Donna can't imagine having the nerve to do that, though sometimes, when she's sitting at her computer, she thinks about the jewellery business. The one she wishes she had. The one her mother talked her out of. The one she might set up in years to come. There's plenty of time, of course – she can earn some money in her bank job, and *then* start her jewellery business. She's only twenty-five.

Julia, too, is thinking about Gabe. Will he be there tonight? He's been texting, and she's been enjoying it more than she expected. He's Anya's ex, of course, but Anya won't mind – she's loved up with her new boyfriend and has probably forgotten all about her fling with Gabe.

Kathleen, Donna's mother, pops her head around the door to say she's going out. She takes in the foursome. Julia retying her ponytail, her hair still as blonde as when she was ten. Eleanor with her doe eyes and her red lipstick, busy on her phone. Anya in a purple satin top, a mischievous look in her eyes. She's up to something. What do these girls see in Anya? She's fun, Donna tells Kathleen, every time she asks. And she can be funny when she's not slagging people off. And she's generous with money. It doesn't sound like a true friendship to Kathleen, and Anya's teasing sometimes seems cruel, especially towards Donna, especially about her permanent single status, but Donna tells her mother it's just how Anya is.

Donna's on the couch beside Julia, dressed as though she's off to the library on a Saturday afternoon. Kathleen smiles inwardly. *Never stop being yourself*, she silently tells her daughter. Out loud, she tells her Andy's upstairs in his room, and to enjoy the night. She's about to go in to kiss Donna goodbye, but decides against it. It'll only embarrass her daughter. Instead, she waves and shuts the door.

*

Can Andy give us a lift to Club 92, Anya wants to know. Or is he too busy playing video games?

Donna hears the undercurrent of a taunt but doesn't say anything. You can't, not with Queen Bee Anya. Not for the first time, Donna wonders why she lets Anya use her for somewhere to stay. Because it means she's included, she supposes. And because being teased is better than being ignored.

He's going out, she tells Anya, to a party.

Anya's eyes widen. *Really!*

Donna nods. Anya's incredulity grates. Andy is quiet, like Donna, but unlike her he doesn't feel the need to keep up with everyone else. Mostly, he stays in his room, playing *Mario* and watching *Lost* and ignoring everyone else in the house. There's no way she's asking him for a lift to the nightclub, not least because Anya will pretend to flirt with him all the way there, just to entertain the others.

Yeah, he's going to some house party in Blackrock with workmates, she tells Anya.

Anya thinks about Andy's workmates, who are all three years older and have good jobs with plenty of cash. Maybe we should go to that? she says.

Donna is about to say yes, actually, they should, because that's infinitely preferable to Club 92 and she can slip away whenever she likes.

But then Julia gets a text that changes everything.

And that's why Donna doesn't come home.

37

It's after midnight when Julia arrives at Eleanor's. The three kids are fast asleep in the den and Eleanor, in pink silk DKNY pyjamas, leads her into the living room. Julia smiles to herself. Eleanor is the only person she knows who'd bother buying high-end branded pyjamas.

'Thanks for coming,' Eleanor says. 'I'm ridiculous, I know.'

'Have you heard any more noises?'

'Maybe. I'm not sure. Juju, I might have imagined it. I'm sorry for dragging you out.'

Julia sits beside her on the couch. 'Right, do you want me to go up there?'

'Oh god, you wouldn't, would you?'

'Of course! I know you'd do the same for me.' And they both burst out laughing, because this is not one bit true and suddenly it feels like the old days. 'I reckon there's nothing there and the only way to reassure you is to prove it. I don't mind.'

'God, I couldn't in a fit.' Eleanor shakes her head. 'You know the way mothers are supposed to have a primal instinct to protect their kids and, like, jump in front of a tiger if it attacks? I always worry that I wouldn't.' She grits her teeth and Julia laughs again. 'Anyway,' she continues, 'I think you're *insane*, but if you want to go up there, I won't stop you.'

Which is how Julia finds herself clambering into the

Jordan-Keogh attic at half past midnight when she should be home in bed. Fully floored and floodlit by multiple lights, it's a room in its own right. Neat boxes with neat labels line both sides and there's an ordered, almost clinical feel to the space. It is the opposite of a spooky, dusty attic and it doesn't take long for Julia to climb back down to the landing and confirm that it is indeed devoid of concealed strangers. Eleanor is visibly relieved.

'You're a good friend.'

'Well, got a bit of making up to do on that front, don't I?'

'You mean because you've been away?'

Julia nods, even though that's not what she means at all. Her mind is on the night when none of them was a very good friend to Donna.

'Well, I for one am glad you're back. Especially after—'

A sound from downstairs interrupts them – the creak of a door. Eleanor freezes, but when a small voice drifts up the stairs she relaxes.

'Oh, bloody hell, one of the kids is up.' She moves across the landing just as a tousled head peeps around the corner. Julia smiles and waves at Georgia, Eleanor's three-year-old.

Georgia lifts her hand to wave back, but her fingers are clutched around something.

'What is it, pet? Did we wake you?' Eleanor asks.

'I want water.'

Eleanor reaches for her hand. 'Come on, let's get you some water and then you can go back to sleep in your own bed—' Eleanor stops suddenly. 'Georgia, what's in your hand? Where did you get that?'

Her voice is urgent, panicky.

Julia steps forward to see what Georgia's holding. At first it doesn't make sense – why is Eleanor so shocked? Then her eyes adjust. And her blood runs cold.

38

Then

THE TEXT ON JULIA's phone – the message that alters the course of Donna's life – is from Gabe.

Why is he texting *Julia*? Donna wonders. It sends an uncomfortable feeling curling through her stomach. But then Julia explains. Gabe is doing a painting for Julia's mother, one she's buying for her mother's birthday. He wants to check some details with Julia, and it seems he's also going to Club 92. Now the feeling in Donna's stomach becomes a fizz of anticipation. He's off limits, she reminds herself. But still. She'll get to see him. To chat to him. And Gabe is always lovely, even to people like Donna who everyone else ignores. Perhaps she'll go to the club after all. She gets up to go to her bedroom. Maybe she'll change out of the shirt and into a strappy top.

On her way past Andy's room, she peers inside. He's at his computer, playing some game. He turns when he hears her. *What?* he says. Impatient. She asks if he's going to a party and he says he is. He's driving, though, he can't be bothered with drinking and taxis and all the rest. Taxis are a nightmare, she

169

agrees, it's impossible to get them. He doesn't reply; her effort to connect is redundant. She goes into her room.

Down in the living room, Anya is on her fourth drink, slightly irked that Donna is still on her first. They're twenty-five, for goodness' sake. They have all the time in the world to be sensible. Julia and Eleanor are composing a let-you-down-gently reply to Ian Keogh, both absorbed in Eleanor's phone. Anya takes the bottle of vodka, pours a good measure into Donna's glass and tops it up with Coke. Now maybe Donna will have some fun, she thinks.

Julia helps Eleanor with her text, then turns to her own phone. So Gabe is coming along tonight. That's interesting. He could chat about the painting another time. A nightclub is hardly the best place ... Is she reading this right? The texts, the phone calls, the bumping into each other in pubs in town ... It's always hard to tell, but this time she thinks she might be right. Gabe is interested. And Julia is interested too.

Eleanor, text sent, turns back to the bottle of vodka, topping up each of their glasses, though Donna's is pretty much full to the brim. Eleanor knows what happens when Donna drinks too much. She's seen it once or twice, when Donna threw caution to the wind.

Donna arrives back in the living room, now in a pink strappy top. She's pinned back her curls and put on lipstick. You look amazing, Eleanor tells her, and Donna flashes a self-conscious smile. Julia nods agreement and knocks back her drink. Donna smooths her hair, then glances down at the black work shoes peeping out beneath her jeans. Sensible, boring, the kind of shoes the others would never wear.

Anya catches the glance. Here, she mutters, rummaging in a bag, pulling out pink kitten-heel mules. I brought options. You can wear these.

And when it's time to leave, Donna doesn't feign a headache. She puts on her coat, calls goodbye to her brother and heads out the door. And fate takes another irreversible turn.

39

Eleanor hunkers down to her daughter. 'Can I hold it?' she asks. A nod.

Eleanor takes it from Georgia and stands to show Julia. A little smaller than a computer mouse, made of some kind of green stone, it nestles in Eleanor's palm. A paperweight in the shape of a rabbit.

'That's what was in Chris and Anya's bathroom,' Eleanor whispers, more because her voice has deserted her, Julia thinks, than any worries about Georgia hearing.

'We never saw that one, though . . .' Julia says. 'We only heard about it from Chris's sister. It might not be the same one?'

'Come on, how many green stone paperweights in the shape of a rabbit do you see every day?'

None, Julia has to admit.

Eleanor kneels again. 'Sweetheart, where'd you get this?'

'Mine.' Georgia reaches for it.

Eleanor closes her fist around it. 'You can have it back tomorrow, but I need to check something first.'

Georgia's face crumples and her cheeks go red. If she's anything like Isla was as a toddler, the roar is only seconds away. Eleanor is quick to react. 'Tomorrow, we'll go to Smyths and you can pick out two presents. How about that?'

Georgia's face relaxes. 'And have my rabbit back?' She pronounces it 'wabbit'.

'Sure!' Eleanor says. 'But first, I need to know where you got it.'

Georgia puts a finger to her lip, miming deep thought. 'In my bag from pre-school. But I didn't taked it,' she adds quickly. 'I don't take the toys home by purpose.'

Eleanor looks up at Julia. 'We've had a few issues with toys finding their way into her pockets . . .'

'Mummy, I didn't taked this one.' Georgia stamps a foot. 'It was in my bag itself.'

'Jesus.' Eleanor stands. 'Someone put this in her bag as a warning to me.' Her voice goes up. 'Someone got into her pre-school and targeted her because she's my daughter. Oh my god, Julia!'

Julia puts a hand on her arm. 'Hold on now. Let's not get carried away.'

'It can't be a coincidence.'

'Could we get a photo of the one from Anya's bathroom, do you think? Would Chris have one?'

'I'm guessing the police took a picture, but I doubt if Chris did. That would be weird . . . Maybe the sister – Lynn – can describe it? She seemed pretty clued in.'

Julia checks the time on her phone. 'We'll have to wait until morning to text. It's nearly one.'

'Do you want to stay here? I'll make you a hot choc, like the old days? I really don't want to be on my own, Juju.'

Julia nods and relief spins across Eleanor's face.

'You're a true BFF, as my kids say. And tomorrow morning we'll message Lynn to ask her to describe the paperweight from Anya's house. She definitely said it was a rabbit made of green stone, didn't she, and—' She stops. Her eyes widen. 'Oh god, Julia, I've worked it out.'

40

'Worked what out?' Julia asks.

'The green stone. Look what kind of stone it is.'

Julia doesn't know much about stones or gems or crystals – that's Isla's domain. But suddenly it hits her.

Eleanor nods. 'It's jade, isn't it?'

'I . . . I honestly don't know. Maybe . . .'

'How many other green stones are there? It's not emerald. It's jade. This is about us. You and me and Anya and Donna. Oh god.' Her voice is shaking.

Julia swallows. 'What are you saying?'

'This is about what happened to Donna.'

'That was a horrible thing, but it was an accident.'

'I know, but we let it happen. We should have taken better care of her. And someone is trying to . . .'

'What?'

'I don't know. But what if Anya's death wasn't an accident? What if the videos are real? What if someone put this in Georgia's backpack to send me a message?'

'Eleanor . . .'

'What else could it mean?'

'Listen. Your attic is empty. The videos are almost certainly fake.'

'*Almost* certainly. You admit it. They could be real.'

Julia shakes her head. 'It's too fantastical. I can't see how someone would get into the house.'

Eleanor grits her teeth. 'OK, what about Anya's death?'

'An accident.'

'And this?' Eleanor holds up the paperweight.

'A coincidence.' But even as Julia says it, she knows it's not credible. 'OK, we contact Lynn in the morning and we go back to the police to give them an update. Even if there's some logical explanation, it's better to report it.'

Although it's only seven o'clock when Eleanor messages Lynn on Monday morning, Lynn phones her back immediately. She can do one better than describe the paperweight, she says, she can show it to them. Chris is still staying with their parents, she explains, but Lynn has a key to the house he shared with Anya and can swing by to pick up the rabbit. She and Eleanor agree to meet at ten in the Mellow Bean in Blackrock, near where Lynn works.

'She's keen,' Julia says, having heard Eleanor's side of the conversation.

'She's bored,' Eleanor replies, 'and sensing drama.'

'She'll be sorely disappointed.' Julia laughs. 'A pair of lunatics getting excited over a paperweight.'

But Eleanor doesn't laugh.

Julia isn't due in the office until two and Eleanor is free once the kids are deposited at school and pre-school, so at five to ten they arrive in the café and take a table near the window. Julia hasn't been here before, and she looks around now, taking in the mismatched floral-print oilcloths on the tables, the cute bric-a-brac on the shelves and the vintage posters on the walls. It reminds her of her favourite coffee shop in San Diego, but that in turn reminds her of Riley, and of Heather, Riley's mother, and the conversation they had when they met in that same café to talk things through. Julia had prostrated herself in front of Heather, apologizing profusely for what Isla had done. She did not, of course, get defensive or offer mitigating circumstances. She didn't want to dilute her apology with 'but your daughter started it' or 'my daughter was responding to months of bullying', because she's not that kind of person. An apology only has value if the mitigations are left out.

Heather listened carefully, nodding without interrupting Julia's flow. They'd met a handful of times at school events and Heather had always seemed warm and friendly. She looked like an adult version of a cheerleader – blonde ponytail, wide blue eyes and the kind of dewy skin Julia had never achieved even in her twenties.

'So look, as I say, I'm really, really sorry . . .' Julia had finally trailed off, after what felt like a very long one-way conversation.

Heather reached across the café table and touched her hand. 'Hey, it's not easy parenting teens, and don't we all know it.'

The unexpected kindness made Julia well up, and she had to work hard to keep the tears from spilling over.

'Oh, now, don't cry, you'll set me off too!' Heather's eyes were shiny now, and this pushed Julia over the edge. She swiped at her cheek.

'Thank you for understanding.' A shaky laugh. 'After what happened to Riley, I wouldn't blame you if you never wanted to speak to me again.'

'Julia, it's *not* your fault,' Heather said, emphatic now.

Julia shook her head helplessly. 'Maybe it is, maybe I did something. God, we always blame ourselves. The mothers, I mean.'

'We do. But honestly, please don't.'

Julia let out a small, quiet sigh of relief.

'There's only one person to blame,' Heather continued, 'and that's Isla.'

Julia swallowed. Of course it was Isla's fault, and what happened was horrific, but somehow hearing Heather speak about her child like this felt . . . uncomfortable.

'I know. Look, I need to say, she's not a bad kid, she just made a stupid decision,' Julia said, heading down the defensive route she swore she'd avoid.

Heather sat up straighter, frowning now.

'A stupid decision that has my daughter at home, refusing to get out of bed.'

Julia felt her cheeks flood with heat.

'What Isla did was terrible, but she'd had months of' – she stopped, wary of using a touchpaper word like 'bullying' – 'negative attention from Riley and eventually she'd had enough. It's no excuse, she went too far, but—'

'Negative attention? What exactly do you mean?' Heather's eyes narrowed.

Julia should have stopped there and, later, she wished she had. 'Well, criticizing how she looks, asking her if there's any treatment for freckles, offering her teeth-whitening strips. Confiscating her food to "help get a thigh gap", which Riley said was for her own good because "people were talking" . . .'

Heather tilted her head, faux confusion all over her face. 'I'm sorry, you're saying Riley tried to help Isla with some basic wellness tips and you're calling this negative attention?'

Julia could feel herself starting to shake. 'It's just—'

Heather cut her off. 'Your daughter nearly gets my daughter killed, and instead of apologizing, you come to me with this? You're trying to blame *my* daughter?'

'No, I *am* apologizing. I'm just saying that there were

mitigating circumstances. Isla didn't do what she did for fun – it was a reaction to months of provocation.'

'Wait, you're claiming what your daughter did was justified?'

'Of course not! What Isla did was stupid – she should never have taken Riley's phone. But Riley had done the same to Isla. I mean, one time she took her phone, found some unflattering selfies on the camera roll and posted them on Isla's Snapchat.' Isla had been devastated at the time, but now, of course, it sounded weak.

Heather stared, her eyes cold. 'That's hardly the same thing.'

'I know, but—'

Heather slid back her chair. 'I thought I was coming here for an apology. And to hear how Isla will be punished. To discuss what we'll say to the police. To see if you can give me any reason at all to continue keeping Isla's name out of it. But I can see we're poles apart. You'll be hearing from my attorney.'

And with that, she stalked out of the café. Which is when Gabe took over negotiations and Julia decided to move to Ireland.

Now, in Dublin, on a bright September morning, she's in a similar café, but this time opposite Eleanor and Lynn. Lynn, who, now that she thinks about it, gives her slight Heather vibes. Same shade of yellow-blonde hair, same liberally applied perfume, same darting, watchful eyes.

And Lynn is in her *element*. Clearly bored at work, she seems delighted with a chance to pop out and meet with Eleanor and Julia.

'So what's it all about?' she gushes. 'You were very vague on the phone, but I had a feeling you think there's something more to the story? You think Anya was cheating on Chris, don't you? And that's where the rabbit came from?'

Eleanor and Julia exchange a glance.

'Yes,' Julia says quickly, because that sounds a little more rational than 'we think someone is hiding in attics and trying to hurt us for something that happened decades ago'.

Lynn nods sagely. 'Me too.' Her eyes gleam with drama. 'Chris has no idea, poor sod. But I never trusted that one.' A pause. 'Sorry, I know she was your friend.'

Julia ignores this. 'Can you give me the paperweight?' It sounds abrupt, she realizes too late, as Lynn's eyes narrow.

Eleanor jumps in. 'Lynn, I meant to say, you're *so* good to be helping us and taking time out of your busy day. Anya always said you were kind and thoughtful, so I'm not surprised.'

Lynn flashes a smile at Eleanor and pulls a green paperweight from her handbag. Julia and Eleanor exchange another look. It's exactly like the other figurine. The snub nose, long ears, curled-under paws, all in a green stone that looks very much to be jade. Julia lets out a quiet breath.

'So . . . what you said about cheating – you think the paper-weight was given to Anya by someone she was seeing? Any idea who?' Eleanor asks.

'I don't know who, no.' Lynn sounds disappointed in herself. 'And obviously, that's not what gave the game away – I mean, she could have bought the rabbit herself.' She tucks her hair behind her ear and leans closer. 'But there were other hints.' A knowing nod. 'Things Chris said.'

'Like what?' Julia asks.

'That Anya seemed to be withdrawing from him, but also happier than he'd seen her in ages.'

'So he *did* think she was cheating?'

'No. Chris isn't the sharpest tool in the box. He'd be sitting at the kitchen table in my mother's house, telling us all this, scratching his big lump of a head, while my mother and myself are rolling our eyes and thinking what a dimwit he is.'

Julia frowns. 'It doesn't sound . . . conclusive.'

'Well, *you'd* know best, you're her friends.' Lynn's eyes dart from Julia to Eleanor. 'Was she seeing someone else?'

'She certainly hadn't said so, but we'd not met up in a while.' Eleanor's voice is hoarse and she clears her throat. 'We were supposed to have drinks the night we found out she died . . .'

Lynn looks disappointed that they can't offer more.

'Well, Chris told us she was working late a lot – classic stuff. I mean, if you were watching on TV, you'd be screaming "Affair!". Honestly, if Glyn ever cheated on me, I'd castrate him, and he knows it.' A laugh. 'Keep them scared, ladies. But I think Anya saw a man with a nice house and a fat salary and she threw herself at him.'

'I don't think Anya needed to throw herself at anyone, to be honest. Her accounting firm was pretty successful.' Julia wonders, as she says it, what will happen to Hase Accounting with Anya gone.

'Well . . .' Lynn tilts her head from side to side, wrinkling her nose. 'It *was* successful until a massive problem a couple of years back. Chris told me all about it. Anya had an employee who was offering to do customer accounts on the side for a reduced rate, cutting out Hase. She caught him and got advice from some bigwig consultant on how to deal with it, only the bigwig consultant was a fucking liability.' Julia can feel the heat creeping across her face. Lynn keeps talking, oblivious. 'Gave her bad advice, told her she could fire the guy, and of course he took a case for unfair dismissal and won. Hase's reputation was severely damaged. And it turned out the guy really was embezzling from her all along. Anya should have sued that consultant, taken her for every penny.'

Eleanor folds her arms resolutely. 'Well, I can tell you—' But Julia cuts her off. They don't need to tell Lynn any of this. Apart from not wanting to hold up her hand as the 'fucking liability consultant', they're here to find out about the paperweight.

'So no idea who Anya was seeing?' she tries one more time.

'No. But I do wonder if she was thinking about children. That magazine, open on the page about eating for fertility.'

An image of Shirin finding Tony's baby-scan picture flashes across Julia's mind. 'I presume she wasn't pregnant – they would have discovered that, wouldn't they?'

'I don't know,' Lynn says, sitting forward in her seat. 'If it was very early days . . .'

'It's kind of a moot point, I suppose,' Julia says. 'If we're just trying to find out who gave her the paperweight. Who she was seeing,' she adds hurriedly.

'I know, I'm *dying* to find out.' Lynn catches herself. 'For poor Chris's sake, of course.'

For the gossip, Julia thinks.

Eleanor picks up the paperweight. 'I have some ideas . . . I don't want to say much yet, but, Lynn' – she widens her eyes – 'do you think I could borrow this?'

Lynn looks like she wants to say no.

'It's just . . . my hunch . . . it's something to do with when we were all in college,' Eleanor explains. 'I think it might give us a clue to who she was seeing, and we can meet up again to report back once I confirm.'

This is enough for Lynn. 'Sure. Take it.'

Julia smiles inwardly, impressed with Eleanor's charm. She'd forgotten how good Eleanor could be at winning people over.

Lynn watches Eleanor examine the paperweight. 'You can keep it. Chris won't notice or care. He's still distraught. Poor fella. No clue that she was running around behind his back.'

Julia thinks this is harsh, considering they have absolutely no proof that Anya was cheating. Then again, thinking back to Anya's track record, there's every chance she was.

41

Then

THE FOUR GIRLS ARE at the club now, the 'club of love', as it's affectionately known by its south Dublin clientele. Older teens, finally legally allowed to drink but with no money to do so. Young twenty-somethings high on first jobs and steady incomes. Flashing lights, heaving dance floor. Dark red booths and drink-slick tables. The Killers booming from the speakers. The queue at the bar six deep and growing. As one, they smile, and make their entrance. Heads turn. Anya with her ebony hair and satin top, worrying suddenly that her boyfriend and the boy she's seeing will both be here. Eleanor, dark waves framing her carefully made-up face, wondering if Ian Keogh will text again and half wishing she hadn't put him off. Julia, swishing her white-blonde ponytail, looking for Gabe. And Donna, curls clipped back, lipstick on, also quietly seeking Gabe.

Donna's happy. Woozy, but happy and light. She thinks she might dance. She doesn't usually dance. If she does, it's because the others tease her into it, then go on to tease her about her dancing skills. Why is it assumed that everyone loves dancing? she wonders now, as she scans the dark booths. But maybe tonight, she can be one of them.

*

Anya goes to the bar. She doesn't ask them what they want. The others find a spot beside a ledge, somewhere to throw their bags and get their bearings. Anya arrives back with a tray of drinks. Four double vodkas, four bottles of Smirnoff Ice as mixers, and a shot of Baby Guinness each too.

Let's get locked! she shouts over the music, then nudges Donna. Look at you, Donna, all done up – maybe tonight's the night you'll get your first snog.

She turns to Julia and Eleanor and pulls a face that somehow means 'here's hoping', 'who knows' and 'as *if*' all at once.

Donna eyes up the tray. She never mixes her drinks. But it's just spirits and spirits, she thinks. Or is Baby Guinness made with liqueurs? Kahlúa and Baileys? She's not sure, but right now she's feeling good and she doesn't care. She won't have beer and she'll be fine. Anya raises a shot glass and the others follow suit. Down in one. Then on to the vodkas.

JADE are ready to party. And Donna is ready for Gabe.

Julia is also ready for Gabe.

He's texted again, to see if she's arrived. He's outside in the queue, and the bouncers are saying it's full. Julia's stomach plummets in disappointment and Eleanor asks what's wrong.

Gabe can't get in, she tells her friends, watching for a reaction from Anya, and missing the reaction from Donna.

Anya flicks her hair. God, I hope he's not trying to get back together with me, she says. He knows I'm seeing someone. *Two people*, she thinks, but doesn't tell the girls. They wouldn't approve. They're judgemental about cheating, especially Donna, which is mostly because she's never gone out with anyone, so has no idea what she's talking about. *Let's see if she finally loosens up after those double vodkas*, Anya thinks, watching her smiling, swaying friend.

Donna is feeling it now, though she doesn't know about the doubles. But in the way these things always go, the more she drinks, the less she cares. Her early warning signal is off, her caution's in the wind, and she's going to have the time of her life, Gabe or no Gabe.

Julia's phone beeps again. Gabe is going to a party, in town, on Wexford Street. He's got a lift, he says, and they'll fit if they come now. She tells the girls.

Anya is not going to any party on Wexford Street, she says. All the way into the city centre? It'll be impossible to get home, she points out, the taxi shortage is a nightmare. Hadn't Julia walked home from town last weekend? Julia and Eleanor could do what they liked, Anya and Donna were staying put, and would walk home to Donna's. *Right, Donna?*

But Donna has other ideas. Buoyed by vodka, emboldened by shots, Gabe on her mind, she says no to Anya. She's going to the party on Wexford Street.

And so Julia, Anya, Donna and Eleanor pile into the waiting car, to go to the party with Gabe.

42

'WILL WE ORDER MORE coffees,' Lynn says, 'and I'll see what else I can remember? Glyn always says I'm great at seeing things other people don't. Intuitive.' She raises a finger to summon a server.

Julia grimaces. She really wants to have a proper look at the two paperweights to see if they're identical, and she *really* needs to get home to change – she's still in last night's clothes.

Eleanor gives her a tiny nod of understanding and pushes back her chair.

'I have to do my pre-school pick-up in a bit. Otherwise I'd love to stay and chat.'

Lynn juts her lower lip in exaggerated disappointment. 'You'll keep me in the loop if you discover anything?'

'Absolutely.' Eleanor smiles. 'And if you think of something, let us know.'

Lynn still manages to keep them talking for five more minutes at the table, and another five outside the café, but finally her phone rings and she mouths the words 'my supervisor' before scurrying down the street towards her office.

Huddled together under the green-and-white-striped café awning, Julia and Eleanor compare the two paperweights and confirm what they already know – they're identical.

Eleanor's eyes are saucers. 'This is about JADE. About us. About Donna.'

Julia wants to tell her it's not, to say it's ridiculous to think someone from their past is trying to hurt them. But she can't.

'OK.' She looks at her watch. 'I'm going back to Brentwood to see Gabe and get changed for work. You do your school pick-ups and we'll go to the Garda station at six. Does that work? Will Ian be home?'

He will, Eleanor confirms, and they hug goodbye, Eleanor taking the two rabbit figurines with her.

Gabe is surprised to see Julia and makes coffee while she tells him the story. She waits for him to laugh. To roll his eyes. To tell her that she and Eleanor have lost the plot. But he does none of these things.

'Wow. That's a bit creepy all right.'

'There has to be a simple explanation.' She waits for him to provide it. He does not.

'Maybe, but what? It's clearly not a coincidence.'

Julia shakes her head, lost for answers.

'Luca's still obsessing about it too,' Gabe continues. 'He said it again at breakfast this morning – that the man is in his room every night.'

'Oh god . . .'

A pause. 'Do you want me to check the attic?'

She nods, then manages a smile. 'Now, this isn't because you're the man. I went up last time, so it's your turn.'

'Sure.' He smirks and pats her arm with mock condescension. 'I'll go do manly stuff, you make more coffee.'

She stretches to swipe him with a tea-towel but he's already halfway out the kitchen door.

As the coffee hits the bottom of her cup, the doorbell rings. Alastair is on the step, with Mavis the dog at his side.

'Hey, Julia, I was just passing and thought I'd pop by with an update on the video thing we talked about on Saturday night?'

Her mind goes back to their encounter in his back garden, and she cringes, her face burning, but if Alastair feels awkward, he doesn't show it.

'Oh yes, great – what did you find?'

'Nothing on the IP side, I'm afraid. As I suspected, it's not something the general public can do – we can't just ask TikTok for the IP address, and without the IP address we can't get a location. But also, whoever it is probably uses a VPN to mask their location, so getting the IP wouldn't be much use anyway.'

'Ah, I see.' Julia slumps against the doorway.

'However, I have one colleague who is very interested in deep-fakes and AI and video editing, and she's taking a look at the clip. So I'll come back as soon as I have anything from her.'

'Thank you. And sorry about the other night.' Her face heats up even more. 'In your garden.'

He waves it away. 'If I was seeing videos of my house on the internet, I'd be paranoid too.'

She smiles.

'Hey, want me to have a look around for you now?' He steps forward, nodding towards her hall. 'For peace of mind?'

'No, gosh, no, it's all fine.'

'Crap, sorry.' He holds up his hands. 'I'm doing it again, aren't I? Overstepping.'

'Not at all. I know you're trying to help.'

He waves goodbye and heads down the drive, Mavis trotting after him.

Gabe comes down the stairs, brushing dust from his shoulder, more for effect, she thinks, than to remove the presence of any actual dust.

'Nothing to report from the attic. Who was at the door?'

'Alastair. I'm mortified about the other night. He's being really kind, getting a colleague to examine the video, after I accused him of being the intruder.'

'Hmm. Does he have a little crush, maybe?'

'Oh my god, stop!'

'Well, he did break up with a fiancée a while ago, didn't he? Might be lonely?'

'Gabe, you've broken up with half a dozen women in that space of time and nobody goes around calling you lonely,' Julia says. 'I think he genuinely just wants to help, and since he works in IT . . .'

'It doesn't sound like he's great at his job, to be honest, if he can't even get an IP address.'

Gabe, who barely knows how to change a password. Julia shakes her head. This is something Gabe does. If he thinks anyone is interested in her, he can't help criticizing them. It's occasionally endearing but often irritating and, today, it's mostly irritating.

'Oh, give him a break. Anyway, thanks for checking the attic. Should we bring Luca up there, to reassure him?'

'I tried, but he froze completely and got upset. He's terrified.'

'I know.'

'I'm really worried about him, and I keep wondering if we should, I don't know, move again.'

'Wait, go back to the States?'

He looks stricken. 'God, no. Move somewhere else in Ireland, fresh start, cut ourselves off from everyone, go somewhere no one can find us . . .'

'Gabe, we just moved here. My work is here. Our friends, the schools.'

'I know.' An expression she can't read skims across his face. 'I'm just worried.'

'What are you not telling me?'

'Nothing.'

With zero reassurance and a resigned sigh, she heads upstairs to change.

Her room is cool and calm and, before she does anything else, she sits on the side of the bed to take a minute. There is no sound. No creak, no gurgle. No footsteps from the attic. She lets out a long breath, exhausted from all of it – all the listening, being constantly primed.

Then suddenly, someone touches her ankle.

Someone is under the bed.

43

Then

ANYA HAS LOST EVERYONE. Eleanor spotted some girls from work as soon as they arrived at the party and went to tell them some gossip. Julia went out for air an hour ago and hasn't come back. Donna is nowhere to be seen. Maybe she's gone home? She wouldn't, surely, not when Anya was supposed to be staying with her? Then Anya sees her through a fog of cigarette smoke. Sitting on the floor of the living room, knees hunched to her chest, arms wrapped around her legs. She looks like a miserable, lost child. For god's sake, they're at a party. Exasperated, Anya makes her way over.

What are you doing on the floor? she snaps. You look like a wet blanket. Nobody will want to talk to you with a face like that.

Donna raises her chin, and Anya sees the tears now. Her irritation flares. Donna is literally the most annoying person in the world.

Through the blur of tears, Donna sees Anya's disapproving face, hears her disapproving words. Anya's right. She doesn't even know why she's crying. There's nothing wrong. It's just . . . everything. Life. Her parents. Her dad never stops going on at her and Andy. And her mum should step in, but she doesn't. Her dad's not violent. But the constant put-downs are exhausting. Especially for Andy. And work . . . The bank job her mum is so proud of . . . Donna hates it. But none of that explains why she's crying now, does it? Her parents haven't suddenly changed . . . On some level, Donna knows it's the vodka, but not really, because that's how vodka works. And now here's Anya, being cross with her. God, Anya is always cross with her.

Anya hunkers down. What is the point of wing-women at a party, she asks herself, if one of them looks like she wants to throw herself out of the window?

Donna, come on, she says out loud. Snap out of it. You're never going to meet a guy like this. Weeping drunk girl isn't a great look.

Donna dips her chin, and a tear spills over.

Anya wants to shake her.

What is even wrong with you?

Donna bites her lip. Anya is the last person she can talk to about her work and family problems. Julia, maybe. They're not as close as they used to be, but Julia would listen. Anya likes glittery, juicy problems about outfits and boys. Donna considers her clothes, her single status and, with a lurch, realizes these are also her problems. *God*.

There's a guy I like, she says to Anya, but nothing will ever happen.

She puts her hand over her mouth. Did she really just say that? To Anya? If she finds out who Donna means, there'll be war.

Anya looks at Donna with her hand over her mouth, as though she's the first person in the world to like a boy.

Who is it? she asks.

Donna shakes her head.

Well, you're not going to meet anyone sitting here looking miserable, Anya says. Every guy in the place will run a mile. And your mascara is streaked all over your face. Donna, you're a mess!

Donna feels another tear spill over and trickle down her cheek, making her mascara worse. She just wants to go home. Even if she sees Gabe, she can't talk to him looking like this.

I'm sorry, she whispers. You're right, I *am* a mess.

She looks down. Below her jeans, the pink kitten-heel mules peep out. She manages a watery smile and looks back up at Anya.

But at least I'm a mess in nice shoes. Thank you for the loan.

Anya sighs and squeezes Donna's hand.

They *are* fabulous shoes, in fairness. And they deserve a fabulous face. Want me to fix your make-up?

Donna nods.

Anya squints closer. It's not as bad as I thought, she says, and you're lucky, you can get away without foundation. I wish I had your skin.

Donna sniffles, pleased with the unexpected compliment.

Anya stands and pulls her up by the hand, then puts an arm around her.

Let's go and find a bathroom, and I'll give you some pointers on what to do if you happen across this boy you like, whoever he is. Deal?

Donna smiles, feeling lighter. Deal.

44

THERE IS SOMEONE UNDER the bed.

Julia jerks her legs up, knees to chest, before logic and sense kick in and she realizes it's the rabbit. Basil is under the bed and she has almost died of fright. She laughs because it's ridiculous and, if she doesn't laugh, she'll cry.

Before she can summon the energy to get changed, she hears the doorbell again, and the sound of Gabe's footsteps in the hall as he goes to answer. Wondering if Alastair is back, she sticks her head outside the bedroom door to hear. But the voices are unfamiliar and, curious now, she goes halfway down the stairs and sees that there are two uniformed gardaí on the doorstep. Heart in mouth, brain scrambling over what could be wrong (the kids? Her parents?) she takes the rest of the stairs two at a time.

'What is it?'

Gabe answers before the gardaí have a chance. 'It's Tony. They're trying to find him.'

The garda closest to the door picks up.

'His siblings are worried about him. They haven't been able to reach him since Friday, which is out of character, apparently. They chat on the family WhatsApp group every day.' The police officer's face registers his feelings on this. He clearly doesn't chat to his family on WhatsApp every day. 'Have you seen him at all?'

Julia shakes her head. 'Um, do his family know he's moved out, though?'

The garda nods. 'They do now. They were surprised, but nevertheless convinced he'd never cut contact like this, not let them know where he is.'

'Surely he's staying with his girlfriend?'

'His wife believes so, but his phone is out of service, no credit card transactions, no trace of his car, and nobody knows who this girlfriend is, so the family is concerned.'

The other garda hands Gabe a card. 'Call us if you think of anything, won't you?'

'Sure. Sorry we can't be of help,' Gabe says, with a wish-I-could-do-more shrug that reeks of uncharacteristic faux concern.

'I hope he's OK,' Julia adds as the two gardaí step away from the doorway.

Once the door is closed, Julia turns to Gabe, eyes wide. 'Wow, what do you think is going on there? I really hope nothing's happened to him.'

'Who knows? I wouldn't wish ill on anyone, but . . .' Gabe holds up his hands in a *what can you do?* gesture. 'He was kind of a dick.' And with that, he walks off.

When Julia arrives at the Garda station at six that Monday evening, Eleanor is already waiting for her, both rabbit figurines in her hand.

'They're going to think we're mad, aren't they? Turning up like characters in a kids' mystery book with our "clues".'

'Yup.' Julia blows air through her teeth. 'Let's go make idiots of ourselves.'

Detective Connell isn't working tonight so Eleanor and Julia sit down with Detective Stilwell instead, a tall woman with dark hair and a soft midlands accent.

Her expression is unreadable throughout the telling, which Julia and Eleanor do together, finishing one another's sentences. Stilwell takes notes but makes no comment until they finish. The two figurines sit on the desk between them.

She asks some questions then, her tone neutral – has Julia searched her attic? Could Isla's friends have made the videos? Has Georgia any idea where the paperweight came from? It sounds as though she's taking them seriously, Julia thinks, but maybe that's just her natural Garda demeanour. Maybe Stilwell will be in the pub tonight, telling her pals about the two women with their story of attics and revenge and rabbits.

Stilwell asks if they're sure Anya hadn't seen the video of her house. They don't know, they say, but logic suggests she'd have told someone if she had. Stilwell pauses, examining the figurines for a moment, before looking back up at Julia and Eleanor.

'OK, then. If you think this might be about your friend Donna, we'd better hear how she died.'

45

Then

IT'S THE HAPPIEST DONNA has ever been.

She is floating.

Euphoric.

The music sounds different tonight. She doesn't pay attention to music any more, but this is a beautiful night with beautiful songs and she wants to dance.

No, wait, she doesn't want to dance. She wants to stay right here. Right here with Gabe, whose hand is on her lower back, whose voice is in her ear. How did she get here? It's a blur. Anya fixing her make-up, the pep talk on chatting to boys, the extra shots of vodka to buoy herself, the ending up – somehow – beside Gabe. *With* Gabe.

In her pocket sits a piece of paper with his phone number. He said he'd key it into her phone, but she couldn't find it. Or her coat. And it didn't matter because he took a slip of cigarette paper from the packet in his pocket and wrote his number on that.

She can smell him. A mix of tobacco and Ralph Lauren Polo, and something deeper that's Gabe's own scent, and right now she'd die happy, inhaling that smell. He's a head taller than her and, if she steps just one inch closer, her head will be resting on his chest, and that's what she wants, only not really because what she really wants is to kiss him.

They're by the window, in a fourth-floor living room, at the edge of the party, oblivious to the pushing bodies and spilt drinks. She doesn't know where the others are and she doesn't want to know. He's talking. She has no idea what he's saying. It's so loud, she can't hear a thing, but she doesn't care because when it's this loud and this late and you're this drunk, you're not supposed to be able to hear anything.

The words don't matter.

All that matters is Gabe and his hand on her lower back and his face just above hers, leaning closer now. She inches nearer, stretching up, and then it happens and his lips are on hers and it's like a movie in her head and all the clichés are true because there *are* fireworks going off and she never, ever wants this to end. Except then she stumbles and reaches for the wall and Gabe looks at her and she can see concern on his beautiful face.

He says something and she hears it this time. He's worried about her, worried she's too drunk for this and she'll regret it. She'll *never* regret it, she wants to tell him, this is the best moment of her life. But she says none of that because it's true, she *is* too drunk and now, suddenly, a surge of nausea rears up and she puts her hand over her mouth.

I'll get you some water, Gabe says, still looking worried, and he goes and then he's gone.

Anya is on the third floor, in the kitchen, when Gabe comes in looking for a clean glass. For Donna, he says, she's had a little too much to drink. He smiles, and something in that smile tells Anya there's more to this. Donna and Gabe? She wouldn't. *He* wouldn't. But it's there in Gabe's smile. In his eyes. Is that who Donna meant? The boy she likes? Anya watches him fill a glass and leave, to look after Donna. She's starting to regret giving out her tips on boys.

Julia is on the second floor in the games room, marvelling at this house with its stairs and its storeys. There's even a roof garden, someone had said, but Julia won't go near that – heights are not her thing. She wonders where Gabe is; she hasn't seen him since they all piled out of the car and now her phone is dead. She hasn't seen anyone else either – not Donna, not Anya, not Eleanor, and she's starting to feel tired. She sips a warm, flat Coors Lite and wonders how they'll get home.

Eleanor appears and rushes towards her. Juju! I thought I'd lost everyone! I'm kinda bored? If we go now, d'ya reckon we'd get a cab? Before the big rush when the clubs close?

Julia checks the time and nods. If they leave now, they might not have to walk home. They just need to find Anya and Donna.

Upstairs on the fourth floor, Donna is in an en-suite bathroom, being violently ill. Vodka and Smirnoff Ice and shots, and she's never drinking again and, if this feeling could just go away, dear god, she promises she'll be good. The toilet bowl is cool against her sweat-slicked forehead and she kneels there, resting her head. Spent. Gabe will be looking for her. But she can't move. She just wants to sleep. Right here on the cool bathroom tiles on the fourth floor of a stranger's home.

Gabe is searching for Donna. He tries the fourth floor, by the window where he left her. He asks around but nobody noticed the girl with the sandy curls and the pink strappy top. He tries the third floor, back to the kitchen, where Anya is.

Have you seen Donna? he asks her.

A beat. Then: Donna left already, Anya tells him, before she can stop herself.

And she probably has, Anya thinks, considering Gabe can't find her. And now with his full attention on her, Anya adds that she's stuck. She was supposed to stay in Donna's house. She's stranded. She'll never find a cab to take her all the way back to Bray.

Gabe puts his arm around her. He won't leave her stranded, he says, she can stay in his house.

Can we go now? Anya asks.

Gabe nods. Sure.

Downstairs, they find Eleanor and Julia.

There you are! We're ready to go, Julia says. If we're quick, we might get a cab before the rush. Where's Donna?

She left already, Anya says, with just the tiniest flicker of guilt. And in fairness, it's probably true. Donna more than likely went home.

Julia is surprised. Donna doesn't like going home on her own. Eleanor pulls her arm. It's perfect, she points out, because if there are four of them, they don't need a six-person cab. But they need to hurry before the rush.

Outside, the street is thronged. They push through queues of people waiting to get into clubs and move to the edge of the path. There's a rank a few feet away and, just then, a cab pulls up. It's magic. It's a miracle. They run towards it.

Julia hesitates. Are you sure Donna went home?

Anya looks at her. I'm sure, she says, tired now. I saw her get in a taxi. Let's go.

Eleanor pushes Julia forward.

And they go home.

Donna emerges from the fourth-floor bathroom. Her legs are shaky and her stomach churns but she thinks she won't be sick again. Now she just wants to go home. Where are the others? She looks at her watch. She's been in the bathroom an hour. They must be looking everywhere for her. She moves through the floors, but they're nowhere. And Gabe. Gabe is gone too. Stumbling slightly, she makes her way outside. She'll get a cab. On her own. She hates being on her own, but she just wants her bed now. Why are there so many people? Are they trying to get into the party? It dawns on her then. They're trying to get taxis. There are dozens and dozens of people in the queue. God. What is she going to do? Suddenly Donna feels like crying. She's sick and she's cold and, somehow, she's still drunk. She goes back inside for water and warmth, wondering where she left her coat. Retracing her steps now, back through the rooms, searching. On the fourth floor she finds it, with her phone in the pocket. A brain wave. She'll call Andy. He'll pick her up. She searches for his number and hits Call.

Andy sounds grumpy. Impatient. But he always sounds grumpy and impatient. Is he still at the party, she asks? Yes, but he's leaving now. Could he pick her up? He can't hear her, he says, the signal is bad. She tries again, but he still can't hear her. The call drops.

She moves towards the stairs to the roof to get a signal.

It's cool outside but not cold, not now that she has her coat. She tries her brother again. Andy doesn't answer at all this time. Maybe he's driving. She'll try Julia. Not that Julia can drive or collect her, but just to have someone to talk to. Julia's phone goes straight to voicemail. Then she has another idea. She'll call Gabe. In her jeans pocket sits the thin scrap of paper with his number. She pulls it out and begins to type the digits into her phone, squinting in the wan moonlight. But the paper is pulled from her hand by a gust of wind and, without thinking – maybe it's the drink, maybe it's the primal need to talk to Gabe – she reaches for it. And she reaches too far.

46

THERE'S A MOMENT OF silence when Julia gets to the end of the story, then Stilwell clears her throat. 'So your friend Donna fell from the roof at a party and died.'

Eleanor nods. 'Yes.'

'And no foul play suspected?'

'No. She was on her own, CCTV showed that. We don't know why she went up on the roof, but you can see that she drops something and reaches to grab it, and then she—' Eleanor's voice deserts her.

'You've seen the footage?'

'Oh god, no. I wouldn't be able to sit through something like that. But the police at the time watched it, of course.'

'So, if it was an accident, what makes you think someone would target you?'

Julia and Eleanor glance at each other. This is the stuff they never say.

'I suppose . . . I guess we've always felt guilty.' Julia pauses. Eleanor nods at her to continue. 'Anya told us Donna had gone home and, looking back, I wish we'd probed that. We were so eager to jump in the taxi, to get home ourselves, we didn't try very hard to make absolutely sure Anya was right. There was just this one taxi and if we didn't get it . . .'

Stilwell looks confused and Julia explains. 'You're younger

than us so you probably don't remember, but back then there was a major taxi shortage in Dublin. Queues at ranks a mile long, people piling in with strangers, people walking home for hours because there were no cabs. It's no excuse, of course. We should have made sure she was OK.'

'To be fair, we genuinely thought she'd gone home. Anya said so.' Eleanor sounds defensive. Maybe this is why she's always found it easier to say Donna's name. Maybe she doesn't worry the way Julia does.

'Did you ever ask your friend Anya about this?'

'Oh, of course!' Julia says. 'I mean, not in a way that would make her feel guilty. More in a "but didn't you see her get in a cab?" kind of way.'

'And what did Anya say?'

'She told us that Donna had *said* she was going home. The thing is, I'm certain that on the night, what she actually said was that she'd *seen* Donna get in a cab. There's quite a difference between "Donna told me she was going home" and "I saw Donna get in a cab," and I know if I'd heard the former rather than the latter I'd have checked on Donna.' Julia looks down. 'Maybe that's just something I tell myself . . . but . . . no.' Emphatic now. 'I know Anya said she'd seen her get in a cab. And then she changed her story. I don't know if she even knew she was lying afterwards. Maybe she convinced herself the second version of the story was true, because, I suppose, the alternative – that Donna's death could have been prevented if Anya hadn't lied on the night – was too much.'

'She made a fuss about being stranded,' Eleanor adds. 'She was supposed to stay in Donna's that night and she had to stay at Gabe's instead.'

'Gabe?'

'Uh, my ex-husband. He and Anya had dated, and they were

still friends. We all were. So when Anya realized – or thought – Donna had gone, Gabe stepped in and offered her a bed in his house.'

Stilwell tilts her head. 'And he went on to marry you?'

Julia nods. 'We got together a few months later and, soon after that, we left for San Diego and eventually got married.'

'OK. So who might know that Anya claimed to have seen Donna get in a cab and then changed her story?'

Julia and Eleanor look at one another.

'Us. Gabe. Lots of others too – we told people at the time. Not to get Anya in trouble,' Julia adds hurriedly, 'but because we genuinely thought she'd seen her get in a cab. So our other friends knew. The police. Donna's family. You see, she'd tried to phone her brother for a lift home.' Julia's throat tightens. This bit always gets her. Picturing it. Donna phoning Andy, Andy trying to hear her. Donna all on her own, making the call, because her friends had left her behind.

And now she can't hold it in any longer. Julia begins to cry.

47

The tea scalds Julia's tongue, but it's exactly what she needs after the Garda station visit. She and Eleanor are perched on a stone bench by the fountain outside Dundrum Shopping Centre. It's getting dark already, but still shoppers and cinema-goers mill past, eyeing up menus in restaurants and food vans. Julia pulls her coat around her. 'So what are we thinking now?'

Eleanor twists a tennis bracelet on her wrist. 'I know I'm the one who said the videos are linked to what happened to Donna, but . . .'

'You were hoping the visit to the guards would knock that on the head?'

'Yeah. I didn't expect her to look into it. I was hoping for "sounds like an elaborate prank".'

'It still might be. I mean, logically, who from back then could possibly want to get at us? And why now? What's changed?'

Eleanor gives her a funny look.

'What?'

'You've moved home, that's what's changed. Maybe someone read about your seven-figure business sale in the paper and got mad that things have worked out a little better for you than they did for Donna.'

'Eleanor. That's not fair.'

'God, I don't mean *I* think that, but someone might. Right?'

'But who? The friends who were closest to Donna, who were most upset at her death, were you, me and Anya.'

'And Gabe, I suppose.'

Julia smiles. 'Imagine it turned out to be Gabe. I can see the headlines: "Tech-phobe middle-aged dad figures out video editing in order to scare ex-wife for unspecified reasons".'

'Well, he wouldn't need to do any editing' – Eleanor raises her eyebrows – 'he lives in your house.'

Julia rolls her eyes. 'OK, but joking aside, of all of us, Donna was the one with fewest "other" friends. Our little group was everything to her.'

'JADE.' Eleanor whispers it.

'Yep.'

'What about her family – her brother? Did you stay in touch with him?'

'No, but I barely stayed in touch with anyone.' Julia picks up her phone. 'Let's look him up online.'

Eleanor peers over her shoulder. 'Jeez, you have so many apps. What are *Roblox* and *Township* and *Smobik*?'

'Oh god, they're not mine. *Roblox* is a game Luca added, and I imagine that's what the other two are as well.'

'He just puts games on your phone without asking?'

'Eleanor.' Julia injects a hint of warning into her tone. 'Give it three years, that's all I'll say. OK, let's find Donna's brother.'

She types 'Andy Wilson Straub' into Google. A number of search results come up – a LinkedIn profile, a Facebook account and some newspaper articles all referencing a local councillor called 'Andrew Wilson Straub'. She clicks in, but it's soon clear this is not Donna's brother – Andrew Wilson Straub is about ten years too old and originally from Kentucky. The next results bring up social media accounts of people with similar names – Andrew Wilson, Andy Straub, Alex Wilson Straub. She checks each LinkedIn and Facebook profile just in case, while trying to conjure up a memory of Andy.

He was three years older than Donna, and Julia hadn't encountered him often on her visits to the house – he spent a lot of time in his room playing video games. Donna used to play too, Julia remembers. She idolized Andy, while he mostly ignored her. Pretty standard sibling stuff, Julia thinks, aware of just how little interest Isla shows in Luca. So Donna got into gaming, in a bid to connect with Andy. She never said as much, especially not in front of Anya, who was adamant that video games were for nerds. But Julia knew. She'd grown up with Donna and knew her best.

Andy was a different story, though. Anya used to call him a 'grumpy git', and the last few times Julia met him did nothing to dispel this assessment. He either grunted at the girls or said nothing at all. In hindsight, he was probably shy and awkward and didn't much like having four loud girls descend on the kitchen when he was trying to make a sandwich. The main impression she had at the time was nerd. Awkward. Lumbering. Stretched jumpers and saggy jeans. Wire-rimmed glasses and pasty skin. An indoor person. Not quite a recluse, but almost. God, teenage girls were harsh. Andy was probably no more a recluse than Isla is now – he was just a guy who didn't engage with his younger sister's friends. Would she recognize him today? she wonders. His image swims in her memory. There's an impression – the glasses, the clothes – but nothing distinct.

'We need more information if we're going to track him down. I don't think I'd recognize him, even if we did find him online. Would you?'

Eleanor shakes her head.

'I don't think so. Should we try Donna's mum?'

Julia's chest tightens.

'Are you in touch with her?'

'Not for a few years. I used to call in to see her until the kids were born and things got busy . . . I feel bad now.'

Julia bites her lip. She has never visited Donna's mother. Not once. She hadn't known what to say and it was easier to stay away. *Of course it was.* She looks at her friend now. Eleanor might not handle late-night creepy noises, but perhaps that's not what real bravery is about.

'She still lives in the same house, I know that,' Eleanor continues. 'Donna's dad died last year and Mum went to the funeral.'

Christ, that poor woman. Her daughter gone, and now her husband too. And they're going to chase her down to find out if her son is trying to get some kind of revenge.

Julia sips her cooling tea. 'Maybe your mum would know what happened to Andy, where he is now?'

Eleanor nods and pulls out her phone to text. The reply comes swiftly, in the form of a voice note, which Eleanor plays, mouthing, 'My mother hates typing.'

Mrs Jordan's voice rings out clear as a bell: 'Hi, darling. Goodness, that's a blast from the past. I don't know where Andy is now, but I think he worked in Nintendo or Sony or Stich – one of those video-game companies – and was doing great until he decided to give it all up or he had to quit for some reason, I'm not sure which. Or maybe he was fired? I shouldn't say things like that without knowing. Ignore that bit. Pity you can't edit voice messages. Anyway, are you and Ian coming over on Sunday?'

Julia nods towards the phone. 'Could we send your mum to chat to Donna's mother? She'd be great.'

Eleanor gives her a look. 'I know you like to avoid tricky conversations, but I think we're a little old to be turning to my mum for help.'

'Fine. What would we say to her, though? To Donna's mother?'

'We could tell the truth, or a version of it – that Anya died, that it's resurrecting some memories about our friendship, and we wanted to reconnect with Donna's family.'

Julia screws up her face.

Eleanor nods. 'I know, I know, it's not the most palatable. But it's not doing any harm either. And our motives are reasonable, even if we're not telling Donna's mum why.'

Julia nods agreement. 'So do we just turn up?'

'We should phone first and ask if we can call over.'

'But where will we get her number?'

Eleanor smiles a sad smile. 'The landline, I mean. I never deleted it.' She nods towards her screen, open on a contact that reads 'Donna Home Phone'.

It's pitch dark and after nine when Julia arrives back in Brentwood. The only sound is the click of her heels as she makes her way towards home. Luca's words come back to her. *It's like the houses have eyes.* She puts her head down and keeps going. This is not where she's supposed to be tonight, and she'll go back to the apartment later, but right now she really wants to see the kids. A sound catches her attention. A crush of grass, coming from her left. Only it's stopped now. She listens but keeps walking, trying to hear above the clack of her shoes. Annoyed at herself for wearing heels. They're so noisy, and also . . . also, she wants to run now. Ridiculous as that is, she wants to run and be indoors. A crack of a twig sends adrenaline coursing through her. Who the hell is out there, standing, watching? She picks up speed, half walking, half running, and now she's at the gate to their house and she's letting out a breath. He can't get her once she's inside. She laughs quietly. This is crazy. There is no *he*. And anyway, she reminds herself as she puts the key in the door, if this is something to do with Donna – if this is Andy Wilson Straub playing his own live version of a video game, he's not inside the gates of Brentwood.

48

On Tuesday morning, everything goes wrong. Not in a big way, just in that everyday Tuesday-morning way. Julia wakes in the apartment, confused about where she is, before remembering getting a cab here from Brentwood late last night. Her head is pounding but there's no paracetamol in the medicine cabinet. She spills a full cup of coffee on her laptop when she's rushing to connect to a conference call and, despite wiping, shaking and turning it upside down on a towel, it shudders and dies. She connects to the meeting on her phone instead, noticing a text from Gabe (the locksmith's been, her keys won't work, but he has a new set for her) and messages from Brentwood neighbours Drew and Shirin, plus one from Eleanor. She walks over to the coffee machine while on her call, to discover *now* they're out of coffee. Great.

After her meeting, under-caffeinated and cross, she messages Gabe to ask if she can use his computer for the morning and could he let her know the password. He keeps his brand-new Apple iMac in the small third bedroom he uses as an office. Only, when she walks through to the office, it's not there. In its place, sitting disconsolately on the huge desk, is the old refurbished laptop they let the kids use for school projects.

'Where's your computer gone?' she texts Gabe, wondering if Tuesday could get any worse.

He hasn't seen her first message yet. He's probably in the studio with his phone on silent. With a sigh, she sits at the desk and opens the laptop. It's clunky and old, but at least she knows the password.

She checks her other messages while she waits for the machine to power up. Shirin asking if Julia would like to grab a cup of tea or a drink. She would, she replies, even though every instinct tells her it will be awkward. What do you say to someone whose husband has just left and now seems to be missing? But on this front, she needs to take a leaf out of Eleanor's book, she reckons, thinking again about Donna's mum and her own failings. Drew, too, wants to socialize, it seems – he's inviting her over for drinks with a few other neighbours on Friday night. She wonders briefly if the invitation extends to Gabe and answers that yes, she'd be delighted to go along. Eleanor is asking if lunchtime today works to visit Donna's mother. She's made the call and Mrs Wilson Straub will be there. With a curl of guilt winding through her stomach, Julia says yes, then sits back on the chair, staring at the laptop screen, thinking about Donna's brother. She should go straight to her work email, but she goes to Google instead, to do another hunt for Andy Wilson Straub.

As soon as she clicks into the Google bar, the search history appears. Gabe's search history. She frowns, trying to process what she's seeing.

> what drugs cause loss of memory
> does ketamine stay in system
> side effects of ketamine and ghb

She closes the laptop.

Ten minutes later, she's in Brentwood, rummaging for her keys before remembering that the locks have been changed. She rings the doorbell and Gabe answers, paintbrush in hand, dots of blue paint punctuating his stubble.

'Oh, hey, what's up?'

'I was just on the laptop in the apartment and there was some weird stuff about ketamine and GHB.' She pauses, not even sure what she's asking. 'I . . . I'm just worried one of the kids is googling drugs. But maybe it was you?'

He blinks. 'Oh. It was in a true-crime podcast I was listening to. Somebody had been drugged and they had no idea what happened and I just wondered how realistic it was.'

He turns, walking back through the hall. A tiny splash of paint slips from his brush and on to the marble floor. 'Coffee?'

'Sure.' Quietly relieved, she steps in and stoops to clean the fleck of paint from the floor, mopping it up with her finger.

'Oh, by the way' – he picks up a bunch of keys from the hall table – 'these are for you. I even put a Mission Beach key ring on them to remind you of home.'

Home. Dublin is home now. Or is it? She slips the keys into her bag.

'Great. Was it expensive?'

'Not sure yet. It was Pauline who let the guy in and he didn't leave a bill. I'll text him for it. I got a full set for us and for Raycroft – patio doors, balcony door, back door, garage – but just front door for Pauline. She seemed a bit put out by that, asked why she wasn't getting a full set.'

'Crap. I hope she doesn't think we don't trust her.'

He waves it away. 'She'll be grand. I got one spare front-door key too, to give to a neighbour in case we're locked out. Shirin, maybe?'

Julia bites her lip. 'Much as I like Shirin, I don't feel comfortable giving a spare key to any of our new neighbours right now . . .'

Gabe holds up the single key. 'My parents, then? They're a bit far away to be of any use, though.'

Julia reaches for the key, the answer suddenly blindingly obvious. 'I'll give it to Eleanor.' The realization that Eleanor is probably the one person in the world she completely trusts right now is both heartwarming and sad.

'And the attic bolt?' she asks.

'Raycroft still haven't said if we can do it. A concern that someone could get locked *in*, which is a bit daft.' He jerks his head towards the kitchen. 'Want anything to eat with the coffee?'

'No, I'm grand, but back to what I was asking about your Google search – where's your iMac, anyway?'

Another flicker in his jaw. *What the hell is going on with him?*

'It's in for repair.' He moves into the kitchen and presses the switch on the coffee machine.

'Already? It's brand new.'

'Yeah, something glitchy with it. I'm sure it'll be back in no time.' And again he turns away.

He's lying. For whatever reason, her ex-husband is lying to her.

49

Shirin is outside her gate when Julia reaches the end of the driveway.

'Oh, hi! I thought you were in the apartment at the moment, hence the text earlier. Otherwise I'd have called in.'

'I am, I just popped by,' Julia explains. 'I heard about Tony . . . the police came yesterday . . . Any news?'

'Not a thing. He's probably tucked up with Molly, ignoring all his calls.' She rolls her eyes.

'The guards said his phone is out of service, though?'

'Yes,' Shirin concedes. 'To be honest, if I wasn't still so mad at him, I'd probably be a little worried. Tony and his siblings live in each other's pockets. It *is* odd that he hasn't been in touch with them.'

'Or used any credit cards . . .'

'I know. But if he'd been in any kind of accident, he'd have shown up in a hospital. Or, well, a morgue, I suppose.' She grits her teeth. 'Gosh. On Friday night, I'd have happily bashed him over the head with a golf club, but even I'm not angry enough to wish him dead.' A pause. 'I *think*.' She laughs.

Julia laughs too, marvelling at the change. This is a very different Shirin to the shell-shocked person she saw on Saturday. 'Anyway, I'd better get inside. I have someone calling for lunch.' This is followed by a conspiratorial smile that misses its mark, as Julia has no idea who's coming for lunch. 'I'll be in touch about that drink. And in the meantime, if Tony *has* fallen off the face of the earth, I hope nobody expects me to give a flying fuck.'

With a toss of her ponytail, she turns to walk up her driveway, leaving Julia open-mouthed in her wake. *Good on Shirin*, she thinks.

Her phone beeps. A text from Eleanor, who'll pick her up at twelve thirty to go to Donna's mother's house. Julia lets out a shaky breath, wishing for it to be over.

Nothing has changed in twenty years. The way the light casts through the stained-glass window in the front door, colouring the pine floorboards in the hall. The long, narrow runner, now faded to pink. The phone seat, where Donna used to sit for hours, chatting. The smell of polish and lavender. Julia gazes around, taking it all in, while Eleanor does the talking. They're sorry for her loss, sorry about her husband's death. How is she doing? They have such fond memories of coming here. Sleepovers and popcorn. *Dawson's Creek* and *Ally McBeal*. Staying in and getting ready to go out. Tops from A|Wear and Body Shop White Musk. *And smoking cigarettes up the chimney*, Julia thinks, but Eleanor doesn't say that. There are some things you still don't say to parents.

Mrs Wilson Straub invites them through to the living room, her hands fluttering as she gestures to the couch. Not the same couch – the floral print of old replaced by a more contemporary grey. Julia looks at Donna's mum properly now, at the thin dark hair hanging limply to her shoulders, at the tiny face and watery blue eyes. Mrs Wilson Straub has been aged by more than time. Julia swallows a lump of guilt.

'I made tea,' Donna's mother says, gesturing at a coffee table on which sits a small white teapot. The cups – dark blue Denby that Julia remembers from her own house too – are on matching saucers, and there's a plate of sliced cake. Banana bread, she thinks; that was Donna's mother's speciality, served up when they'd stop off here on the way home from school. A wave of nostalgia swamps her now and her hand shakes as she picks up a cup of freshly poured tea.

'Thank you, this is lovely, Mrs Wilson Straub,' Eleanor says, sliding a slice of banana bread on to a small plate.

'Oh my goodness, that name is such a mouthful. Just call me Kathleen, please. So, how are you, girls?' she asks. Not 'how can I help you?' or 'what do you want?', just a simple, kind 'how are you?' and the guilt kicks in again. Of course she'd ask how they are. She was a constant in their lives for over a decade, all through secondary school and on through college, longer for Julia, growing up here in Kerrybrook. The open house, the welcome in, the smile, the banana bread. And Julia hadn't called once since Donna died.

'We're OK, thanks,' Eleanor says, 'though still quite shook up about Anya.'

'Dreadful. Awful thing to happen.'

Eleanor glances at Julia. 'It stoked up a lot of old memories. We've spent a good amount of time in the last two weeks reminiscing, haven't we, Julia?'

Julia nods and forces a small smile, and Kathleen smiles back.

'We're remembering Donna, of course, and all the lovely times we had here.' A pause so brief only Julia hears it, and only because she knows Eleanor is gearing herself up. 'And Andy, of course! How's he doing?'

Kathleen's smile drops and her cup clatters on to the saucer. She clasps her hands on her lap, looking down. Silence.

'Mrs— Kathleen, are you all right?' Eleanor asks.

Still silence.

Eleanor makes to stand, half hovering over the couch, as though not sure whether or not to go to her. Kathleen looks up and Eleanor sits back down.

'You couldn't know, I suppose. But Andy left. It was about . . . oh god, ten years ago now. Himself and his dad had been at odds for a long time. Since Donna . . . before that, even. Joe, God rest him, thought Andy was wasting his time, sitting in his room with his computer and his video games.' She glances at Julia, then back to Eleanor. 'He wasn't, you know. He got himself a very good job in game design in Stich.' A small sigh. 'But you remember what Joe was like.'

Julia does. Donna's father was sport mad – soccer, Gaelic, rugby – and couldn't understand why his children didn't follow his passion. Donna got a dispensation of sorts. It was the nineties, and men of Joe's generation didn't necessarily expect girls to play football or rugby. But Andy was a big disappointment to him. *He's sitting at that bloody computer again, playing his stupid games.* Julia remembers it like it was yesterday.

'It all came to a head one night. Joe was at him again: when would he get a proper job and get up off his lazy behind and find somewhere to live. Andy told him to back off, and things escalated. It wasn't Joe's fault really' – she looks from Eleanor to Julia, her eyes so sad now – 'Andy was a nightmare to live with by then. Surly and difficult. I remember, God forgive me, I used to be grateful that he stayed in his room. But that night it got out of hand. Shouting and arguing, and then Joe went too far.'

Kathleen looks down at her lap again, clasping and unclasping her hands. When she continues her story, she doesn't look up.

'Joe called him useless and said . . . and said if he wasn't so useless he'd have collected Donna from the party that night and she'd still be alive. He said, "It's your fault she's dead," and Andy just stared at him and' – her voice cracks and she takes a moment to compose herself – 'he walked out of the room and up the stairs. And the next morning, Andy was gone.'

'I'm so sorry,' Julia says, and her voice sounds strange. She realizes it's the first time she's spoken since they arrived.

'We thought he'd come back. Joe said he'd never manage on his own – I mean, he couldn't boil an egg. But he didn't come back.'

'Where did he go?'

A helpless lift of her bony shoulders. 'We don't know. He was working in Stich at that stage, but by the time stubbornness gave way to worry and we tried to get in touch he'd left. His phone number was out of service and we couldn't track him down.'

'*What?*'

Kathleen nods. 'I haven't seen him since.'

And now there are tears flowing freely down her paper-thin cheeks and Eleanor is on her feet and pulling her into a hug. Julia swallows against the tightness in her throat. *Good god, how can one woman go through so much?*

They're sitting again, and Kathleen has produced fresh tea and a box of tissues.

'Sorry,' she says with a small laugh. 'What must you think of me? It's just . . . they've all gone. First Donna, then Andy, now Joe. I'm on my own. And you don't want people to think you're this lonely old lady, so you put on a brave face' – a smile – 'but the truth is, that's what I am. Lonely.'

Eleanor reaches over and squeezes Kathleen's hand as Julia swipes at a rogue tear in the corner of her eye.

'Donna was such a good girl. I still miss her dreadfully. She idolized *you*.' Kathleen nods at Julia. 'I remember the two of you cycling around the green when you were small, and Donna coming home full of *Julia this* and *Julia that*. She used to learn as much as she could about anything you were into so she'd be able to talk to you. Music especially. Madonna, and that band Bon Jovi, right? And the other ones, Europe?'

'Ha, Bon Jovi more than Europe!' Julia lets out a laugh that turns into a sob. 'I didn't know that. I thought she was just into all the same things I was.'

'Well, by the time she'd finished reading every issue of *Smash Hits* and taping songs off the radio so she could learn the lyrics, she was.'

Julia's heart contracts. This is a different Donna to the one she knew. Or maybe it's the same Donna through a different lens. Guilt wraps around her like a cold fog. Did she know, on some level, that Donna was trying so hard? Maybe. Sometimes Donna was irritating. Sometimes Julia was impatient. Sometimes, when Anya was mean, Julia didn't speak up. She was never mean to Donna herself. But, she thinks now, bystanders who don't intervene are just as bad.

Kathleen is watching her intently, as though reading her thoughts.

'You were never as close as when it was just the two of you, here in Kerrybrook, on your bikes. But she understood that. Secondary school and college are all about making new friends.'

'She didn't really . . . she—' The words are strangled and won't come out. The truth is, Donna didn't make new friends. She latched on to Julia's friends.

Kathleen's voice is soft. 'She didn't need to make new friends, though, because you did that for her, Julia. You never let her go. She idolized you to the day she died, and I'll always be grateful for your friendship.'

Tears roll down Julia's face. She has no words. Eleanor puts her arm around Julia's shoulder, squeezes it and gives a shaky laugh. 'OK, I'm crying now too. What are we like!'

Julia wipes her eyes and works to compose herself.

'Donna loved you so much,' she says to Kathleen. 'And she adored Andy.'

'She did. And he used to roll his eyes every time she asked if he wanted a game, but you never saw him move quicker than when he was switching on that console after she said it. I always suspected she only played to spend time with him, but sure, look, it worked. They had great craic together. Poor Andy, wherever he is now.'

'You have absolutely no idea?' Eleanor asks. 'He never got in touch at all?'

'He texted soon after he left. Said we should all take a break from each other. I didn't tell Joe this, but I replied to it, asking him to come home.'

'And what did he say?'

'He didn't write back. Blame is too big. Words like that, you can't take them back.' She looks at both of them in turn. 'Girls, if anything ever happens to you, God forbid, don't ever lay blame on someone close to you. It cuts deeper than anything, and you can't unsay it.'

Julia nods, thinking about Isla, about Riley.

'I'm so sorry,' she says now to Donna's mother. 'For everything.'

And Kathleen nods and smiles, and Julia knows more clearly than anything she's ever known that Donna's mother forgives her.

50

'GOD.'

'I know.' They're walking back down Donna's street towards Eleanor's car and Julia feels like she's been crying for hours, though they were only there for forty minutes. 'Eleanor, you were so great. I could hardly speak.'

Eleanor waves a hand, brushing it off. 'That poor woman. But what do we do next to find Andy?' she says, unlocking her Jeep.

'Well, Gabe has a pal in Stich. I could ask him to put us in touch? See if anyone there today knows where Andy went.'

'It's worth a try. Right, I'll drop you home. Apartment?'

'Yep, thanks. Eleanor . . .' Julia touches her friend's arm before they get in. 'You know something – I wouldn't worry so much about saving your kids from tiger attacks. Staying in contact with Donna's mum, checking on her' – she feels her throat tighten again – 'that's a lot braver than climbing into an attic.'

Gabe is quick to send her his friend's contact details but curious, too, about what she's up to. She explains briefly in a text, aware that as soon as she mentions Donna's name he'll clam up. And sure enough: two blue ticks but no reply. No matter. She messages Gabe's friend to ask about Andy Wilson Straub, one-time staff member of a company with literally thousands of employees. This is a long shot and, unsurprisingly, the friend doesn't know Andy. He does, however, have a colleague in reception who's been there since the office first opened and he'll message her to ask.

Julia paces while she waits, conscious that Gabe's friend might not get back to her this afternoon but unable to concentrate on anything else. In Gabe's office, she opens the kids' laptop to search 'Andy Wilson Straub Stich Dublin', but nothing comes up. She sits back on the chair, stretching her arms, thinking. Has he wiped all his social media, or did he never have any to begin with? Her eyes roam around the office, and a box in the corner catches her attention. One of Gabe's, not yet unpacked from the move. The sticker on the outside says 'GABE'S DOCS/FILES', and she knows she shouldn't, she absolutely shouldn't, but the search history is fresh in her mind and Gabe's explanation doesn't ring true, and she's halfway across the room before she can talk herself out of it.

She kneels to open the box. What is she looking for? Maybe she wants to find nothing and have her mind put at ease. She begins pulling out files and loose pages, recognizing bank statements, pension documents and tax files, just as she expected. A familiar logo catches her eye, and a business name, Hase Accounting. Gabe used Anya's firm too? This, while not known to her, is also not surprising. God, Gabe sold so few paintings he can't really have needed an accountant, and yet Julia knows Anya would have had no qualms taking a fee from him. As well as asking for a painting, she thinks, remembering the one from the video. She picks up the invoice, to take a peek. Sure enough, a bill for €600 for work carried out by Hase Accounting, signed off by a clearly unabashed Anya Hase and by her former employee Vincent Gale – he of the 'fucking liability consultant' debacle.

As she stares at Anya's signature, for the first time Julia feels a pang of true sadness for the disintegration of her relationship with her childhood friend. She'd been so busy being angry, she'd never grieved the loss. Anya had been a friend for thirty years. And now she's dead and there's no way to make up. Would Julia be thinking like this if Anya was still alive? Probably not. And that's sad too. She puts the invoice on the floor and keeps digging. At the base of the box, she finds the bill from the law firm again, the one she's already seen in the kitchen drawer. Why is Gabe burying it here, underneath everything else? A text interrupts her thoughts.

Hi Julia, my name is Bláthaín and I hear you're looking for people who might have known Andy Wilson Straub. I can tell you about Andy. Are you free for a call?

51

BLÁTHAÍN PICKS UP AFTER one ring, and sounds much younger than Julia anticipated. Having heard she'd been in her job for twenty years, Julia somehow expected the receptionist would be older, until she remembered that she, too, has been in the work-force for twenty years. After a brief greeting and zero small talk, Julia asks Bláthaín about Andy.

'He was with us back when the offices first opened. I remember him well. Quiet guy, came off as rude, but I reckon he was just awkward. Hung out with the Level Design gang. Didn't speak to anyone outside the department. It was like those guys had their own code, you know?'

'Yes, I knew him a little a long time ago. That sounds about right.'

This seems to remind Bláthaín that she has no idea who Julia is.

'You're searching for him for some reason?' A note of guard-edness has slipped in.

Julia opts for something close to the truth. 'I was very good friends with his sister, who sadly died a long time ago. I've just moved back to Ireland and I'm trying to reconnect with old friends.'

'Oh god, I had no idea his sister had died. He really was very quiet. Subdued, you might say. What happened to her?'

'An accident. She fell from a high building.' *And his dad blamed him.* No wonder he was subdued.

'Christ. Poor Andy.'

'Do you know where he went after he left Stich?'

'No, sorry. He handed in his notice nine or ten years ago and told us he was taking a break, thinking about doing something completely different.'

Damn.

'I did see him in a pub once.'

'Oh yeah? Where?'

'At least, I *think* it was him.'

'Go on?'

'It was about five years ago, in Harry's on Exchequer Street. I was on a first date with my now-girlfriend, in her local. Andy was sitting at the bar on his own. I recognized him and, when he turned around at one point, I waved, but I don't think he saw me.'

'Right.' Julia's still on the floor beside Gabe's document box and her knees are getting stiff now.

'The thing is, I wasn't a hundred per cent sure afterwards if it really was him. He'd toned up, looked really healthy and fit. The Andy I knew was kind of slouchy and looked anything but healthy and fit. But his face . . . that looked the same, just a . . . less pasty version. My girlfriend asked me if I knew him and said she'd seen him in the bar pretty much every time she'd been in. I wondered if he had a drink problem, but he seemed to be sitting over a Coke for the night.'

'Uh-huh.' Julia moves from kneeling by Gabe's document box to sitting at the desk.

'I've been back there over the years, but haven't seen him since,' Bláthaín adds.

'So, possibly a regular in Harry's, at a point in time. OK. But no way of knowing where he'd be working now?'

'No. He said he was switching careers, to do something

completely different. And I'm about the only person left from when he worked here. Sorry.'

'No worries, I really appreciate you taking the time to chat.'

Julia says goodbye and slumps back in the chair. This feels like a dead end. And maybe it was never a runner anyway – maybe none of this has anything to do with Andy. She and Eleanor have been chasing this angle for three days now, without any real reason to think it will lead them to whoever is posting the videos. Nevertheless, it can't hurt to go to Harry's bar and ask some questions. She texts the update to Eleanor and they arrange to visit the bar the following evening.

Her phone rings just as she finishes her text chat with Eleanor. It's Isla and she sounds panicked.

'Mom. You have to come home. Now.'

52

'What's happened? Are you hurt? Is Luca OK?' Julia grabs her keys, phone still clamped to her ear. 'Where's your dad?'

'He's at the store, but he's not answering his phone. Can you come home?'

'I'm on my way, but Isla, please tell me what's wrong.'

'It's another video, and I don't know how they did it, but they could only have taken it inside our house. It's not one of my videos that I already put up. And there's another thing. But just come.'

'OK, on my way. Screen-record it, but don't message the person.' A breath. 'And lock the doors.'

Ten minutes later, Julia lets herself into the house in Brentwood. Gabe's car's not in the driveway; he must not be back yet. Luca's in the den watching TV, his small form cross-legged on the wooden floor, Basil on his lap. She slips quietly past and through to the kitchen, where Isla is sitting at the table hunched over her phone. On the stovetop, a saucepan of chip oil bubbles, and beneath her worry about what's coming in the video, Julia feels a flicker of irritation at Gabe for leaving the hob on. She switches it off and walks over to her daughter. Isla glances up, then presses Play.

Something about the image on-screen strikes Julia as odd.

'Wait, why doesn't it have all the TikTok stuff? The Like button and all that?'

Isla's voice is low. For the first time, she sounds scared. 'It's not *on* TikTok. This one was sent to me by text.'

Julia goes cold. 'Wait, to your phone number? Someone has your number?'

'Yeah.'

Fuck. Julia takes the phone and clicks into Isla's texts. The video's come from an Irish mobile. Ten digits, no name.

Anger surges through Julia and she hits the call button, with no idea if it's wise or what she's going to say. It's a moot point: the number is out of service.

'And, Mom, it's not one of my videos. Watch.'

The opening is the same as all the other videos, but in the kitchen, the camera zooms in on one photo – the snapshot of Julia, Anya, Donna and Eleanor at their Debs graduation ball. Isla may not have posted a video that included the Debs photo, but the earlier part of the clip is similar to the others . . . Maybe someone had tacked on the Debs photo at the end? But how would anyone have an image of her photo? Then she remembers. Eleanor shared it on Facebook. Where any one of her 600 friends could access it.

'OK, first of all, the thing to remember is we've changed the locks. So even if someone *had* keys and was getting in to film these clips, as of yesterday, it is *impossible* for them to do that. Who might have your Irish phone number?'

'Um, girls in my class. There's a class chat group and a smaller group for a few of the girls I have lunch with. And there's a WhatsApp for the school soccer team, so anyone who's in that, I guess. I don't think anyone else would have it . . .'

Julia hides her surprise at the lunch-girls news and the soccer-team news. Isla hadn't mentioned either of them, and she is *not* going to ruin it now by making a big deal.

'OK. I don't know who sent it or how they got your number, but it must be an old video of yours that's been edited.'

'Mom, I never posted a video like this.' Her voice shakes. 'I don't know where they got it.'

Before Julia can explain about Eleanor and the Debs photo, a small, serious voice interrupts.

'I told you.'

Luca is standing in the doorway, cradling his rabbit. 'He lives here, in the attic. He comes down when we're asleep. He watches us.'

'Luca, stop!' Isla yells. 'You're giving me the creeps. Mom, I hate it here. I hate this house – can't we go home?'

'Isla, honey. This is home.'

'But I *hate* it! Why do we have to do what you want, all the time? What about us? Don't we count?'

'It's not for me, it's for all of us.'

'Yeah, right. How is it for anyone but you? You're the most selfish person I ever met.'

'That's not true. We're here because of—' *Stop. Breathe.*

'Because of *what*?'

'Because it's better for all of us.'

'*I hate you.*' Eyes brimming with angry tears, Isla storms out of the kitchen and stomps up the stairs. Luca, brushed sideways in her jet stream, turns and walks away. Julia slides on to a stool at the island and rests her face in her hands.

How much longer can she take being the bad guy? Should she just tell Isla what happened to Riley? Head in hands, her mind goes back to that day. Heather standing on her doorstep, calmly informing her she had something to tell her. Julia had invited her in, asked her to sit, habitual politeness kicking in, feeling sick to her stomach as she tried to make sense of what Heather was saying. Isla had taken Riley's phone, Heather said. She'd messaged a boy who Riley had been chatting with on Snapchat. Joshua was his name. Twelve years old, a sixth grader at a nearby school. Not their school, a private Catholic school, about five miles away. Riley liked Joshua, and they'd been chatting for a while though had yet to meet in real life. Joshua wanted to, but Riley was playing it cool. Telling him she'd meet, but then changing her mind. She was into him, she told her friends, but wanted to keep him dangling. Then Isla sent a message to Joshua on Riley's phone, pretending to be Riley. Heather showed Julia the message:

hey come over xx my moms out all day xx

Julia winced, angry and embarrassed that Isla would take her friend's phone and betray her trust.

'I'm so sorry. I'll speak to her. Obviously, she shouldn't have done that. But I think Riley's taken her phone in the past and posted photos—'

Heather cut her off.

'I'm not finished.' Seething now, her jaw tight, the words came in a hiss. 'Joshua asked for our address and Isla gave it to him. *She gave him our address.*' Every word enunciated, laced with cold fury. 'And Riley went home with no idea. And an hour later, Joshua showed up at our house.'

'OK. I'm really sorry.'

'You will be. Joshua's not a twelve-year-old boy. He's a middle-aged man, six feet tall, and he barrelled his way into the house as soon as Riley opened the door.'

Julia's hand flew to her mouth. 'Oh my god. Is she OK?'

'No, she's not OK. She's been assaulted by a stranger. How could she be OK?'

'A-assaulted? You don't mean she's . . .'

'I do.' Heather stood. 'We've been to the police, and she's

home now with my ex-husband, shaking under a blanket, not able to talk or get up or leave the house. I don't know how she'll ever recover, and that's on you. On your daughter.'

'God, Heather, I don't know what to say.' Julia was crying now. 'I'm so, so sorry. If I could swap places with Riley, I would.'

Heather shook her head, dismissing it, but Julia knew with every ounce of her being that she would switch. *Christ almighty, poor Riley.*

'Did the police get him?'

'No. He left our house, left Riley lying on the floor, deleted his account, and the police haven't been able to track him down. She's terrified he's going to get at her again. Or get someone else whose friend is stupid enough to do what Isla did.' Her eyes narrowed. 'We haven't told the police who took Riley's phone, so they don't know who sent the message.'

Julia dug her nails into her palms, waiting for whatever Heather would say next. Would Isla be in trouble legally? At age twelve? Could they prosecute her? Shame took over then. How could she think like that after what had happened to Riley? What kind of person even goes there? *A parent protecting a child.*

'Riley knows it was Isla. She's the only one who had access to her phone.' Heather paused. 'I need to think about it. About whether or not we'll give her name to the police. Or the school.' That's when Julia realized to her shame that she was more frightened of the school – the parents, the teachers, the kids – finding out than she was of the police knowing. But she couldn't bring herself to ask for mercy. Not with knowing what Riley had been through.

'I'm going now,' said Heather. 'I need to be home with my daughter. But we'll talk soon. This isn't the end of it.'

It certainly wasn't the end of it, but it was the start of the end of their time in San Diego. A week later, Julia and Heather had the showdown in the café and Gabe took over negotiations. A week after that, they heard Riley had been checked into a psychiatric hospital. Isla continued with her life, oblivious to what she had done. Riley had gone to stay with her dad – that was the story that spread at school, and Isla believed it. 'I think her mom got tired of dealing with her,' Isla said to Julia, and Julia cringed inwardly but kept her lips sealed.

Meanwhile, Gabe was shell-shocked after his first meeting with Heather.

'Jesus, that was horrendous.'

Julia couldn't help feeling just a tiny bit gratified that Gabe now had first-hand experience of being the punchbag. Heather had every right to punch, but Julia was more than ready to share the load with her ex-husband.

'She gave you hell, I take it?'

Gabe's eyes widened. 'No, she was nothing like you said – she was just . . . broken.' He ran his hand across his head. 'God, I felt awful for her. She was trying not to cry the whole time I was there, and kept telling *me* not to feel bad.'

Julia bit her lip. 'I hate jumping to this, but has she decided yet whether or not to give Isla's name to the police?'

'She's struggling with her conscience. She feels she has a moral obligation to tell the truth, but she said she doesn't want to cause any more hurt. She's battling with herself, trying to find the best solution, to see if there's a way to keep Isla's name out of it.' A pause. 'Maybe we should just tell Isla the truth.'

'Absolutely no way. It will destroy her.' Julia shook her head. 'Knowing her friend was assaulted and is now in a psychiatric hospital for something she did? She thought she was playing a harmless prank.'

'It wasn't harmless, though.'

'But that doesn't make Isla a terrible person – it's basically moral luck.'

'It's what?'

'Moral luck? Like, if someone forgets to turn off the gas and the building blows up, he's a monster. If someone forgets to turn off the gas and the building doesn't blow up, he's just a regular person. The outcome was obviously tragic for Riley, but it doesn't make Isla a monster. If she finds out, the guilt will eat her up for the rest of her life.'

'Is this about . . .'

'Donna? No!'

Maybe.

Eventually, Gabe came around to her way of thinking and they agreed not to tell Isla the truth. He met with Heather again, keeping the lines of communication open. Working his charm to deter her from telling the school what Isla had done. That part made Julia uncomfortable, but not enough to stop it.

Meanwhile, Julia hatched an escape plan.

And now here she is, in her oversized kitchen, with a daughter who hates her, watching a video taken by someone who may or may not be creeping around their house. Maybe Gabe is right. Maybe they should move again.

53

THE POLICE HAD COME on Tuesday night and searched the attic. To nobody's surprise, there was nothing there. Luca couldn't be convinced to go up to see for himself, and when the garda climbed back down and said it was empty, Luca just nodded and said, 'He'll be back later,' in a solemn tone. Detective Stilwell took a look at the text on Isla's phone and tried the number, but it was still out of service. Most likely a pay-as-you-go phone, Stilwell said, and the sender had probably destroyed the SIM. Julia asked about the IP address request that Detective Connell had instigated, and Stilwell said she'd check, but that there was unlikely to be an update so soon.

So, once Stilwell had left, Julia had texted Alastair to see if his colleague had made any progress, and he'd said he'd call around with an update. Which is why at 11 a.m. on Wednesday, Alastair is sitting opposite Julia at her kitchen table with a notebook and a laptop, and a takeaway cappuccino for each of them.

'I know you have that big fancy coffee machine,' he says, 'but sometimes takeaway coffees are a nice treat, aren't they?'

'How did you know about my coffee machine?' The words are out before she can stop herself.

Alastair flushes pink. 'You said it? When I offered a contact name for the garbage disposal?'

Shit. She had. God, she must sound like a paranoid lunatic.

'Sorry, don't mind me. I'm addled with all this video stuff . . .'

'And I need to learn to dial things back on the nosiness front.' A sheepish grin. 'My ex used to say it was my way of bonding with people but that it just comes off as "unacceptably nosy and monumentally annoying".'

Ouch.

Alastair smiles at Julia's expression. 'I know. I think we reached a point where everything I did embarrassed her. And it's rubbed off on our daughter now too.'

'Oh god. Maybe she means it in that kind of pre-teen half-jokey eye-roll way?'

He shakes his head. 'No, she literally can't bear to be around me. I can't do anything about it, though, because she chose to live with her mum, and the more time she spends with her, the more it colours her judgement. I should have fought harder back when we broke up . . .'

'How long ago was that?' Julia wonders why she's probing, having put up with questions about her own break-up for years. But Alastair seems eager to talk, and it strikes her that perhaps he doesn't get to offload like this very often. Gabe certainly didn't. When they broke up, she had Eleanor and Anya by phone, and she had colleagues and mom friends in San Diego. She had Milena, the yoga instructor she'd bonded with – they'd talk over coffee about Milena's unsuccessful search for love and Julia's unsuccessful marriage. She had her sister in Perth and, to an admittedly less useful extent, her brother in Jakarta. Gabe had nobody.

'We broke up early last year,' Alastair says. 'We were only months from the wedding. That's what triggered it – the wedding. I couldn't afford the venue we'd booked or the kind of wedding she wanted and it took me far too long to admit it. When I finally did, she walked out.'

'Oh, I'm so sorry.'

'I know what you're thinking and you're right – it doesn't paint her in the best light. It wasn't just about the wedding, though, it was a wake-up call – she realized she wasn't going to get the kind of life she envisioned, married to me.'

'That's awful, all of it.' Julia can't quite imagine being with someone who attached such importance to money. Then again, it had never come up – she'd always earned more than enough for her and Gabe to live well. Gabe had never had to worry about money at all.

'It was pretty bad all right,' he says grimly. 'The irony is, I came into some money – a decent bonus in my new job – and offered to give her what she wanted: the big wedding, the fancy venue. But it was too little too late. And I suppose that's OK – it probably wasn't meant to be if money was such an important element of the relationship. Plus, what with me being so *monumentally annoying . . .*'

'Hey, don't let her words define you. You give more than you take, which says a lot about anyone. Look, aren't you in my kitchen right now helping me with my video problem?' She gestures at his laptop and notebook.

'And getting sidetracked telling you my woes . . . Right, back to business. So my colleague who's looking into it hasn't been able to say yet if the video is real or fake, but she reckons it could also be useful to examine the clip to see if the person gives themselves away somehow.'

'How do you mean?'

'Walking past a mirror with their mask up, filming something revealing – their own shoes, maybe.' He holds up his phone. 'She spotted something in the video of your friend Anya's house and asked me to show it to you. Here's a screenshot.'

Julia takes Alastair's phone. The screenshot shows the huge

mirror in Anya's hall, with the reflection showing the wall opposite. A blank white wall, with something blurred but familiar at the outer edge of the frame. Julia zooms in.

'My colleague was hoping that photo might give something away,' Alastair continues. 'If the video is Photoshopped, there's a chance that some components are from the TikTok person's own home. And if we had a photo in which they actually appeared . . . that would be pretty amazing, right? Long shot, I know . . .'

Julia stares at the zoomed-in photo in the reflection, at the blur of fuchsia, red, jade and biscuit.

'It's Anya's photo.'

She points across the kitchen to her own copy of the Debs picture, swallowing a lump of emotion. *Anya had the Debs photo on her wall?* There's something so horribly poignant about that. All that wasted time fighting. *God.*

'Ah. Figured it was a long shot,' Alastair says. 'We'll keep looking. Maybe future videos will give us something useful.'

'Yeah, I was hoping for no more videos at all . . .'

'I understand, but more videos might tell you the purpose and, once you know that, you'll know who it is.'

'True . . . I'm assuming they're trying to scare me, maybe because of something that happened a long time ago . . .'

'Oh?'

Julia hesitates but decides against telling him about Donna, for now at least.

'It's probably not that,' she says. *Although with the Debs photo in Anya's video . . .* 'Anyway, for now we'll just keep all the doors and windows locked, and keep the police updated.'

'If you need me, give me a call any time.' He grins. 'I'm pretty handy with a crowbar, though only at holding it while trying to look tough.'

Julia puts her hand to her face. 'Sorry again. I'm mortified.'

'Eh, I'm the one who was standing there with a crowbar! Right.' He gets up to leave. 'I'd better take Mavis for a walk or she'll be barking the house down.'

Isla's in a mood when she comes in from school, stopping short when she sees Julia in the kitchen. 'Oh,' she says, dumping her bag on the floor. 'It's you.'

'Yep,' Julia says breezily. 'My turn. Your dad's in the apartment.' She plasters on a smile, trying to ignore the obvious displeasure on her daughter's face.

'Where's Pauline?'

'She's coming over a bit later because I have to pop out this evening.'

'Great,' Isla says, meaning very much *not great*. 'Where's Luca?'

'Tennis. His friend's mother's dropping him home.'

'Where's my PE gear? I need it tomorrow.'

'It's washed and dried and back on your bed. If you could try to remember to put it in the wash yourself . . . just in case your dad or I forget . . .'

Isla ignores this and cranes her neck to see what's in the wok. 'What's that?'

'Satay. Or it will be,' Julia says, tossing chicken pieces in the hot pan.

'I hate satay.' And with that, Isla stomps up the stairs. Julia bites down the urge to shout after her to *get back down the stairs this minute* and *lose the attitude* and actually, *cop on and stop being such a brat*. That's not going to help. And, she reminds herself, on top of everything else, Isla's rattled about the video sent to her phone yesterday. But right now she's sorely tempted to ship her off to boarding school, just as her own mother used to threaten her when she was a child.

The doorbell rings, and Julia glances at her watch. Luca, she reckons. She wipes her hands on a tea towel and goes out to answer. Luca trudges into the hallway without looking at her, grazing beneath the kiss she tries to plant on his head. Behind him, Eimear, his classmate's mother, makes a face that means *I know what it's like, my kid does this too.*

'Hey, say thank you for the ride home!' Julia calls after Luca.

But Luca's gone. Eimear waves it away.

'Don't worry. He's probably tired. He was very quiet in the car.'

'Yeah, September's exhausting . . .'

'He said something about a man in the attic?'

'Oh Jesus.' Julia tries to laugh but thinks she might cry. 'Yeah. Long story short, someone's been posting videos on social media that look like they were made in our house, and they show someone creeping out of the attic.'

'Oh, like the *Loft* thing?'

'Exactly. Poor Luca's terrified. I don't know . . . I might get Gabe to take him to his parents' at the weekend or something. Give him a break from all this.'

'Good idea, and they're off school Friday for the in-service day. Maybe the rest will do him good.'

Julia had forgotten that. She makes a mental note to suggest a trip to Gabe – Isla won't object to missing a day of school, she's certain of that.

'Are you doing anything nice yourself?' she starts to ask Eimear, before being interrupted by a shriek from the kitchen and the sound of two smoke alarms going off.

'*Shit.* The chicken!'

'Go!' Eimear says, waving her off, and Julia rushes through to the kitchen to find the wok belching black smoke. She grabs the handle and flings the whole thing into the sink, running cold water on it while trying to remember if this is the right thing to do. Luca's eyes are scrunched shut and his hands are over his ears. Julia climbs on a stool to hit the button on the kitchen smoke alarm, then runs upstairs to do the same with the one on the landing. For some reason, the smoke alarm in the hall isn't going off. She stares at it for a moment, berating herself for not testing the batteries on all the alarms as soon as they moved in. She adds it to the long list of things she's doing wrong. From upstairs comes the sound of the bathroom door as Isla slams and storms her way around. Back in the kitchen, Luca has the chess set out.

'You can be white,' he says. And although she has to meet Eleanor in less than an hour, and although there's no dinner, Julia's ever-present mom-guilt won't allow her to say no. She sits opposite Luca, touches the queen and dials the number for pizza.

54

From outside, Harry's bar looks not just closed but borderline derelict, an anomaly on Dublin city centre's Exchequer Street. Nestled between a glossy department store and a gleaming coffee shop, the paint-flecked front door and barred windows no doubt irritate the neighbours. But Harry's is a Dublin institution. The people who drink here – musicians, millennials, shoppers, stag parties – happily share space with older customers who've quite possibly been on their bar stools since the pub was built in 1884. Julia pushes the heavy door, holding it for Eleanor to pass through, and follows her in. The pub is dark, thanks to shutters on the windows, and already bustling with Wednesday evening drinkers. Julia and Eleanor make their way to the bar and perch on the only two vacant stools. A pale, dark-haired girl with a name tag that says 'Niamh' approaches. She looks not much older than Isla, and suddenly this feels silly. How is anyone going to know who they're looking for, with only a vague description and no photograph? Julia asks about wine and Niamh slides a sticky laminated menu into her hand. There are three reds and three whites, all sold in quarter bottles. Eleanor, peering at the menu, wrinkles her nose and says she'll have a gin and tonic.

'Two gin and tonics, please,' Julia says and, without responding, Niamh pushes a Slim Jim glass against an optic beneath a bottle of Gordon's.

Eleanor, who prefers her gin overpriced and in a fish bowl, wrinkles her nose a little more, then casts about the bar, taking in her surroundings.

'Do you know, I think I came here on a date once! It was when Ian and I broke up for two weeks that time. One date. Here. A god-awful guy who informed me girls wear too much make-up and I'd be prettier without it. That's all it took for me to realize I wanted to get back with Ian.' She rests her eyes on Julia. 'How about you? Any potentials since you moved back?'

Julia laughs. 'God, no. Between the kids and the job and the *slight* issue of the attic videos, I wouldn't have time, even if there was anyone remotely interesting.' She wraps her hand around the gin and tonic Niamh has just placed in front of her. Two lonely cubes of ice float in the glass.

'And in San Diego?' Eleanor takes a tentative sip of her drink. 'You never say much about that side of things . . .'

'Because there's nothing to say. I literally don't have time to date. Not then, not now.'

Eleanor shrugs. 'I mean . . . you could make time? Are you being a bit of a martyr, maybe?'

Julia stiffens. 'Hey, that's not fair.' This, from Eleanor, who settled down with Ian as soon as she came back from her travels. Eleanor, who has never had to contend with dating apps. Eleanor, who, as usual, is proffering advice on something about which she has absolutely no clue. Julia's nostrils flare and she swivels on her bar stool, ready for defence.

But Eleanor's eyes are soft. 'It's OK to choose *you* sometimes. That's all I'm saying. Now, we'd better get on with our questions.' She inclines her head towards their young bartender.

Mollified, Julia nods agreement. She raises her voice slightly, addressing Niamh. 'Excuse me, have you worked here long?'

Niamh eyes them suspiciously. 'Since the summer.'

'Is there anyone around who's been working here longer? We're looking for an old friend who used to drink here.'

'Mike!' Niamh calls as she taps something on the till, and a short man ambles over from the far end of the bar. 'These are looking for someone.' She sticks a docket and a credit-card machine in front of Julia and moves away to serve another customer.

Mike puts his hands on the bar. 'Yes?'

Julia launches in without preamble. 'We're looking for someone who used to drink here, or maybe still does. His name is Andy Wilson Straub.'

Mike shakes his head. 'Sorry, nope.' He starts to move away.

'Can you think about it for a moment?' she asks. 'It's important.' On some level, she's aware that she sounds abrupt. Demanding, almost. But this bar is their only lead and this barman is not pausing to think for even a second.

'Already said, don't know.' A slightly irritated shrug.

'It's such an institution, Harry's,' Eleanor says. 'I remember coming here twenty years ago on a disastrous date. Have you been here long yourself?'

'Not far off that, actually. Nineteen years next May,' Mike says, with some pride.

'Wow. I'd say you could tell some stories!'

'Ha. Between the politicians who think no one will recognize them and the journos fishing for stories and the odd celeb, I've seen it all. Did you know Katy Perry came in once?'

'Really!' Eleanor's eyes are huge. 'I need to come here more often. We only came in to find an old friend, but now that I'm here' – she glances around – 'I'll definitely be back.'

'What did you say the friend's name was?'

'Andy Wilson Straub.'

'Jays, that's a mouthful. Sounds like a musician or something.'

'No, he works in gaming, or at least he used to.'

'The name doesn't ring a bell . . . Have you a photo?'

'We don't, unfortunately . . .'

Mike tilts his head, puzzled, no doubt, about why they have no photo of their 'old friend'.

'It's been a very long time,' Eleanor explains. 'We were good friends with his sister and she died and we're trying to reach him.'

'Ah. Right.' Mike's face softens. 'What does he look like?'

'Brown hair, medium height, quite fit and toned, as far as we know.'

Mike laughs and leans closer, cupping a hand to the side of his mouth as he nods towards the other customers along the bar. 'Fit and toned? Probably not a regular here, then. Any other details?'

'He was a gamer. Loved video games when we knew him. We don't know if he still does.'

Mike's face changes. 'Hang on, there might be someone. Did you say Andy? Would he go by Andrew?'

'He might, absolutely.'

'There *was* an Andrew. A regular. Lived in an apartment next door, above the coffee shop. Big, fancy place it was; I was in there once. He was a gamer fella. Used to play on his phone when he was here but had a ton of computer stuff for games in his gaff. Big fancy chair for sitting in too, with a headset thing. Could that be your guy?'

Julia sits forward on her stool. 'Maybe . . . What age would he be?'

'Early forties when I knew him. Had a drink for his fortieth in here, all on his own. I remember he was always on his own. So he'd be' – he looks up, doing a calculation – 'maybe forty-eight or forty-nine now?'

Julia and Eleanor exchange a glance: the age fits.

'You wouldn't by chance know where he worked?' Eleanor asks.

'I don't think he said. He mentioned that he *used* to work for one of those big American companies, but he left because they wanted him in there all hours of the day and night.'

'Stich?'

'That's the one.'

A fizz of excitement bubbles up in Julia's stomach. But just as quickly, it deflates.

'Wait,' she says. 'You said when you "knew him" – do you mean he doesn't come in any more?'

'Not for a few years now. He moved out of the flat. Sold or gave away all his furniture. Gave me a couch. That's how I was in his gaff that one time – me and the brother went in to take the couch. Massive thing. Bloody hard work getting it down those stairs.'

'When was that?'

'December four years ago, middle of lockdown. Gave the couch to the missus for Christmas.' A grin. 'Got an earful for that, though not as bad as when I gave her a hoover.'

'And do you know where he moved to?' Eleanor asks.

Mike scratches his head. 'I can't remember now. Somewhere fancy in south Dublin. And for whatever reason, he didn't need his furniture – moving somewhere furnished or moving in with someone, I suppose. There was something about needing space for his son.'

'Can you remember anything else about him?'

Mike shakes his head, wiping the bar with a disturbingly

discoloured cloth. 'A very quiet fella, head stuck in his phone. Never gave much away. If it wasn't for the couch, I don't think I'd remember him at all.'

Julia and Eleanor share a taxi home, though the route from Exchequer Street to Morehampton Road to Foxrock is somewhat circuitous. They go through everything Mike said, with Julia making notes on her phone.

'It paid off!' Eleanor says, eyes gleaming, as they pull up outside her house. 'I feel like Miss Marple.'

'Thanks to your charm,' Julia says. 'He looked at me like I was his old school principal. I wonder, though, after all this, if it's really the same Andy . . .'

'It *has* to be him. Same workplace, same first name, same hobby, same description – and don't forget, all of this is because that colleague of his saw him in the pub and heard he was a regular.'

'OK, but all we know now is that he lives in "south Dublin",' Julia says. 'Where do we go from here?'

55

LUCA IS NOT SURPRISED, not any more. It's the same every night now, waking up as soon as he hears the noise, the creak from the landing. His eyes dart to his bedroom door. It's shut tight, just like he left it. He leans over the side of his bunk: 03:11 is the time on his Alexa. The middle of the night. Everyone asleep. He leans further and sees Basil is in his nesting box and lets out a quiet breath. But any relief is short-lived.

A footstep.

The man is outside his door.

Luca's eyes go to the vent in the wall, the one that leads to the landing. A flicker. A shadow. Maybe he's imagining it. He stares, adjusting to the darkness. And that's when he sees them. Shining in the landing light. White and black, but mostly black.

Eyes staring back.

Luca buries his head under his duvet so he can't see the vent any more. But he can sense something else now. The man has somehow opened the door without making a sound and he's here in the room, just inches from where Luca is lying in his bunk. He freezes, staying as still as he can, pretending to be asleep. Holding his breath, afraid to make a sound. But that's not right. If he was asleep, he wouldn't be holding his breath. He lets out a very slow, very quiet whisper of air. The man is right there, he knows it. If he opens his eyes he'll see him. Saliva sits in his mouth and he needs to swallow, but if he swallows the man will know he's awake. Under the duvet, he curls his hands into small fists, digging his nails into his palms. Hold on. Hold tight. He'll go soon. He always does.

A whisper of breath.

But it's not Luca's.

It's his.

And if Luca is still alive after this, if the attic man doesn't take him tonight, he's going to tell his mom that this is *it*. This is the end. He is not staying in this house one more night. And he is never sleeping in this bedroom again.

56

JULIA WAKES WITH A start, her heart pounding in her chest. A noise. Footsteps? From above? She turns her head to check the time: 3.33 a.m. Adrenaline pumps through her body; everything tingles. It's fight or flight, but she can do neither. She's frozen. And now the door handle is turning. Her limbs are numb. She can't move, she can't even turn. Light from the landing. A shape. A small shape. A Luca-sized shape, because of course it's Luca and how did she think it could be anyone else? He crawls in beside her.

'He was in my room,' he whispers. 'I felt his breath on my face.'

Long after Luca slips into sleep, Julia lies awake, staring at the ceiling.

Thursday morning dawns in a bleary fog after a bad night's sleep. Luca's foot is cold against her leg, kicking sporadically, as he has done for hours now. His eyelids flutter awake and at first he looks confused.

'You're OK, pet. You came into my room in the middle of the night. Do you remember?'

A nod. 'The attic man was back.'

She swallows, reluctant to remind him of what he said. 'What makes you say that?'

'I heard him. And I kept my eyes closed until he went out of my room, but I could feel him breathing on me.'

'Luca, remember the police came on Tuesday night and searched the attic and said nobody was there? And you know we lock all the doors and we changed the locks? So could it be your imagination?'

An emphatic headshake. 'I hear him all the time, and last night I felt him breathing. And now you think I'm lying, and that's making it even worse. And I'm not staying here. I'm not going back into my room, and I'm not going to live in this house any more.'

They need to fix this. Julia *will* fix this.

'We're going to find whoever made the videos, and all of this is going to go away. So, we'll make the videos stop, and then you'll stop hearing noises. Does that sound like it will work?'

His mouth is set in a tight line. No answer.

'Eleanor and I are working on finding whoever's making the clips, and Dad's helping too, and the police. So it won't be long now. And if your dad's OK with it, you might be going to Granny and Grandad's for the weekend!'

'OK . . . so I don't have to stay in my room tonight?'

'You don't.' If Gabe can't take them away, she can bring Luca to stay in the apartment.

'All right. Can I have Coco Pops for breakfast?'

Her turn to nod. Who is she to say no to chocolate for breakfast when they've just moved halfway around the world to what's fast becoming a haunted house?

While Luca finishes breakfast and goes in search of a yet-again-missing Basil, she makes a call.

'Alastair? It's Julia. I hope you don't mind me calling so early, but I'm getting desperate to figure out who's making the videos and I thought of another way you can help, if you're on for it?'

'Sure, what do you need?'

'There's a guy who used to work in Stich years ago, and he left, but nobody knows where he went. He's not on social media, but I feel like he must be traceable somehow. Would you or your colleagues be any good at that kind of online searching? Only if you've time.'

'I'd be more than happy to. So, a bit of armchair detective work? Like those people who found the Golden State Killer in California?'

She can hear the smile in his voice and she knows he's joking; nonetheless, the words make her shiver. Bloody hell. But Andy Wilson Straub is not a killer. Andy Wilson Straub is Donna's big brother, and if he is somehow behind the videos, it's just to scare them. It's not like he's going around murdering people. A thought nudges in. *Anya is dead.* She pushes it away.

'Yes, like that, but in a far less dramatic suburban Dublin way. OK, do you want to give me your email and I'll send you through everything I know about this guy?'

Alastair spells out his email address and they say goodbye and Julia lets out a breath. It feels good to be doing something.

As soon as she's dropped Luca to school, promising she'll keep searching for the missing rabbit, she phones Gabe to see what he thinks about taking the kids to their grandparents' for the weekend. He agrees more quickly than she expects. He's not particularly close to his parents and rarely in a rush to visit, but it's a mark, she supposes, of the mess they're in that he says yes so readily. It means he won't be able to go to Drew's drinks tomorrow night, she reminds him. He wasn't going to go anyway, he says, since he wasn't invited. Julia is almost certain he *is* invited, even though it wasn't explicitly mentioned in Drew's text, but Gabe says he doesn't care, the barbecue was quite enough socializing for him. Julia's surprised. Normally he's up for meeting people and says yes to everything. This isn't like Gabe at all.

At home, after a renewed but unsuccessful search for Basil, she clears the breakfast dishes, eyeing up the chip pan that's still on the hob since Tuesday evening. She can't really leave it there till Gabe takes over on Sunday, but the thought of lifting the lid and smelling two-day-old oil turns her stomach. Maybe, at the risk of being petty, she *can* leave it for Gabe. Or for the kids. Perhaps her chip-eating chore-averse kids would clean it if it sat there long enough? Only one way to find out, she decides, bypassing the hob and opening her laptop.

Once her inbox is clear, she begins yet another project plan for yet another round of redundancies. She stares at her spreadsheet. At the numbers. The numbers who are really people. People with mortgages and childcare and bills. This is her job, and someone has to do it, but this morning she's unable to muster the appetite. The battery symbol turns red, warning her that her laptop is running low on power. She hunts for her cable, but it's not in her work bag or her bedroom or any of the usual spots. It's a sign, she decides, closing her laptop. Her boss won't be happy if she misses her deadline, and she sits for a moment, pondering, but finds it's so far down her list of worries it almost doesn't count. She moves on to a more practical and achievable goal – replacing the batteries in the smoke alarm in the hall.

Armed with two triple-A batteries, she drags a stool to the centre of the hall and climbs up. But to her confusion, there's no battery compartment on the smoke alarm, just one small port to the right and what might be a charging port on the left, although it's too small for a USB cable. Admittedly, this is her first time checking, but aren't smoke detectors usually battery operated? With a little effort, she manages to detach it from the ceiling to take a closer look, carrying it through to the kitchen for better light. That's when she realizes it's different to the one on the kitchen ceiling. A brighter white plastic, and no visible supplier details. She inverts it now, to examine the underside, and there she finds a sticker with the brand name, RyCo. Still none the wiser, she googles RyCo, hoping for a quick explainer video. Her eyes widen at the first result. It doesn't make sense. She looks at the next result, but it's the same. Confused and suddenly frightened, she jumps back from the kitchen counter and her phone clatters to the floor.

57

JULIA PICKS UP HER phone, swallowing as she stares at the search results.

RyCo do not make smoke detectors. Of course they don't. It all makes perfect sense now – the missing battery compartment, the pinhole on the right-hand side, the absent beeps during yesterday's burnt-chicken drama. RyCo make cameras. Spy cameras that *look* like smoke detectors.

Within ten minutes, Julia is knocking on the now-familiar door of the Garda station, and three minutes after that, she's sitting at the same messy desk as before, but this time opposite a different garda, as Stilwell is out on a call. She hands over the smoke detector and explains her story. The garda, a man about her own age, with large ears and jowly cheeks, examines it.

'If you or your husband didn't install it, it's possibly in place since the previous tenant's time?' He taps the plastic. 'What I'm saying is, it's not necessarily the case that someone installed it surreptitiously while you've been living there.'

Julia nods uncertainly. She hadn't thought of that, though now of course it sounds like the most logical conclusion. Or it would, if it weren't for the TikTok video campaign.

'So it might not indicate any actual spying,' the Garda goes on. 'Lots of people use cameras like this for added security, you know? People who don't trust their nannies or their house-mates. People worried about landlords letting themselves in uninvited – we get calls about that a good bit nowadays.' He leans forward, picking up the smoke detector again. 'People worried about other intruders – a sense that someone's been in while they're out. When you really think about it, you'd be sur-prised how many people have keys for any given residence. Previous tenants, previous owners, management companies, letting agents, nannies, cleaners, neighbours, builders, babysit-ters, housesitters.'

Julia shudders. She still has a key for their house in San Diego – a spare she never thought to give to the real estate agent. It's all very well that the locks are changed now, but how many people had access before?

The garda nods, as though acknowledging her silent thoughts. 'Anyway, that's the most likely scenario – a camera installed by the previous tenant.'

'Even still,' Julia says, 'the idea that Hugo – that's the tenant – can see inside our house is horribly creepy. I had a quick look at the RyCo website and, if I understand correctly, the camera sends a feed to an app on the owner's phone. Can the guards work out where the feed is going? As in, whose phone is on the receiving end?'

The garda says he'll look into it but doesn't sound confident. Maybe the RyCo people can help, he suggests, if there's some sort of inbuilt code or identifier to link the hardware and the purchaser's app. Even as he says it, she sees how unlikely it is. If the feed is going out from the camera to a phone, it could be any phone – there probably isn't a way to know.

He asks her if the video clips on TikTok have come from the smoke-detector camera.

She slumps in her seat as reality hits. 'No,' she tells him. 'The video clips all show a sweep of the house. It's not possible that they came from this one static camera in the hall that was pointed' – she thinks for a moment about where the pinhole camera was – 'at the front door.'

After the garda station, Julia goes straight to the apartment to tell Gabe. At the rate work is going this morning, *she'll* be the next number on a redundancy spreadsheet, but she finds she doesn't care. Gabe leans against the kitchen counter as she tells him about the spy camera, his face moving from confusion to shock and then something else – a kind of dawning realization.

'So that's how he did it,' he says, almost under his breath, shaking his head in wonder.

'That's how who did what?'

He looks at her, opens his mouth, but takes a moment before answering. 'The attic guy, obviously.'

'That's not what you were going to say.'

'It is. What else would I say? That's what we're talking about, isn't it?' He turns to rummage in a drawer, his back to her now.

'Well, that's *not* how he did it. This was a static camera. It doesn't account for any of the attic videos. It was pointed at the front door, so that's all it would have captured – anyone coming in and going out,' she says to his back. 'And audio from the hall, I suppose, though who knows, since we don't know where the feed is going and who's looking at it. It basically means someone – either the TikTok guy or someone else – has been spying on us. Or,' she concedes, 'it could have been there since Hugo's time. He might have installed it for whatever reason and forgotten to take it with him. I think maybe it's time we get in contact with Hugo . . . Would the letting agent give us his contact details, do you think?'

Gabe closes the drawer and faces her again. 'The guy from Raycroft Estates? Not the gobshite I was dealing with – that guy didn't know his arse from his elbow.'

'Oh, I think Alastair said something similar – someone called Clive Gannet who we should avoid? Was that him?'

A shrug. 'Maybe . . . I don't remember his name.' His eyes light up. 'Actually, the guy I was dealing with might be the *best* kind of person to give out confidential information we're not supposed to have.' He picks up his keys. 'Anyway, I'd better head – I'm meeting a buyer about some paintings.'

'Sure. Oh – do you have a spare laptop cable, by chance? I can't find mine.'

'Yep, there's one in my bedroom. You can take it.' A beat. 'On another note, have the police said anything more about Tony next door?'

'Not that I know of.' She hesitates, thinking about Monday night's visit to the garda station with Eleanor. He needs to be in the loop.

She tells Gabe what happened, about the jade rabbit paperweights, and Andy, and the possible link between the attic videos and Donna.

Gabe lowers himself on to a kitchen chair. 'Wow.'

'Yeah.'

'I guess we never talk about that night.' He sets his keys quietly on the table.

'I know. What is there to say . . .?'

'I was there.' He's staring into the distance, as though talking to himself. 'I was the last one to see her alive.'

'Yeah.' Julia sits opposite and rests her hand on his. They never go here.

'Did you know . . .' He trails off.

'That you kissed her?'

258

He nods.

Julia gives him a watery smile. 'Yes. You told Eleanor and she told me.' She squeezes his hand. 'You were some man for play-ing the field. Playing the group. Should we set you up with Eleanor to complete the circle?'

He smiles. Then, softly, sadly: 'I liked her. Donna.'

Julia swallows, her eyes damp. 'Me too.'

Ten minutes later, Gabe has gone to meet his buyer and left her to lock up. She should go too, but something's not sitting right. Something Gabe said? Something about that last night with Donna? No, that's not it . . . She casts her mind further back to his response to the smoke-detector camera. What did he mean by 'so that's how he did it'? Was it really a reference to the TikTok guy? She gets up off the couch and goes through to the office. The kids' old laptop is still there in place of the iMac. She opens it and clicks into his search history, squirming as she does, reminding herself that it's a shared laptop in a shared apart-ment. There's nothing out of the ordinary in his most recent search results anyway – he'd googled the dinner menu from Fallon and Byrne, opening hours of a gym in Stillorgan, and reviews for *Succession* – that makes her smile. Gabe is always about three years behind everyone else when it comes to TV. She types Tony's name into Google and clicks on the news tab. The first result tells her nothing new:

Gardaí Issue Appeal for Missing Dublin Man
Family 'desperately worried' about sixty-two-year-old Tony Hudson,
missing almost a week.

She reads on, scanning quickly through that first article and going on to the next and the next. They all say some version of the same thing – no trace, no leads, no clue, no sign. Poor Shirin, she thinks, pushing back the chair. Or not, judging by the new spring in her step.

She's about to leave when she remembers the laptop cable. Gabe's bedroom is neater than usual, his dark grey duvet pulled tight across the bed. No sign of a cable. She looks in the wardrobe, on the bookshelves, then under the bed, and that's where she finds it. As she's crouched, on the carpet below the nightstand, a corner of yellow paper catches her eye. She reaches down to pick it up. It's a Post-it note, sticky now with carpet fluff. A handwritten note, like something you'd jot down during a phone call. 'Date set Sept 9th'. It means nothing. *Wait, it does mean something*. That's when Gabe was in New York. A date for a meeting with a customer, maybe? Something about the wording makes her think it's more than that.

It's almost midday when she gets back to Brentwood, distracted and unfocused. She spends twenty minutes trying and failing to find Basil, then ten minutes trying and failing to focus on work. Her boss has emailed, looking for an update on the plan she was hoping to start that morning. God. Had she been as exacting when she ran her own business? She marks his email unread and doesn't reply. Deciding she'll catch up on work tonight, she calls into Shirin instead, to see if there's any update on Tony. Shirin seems delighted to see her and invites her in.

'Tea is all I can offer, for obvious reasons,' she says, gesturing at the spot on the counter where the coffee machine used to sit. 'I should buy a jar of instant, I suppose, but I'm resisting on principle. It feels like giving in.'

'Don't give in on my account,' Julia says. 'Tea is perfect. I take it there's no news on Tony?'

'Nothing. The family are doing their nut. Convinced I must

know where he's gone. Sure he's dead in a ditch or kidnapped. I told them I hadn't had a ransom note but I'd be sure to pass it on to them if one arrived.'

'You did not!'

Shirin smiles. 'Fine, I didn't say it, but I wanted to. Pack of ninnies. He's a grown man. Milk?'

Julia declines. 'On another note entirely, could I ask you about Hugo, who used to live next door?'

Shirin is busy cutting pieces of what looks like ginger cake but as Julia's words hit air, her hand stops mid slice. It takes a moment for her to look up.

'Hugo? Why?' She's guarded now.

'I found a camera in our hall this morning. It might have been there since Hugo lived in the house. That's what the guards said anyway.'

Shirin's mouth drops open. 'Oh.'

'What is it?'

'It's . . . it's nothing.' She turns back to the ginger cake, her cheeks flushed.

'Would you have contact details for Hugo? A surname?'

'I don't think so.'

'Not even a surname?'

'He wasn't here that long. Honestly, until you arrived we hardly knew anyone. The barbecue was the first get-together we had.'

'Ah, OK, I just assumed everyone knew everyone. I'm sure the police will track down Hugo anyway.'

'They will, of course,' she says, more cheerfully now, placing a plate of sliced ginger cake between them. 'Now, isn't it great to be able to eat without some fucker telling you you'll put on weight?'

And then the doorbell rings.

58

Shirin pads out in bare feet to answer the front door.

'Don't judge me if it's another delivery,' she calls back over her shoulder as she reaches for the latch. 'Shopping is my therapy.'

But there's no courier at the door and no package. Instead, there's a young woman who looks like she could be Shirin's daughter – or, at least, looks as Shirin might have looked twenty years earlier.

'Hi,' the woman says. 'Shirin?'

'Yes?'

'My name is . . . This is awkward. My name is Molly. I know your husband. I was wondering if we could talk.'

Molly nods hello to Julia and stands just inside the kitchen, clasping and unclasping her hands. She's tall, with dark hair cut in a shoulder-length bob and a nervous expression. Julia can't help glancing down at her belly, but if Molly is showing already, it's hidden by a loose-fitting A-line dress.

Julia pushes out her chair.

'I'll leave you to it, Shirin,' she says quietly.

Shirin touches her arm. 'Please. Stay.' Then she turns back to the visitor, arms folded.

Molly's eyes dart from Julia to Shirin. 'I . . . I'm not sure where to start.'

'Maybe with whatever message my coward of a husband has sent you to tell me.'

'Tony? No, there's no message – I haven't seen him at all.'

'Isn't he staying with you?'

'No. I don't know where he is,' she says miserably. 'I had no idea he was still with you until I saw the news report that he was missing. I saw his photo, and his name, and then a reference to his "distraught wife". I wanted to kill him there and then. I am so sorry.'

'*Come on.* It's the oldest story in the book. You really believed this sixty-two-year-old man was young, free and single?'

'I didn't even know he was sixty-two,' Molly says, gritting her teeth. 'He told me you were separated. Living in the same house but leading separate lives.'

Julia winces as the words come back to her – the overheard conversation as she crouched in Tony's en suite.

'Stop. You look like a smart woman,' Shirin scoffs. 'How could you believe such nonsense?'

'He made it sound so plausible,' Molly says, close to tears. 'He said the house and all the money belonged to you, your family, and that you'd threatened to cut him off without a penny if he divorced you.'

'Ha! He really said that?' Shirin shakes her head. 'Well, it's true that we got our first rung on the property ladder from my parents, and we bought this house when I sold my business, and' – she pauses as though considering something – 'he wouldn't fare well in a divorce, that's true, but good god, he never asked for any kind of separation.'

Molly blinks back tears and Julia almost feels sorry for her.

Shirin narrows her eyes. 'I suspect Tony enjoyed his life here far too well to risk losing even some of it. He was stringing you along.'

'But he said he had something that would force—' Molly

stops, swallowing visibly. 'You're right. I'm an idiot. I'm so sorry.' She looks around the vast kitchen. 'He also said that you've no children? Was that . . . The papers haven't mentioned . . .'

'No children.' Shirin's voice is tight. 'You'll have the honour of making him a first-time father.'

Molly shakes her head. 'No, neither of us ever wanted children. And obviously, now that I know he wasn't actually separated, I don't want anything to do—'

'I know about the baby.'

'The baby?'

'I found the scan, the same night I found the texts on his phone.'

Molly looks baffled. 'There's no baby . . . It wasn't my scan.'

Silence, as her words sink in.

Julia bites her lip. Was there someone else too? 'Shirin, do you still have the scan?'

'Somewhere, I guess. He didn't take it with him anyway, though it's all a bit of a blur. He was packing, throwing things into the car, texting.' A dagger-look at Molly. 'Texting you, I assume.'

Molly's cheeks redden. 'Yes, he did text that night. He said he was leaving, that you'd found out about us. I didn't see it until the following morning and, as I say, I haven't heard from him since.'

A crease of confusion crosses Shirin's face.

'Why do you want to see the scan?' she asks Julia.

'There are probably details on it – small print at the top showing the mother's name, the clinic, the date. It might shed some light . . .'

'On who else he was seeing. God.'

Julia nods. Both women now look truly miserable.

'I should go,' Molly says. 'I wanted to call by to apologize to you face-to-face. I'm so sorry. If I'd known, I'd never—'

'Fine.' Shirin's tone is still sharp, but the fire has gone out of it. 'And you really haven't heard from him?'

A headshake. 'Nothing since Friday night.'

'Me neither,' Shirin says. 'Gosh. Maybe his family are right. Maybe something's happened.'

As Shirin sees Molly out, Julia is trying to decide if she should confess what she overheard in the en suite. It certainly doesn't help Shirin to know what Tony said to Molly or to realize that Julia has known all this time. And some of what Tony said made no sense anyway. She casts her mind back, recalling his words.

He's not on the scene. They've split.

She remembers briefly thinking he meant her and Gabe, especially after his odd interrogation about their divorce. But that doesn't really add up, not then, not now. Then she remembers what else he said and her skin goes cold.

59

SHIRIN IS STILL AT the front door, speaking to Molly. Julia's mind is whirling, trying to make sense of Tony's words.

You know what I saw on the footage. The camera's still there.

It might not be the same camera, but realistically, it would be a fairly big coincidence. So maybe he had been talking about Gabe and Julia after all, when he mentioned a split? Had he been spying on them, and if so, why?

Should she ask Molly? Even if it means further embarrassment for Shirin? Fuck it, she has to find out what's going on.

'Molly?' She rushes out to the hall. The two women turn towards her, surprised expressions on their faces. 'Look, this is awkward, but did Tony have some kind of camera installed, to spy on . . . anyone?'

Molly's hand flies to her mouth. A small nod.

Shirin takes a step back. 'Oh god.'

'Can you tell me where the camera was?'

Molly looks from one to the other. 'I told him not to do it. It's completely illegal and immoral, but he was desperate to get proof. It was going to be his ticket out. And he told me he'd begged for divorce, but that you had a rigid hold on everything and he'd be jobless and homeless, and I said he could move in with me, but my place is, well, nothing like this and he—'

'Where is the camera?' Julia's tone is steely.

'The house next door,' Molly whispers.

Shirin lets out a small cry.

'My house,' Julia says, pointing.

'Oh. Sorry. I didn't know.'

'Why the fuck would Tony be spying on my house? How exactly does watching me, my ex-husband, my children, help him get his divorce?' She glares at Molly and then at Shirin.

'He wasn't spying on you.' Shirin sounds lost. 'He was watching me.' Her eyes meet Molly's and Molly nods.

Julia is perplexed. Shirin and Gabe? It doesn't make sense. They've only known one another a few weeks. She remembers what Gabe said earlier when she told him about the camera: *So that's how he did it.*

'Just tell me. Shirin, please. Why were you in my house – *when* were you in my house?'

'It wasn't your house at the time. It was Hugo's.' Shirin lets out a slow breath. 'Remember I told you I caved one time, had an affair of my own? It was with Hugo. I can't believe Tony installed a camera. My god. Years of cheating on his part, and this one time I . . . this is how he responds.'

'Wait, so you were seeing Hugo, and Tony installed a camera in our house – Hugo's house – to prove it? Did he ever say it to you?'

'No. I had no idea he knew.'

Molly speaks up. 'He was keeping it in his back pocket, as leverage to get what he could out of the divorce. I'm sorry. It sounds so sordid now.'

Molly turns to Shirin. 'You two were in there for a dinner one night, and he replaced the real smoke detector with the camera while you and Hugo were out in the garden.' She looks at Julia again. 'How did you know?'

'I found it. It's with the police now,' she says flatly. 'Look, I'm going to go.'

'I'm sorry,' Shirin says, touching her arm. 'I know it's an awful invasion of privacy and you're the innocent party in all this, but I'm sure he never watched you.'

Gabe's words flutter through her mind. *So that's how he did it.* She shakes her head and walks past Molly, down the steps. 'Yeah, I'm pretty sure he did.'

60

GABE IS SHOCKED AND speechless and outraged and says all the kinds of things you'd expect when she phones to tell him that Tony was behind the camera.

But she hears it.

The false note.

'You'd already guessed, hadn't you?' she asks.

'No? Why would I think it was Tony?' Gabe says, and she can picture his wide-eyed-innocence expression down the phone line, the one he uses when she asks who put the empty milk carton back in the fridge.

'You said "so that's how he did it" when I asked.'

'Meaning the attic guy,' he says.

But of course now they know it had nothing to do with the attic guy.

They move on to discussing logistics: Gabe's going to pick up the kids from school, he says, then swing by the house so they can pack, and then he'll take them to his parents' mobile home in Wicklow for the weekend.

'The break from the house will be good for Luca,' Julia says. 'Tell him I'll FaceTime with Basil every night.'

'You won't be able to. There's no 4G and patchy mobile coverage.'

'Isla won't be impressed . . .'

'It'll be no harm to be offline for a few days. Are you OK to stay in the house on your own?'

She realizes then that she's not. She's going to stay in the apartment, she decides. She'll stay in the apartment tonight, and check on the house tomorrow evening before she goes for drinks at Drew's. And by then, perhaps Alastair will have made some progress on finding Andy or the police will have some answers or . . . or, she realizes, they'll move. They'll find another house. When things go wrong, you just move. It's not running away, it's a practical response, and Julia is expert at practical responses. If you're lucky enough to have money and privilege, there are options. Feeling a weight lifted, she phones Pauline to tell her she doesn't need her this afternoon or tomorrow. Although she's flexible, Julia can't help feeling bad cancelling at such short notice. But Pauline doesn't seem surprised at all; it's almost like she expected it. Perhaps she's picking up on the stress in the house. In fairness, it would be hard to miss.

It's only when Gabe arrives with the kids on Thursday afternoon that Julia remembers Basil is still missing. Shit. That's when she decides a fib won't hurt. Basil is, no doubt, snuggled up in some cosy spot inside a wardrobe or under a bed, but Luca won't go to Wicklow if he knows the rabbit is missing. So Julia says she found him and dropped him to the apartment already, since that's where she's staying tonight. Luca seems to accept this and makes her promise to send a photo of Basil before he goes to sleep tonight. Of course, she says, certain she'll find the rabbit before she leaves for the apartment. The kids hug her goodbye: Luca tightly, Isla less so, and she watches with a mix of relief and unease as the car heads for the main gates of Brentwood.

Back in the kitchen, she surveys the mess. Discarded schoolbags and jackets on chairs. Isla's mucky football boots in the middle of the floor. The chip pan still on the hob. Everything but the rabbit. She's not worried. Basil will appear in his own good time.

But at nine o'clock, he still hasn't shown up. And, as Luca has told her, rabbits can't live very long without water. Meaning Julia can't leave the house in Brentwood until she finds him. It's dark out now, and she's flat on the floor, under the bed in Isla's room with a torch, searching here for the third time. She tries Isla's wardrobe next, pulling tentatively at a pile of clothes, bracing herself for warm fur. Next is Gabe's room, then Luca's, then hers. Still no sign. Tired now, she flops on her bed, and curses silently. She can't go to the apartment without the rabbit. Despite all her fears, she's not going to leave her son's pet to die. Shadows creep across the wall and she lies still, staring at the ceiling, psyching herself up to search again. That's when she hears it. Faint at first. The noise that woke her those other times. The dream that maybe wasn't a dream. Footsteps. Light footsteps. Above her head. There's someone in the attic.

61

JULIA IS FROZEN, LISTENING to the footsteps, willing herself to get up. To get out. To leave this house and never come back. But she can't move. The footsteps stop. Then start again. Are they moving towards the hatch? Oh god. But they're too light to belong to the man from the videos. It sounds more like a child. A child or . . . of course.

She jumps off the bed and, before she can change her mind, she runs to the landing and opens the hatch. The ladder comes down easily and clicks into place. Deep breath. Up the ladder. Into the attic. The light. *Where's the damn light switch.* Jesus Christ, she can't do this in the dark. Her fingers find it. Light fills the attic. And there he is. A laugh that might be a cry of relief escapes her and she reaches across to scoop him up. At least Luca will get his goodnight photo, she thinks, as she brings the rabbit back down the ladder. The footsteps. The tiny footsteps. A rabbit with yellow fluff in his fur, just like Luca had tried to tell her. How did Basil get up there? It doesn't make sense, but her brain is too tired now and she pushes that worry away for another day.

On Friday evening, Julia's in the apartment, feeling lighter than she has done in weeks. She's away from the house and she has a plan. If they don't resolve this attic stuff by the end of the weekend, they're moving. Everything is better with a plan. She hasn't told Gabe yet – he's with the kids in a valley in Wicklow with terrible phone coverage and wonderful walks. But Julia's had a day in the office that felt almost normal and now she's getting ready for drinks at Drew's house, humming as she puts on mascara. She wonders if Shirin will be there, and Alastair, and if he'll have any news about Andy Wilson Straub. It's hard to put her finger on why, but she senses they're close to resolution.

Her phone beeps with a message from Shirin. She's found the scan, she says, attaching a photograph of it. Julia zooms in to read the tiny white print on the top-left corner:

Dr Siegler-Barrows, Marina Clinic

OK, clearly the doctor's name, not the mother's name. Where has she heard it before? It takes a moment, but then it comes to her. Tony said it, at the barbecue. He asked Gabe if he knew Siegler-Barrows. So perhaps, as she suspected, it is Tony's baby, with someone else entirely. Would the mother's name be on the scan too? She thinks it was on her own scan printouts, though it's a long time ago now.

She squints at her phone screen, zooming further.

And then her breath stops.

There it is. In tiny print, halfway down the left-hand side. The mother's name.

Heather Walters.

She stares, standing stock-still, as the pieces fall into place.

Gabe taking over negotiations, spending time with Heather. Heather backing down on her threats to take things further. Gabe's caginess. The sense that he's been keeping something from her. Her mind whirrs across dates. The X on the calendar. A due date.

Oh Jesus, Gabe.

She stabs at the phone, flustered, finding Gabe's number. It goes to voicemail. Because of the coverage in the mobile home or because he's avoiding her? Jesus Christ. His children were going to have a new sibling, and he hadn't even told her? With Heather Fucking Walters? Christ, did that make Isla and Riley some kind of stepsisters? Oh, good fuck. She's going to kill him. When she finally gets hold of him, she's absolutely going to kill him.

A sudden sick feeling takes hold. Was it a one-night stand, or is he in a relationship with Heather? If he's still with her, what is he doing in Ireland? Does he want to move back? And if so, when was he going to tell Julia? Furious now, she goes to his bedroom and grabs the Post-it from the floor. Was the September 9th note about a prenatal appointment? She flings the Post-it on the bed and pulls open his nightstand drawer. Rummaging through a disarray of receipts and notebooks, right at the bottom of the drawer, she finds something. Two photos. One, a selfie of Heather and Gabe in what looks like an upmarket bar. Heads together, drinks raised, both smiling. The next picture makes her nauseous. Gabe and Heather again, another selfie, but this time, curled up together in what looks like a hotel bed.

Julia sits on the floor, staring. Thinking. What must Heather make of this move to Dublin? Would she want Gabe to move back? She must hate Julia more than ever. This brings Julia back full circle – could the attic videos have something to do with Heather and Riley after all? But how would they do it, even with all the Photoshopping skills in the world? It has to be someone who has access to their house. Someone with a key. But besides Gabe and Julia, who else has a key? She stops for a moment, trying to pin her scurrying thoughts. Eleanor does, but only for the new lock, and anyway, Julia knows with every fibre of her body, it's not Eleanor doing this. Pauline has a new key and had an old key, but Julia can't imagine her trying to terrorize them.

Unless there's some link between Pauline and Andy? Pauline and Donna? That rings a distant bell. Something about Pauline's sons? But it's surely not her housekeeper's sons. Who else had keys, the old keys, before they changed the locks? Raycroft Estates? This 'inept' Clive Gannet who Alastair dealt with, the temp who Gabe met – possibly the same person? Someone like that might give out a key in error? To Andy Wilson Straub? And Hugo might have kept a key . . . What if he'd left spares with neighbours? She types a quick message to Shirin, skipping any response as yet to the baby scan.

> Shirin, sorry to be so direct, but do you think you could contact Hugo for me? I don't have a number for him but need to ask him who had keys to our house.

No blue ticks, no reply.

It's only as she's walking from the apartment to Brentwood that the rest of it dawns on her. If the scan was Gabe's, it was never Tony's. She remembers now: Gabe losing his hoodie, Alastair handing it back. The same evening Gabe got a letter from America. Did Gabe shove the scan into the pocket of his hoodie when they were leaving for the barbecue? He must have done. Then Shirin found the scan and assumed it was Tony's, read his texts, discovered the affair, and Tony left. Would he have left if Shirin hadn't confronted him? Would she ever have confronted him if she hadn't found the scan? And now Tony's missing. All because of a dropped hoodie. The flap of the butterfly's wings.

It's dark when she knocks on Drew's door. From inside comes the sound of jazz music and the house is lit up, but she can't see in as the living-room curtains are drawn. At first she's not sure if the doorbell rang. She's about to try a second time when the door is opened by Drew. He's wearing a black shirt with black jeans, and a wide smile. He's quite handsome, Julia thinks, as he welcomes her and brings her through to the living room. Music plays from a speaker and an open bottle of wine breathes on a coffee table, but there's nobody else here. Julia looks at her watch. She's fifteen minutes late, yet somehow she's also first to arrive.

'Am I too early?' she asks, as Drew closes the door behind them.

'Not at all, perfect timing. What would you like to drink? I've opened a nice bottle of red there, but I have white, rosé, gin and tonic . . . Beer? . . . And Redking whiskey, of course.'

Julia opts for a glass of red and takes a seat on the black leather couch, which is more comfortable than it looks.

'If you're still getting things ready and I've turned up far too early, please do just leave me here!' she says as he hovers over her.

'Nope, there's nothing to do – I've some finger food in the oven and the timer's set. So how are you?'

They make small talk and time ticks by, and Julia becomes increasingly confused about where the others are. Her phone beeps with a text from Alastair and she wonders if he's found something, but she can't pick it up to read without appearing rude. Meanwhile, Drew is full of questions – where they lived in San Diego, how it compares to Ireland. She explains that she's not back that long, so it's hard to make comparisons yet. This leads to lots of questions about why she moved, where she grew up, and if she's still in touch with friends of old. That's a tricky one, a place she doesn't want to go. Just one friend, she tells him, keeping it simple. Her phone beeps with another text from Alastair, and she's itching to answer.

In the meantime, she turns the questioning on to Drew, asking him how he got into personal training.

'It was a journey,' he says. 'I started getting into fitness for myself, then realized I could help other people too. I think I told you before, I was a video-game nerd when I was younger, never out of my bedroom. It all came to a head a few years ago and I realized I needed to make a change.' He points to the tattoo on his arm; the letter 'D' with the bird flying above it. 'Set myself free.'

'I knew someone like that once,' she says, remembering Andy's indoor existence at his computer screen.

And then it hits her, like a punch in the stomach.

Drew. Andrew. Andy.

She stares at him, frozen.

But it can't be.

She's letting her imagination run away.

He couldn't be Andy, could he?

She looks at Drew, trying to remember, but Andy's figure is always an indistinct huddle at a computer screen. She could pass him in the street and not recognize him. Twenty years and a fitness glow-up later?

Her phone buzzes a third time.

Why is Alastair messaging her when he should be here?

'Alastair and the others must all be delayed,' she says, hearing a small shake in her voice.

Drew laughs. 'I didn't invite Alastair. I'm sure he's grand, but—' He shrugs.

'Oh.' Of course. She'd just assumed it would be similar to the barbecue; Drew had never actually said that he'd invited Alastair.

'Shirin's coming, I assume? Obviously not Tony . . .'

'No, it's just you.'

'Oh. And your girlfriend, right?'

'She can't make it now, so it's just you and me.'

A cold sensation slips across her skin.

'Oh. That's a pity. She doesn't live here, then?'

'No. We're not together all that long. She's been called into work tonight. Last-minute thing.'

'Right.' She sips her wine, trying to think of something to say. 'Did you grow up around here?' she tries.

'Yep, Dublin born and bred.'

'Drew is an unusual name. Is it short for something?'

He tilts his head, an unreadable look on his face. 'It's a family name.'

'Do . . . do you have siblings?' Why is she doing this? She should just go.

A beat. 'No. But I imagine you know that?'

She shakes her head, her mouth dry. *Fuck*.

'You don't have to pretend, Julia.' He stands and walks towards her.

62

JULIA JUMPS UP FROM the sofa, stumbling slightly.

'I have to go, I feel quite sick . . .' Dammit, she's left it too late. What if he's locked the door? What if she can't get out? Fuck, how did she not make the connection sooner?

Drew is still walking towards her. He leans down and picks up the bottle of whiskey from the coffee table. He turns to face her, the bottle raised.

'Drew . . . Andy, I'm sorry. I'm really sorry. We never meant it to happen. We loved Donna, and I'll never forgive myself for leaving her that night.'

His face changes.

'You have every right to be angry,' she whispers, her voice deserting her. 'But I need to go now, and we can talk again when we've both had time to . . . to digest, and when it's daytime and . . .' *When I'm not alone with you.*

'Who's Andy?'

'What?'

'And who's Donna? Are you OK, Julia?'

She glances at the bottle in his hand.

'I don't know who Andy and Donna are,' Drew continues. 'I was about to show you the name on the label. Drew Redking. My great-grandfather. And my grandfather.' An eye-roll. 'And my dad. If I'd had a brother, they'd probably have called him Drew too. The Redkings are very into tradition.'

'The Redkings?'

'My family? The whiskey makers?' He laughs. 'Oh my god, have I literally just met the one person in Ireland who doesn't know anything about my family? We're like the Guinness family, only, well' – he holds up the bottle again – 'whiskey.'

Her mouth drops open.

Drew smiles and shakes his head. 'God, you must think I'm an awful eejit, assuming you knew who I was. You're gone twenty years, you don't know what I'm talking about, do you? The scandal with my dad's affair? My stepmother's drunk-driving charge? My cousin's boy band antics? No?'

'I've heard of the Redking family, I just didn't click . . .'

Drew flushes. 'I never thought I'd become *that* guy – the one who thinks everyone knows who he is, and yet here I am. Bloody hell, sorry.' A grin. 'Let's start over.' He reaches out his hand. 'I'm Drew Redking, of the Redking whiskey dynasty, living a very different life as a teetotal personal trainer, much to my father's disgust.'

Julia takes his hand. 'I'm still the same person I was five minutes ago, only slightly more enlightened and utterly embarrassed.'

'So who's Andy?'

'That is something I'd very much like to find out,' she mutters, and picks up her phone to check Alastair's text.

63

WHEN HE HEARS WHERE she is, Alastair says he'll call by. That it's a social occasion to which he wasn't invited doesn't seem to faze him, though Drew looks slightly uncomfortable when Julia gives him the update.

'Shit, I should have asked him along. It's just that he talks a lot, asks a lot of questions. I thought it was because of my family, but' – a sheepish smile – 'maybe I need to stop assuming everyone reads the gossip mags.'

'I think Alastair asks questions of everyone as a way to connect.' She grins. 'He probably knows as much about the Redkings as I do.'

And indeed, Alastair arrives, slightly out of breath, and launches straight into his update.

'So, you were right – Andy Wilson Straub has no social media, but I figured it's hard to avoid the internet completely, so me and the guys at work dug a bit deeper. And eventually we struck gold.'

Alastair sits on the couch, accepting the beer Drew offers.

'We decided to try individual websites that even people who don't use social media might use – buy-and-sell websites, discussion forums, death announcements, that kind of thing. If you google someone's name, they won't typically come up just because they've used one of those sites, but if you go into each website one by one and search under the name, you can find people.'

Julia shakes her head. 'Why didn't I think of that? It makes so much sense.'

'It took a while, but between us we got there. We found an A. Straub on DoneDeal selling a guitar, an Andrew Wilson on Adverts, selling a mountain bike, and an A. W. Straube – with an 'e' – on RIP.ie, writing a note of condolence for a cousin with the same surname.'

'Wow, I could kiss you!'

Alastair's cheeks pinken. 'Well, let's wait and see if any of these pan out.'

He pulls a laptop from a bag and asks Drew for the Wi-Fi code. Drew provides it, looking slightly bewildered.

'So maybe we should try all three and you can see if any of them look like your guy?' Alastair continues. 'No pics on any of the profiles, but there rarely are on sites like this.'

Julia leans in to look at the screen and Alastair narrates.

'A. Straub selling a guitar. No indication of his first name. Most of what he's sold to date is music-related, plus some plug-in heaters and a TV. Based in Dublin 2.'

'I don't think Andy was particularly musical, though I suppose that could have changed . . .' Julia pinches her chin. 'Dublin 2 doesn't sound quite right, does it? Exchequer Street, where he lived before, is in Dublin 2, and Mike the barman said he was moving "somewhere fancy in south Dublin".'

'Then again, that could mean somewhere up around Stephen's Green or Merrion Square?' Drew chimes in. 'Not that I have a clue who Andy is or what you're doing . . .'

'I'll explain it all in a sec,' Julia says. 'But let's see the next person.'

Alastair clicks into another tab. 'Right, Andrew Wilson, selling a mountain bike. Lives in Dalkey. No Straub in the name, so this one's a long shot, I guess. But Dalkey would count as somewhere fancy in south Dublin, I think?'

'Definitely. Now, the Andy I remember wouldn't know one end of a mountain bike from the other. And with no Straub in the name . . . Then again, Straub was his dad's name and maybe he dropped it after they fell out . . .' Julia lifts her hands. 'God, it's all speculation.'

'OK, A. W. Straube. He – or she, I suppose – isn't selling anything, it's RIP.ie, but we can see that they and the deceased relative both worked for Bryce and Lloyd, a law firm.'

Julia tilts her head. 'Maybe? I don't know why he'd move from tech to law . . . It's as likely as it is unlikely, I suppose? Do we know where this person lives?'

'No. Bryce and Lloyd are based in Dublin 2, but that doesn't tell us anything – I suppose A. W. Straube could live in, like, Kerry or Donegal, and work remotely.'

'Hmm.' Julia picks up her phone to flick back through the notes she made after the conversation with Mike in Harry's.

Stich. Gamer. Loner. Nice flat. Couch.

'Wait! Go back through the two on the buy-and-sell websites. See if either of them was selling or giving away furniture in December 2020?'

Alastair flicks back to A. Straub. He hadn't been selling anything in December 2020: his first listing was from 2023.

'OK, try Andrew Wilson.'

Alastair scrolls and Julia begins to feel dizzy, trying to read as the entries fly past.

'Bingo!'

'What is it?' Julia leans closer.

'November 2020. Table, chairs, bed, couch, all for sale.' Alastair runs his finger along the screen. 'Everything sold, except the couch – withdrawn from sale December 2020.'

'Because he gave it to Mike the barman. Oh my god, that's him.'

The fizz is back. And with it, a small tinge of dread.

64

'OK.' JULIA PACES. 'DOES it include an address? The mountain-bike ad?'

Alastair shakes his head. 'No, just Dalkey.'

'Right.' Julia is still pacing. Thinking. 'But if we successfully bid on the mountain bike . . . he'd have to give us his address?'

'Exactly.' Alastair nods. 'So, what do you think – will I offer the asking price for the bike and see what happens?'

Julia hesitates for only a second. 'Do it.'

As they sit waiting for Andrew Wilson to respond to the offer, Julia tells a baffled Drew about the attic videos, and that they're trying to track down an old friend's brother. She doesn't say anything about Donna's death, and she can feel both men looking at her curiously, trying to understand why she thinks Andy would be responsible for the clips. But she can't. It's not even about trust any more. It's about Donna. It's about struggling to say those words – *she died, it was our fault*. Because in truth, if Andy is targeting Donna's old friends, maybe he has every right to.

Alastair startles suddenly, sitting up straighter.

'A bite! He's accepted the offer! OK, what now? Will I say we can pick up tonight and get his address?'

'*We?*' Julia repeats.

'Yeah.' A grin. 'A team-up. Like the Goonies, only older. *Much* older. And don't forget, I'm handy with a crowbar.'

Julia reminds Alastair that they've both been drinking and that travelling to Dalkey at nine o'clock at night to buy a mountain bike might seem a bit strange or even unnerving to Andrew Wilson.

'Well, we don't need to say we'll *collect* it tonight – how about we arrange to pick it up tomorrow and, once he gives me the address, we go over there tonight?'

Julia points out again that they've been drinking.

'I haven't,' Drew says. 'My car's outside. And lookit, I'm curious now too to see where this goes – if this guy's really been making your attic videos.'

'I need to let the gardaí know,' Julia says. 'They should really be the ones to handle this.'

'Do that. But it doesn't mean we can't call over tonight to see for ourselves?'

'What if he's dangerous?'

'That's why you have two strong bodyguards by your side.' Drew grins. 'OK, one strong bodyguard and Alastair.'

Julia is almost sure this is a giant mistake, but it can't hurt to stand on the doorstep and ask a few questions. Andy can hardly do anything if there's three of them. He'll either admit that he's been making the videos and maybe they can clear the air, or he'll deny it. If it *is* him and he lies about it, maybe the confrontation will be enough to get him to stop. That, or the police landing on his doorstep. She picks up her phone and leaves a voicemail for Detective Stilwell, though she doesn't mention they're going to doorstep Andy tonight. If Andy admits to making the videos and agrees to stop, she can tell Stilwell she made a mistake. He doesn't need police arriving at his door after everything he's been through.

'Got it!' Alastair says, looking at his laptop screen. 'Four Sanchester Drive, Dalkey.' He stands and shrugs on his jacket.

Julia stands too. 'What if it's not the Andy I knew?'

'Then we'll have an ongoing research project and possibly a new mountain bike,' Alastair says.

'Actually,' Julia says to Drew, 'if we could take a small detour, there's one person I'd like to pick up on the way.'

65

Eleanor is more nervous than Julia, but not enough to stay at home and leave them to it.

'This feels like walking into a spider's web,' she says, as she slides into the back seat beside Julia.

'We're only going as far as the front door, to find out if it's him.'

'And if it is?'

Julia tells her about the voicemail for Stilwell, and the plan to let it go if Andy agrees to stop.

'If he's literally been inside your house, that's breaking and entering,' Eleanor says. 'I don't think you can keep it from the police.'

Has he been in the house, though? Julia still can't decide. One minute she thinks someone's been in, moving from room to room when they're not there. The next, she thinks it's all down to video editing. Luca's face appears in her mind. *I saw his eyes in the vent.* She shakes herself. Maybe they'll have the answers they need in the next twenty minutes.

Andrew Wilson's house does not look like the home of a masked intruder – it's a two-storey redbrick townhouse on a leafy road in picturesque Dalkey. A silver Lexus sits in the driveway, gleaming under the moonlight. Ivy winds its way around the portico at the front door, and through the glass panel on one side a polished walnut floor is visible. Andy seems to have done well for himself.

Julia and Eleanor stand on the doorstep while Drew and Alastair wait at the car, leaning on the bonnet, arms folded.

'We're ready to pounce if needed,' Alastair stage-whispers. 'Just give the word.'

'Why do I feel like we're in an episode of *Slow Horses*,' Eleanor says out of the side of her mouth.

At any other time, this would make Julia laugh, but right now her stomach is a knotted coil. Sucking in a breath, she presses the bell. It chimes, echoing through the house, and at first there's nothing. No sound, no flash of a porch light. Then they hear what might be a kitchen door opening, and a shuffling sound, with a strange clack accompanying it. Eventually, a shadow appears behind the fanlight and, slowly, the door is opened.

66

THE MAN COULD BE anyone.

He could be Andy, but he could be someone else entirely. He's trim and fit, mid to late forties, with dark hair going grey and a surprised look on his face. Julia takes in his features, trying to place them on the awkward, lumbering figure she remembers from Donna's house, and yes, she can get there. It could be Andy.

Beside her, Eleanor tenses and grips her arm. She can see it too.

'Andy?' Julia says, her voice coming out in a croak. 'Andy Wilson Straub who used to live in Kerrybrook?'

'Yes?' It's clear he hasn't recognized them.

'We're . . . we're Julia Birch and Eleanor Jordan. Donna's friends.' The last word is smothered as her voice trails away.

He looks from one to the other.

'My god. It's been so long. Do you . . . do you want to come in?'

'No,' Eleanor says quickly, gripping Julia's arm more tightly. 'We just . . .' She turns to look at Julia. What are they supposed to say now?

'Can I help you? . . . Is everything OK?'

He reaches for something beside the door and Julia flinches, ready to step back. Then she sees it. A crutch. A pair of crutches. He nods towards his left leg, which is encased in a boot.

'Fell off my bike. Going to be in this for another two months. Sorry, I'm not great at standing for long periods.' He arranges the crutches under his arms and takes the weight off his injured leg. 'Are you sure you won't come in?'

Julia closes her eyes briefly. *It's not him.* Unless this is an elaborate fake cast on a fake broken leg, he's hardly been filming himself climbing out of attics, hers or anyone else's. Maybe he put together videos by splicing Isla's clips with some other TikTok footage, but it's starting to feel less and less likely. Which means they probably don't have the answer, and she should be disappointed, but actually, she's relieved. Andy has been through enough in his life, and, she realizes now, she really, really didn't want it to be him.

'Just for a minute, then,' she says, and turns to wave back at Drew and Alastair. They both step forward, but she puts up a hand to tell them it's OK. And she and Eleanor walk into the house.

67

'So how have you been doing?' Andy says as he makes his way slowly to the living room. 'Sorry for my lack of speed, still not used to these things.'

'How long have you been on them?' Eleanor asks, throwing Julia a look.

'A month already. It's healing a lot less quickly than I'd like.'

Julia and Eleanor exchange glances. Whatever else he may have been doing, he certainly hasn't been roaming around Julia's house.

In the living room, he gestures for them to sit. The room is large and high-ceilinged with narrow bay windows looking out to the front driveway. The curtains are drawn and Julia is conscious that Drew and Alastair can't see them now. Andy removes a stack of *Beano*s from an armchair. 'My son's at his mum's this week, but his stuff is *everywhere* still.' A grin breaks out on his open, pleasant face. It's hard to believe this is the same Andy, Julia thinks, but really, did she ever pay him any attention back then? Did she ever see him?

'So, is there anything . . . Is it a social call?' he asks as he lowers himself carefully into the red-and-white-striped armchair.

'We . . . we've come to talk about Donna,' Eleanor says. 'We should have come twenty years ago. We want to say sorry.'

Whether Andy had anything to do with the videos or not, they owe him this.

'What do you mean?'

'We should never have gone home without her that night. If we'd looked for her, she'd still be alive.'

Julia feels her throat tighten at Eleanor's words.

'Oh god, don't do this to yourself. I've done enough beating myself up for all of us.' There is raw pain on his face and Julia's eyes well up.

'It's not your fault, Andy, whatever . . . whatever your dad might have said. I hope you don't mind me saying that . . .' Eleanor's voice is hoarse. 'We were talking to your mum and she told us what he said.'

He nods and briefly closes his eyes, as though shutting out a painful memory.

'Andy, you couldn't have picked her up that night, you didn't know where she was. We *knew*, and we went home.'

Andy sits forward. 'You knew she was still there?'

Eleanor looks stricken, searching for words but not finding them.

Julia waits, then realizes she's doing it again, just like she did in Donna's mother's house – letting Eleanor do all the heavy lifting, because some things are hard to say, and Eleanor is better at it.

Julia swallows and speaks up. 'No. We thought she'd gone. Anya said she'd seen her get in a cab.'

'And *had* Anya seen her?'

Julia and Eleanor look at each other. This is the subject they mostly avoid. And to Julia's mind, it's always felt like an excuse. They were all to blame, not just Anya. Even if she fudged or fibbed or lied.

'On the night, Anya said she'd seen Donna get in a cab. The following day, after we heard about the fall, Anya said she *thought* Donna had gone home. She claimed she'd never said she actually saw her get in a cab.'

'But she did say it, I remember,' Eleanor says. 'It doesn't matter now that she's gone, but she did.'

'Anya's gone? Where?'

They tell him about Anya's death and he doesn't look anything other than sad.

'It's not down to any of you,' Andy says now, his eyes damp. 'I could have saved Donna and I didn't. She rang me and . . . and she *did* say where she was and I heard her, but I' – his voice breaks off and he swallows visibly – 'I pretended I couldn't hear.' The words come out in a whispered blurt. 'I pretended I lost phone signal. That's why she went out on the roof.' He's crying openly now, tears rolling down his face. 'She went up there to phone me back, because I lied. I *did* hear her, I just didn't want to collect her. I was leaving the party, and too lazy to drive into town. It's my fault she died, and I'll live with that for the rest of my life.'

68

THEY DRIVE BACK TO Brentwood, Drew carefully navigating rain-slicked streets as he and Alastair toss theories back and forth, embracing their new roles as what Alastair is calling 'field investigators'.

In the back of Drew's car, Julia and Eleanor sit quietly. Julia is empty. Spent from crying. Sad for all of them – for Donna, for Andy, for Eleanor, for herself. For the mistakes they made. For the horrible truth that Donna's death was avoidable at multiple twists and turns over the course of that night. If Donna had stayed home, as she sometimes did. If Gabe hadn't invited them to the party. If Julia hadn't said yes. If Donna hadn't come too. If Anya hadn't lied. If Julia and Eleanor hadn't been so quick to believe. If Andy had collected her. If Donna hadn't gone up on the roof.

Eleanor reaches across and squeezes her hand. 'Poor Andy.'

'Yeah. Living with all that guilt and blame. At least he has the guts to accept his part in it, unlike Anya.'

Eleanor's eyes widen. 'Is that what you think?'

Julia stares, surprised. 'You reckon she felt some responsibility?'

'A prickly, difficult, emotionally closed-off workaholic who pushed everyone away?' A sad smile. 'She'd never say it, but I'm certain she felt responsibility.'

And somehow, this makes Julia feel even more miserable.

She tunes back in to Alastair and Drew's conversation – they want to do a more forensic (their words) examination of the videos, comparing them to details in Julia's house. They reckon someone should search the attic again. And they think Julia should seriously consider relocating the whole family some-where else, at least until this is resolved. They're keen to help, and intrigued too, she can see, in that way people are when there's drama but no personal risk. Drew pulls into Brentwood and drives to Julia's house first, telling Eleanor he's happy to drop her to her house in Dublin 4. Julia hesitates for only a moment before asking the three of them if they'd like to come in to get started on 'forensically' checking the videos.

In the house, it's Alastair who volunteers to check the attic, while Drew, Eleanor and Julia wait on the landing. Julia closes the door to her own room and sticks her head inside Isla's bed-room. Her daughter's PE gear is on the floor and, on autopilot, Julia reaches to pick it up, to get it washed for Monday morn-ing. How many times does she need to remind Isla to put it in the laundry? She stops. Above her, she can hear Alastair moving around inside the attic. And the insanity of the situation hits her. The stress of the last few months. Everything she did for Isla in San Diego. Moving her family. Setting up home. Starting a new job. Walking on eggshells. The videos. Gabe's baby. She drops the PE gear back on the floor and walks out, shutting the door behind her.

On the landing, Drew clears his throat.

'So, Julia, I've been thinking about earlier – when you called me Andy?'

Oh god.

'You thought I was your friend's brother?'

Julia feels her cheeks flush. Eleanor turns to her, her mouth a bemused 'O'.

'I'm so sorry. It's ridiculous, I see that now. But in that moment . . . obviously, Drew is sometimes short for Andrew, and you'd mentioned you used to be a gamer and that you'd changed career, and we knew Andy had changed career so . . . yeah, you must think I'm an idiot.'

Drew is laughing. 'Sorry, it's not funny, I know. But it's a lot more drama than I expected tonight. I was kind of dreading it, to be honest. The drinks thing was the girlfriend's idea – she thinks I need to get to know people here. But I'm not great at that kind of thing, and then when she couldn't make it and Shirin cried off too, it was all a bit cringe.'

'Shirin was supposed to be there?'

'She got a better offer.' He winks.

Julia has no idea what he means. Above them, Alastair is still lumbering around in the attic.

Eleanor is looking from Drew to Julia. 'Now, I don't know Shirin and I've no skin in this game, but I do love a bit of goss. So, Drew, spill. What's this better offer Shirin got?'

'OK, top secret. Julia, remember I told you Tony was worried about Shirin playing away from home?'

'Yep.'

'Well, Shirin was indeed having an affair – with Hugo, who used to live here. I only know because I do personal training sessions in her house and Hugo arrived one day while I was still there. They were both mortified. She introduced him as an old neighbour, but they were *puce*.'

'Ah, I see.'

His eyes narrow. 'You don't seem all that surprised?'

'Let's just say I've recently become aware of the relationship. Though I hadn't realized it was ongoing.'

'Rekindled in the last week, is my understanding. Cat's away, and all that. I'm telling you, lotta double standards around here!'

Julia clears her throat. 'At the risk of sounding partisan, my impression was that Shirin's affair was a one-off whereas Tony was a serial cheater.'

'Ah, yeah, I'm probably misrepresenting Shirin. Poor woman. That scan that tipped her over the edge. She could take anything but that.'

'She told you about the scan?'

'She tells me everything now.' He makes a face. '*Too* much information.'

Julia says nothing. She'll tell Shirin in person that the scan wasn't Tony's, and then Shirin can tell people the truth of that story in her own time. As for the real mother-to-be . . . Julia's stomach lurches. Gabe is a serial monogamist, falling into relationships without thinking too far ahead, falling back out of them almost as easily. But with Heather? When he was supposed to be protecting Isla? She turns away to try calling him again, but there's either no signal or he's switched his phone off.

Alastair sticks a head down from the hatch. 'Nothing here, unsurprisingly. Not even a lone AirPod, this time.' He grins at Julia. 'Will we examine the videos?'

The others nod agreement, and all four of them set themselves up in Julia's living room to study the clips. Julia opens a bottle of red wine for herself and Alastair, pours white for Eleanor, and sparkling water for Drew. After watching the videos a third time, the foursome get up to walk through the hall and the kitchen, checking the videos against the real-life items in Julia's home – the lamp, the mirror, the whiteboard, the photograph of Julia, Anya, Donna and Eleanor at their Debs.

'JADE,' Eleanor says in a reverential whisper.

'Speaking of jade,' Julia says, 'I should show you guys the paperweights too. Hang on.'

She plucks them from her handbag and lays them on the kitchen island, filling Drew in on what happened to Anya.

'One was in Anya's bathroom the night she died, and the second one, which you can see is identical, was in Eleanor's daughter's bag. And that's how we worked out it's linked to Donna – they're made of jade, and we used to call ourselves "JADE" because of our initials.'

Drew picks up one of the rabbits. 'That's not jade,' he says, 'it's green peridot.'

Eleanor tilts her head. 'Sorry?'

'Maybe I'm wrong, but the girlfriend's big into crystals and gems, and I'm pretty sure this is green peridot.'

Julia looks over at Alastair for confirmation. He shrugs. 'I know nothing about stones and crystals, but there's one other thing I'm curious about. Can I see the video again? The account name is Lepus?'

'Yes. It means rabbit, so obviously another link between the paperweight and whoever is posting the video.'

'It doesn't mean rabbit.' Alastair is shaking his head. 'Or rather, that's not the only meaning.' He picks up Julia's iPad and then the paperweight, frowning and squinting for a few quiet moments. Then he nods. 'I think you might have been on the wrong track all along.'

69

'What do you mean, wrong track?'

'Lepus means "hare" as well as "rabbit", and this figurine is a hare, not a rabbit. See the longer ears? The long legs?'

Julia stares at the figurine in his hand. The legs are curled under and she really has no idea how anyone could tell if they are rabbit legs or hare legs. The ears, now that she thinks about it, are indeed quite long relative to the rest of its body.

'OK, but even if the paperweight's a hare, and "Lepus" means hare, does it change anything? There's still a link between the account name Lepus and the paperweight, even if we're now talking about hares.' *Although no longer linked with jade*, she thinks, if Drew is right about the stone.

'True. Does hare mean anything?'

'No, nothing, no more than rabbit.'

'Wait, it does mean something,' Eleanor says, eyes widening. 'Anya. Her surname is Hase.'

Of course.

'Oh my god.' Julia nods at her friend 'The German word for hare.'

'So this is all connected with Anya,' Eleanor says.

Alastair purses his lips. 'Maybe . . .' A beat. 'There is one more thing I want to check – an idea I have about your friend and the TikTok account, and it might lead us to our guy . . . Just a hunch.'

He types something on his phone. 'It's probably nothing . . . Anyway, leave it with me.'

'But if this is all about your friend Anya, why are there videos of *your* house?' Drew asks Julia.

'There was a video of her house too, but we don't think she ever saw it.'

Drew addresses Eleanor. 'And the hare in your daughter's bag? What could that mean?'

'I don't know. Maybe it's still all connected with Donna . . .'

'But you only thought that because of a jade paperweight that turns out to be peridot,' Drew points out.

'But also because whoever's doing it is targeting all three of us,' Julia says, 'and Donna's death is what links us.'

'Is there anything else that links you, more specifically about Anya?' Alastair asks.

'No.'

Yes.

'Oh god, hang on, there is. Her business is Hase Accounting. And we've all used it at times. She was very pushy about it' – she glances over at Eleanor – 'you used it for your PR business, and Gabe used it for his Irish sales when we were living in the States.'

'And you?' Alastair asks.

'She asked for my help with a problem she had a couple of years ago and it all went sour.'

'What happened?' Drew sits on a high stool, as though settling in for a story. Alastair follows suit.

'One of her employees, a guy called Vincent Gale, was cutting out Hase Accounting, offering to do customer accounts on the side, for a smaller fee. So obviously not the biggest crime in the world, but essentially stealing clients from his employer.'

'And how did you get involved?' Alastair asks.

'Anya wanted my advice. Looking for permission to sack him, basically.'

'And he wasn't too happy with being sacked, I take it,' Drew says, scrolling his phone at the same time. He looks up. 'A bit of a leap that he'd want revenge, though, when he's the one who was stealing clients?'

'Well, you'd be surprised how often people blame everyone except themselves when things go wrong,' Julia says. 'But it was more complicated than that. He—'

Drew interrupts. 'Look!' He's holding up his phone. 'Is this your house on TikTok?'

Julia takes the phone, feeling sick. Two videos in three days? This is similar to the one from earlier in the week, but it zips past everything very quickly this time, focusing in on the photo from the Debs ball before going black.

'Who has access to your house?' Alastair asks, as Julia searches quickly for Stilwell's work number on her phone. As far as she remembers, Stilwell is on duty tonight.

'Nobody apart from Eleanor and our housekeeper. We changed the locks.'

'But maybe it's someone who *had* access, and the video was made before you changed the locks?'

'True . . .' Her call goes to voicemail and she leaves a message for Stilwell.

'Would Gabe have given a key to anyone else?' Eleanor suggests.

'I don't think so, but I can't get through to ask him anyway. His phone's out of service.'

Eleanor frowns and looks like she's about to say something else, but Drew cuts in.

'What about Hugo? He could have kept a key, right?'

Julia nods. 'I've texted Shirin to ask him.'

'Shirin might have a key herself,' Drew says. Alastair looks puzzled, having missed the news about Hugo and Shirin.

'I'll check that with her when she replies.' Julia bites her lip. 'Alastair, you may as well know too. Shirin and Hugo were having an affair. And, to add further drama, Tony had installed a fake smoke-alarm camera to spy on them, here in this house.'

Three jaws drop. Drew looks up at the ceiling. 'Is it still here?'

'No, I found it and removed it.'

Alastair rubs his chin, scanning the room. 'I wonder, are there other cameras?'

Julia hadn't considered that. But of course there might be other cameras. Jesus, the sooner they move from this godforsaken house, the better.

'Yeah, I hope we haven't said anything we shouldn't tonight – in case someone's watching, I mean,' Drew says.

'It doesn't matter. Whoever is watching shouldn't be.' Julia is resolute. 'We're not doing anything wrong, we're just trying to figure out who's doing this.'

Drew nods. 'Sure, but did we let the person know what we know?'

A good point, but there's not much they can do now.

'It's kind of terrifying,' Eleanor says, looking up at the ceiling. 'To think someone can watch you inside your house so easily.'

'I couldn't believe how simple it is to buy spyware,' Julia says. 'I googled the camera and there are so many different types, all on normal websites like Amazon.'

Drew whistles. 'Seriously?'

Alastair is nodding. 'Yeah, you can get anything you want these days. Cameras, apps, the works. I once found something called Smobik on my phone, and it turns out my ex had installed a listening app behind my back. She could hear all my phone calls.' A rueful smile. 'I have no idea what kind of excitement she thought she was going to hear but I fear I let her down.'

Julia freezes. 'Smobik, did you say?' She swipes into her apps and holds up her phone. 'Like this?'

Alastair's eyes widen. 'Oh god. I take it you didn't put that there yourself . . .'

'No. Jesus. I thought it was a game. I thought Luca had put it there. Does that mean someone's been able to listen to all my calls?'

Alastair nods. 'And read your texts. I'd uninstall it immediately.'

Julia feels sick. What has she said? Eleanor is frantically checking her own phone.

'God, that's creepy,' Drew says. 'Who would have access to your phone to do that?'

Before Julia can answer, Alastair's phone beeps with a loud notification. He frowns when he reads it, his expression suddenly apprehensive.

'It's my burglar-alarm app. The alarm's going off in my house. Crap. I'd better go back and see what's going on.' He sounds hesitant – maybe disappointed to be pulled away, or anxious, perhaps, because, as he said himself, he's not exactly a tough guy.

'Do you want me to come with you?' Drew asks.

'No, no, it's OK,' Alastair says, sounding like he means very much the opposite. 'Maybe the wind set it off . . .' He clears his throat and blows his nose. 'It's late anyway, but should we meet again tomorrow night to keep looking into this?'

'I don't want to take up all your free time,' Julia says, without conviction.

'Hey, I have zero plans for the weekend.' Alastair shrugs. 'And it's actually fun.' A sheepish expression now. 'It feels good to be part of something, if that's not a completely dorky thing to say.'

Drew punches him lightly in the shoulder. 'It is completely dorky, and that's a word I haven't heard since the nineties. Spoken like a true Goonie.'

'OK, then, let's meet here tomorrow evening. I'll get some food in.' Julia looks over at Eleanor, eyebrows raised in a question.

'Count me in.'

Julia nods, grateful to her friends, new and old, for the support, and gets up to walk Alastair out.

Drew is on his feet shrugging on his jacket when she returns to the kitchen, and Eleanor is typing a message. She looks up.

'Georgia has a temperature and Ian can't find the Calpol. I'm sorry, Juju, but I'm going to have to go too. Drew's offered to drop me home. Will you be OK?'

'Absolutely, you go. I hope Georgia's all right.'

Drew picks up his keys. 'So to summarize: we think the videos are about your group of friends, and specifically Anya's business.'

'Possibly.'

'And this employee who got fired, what was his name again?'

'Vincent Gale.' Julia sighs. 'It's branded on my brain.'

'And you were saying it was more complicated, before I interrupted you?'

'Oh yeah. I had told Anya to suspend him on full pay and carry out an investigation. She told me she would, but then she decided she didn't want to pay him since she knew he was guilty. So she fired him outright.' Julia shakes her head, still sick at the memory. 'She skipped all the steps, because she was – and I'm sorry to speak ill of the dead – a complete narcissist. She didn't think the rules applied to her.' She glances at Eleanor. *A step too far?* Eleanor's face is impassive.

Drew nods. 'Ah, I see.'

'So Vincent Gale took a case, and won. Quite rightly, I should add, even though he had been in the wrong to begin with.'

'Kinda like those stories you hear where someone breaks into a house and the owner attacks them and they sue the owner?' Drew says.

'You get the gist. Anya had to make a payout and her reputation was badly damaged. She was furious.'

'And presumably Vincent Gale, despite his win, blamed both of you.'

'Exactly. And as far as he knew, I was the one who told Anya to fire him. She said she'd got professional advice, just never told him I'd said to go through the proper steps.' *Fucking liability consultant.*

Drew looks at Eleanor. 'But that doesn't have anything to do with *you*, Eleanor – why would the paperweight be in your daughter's bag?'

'Oh, but it does.' Julia straightens up. 'My god, that's it.'

70

DREW LOOKS EXPECTANTLY FROM Julia to Eleanor.

'Does someone want to enlighten me? The team only works if we all have all the information.' He shakes his head in mock admonishment.

Julia nods for Eleanor to explain.

'Julia's right. I used Hase Accounting to wrap up my PR business. Vincent Gale offered to do it for fifty per cent of the cost, if I went with him directly.'

'Aha.' Drew nods. 'Not realizing you were friends with Anya.'

'Exactly,' Julia chimes in. 'So Eleanor told Anya, and that's what got Vincent fired.' She stops to correct herself. 'Of course, that's not what actually got him fired. He's the person who broke the rules and didn't like the consequences.'

'It's a bit much, though, to get this angry about it, isn't it? Especially if he won a case for unfair dismissal. Did he go back to work at Hase?' Drew keeps pronouncing it 'Haze' and Julia has to suppress an impulse to correct him, after years of hearing Anya insist they say 'Ha-za'.

'God, no. There's no way he could have worked there again, even if legally she had to let him. I'm sure he went and got a job somewhere else, once the court's findings came through.'

'And before that?'

'I suppose he may have struggled to get a job,' Julia concedes.

'Not easy if you've just been fired. It was on social media too. Anya put up some very thinly veiled posts, out of sheer spite. She used the word "embezzlement" even though that's not what was going on. Then she literally called every other accountancy firm in Dublin and told them he'd been stealing from her.'

'Oh. So his friends and family all knew he'd been caught stealing and sacked?'

'Yep. Pretty grim, now that I think about it.'

'Meanwhile, Anya was still running her business and you're selling yours for seven figures . . .'

Julia gives Drew a look.

A grin. 'I googled you, sorry.'

'It's true. And I'm here in this palatial home and Eleanor's in her Dublin 4 townhouse and Anya's in her . . . well, *was* in her lovely house with her boyfriend and her successful business and . . . yeah. I can see how that might grate.'

Drew is on the tablet. 'OK, let's google this guy and see if we can get an address.' He's typing now, and Julia can see newspaper articles come up, but like Andy, Vincent Gale doesn't seem to have any social media. Her phone pings with a text from a mobile number. She clicks in and finds a message from Stilwell. She's picked up Julia's voicemail, and says she and a colleague will call over tonight to check the house again, if it's not too late. 'It's not too late,' Julia replies, feeling a weight lift.

'I'd say Vincent Gale scrubbed everything once his name was in the papers,' she says to Drew, watching him scroll. 'Maybe Alastair and his colleagues can help again, like they did with Andy, or I could try Hase Accounting, see if they have an address on file.'

'If he's moved, that won't be much use . . .'

'True, but there must be some sort of legal or HR file linked to the unfair-dismissal case. It's worth a shot. Eleanor, you have a friend who works in Hase, don't you?'

Eleanor nods and checks the time. 'I'll text first thing tomorrow.' She's inching towards the door to the hall. 'I'd really better go, though. Ian says Georgia's temperature hasn't budged.'

Drew is on his phone. 'Yep, sorry, just texting Alastair to make sure he's OK.' He glances up. 'I feel like he was putting on a brave face earlier, but he looked worried about the house alarm.'

Julia nods. Something tugs at her memory. 'I wonder what he meant about the other hunch he had? Something that would lead him to figuring out who the attic guy is – is that what he said?'

'Yeah.' Drew looks at his screen. 'He hasn't seen my message yet, but I'll ask him if he replies. Right.' He puts his phone in his pocket. 'We'd better go.'

'Juju, are you going to be OK sleeping here on your own? I'd offer to stay, only I'm getting a bit worried about Georgia.'

Julia shakes her head vehemently. 'I'm not sleeping here, no chance. Stilwell and another guard are on their way over to look at the video and check the house, and as soon as they're done I'll grab a cab to go to the apartment.'

'I can come back and drive you, if you like?' Drew offers.

'No, not at all. If I can't get a cab, I'm sure the guards will drive me. That'll give the neighbours something to talk about!'

She walks them out to the front door and hugs Eleanor, holding on to her for longer than usual. The realization hits her then. Eleanor is not just 'not Anya' or 'not Donna'. She's not just the only one left. She's good and kind and loyal, and she's the best friend Julia's ever had and, somehow, during twenty years in America, she forgot this. Eleanor pulls back and smiles at her, rubs her arm and walks down the front steps. On impulse, Julia hugs Drew now too. 'Let us know once you hear back from

Alastair, won't you?' she says, glancing across at the townhouses. Alastair's alarm is no longer going off and his house is in darkness. She bites her lip. He's just asleep, no doubt. Perfectly fine.

They go and she closes the door, facing into her quiet, empty house.

71

JULIA POURS A SECOND glass of wine and sits cross-legged on the living-room couch, trying to get her head around everything that's happened. She goes back over the evening – Vincent Gale, the Smobik spyware app, the green hare. So none of this was about Donna after all. Though maybe, she realizes, it nudged her into confronting some memories she'd long pushed away. And calling to Donna's mother had been the right thing to do. Tiny silver linings. And talking to Gabe about Donna. That's progress. *Gabe.* She needs to tell him it had nothing to do with Donna. And she needs to tell him she knows about Heather. She tries his number again, this time on a WhatsApp video call, and finally, he picks up.

'Hey, all OK?' There's that wariness again, written all over his face, but now she knows why.

'I know about Heather and the baby.'

'Oh god. How?'

'Shirin found a scan the night of the barbecue – that's how she knew Tony was cheating. But it was yours, wasn't it?'

'A scan? There was no scan.'

Not 'there is no baby'; just 'there was no scan'.

'There *is* a scan, with Heather Walters' name on it, so I need you to tell me the rest.'

And so he does. As Julia listens in disbelief, Gabe tells her about fixing things for Isla. About meeting with Riley's mother a second time and a third time, to smooth things over. While Julia was busy getting ready to run away to Dublin, Gabe was busy winning over Heather. His half-formed plan was to charm her, to make it less easy for her to tell people what Isla had caused . . . to create a conflict of interests of sorts. They had coffee. Then drinks. He twinkled and charmed, and it started to work. By May, she'd said she wouldn't be taking things further, she wouldn't give Isla's name to the police or the school. And Gabe, job done, stepped away. Big mistake.

Heather accused him of ghosting her, of using her. Of becoming friends with her just to save Isla. Which, of course, is exactly what he'd been doing. She said she'd changed her mind. Riley'd had a setback at therapy, and Heather'd had a change of heart. She was going to the police after all. Hating himself, but desperate to protect Isla, he'd asked her to meet for drinks. They met in a hotel bar in downtown San Diego. They talked and drank three or four rounds of beers. Gabe played nice, easing back into the friendship, hoping she'd back down again, wondering how long it would go on, pinning his hopes on the move to Ireland – trusting it would bring the friendship to a natural end. And then Gabe, who can hold his drink, woke up in a hotel bedroom, in a hotel bed, beside Heather, with no idea what had happened. And smiling, happy, cat-that-got-the-cream Heather had photos on her phone. Nothing too bad by any standards – a morning-after selfie, with Gabe asleep and Heather nestled in his arms. But not photos he ever wanted Isla to see. Or Julia.

Julia interrupts at this point. 'Gabe, if you slept with her, I'm absolutely furious, but for god's sake, just tell me, don't make up some story about blacking out after three beers.'

Gabe shakes his head. 'I don't remember what happened, but I swear to god, Julia, my gut feeling is that I didn't sleep with her, and I didn't black out after the beers. I think she put something in my drink and set me up.'

'I'm sorry, *what*?' She remembers now, the search results. Ketamine. GHB. 'Are you serious?'

His voice crackles briefly as the call quality dips: '—put me off drinking since. You know me, Julia. There's no way I'd black out after three or four beers. But at the time I didn't realize. Then I was listening to this podcast about a UK woman who spiked men's drinks to steal from them back in their hotel rooms, and I started to wonder. And the more I thought about it, the surer I became that she put something in my beer and claimed we'd slept together.'

'Well, the baby scan suggests her claim is true . . . What happened next?'

The screen freezes for a moment and she misses the start of his sentence, but it's not hard to get the gist when it resumes.

'—pregnant. I still felt it in my gut that nothing had happened, but I didn't want to be the guy who disappears as soon as someone says they're expecting. So I offered to support her, and at the same time broke the news that we were moving to Ireland. I said I didn't want to go, but you were insisting. I needed to keep her on side. I said I'd be back for the birth, that I'd send her money.'

'The X on the calendar. February twenty-fourth was the due date?'

A nod.

'And the money?'

He looks up at her from under hangdog lashes. 'I gave her almost all my own savings, and I did make one payment for her maternity care from the joint account. The transfer marked "SB". I'd applied for a loan and it hadn't come through yet.' He bites his lip. 'And I sold the iMac.'

'God, Gabe, why didn't you just tell me, instead of all the lies? This is way too big to keep from me. As for the money – we have plenty, you didn't need to go behind my back.'

A self-conscious shrug. 'You were stressed enough. I wanted to do this myself, to protect Isla and take some of the load from you. And I really didn't want you to find out.' Gabe grimaces. 'Then that bloody Tony next door started dropping hints that *he* knew. Asking about new relationships, goading me. I couldn't figure it out. I thought maybe he'd overheard me on the phone to Heather, from his back garden, though that didn't really add up.'

Ah. 'It was the camera in the smoke detector. He could see and hear you on the phone in the hall.'

'Exactly. That's how he knew the name Siegler-Barrows. I guessed when you told me about the smoke-detector camera. Tony got great pleasure from dangling that in front of me. Is he still missing?'

'Yeah. It's like he's disappeared into thin air.'

Gabe mutters something then, and the screen momentarily freezes.

'What did you say?'

Gabe shakes his head. He looks exhausted. 'There's one other thing I have to tell you—'

The screen freezes again, and this time the call drops. She tries calling him back, by phone and on WhatsApp, but can't get through. She texts, asking him to tell her what the 'one other thing' is. God only knows what else he's done. She pours another half-glass of wine and begins googling Vincent Gale again, looking for distraction, hoping Stilwell won't be much longer. It's over an hour since she left the voicemail.

She tries Alastair's trick of checking Adverts, DoneDeal, RIP.ie, Boards.ie – anywhere she can think of beyond the usual social media platforms. But there's nothing. The couch is soft against her aching shoulders, and she leans back now, thinking. If it *is* Vincent, how is he making the videos? Has he really been coming into her house? How would he get in? He must have had access to someone with a key; there's no way in without one, she's certain. She closes her eyes and leans her head back, suddenly numb with exhaustion. Numb and foggy and blurred – the wine is getting to her. But she has to think. *Focus*. She sits up straight again and looks at her keys on the coffee table, the red 'R' key ring glinting in the lamplight. Something niggles. Something about the key ring? She reaches out and picks up the bunch of keys, staring at the metal 'R', then puts them back on the coffee table, forcing herself to think through the haze. *Who had keys?* She sends a second message to Shirin.

> Sorry to nudge but I really do need to know if Hugo gave keys to our house to anyone, when he was living here? To you, even?

As she puts her phone down, something makes her look up. A noise? From the kitchen? Not a noise. More a sense that someone is watching. She stares at the connecting doors. Through the glass, the kitchen is in darkness. Her whole body tenses, on high alert. She should get up and check. Fling open the door, flick on the lights. Chase the shadows to the corners. But she can't. She can't make herself move. And that's OK because there is nothing and nobody there. Someone may have *had* keys, but nobody does now, because Gabe got the locks changed. She lets out a breath.

She wades through more possibilities, forcing herself to concentrate. She googles Raycroft Estates, hoping for a list of employees. There are glossy headshots of directors and senior staff and, although she doesn't know what Vincent Gale looks like, he's hardly managed to turn himself into a director of a letting agency. What was the name of the temp Alastair dealt with . . .? Clive Gannet. She googles him, and a number of social media accounts from all over the world come up, but she has no idea what he looks like or if he's still working at Raycroft. She browses the results anyway, waiting for Stilwell's arrival and Shirin's reply, still processing Gabe's news, as tiredness threatens to send her to sleep right there on the couch. Who would have thought there'd be so many people called Clive Gannet, she thinks as she scrolls. It's not the most usual name. There's something about it, though. Something about the name itself that strikes her as important. She tries to order her thoughts. Had she heard it before moving here? No, that's not it. The answer nudges closer, then flits away. She rubs her eyes, trying to focus. To work it out. Clive Gannet. What is it about that name? Clive Gannet.

She jolts upright on the couch, eyes wide open.

Oh my god.

That's it.

She knows who he is.

72

JULIA GRABS A NOTEPAD and pen from the shelf under the coffee table and writes down the name, her hand shaking.

CLIVE GANNET

Then she writes another name.

VINCENT GALE

Carefully, she crosses each letter out, one by one.

She sits back, staring, not quite believing.

But it's right there in front of her eyes.

Clive Gannet is an anagram of Vincent Gale.

Clive Gannet is Vincent Gale.

Oh my god. That's how he got the keys to her house. Vincent Gale was working for Raycroft Estates as Clive Gannet. That's how he got keys, alarm codes, gate codes. Access to all areas. Julia feels euphoria wash over her. Finally the pieces are slotting into place.

He may not still work there, but surely Raycroft will have a current address, even if Hase don't. Would Alastair know anything more about him, having met him at Raycroft? Or even be able to describe him physically? It's late, but she texts him anyway.

Do you remember anything about Clive Gannet from Raycroft? Could you describe him? I've just worked it out . . . his name is an anagram of Vincent Gale!!! I think they're the same person!

There's a frisson of excitement running through her, and a little pride too. Alastair and Drew had worked out so much already – finding Andy, the rabbit that was really a hare, the jade that was really peridot, the meaning of Lepus – Julia can't help feeling glad she'd figured this part out herself.

She tops up her wine, letting the relief wash over her. If Raycroft are still employing Vincent or have a forwarding address, Stilwell can arrest him and Julia can move on. No more attic videos. No more anything. Exhausted but reassured, she rubs her eyes and sets her wine glass back on the coffee table. The red 'R' key ring glints beside it. Is that what was niggling? A link with Raycroft? That's not it, though. It's something else. Something just out of reach. Something unnerving.

As if on cue, she hears a noise from upstairs. A creak. Nothing more than the house settling, but still, the hairs on the back of her neck rise. She pulls a blanket off the back of the couch and hugs it around her, then puts on the TV for background noise, wishing Stilwell would hurry up. If only Gabe was here. Not because she needs a knight in shining armour – Gabe is most definitely not that – but for company.

On her phone, she clicks into TikTok to look at the video Drew found earlier. She goes to the Lepus account and that's when she sees it.

Another new video.

And this time it's too much.

Because this time, as she watches on-screen, she sees something new.

She sees herself.

73

JULIA'S BLOOD FREEZES AS she stares at her phone.

At the unfolding video, taken inside her house.

Her kitchen. Daytime.

And Julia, standing at the island.

Head bowed over something. Her phone, presumably.

Her back turned to whoever is filming.

Oblivious.

Her stomach lurches and she thinks she might be sick. Someone was standing ten feet from her, filming her, and she had no idea. When was it? What is she wearing? A black shift dress. Shit. When did she last wear it? She looks down at what she's wearing now – a green floral wrap dress – when did she last wear black? A week ago, maybe? More? *Fuck.* She has no idea. Were the kids here when it happened?

Suddenly, she's furious. Perhaps knowing they're on the cusp of catching Vincent Gale, there is space now for anger over fear. Or perhaps it's knowing he had been in her house while her kids were possibly there too, in broad daylight. The audacity of it galling and infuriating and terrifying.

A text comes through. Shirin has finally seen her question about Hugo.

Hugo says he didn't give keys to any neighbours. The only person he got to know while he was here was me, never met any other residents.

Shirin had added an embarrassed-face emoji, alluding to the affair, Julia assumes.

Julia takes a shuddery breath and a sip of wine. The video doesn't matter. Tomorrow this will be over.

Calmer now, she replies to Shirin.

Well, except Alastair, I've heard *all* about that bromance. But no worries, I think I have the key question figured out.

Shirin's answer comes through almost immediately.

He says no. He never met Alastair. I'm pretty sure I only met Alastair after Hugo moved out.

Julia stares at her phone. Skin prickling.

But Alastair said he was friends with Hugo? And I thought you all knew him?

Shirin replies:

No, I only met him in July, after Hugo had gone, but before we went to Sicily. What's going on?

Julia swallows.

Which house does Alastair live in?

Shirin replies:

No clue. I've only ever seen him out walking or that night in our house. One of the townhouses, maybe? 🦋

Julia casts her mind back over all of it. Alastair calling in to say he'd brought in her bins. Alastair out walking a dog. Alastair giving her a book, offering numbers for tradespeople. The vermouth. Alastair knowing her nickname. He'd had an answer for everything when she confronted him in his garden that night. But *was* it his garden? She hadn't actually seen him go inside. The house had been in darkness, and *he'd* followed *her* around the back. Did Alastair live in Brentwood at all? But he knew the gate codes, he knew how to get in and out. He'd let Eleanor in that night.

She grabs her phone and calls Eleanor.

'When you called over that night for drinks here, did Alastair let you in? He was arriving in at the same time?'

'Uh, yeah?'

'So he knew the codes?'

'Yep. Why?'

Julia slumps back in the seat. Is her imagination running away with her again? Everything is blurry. It's hard to think straight.

'He was very polite, held the gate open, but said for security he had to ask who I was visiting. I think I told you that.'

'Maybe I have this all wrong . . .' Something dawns on her then. 'Wait, did you tell him my nickname?'

'Juju? Most certainly not!' An indignant click of the tongue. 'Can you imagine if I was going around using your childhood nickname to complete strangers! A grown woman, seller of seven-figure businesses. No, you're Julia Birch to everyone but me, Juju.'

Eleanor is laughing, but Julia is not.

'You never used my nickname?'

'Absolutely not!'

'He said that's how he knew it . . . but he must have heard it somewhere else. Or seen it.' Her mind races. 'Like I thought at first – on the card you sent. Pinned to my whiteboard. I was right all along.'

'Juju, you're not making sense.'

'It's Alastair.'

'What?'

'The person making the videos. I don't think he lives here in Brentwood at all.' She tells Eleanor about the texts from Shirin.

'Jesus, you need to call the police. Why would he be doing this?'

'Because he's Vincent Gale.'

'Wait, what?'

'Think about it. It was Alastair who put it together earlier – telling us "Lepus" means hare, that the figurine is a hare, that it's all linked to Hase Accounting. He didn't figure it out tonight – he's the one who *created* the whole thing.'

'Oh my god. So Alastair's not his name?'

Julia is shaking her head. 'We had no reason not to believe him. A neighbour welcomes you to the neighbourhood, you don't think they're lying about their name or which house they live in. Jesus. Alastair O'Ryan doesn't exist.'

Something strikes Julia then. She picks up the tablet and types, holding the phone to her ear with her shoulder.

'O'Ryan. Orion. Orion is a constellation and the hare sits at his feet. And Alastair . . . Alastair means avenger.'

'OK, get off the phone and call the police. Right now. And get out of there. Stay in the apartment tonight or come stay here. Juju, I'm hanging up now so you can call the police, OK? Call me back once you're out of there and the police are on their way.'

'We changed the locks,' Julia says, and it comes out low and breathless and panicked.

'I know, but just get out of there, OK?'

Eleanor disconnects and Julia stabs at her phone to call Stilwell. Her eyes skitter about the room as her fingers fumble, her stomach churning. In front of her, on the coffee table, are her keys, and something's still not right.

The red key ring.

The 'R' for Raycroft.

The realization hits with a lurch.

They're the old keys. The ones with the Raycroft key ring are the *old* ones. Not the new ones, with the Mission Beach key ring. Yet this is the key she used to come into the house tonight. On autopilot, without thinking, she'd used her old key and dropped it here on the table. How could the old key work if the locks were changed?

Oh god.

It hits her now. The locks were never changed. The 'new' keys must be identical to the old keys. And if Alastair had a set all this time, they still work.

She's going to be sick. She needs the police. Why hasn't her call connected? She looks down. There's no call. In her haste, she's closed her Call screen.

TikTok is still open, though.

And that's when she sees the new video.

And this time, she's wearing a green floral-print dress.

The dress she's wearing right now. And she's sitting cross-legged on the couch, just as she is right now. In horror, she watches herself pick up the keys from the coffee table. Then her phone. Then her head snaps up and, on-screen, her eyes meet the camera. And she understands. He was in the kitchen, filming her through the glass doors. She didn't imagine someone watching. He was there, making this video. Oh, sweet Jesus. Here in her house, tonight. Right now. Her hands fly to her mouth, her phone slips to the floor.

And then she hears a creak.

74

JULIA IS FROZEN TO her seat, her throat paralysed, her mouth dry.

The sound is unmistakable.

The click of the latch.

The hatch swinging open.

Only not in a video now. Now it's real.

A voice in her head screams at her to move, to get off the couch, to grab her phone, to call the police, to run, to hide.

But she can't. She's immobile.

Footsteps now, soft on carpet.

Down the stairs. Stealthy. An animal stalking its prey. A hunter.

On her phone, on the floor, the video plays on a loop. Julia in her green dress, Julia filmed tonight. Inside her house. And now he's here.

With every ounce of willpower she pushes herself forward on the couch and tries to stand. Her legs are too weak, and suddenly it feels wrong. This is more than the paralysis of fear. This is something else entirely. Why can't she move? She slips forward on to the floor, on to her knees, and now she's on all fours, slumped, head bowed.

The creak of the living-room door.

With effort, she lifts her chin. And he's there. Standing in front of her. All in black.

Alastair.

He hunkers down, coming close, and a familiar smell hits her. Medicinal. Eucalyptus. Just like Luca had said.

'Feeling sleepy?' he asks, in the same perfectly normal tone he used to talk about bins and books.

'Why are you . . .? What is this?'

'You know. We worked it out earlier, didn't we? My god, but you are slow, Julia. I can't believe I had to spoon-feed you the answers. Especially when I've been leaving clues for you for four solid weeks now.'

Her mind is mush. 'Clues?'

'The AirPod in the attic, using your nickname, mentioning the vermouth, giving you the book, moving your phone, moving Isla's phone, handing you the name Clive Gannet – all of it. The most fun of all, putting the rabbit in the attic.' A low laugh. 'I enjoyed it – making you wonder, making you worry. Breathing down your neck while you slept. Like a very, *very* slow game of chess.' He reaches out and touches her chin. She flinches. 'And you were so quick to backtrack when you confronted me in the garden that night. All I had to do was look a little hurt and' – he snaps his fingers, close to her ear, startling her – 'you swallowed everything I said.'

'So . . . you're Vincent Gale.'

'The one and only.'

'And . . . and Clive Gannet?'

'That's me. I wasn't sure you'd spot the anagram, but I was thrilled to get your super-excited message to tell me you'd figured it out.'

Her stomach knots further.

'You were here when I texted?' she whispers.

A nod. 'In your bedroom, waiting to come down to see you.'

'You have keys,' she says dully.

'Yes, including a key to your bedroom balcony door. As soon as I left earlier, I came back in through that.'

'How?'

He looks pleased to be asked, ready to show off. 'I've been doing it for weeks. Climbing the garden wall to get on to the garage roof and from there to your balcony.'

She tries to follow through the fog in her brain. 'And . . . then you went up to the attic? You've been in the attic while I've been down here tonight?'

He shakes his head. 'Not this time. It wasn't worth the effort. And I needed to come down to take that final video.' A sly smile. 'I did open the hatch just now, to give you the full effect – the live version of the videos, so to speak. But I didn't go up there. I was literally sitting on your bed when you sent your delighted little anagram text.'

Her mind skitters back. How long ago had that been? Five minutes? Ten? He won't know about the texts from Shirin, but could he have heard her call to Eleanor? Does he know that Eleanor knows too? Her brain feels like cotton wool as she tries to order her thoughts. The recording app. Smobik. But no, she'd uninstalled it. And – the realization slams like a hammer – it has to be Alastair who put it on her phone in the first place. She must stay awake. She has to get out of here.

With huge effort, she slips back on to her heels and pushes herself into a sitting position, leaning against the base of the couch. Her phone is still on the floor. Did he hear the phone call to Eleanor? Not from her bedroom. If that's where he really was . . . She has no choice, she has to believe that she can keep that one card to herself. How near is her phone? She glances over again. More than arm's reach.

'How did you . . . the locksmith? I don't understand.'

'There's no locksmith, and no new locks.' He looks pleased

with himself. 'I gave Gabe my other number. The locksmith he called was me. I turned up when you were both out, brought some random tools, pretended to fiddle about for a while, and handed new keys – *supposedly* new keys – to your housekeeper. Nobody knew they were identical to the old keys.'

And beneath her fear, she feels foolish too. All of them swapping keys and using new ones for no reason at all. How easy it was for Alastair to trick them.

'But you were helping . . . helping me see if the videos were fake or real. Your colleague . . . Anya's video. The Debs photos.'

'And you swallowed it all. I saw your eyes well up when you spotted your Debs photo on Anya's wall. Guess what – it wasn't there. I edited it in.' A snort. 'Do you honestly think Anya would be that sentimental? That woman cared about no one but herself.'

She swallows. 'But why? Why are you doing all this? You won your case. Anya had to pay up.' Her words are slurring.

'I *won*, did I? I lost *everything*.'

'I don't understand.'

'You go around firing people for a living. You're the last person who'd understand.'

'You got a payout.'

'Do you really think it's as simple as that? What good is money when everything else is gone? My fiancée left me. She took my daughter. I don't ever get to see her.' He peers down at her, his face contorted. 'You *know* that, Julia, I told you that, sitting here in your house at your kitchen table. You took my job. Anya took my whole life.'

'*You* did this.' Julia's voice is ragged. 'You're the one who decided to cheat, to steal her clients.'

'Excuse me, Julia, I think you'll find *I* was the one doing the actual work. Sitting there for hours every day, hunched over a computer. Why should Anya get a cut when she wasn't even doing the accounts?'

Because that's how business works, she wants to say, except, what's the point? He's not going to listen. He's decided he's in the right and nothing will shake him.

'I had no money, I had no job, we had to leave our apartment, I couldn't afford the wedding. I lost my child. Anya, breathing down my neck, pouring salt in the wound, spreading lies, telling other firms I embezzled from her. My ex called me an embarrassment. My own flesh-and-blood daughter called me an embarrassment.' He tilts his head, mocking. 'Julia, I *told* you all of this.'

'You . . . you didn't mention *why* they were embarrassed.' She's struggling to summon the words but, somehow – fuelled by anger and hoarse with fear – they come. 'Your ex probably didn't love all her friends and family finding out her fiancé had been fired for cheating his employer.'

'See, you've hit the nail on the head. There was no reason for anyone else to know about it, but Anya leaked it on purpose. Everyone found out. Talk about kicking a man when he's down, when he's at his most vulnerable.' A slow smile. 'That's what appealed about coming into your house. *Her* house. Seeing you at your most vulnerable. Feeling my breath on your neck as you sleep in a bed or lie in a bath.'

'Oh my god. Did you . . .? Was Anya's death . . .?'

'Well, I had to take out the Queen, right?' Another smile. 'And now the pawns.'

'You killed Anya.' It comes out in a whisper.

His smile widens. 'And nobody suspected a thing. I had planned to keep up the campaign a little longer, wait for her to notice her house in the video, creep around for a bit, but that night in the bath with her bottle of wine . . . it was just too easy.

I didn't have to do much at all to hold her down. Just pushed the top of her head. No bruising, no evidence, no suspicion. A workaholic who drank too much and slipped under.' A pause. 'A bit like you, Julia.'

'What?' Everything is swimming now.

'A workaholic who drank too much and slipped under. Metaphorically in your case, no bath required. Just some crushed-up pills in a glass of wine, for a woman who couldn't cope – the stress and strain of the move, the noises in the attic, it all became too much.'

She looks at the glass of wine.

'Accidental or deliberate?' He shrugs. 'Your friends and family can debate that. I might chime in myself.' A pause. 'It won't be long now.'

Everything is fuzzy, it's hard to figure out what to say or not say, but her eyes swivel involuntarily to her phone.

Alastair follows her line of sight and picks up the phone, putting it on a high shelf above the TV. 'No chance.'

Then she remembers something good. 'Stilwell is coming. Any minute.' *The effort to get the words out.*

He's shaking his head. 'Stilwell isn't coming, Julia.'

She tries to nod. 'I phoned her. I left a voicemail. She texted.'

'You left a voicemail on her work phone – I was here when you did that, remember? But she texted you from a mobile.' He pulls a phone from his back pocket. Then another phone. He waves them in the air. 'One for Alastair O'Ryan and one for Vincent Gale.'

'*You* texted?'

'Sure did. Stilwell is nowhere near here.' He sits in an armchair, settling himself. 'I'll stay and watch. It won't be much longer now.'

Julia is tired. Slipping sideways. And then she's flat on the floor. Her limbs won't move and her mind is slowing. What has he put in the wine? She knows nothing about the kind of medication that could make her feel like this. Eleanor will know that he's Vincent Gale, and Alastair will be caught, but it will be too late for Julia. Too late for Isla and Luca. Tears slip down her cheeks and she stares up at Alastair, begging him silently.

'No, no mercy for you. You played God. You arrogant *bitch*. Who do you think you are, sitting on the other side of the Atlantic, deciding who should lose their job and their kid and their life? You should be in your kitchen, minding your own fucking kids.' He's spitting, angry. 'And rich-bitch whore Eleanor. This is on her too. No prizes for guessing who's next.'

'You were in . . . Eleanor's attic?'

'No, that was all in her head. But wait till she sees what the real thing is like.' Calmer again. A sly smile. 'Or maybe I'll go for Georgia. Anya's accident and your overdose might be harder to swallow if Eleanor dies too, so I'll go with Georgia. Her nanny spends a lot of time on her phone when they're at the playground. Getting the paperweight into her bag was a piece of cake. Just think what else I can do.'

'Please . . .'

'The paperweights were my favourite clue,' he carries on. 'The hare for Anya Hase. Except you all thought it was a rabbit, then got stuck on this whole jade thing. One of the few things I didn't know was your nickname for your friend group, but it turned out quite nicely in the end. Are you feeling sleepy, Julia? It won't be long now.'

Julia can't let this happen. And she can't have her kids come home and find her like this, dead on the living-room floor. Believing she did this. Believing – oh god, oh god – that this could somehow be down to them. That the pressure of the last months, that their antipathy towards the move, that . . . No, she cannot have her children find her like this.

A last bubble of anger surges up inside. How can she get out of this? She can't crawl, she can't walk . . . she can't get away from him, she can't get away from whatever drug is inside her body, killing her . . . Or maybe she can.

There's one small way to take some control. She puts her hand inside her mouth, touching two fingers to the back of her throat. Prodding now, harder, as her gag reflex kicks in and her stomach heaves. She tries again, and this time it works and now she's throwing up on the carpet and on Alastair's shoes, and he's leaping out of the chair, surprised and angry. It may be too late, but she had to try. If nothing else, it might show the kids that she tried. That it was a mistake, that she didn't want to die. Grief swallows her now and she collapses again on the rug, spent and broken and slipping away.

75

THE SOUND, WHEN IT comes, is like nothing she's ever heard. A roar. And a thud. A sickening thud of metal on bone, though in that moment Julia doesn't know that's what it is. Has Alastair hit her? She can't feel anything. The drug, whatever he put in her wine, has numbed her. Her eyes are closed and she's drifting away. No fight left. Another sound now. A moan. A cry. Her name. Her eyes flicker open to find Alastair at her level, staring back at her. *You've done enough*, she tells him silently, *let me go in peace*.

But there's something about his stare. Something lifeless. And then hands are on her shoulders and a voice is in her ear. Eleanor's voice. Eleanor is here. Julia needs to tell her to phone an ambulance, that there was something in her drink, that she doesn't know what it is. That she's dying. But it's OK, she realizes, because whatever else happens, her kids will know she didn't choose this, that it wasn't them.

'Ambulance.' It comes out in a mumble. 'Drugged . . .'

Eleanor understands. Through the thick fog of whatever Alastair has given her, Julia hears Eleanor on the phone, shouting her address, telling them to hurry. Eleanor, pulling Julia away from Alastair. Cradling her. Whispering her name as they wait. Maybe it's not too late. Maybe Eleanor has saved her.

Eleanor.

She closes her eyes, with one thought running through her head.

Alastair took out the wrong Queen.

76

When Julia opens her eyes, she senses safety in the hushed voices, the beep of a machine and the clean, clinical smell. She's alive. She made it. *She made it.* She tries to move her head, feeling someone beside her. Gabe. He leans forward.

'Julia? Hi.' A smile. And tears. Gabe is crying.

'Hi.' Her throat is sore, her voice is hoarse. 'The kids? Are they OK? Did they see?'

He's nodding. 'The kids are OK. Terrified, but they know you're in good hands. A very lovely doctor sat with them and told them you'd wake up and not to worry. And they believed her.' His voice cracks. 'I wasn't so sure!' A half-laugh, half-sob. 'Jesus, am I glad to hear your voice.'

'Does everyone know? That Alastair was Vincent Gale?'

A nod. 'Eleanor told the guards.'

'And they got him?'

'He didn't make it.'

'Oh.' She should feel something like sorrow or pity, but all she feels is relief.

'Yeah. Eleanor cracked him across the side of the head with the poker. She's some woman.'

'Is she OK?'

'She is. She says there are things she'll never get over, but this isn't one of them.'

'He killed Anya. Do the guards know that?'

'What? How?'

She tells him, her words coming slowly and in a whisper, her throat still sore and her head still fuzzy. Gabe is reeling.

'God. She didn't deserve that. The police want to talk to you about what happened to you, so you can tell them then. He very nearly killed you too. If Eleanor hadn't shown up . . .'

Julia squeezes her eyes shut and hot tears spill out.

'He tried to make it look like an overdose. I couldn't bear to imagine you and the kids thinking I'd been pushed into some dark place by everything that's happened . . .'

Gabe takes her hand. 'We wouldn't have thought that.'

'But you would. There was nothing to suggest otherwise. The kids would have been . . . Anyway, it's over, and they know the truth. Speaking of truth, we need to tell them about the baby. It'll be their half-sibling.'

'That's what I was about to tell you when our call dropped. It's not their half-sibling.'

She tries to sit up. 'It's not yours after all?'

'It's not anyone's – there's no baby.' He sighs. 'My gut kept telling me she was setting me up, but it was awkward. I didn't want to run from responsibility, and I was still trying to keep her from going to the police about Isla. When we moved here, I felt a bit safer and asked her for a paternity test. She said no, she wasn't going to do anything that could put her unborn child at risk.'

'I'm pretty sure there are non-invasive ways to do it?' A beep draws Julia's attention to the small locker beside the bed. Her phone is charging there, but she doesn't have the energy to check it. 'Don't they just do blood tests on the mother?'

'Exactly, and I said that, but she still resisted, and that's when I knew I was right; she was setting me up. So I got a lawyer and asked for a court-compelled paternity test. I went over for the hearing.'

The Post-it. *Date set Sept 9th*. The invoice from Gallagher and Jonas. 'Wow, OK. Go on?'

'The court ruled that she had to have the blood test, and it was supposed to happen last Thursday. Then on Friday afternoon, my lawyer called to say that Heather had walked away. Admitted there's no pregnancy.'

'But the scan?' She reaches for her phone, to show him the image.

Gabe looks perplexed. 'I've never seen this before. Shirin found it the night of the barbecue? Oh.' His face changes. 'The letter from the US, the one I got that evening . . .'

'Yeah?'

'It was from Heather. Two photos from the hotel, printed out. I hid them in a drawer when you came into the kitchen and stuck the empty envelope in my hoodie pocket. But maybe the envelope wasn't empty . . .'

'Then it fell out at the barbecue.'

'And when Alastair gave it back to me, none of us realized there had been anything in it. The scan had fallen out.'

Julia nods. 'And that's what Shirin found.'

So Heather had gone to the trouble of faking a sonogram printout to extort money from Gabe, to keep him on a string, and had inadvertently prompted Shirin and Tony's split. But after what Heather and Riley had been through, Julia feels no anger any more, only relief that one part of the story is over.

77

STILWELL COMES TO SEE Julia in hospital, to fill in the remaining gaps. Alastair O'Ryan, aka Vincent Gale, is most definitely dead and Stilwell can't say for sure, but she doesn't think Eleanor will face charges. This makes Julia sit up in bed, wincing as her stomach churns. *Eleanor could face charges?*

She bashed an unarmed man over the head with a poker, Stilwell reminds her, reading her mind. But since Eleanor believed Julia to be in imminent danger, and since Julia was indeed lying on the floor with her blood full of lethal drugs, this was a fair assumption. Still, they'd have to go through the motions.

It seems ridiculous to Julia, but boxes must be ticked, she supposes. She thinks of what Drew said, about burglars suing when they're injured during a break-in. Alastair won't be suing anyone any more, of course. This reminds her of Anya, and Alastair's unfair-dismissal case against her.

'He said he pushed Anya under the water. Was he telling the truth?'

'We'll need to interview you formally to hear what exactly he said,' Stilwell says, taking a seat on the plastic chair beside Julia's bed. 'And we'll seek an exhumation of Ms Hase's body, but there's strong indications he was telling the truth.' There's a notebook in her hand and she opens it now. 'Turns out Anya's partner's dog-walker, Eric, had outsourced his duties on a semi-regular basis, unbeknownst to' – she glances down at the notebook and flips a page – 'Chris. Alastair was the stand-in dog-walker.'

'So that's how he got a key to Anya's house?'

'Exactly. We're still investigating, but it looks like Alastair had inserted himself fairly well into Anya's life. He was in her neighbourhood WhatsApp group – using the name Alastair O'Ryan – and when Chris posted looking for a dog-walker, Alastair saw it. He didn't put himself forward, but he saw Eric's response, and that's how he knew to approach Eric, offering to help out.'

'I wonder why he didn't just put himself forward directly as the dog-walker,' Julia muses.

'Perhaps in case he'd encounter Anya face-to-face, who of course knew him from his employment with Hase.'

'Ah yes, of course.'

'So then Eric saw Alastair's face in the newspaper when his death was announced, and turned up in Blackrock Garda station to fill in some gaps.'

'At least he came clean.' Julia slips back down in the bed, tiredness overwhelming her now.

'To be honest, I think he just wanted to be part of the drama – it hadn't dawned on him that Anya was murdered, and that by giving her house key to Alastair, he was partly responsible.'

'God, yeah . . . if he hadn't handed their key to a stranger, Anya might still be alive.'

Stilwell nods. 'Eric should ideally face some kind of charges for it. He's regretting coming forward now, but eager to give us as much information as he can so we'll look more favourably on him.' Under her breath, she adds 'gobshite', and Julia almost smiles.

'Not that it matters now, but why was Eric outsourcing the dog-walking?'

'Sheer laziness dressed up as initiative. He was only giving Alastair half of what Chris was paying him and never stopped to wonder why Alastair would agree to do it for such a pittance.'

'There's an irony there somewhere,' Julia says, thinking about Alastair offering to do Eleanor's accounts for half of what Hase were charging. 'Poor Anya. That must have been terrifying for her. My god. Seeing a stranger suddenly appear in her own house, in her bathroom . . .' Julia swallows, her eyes brimming.

Stilwell nods. 'It probably hasn't sunk in, but you were very lucky not to end up with the same fate. If your friend Eleanor hadn't come over after your phone call, if you hadn't given her a key . . .' She purses her lips.

'And Alastair really was getting into our house. He was in the attic all those times.' Julia's voice drops to a whisper. 'Luca was right.'

'So it seems. We've been looking into his background since Friday night, to see where he ended up after Anya Hase fired him. He'd been temping all over the place, doing office admin mostly, because none of the accountancy firms would hire him, but he became quite the jack of all trades – working for removal companies, cleaning companies, letting agents. You might spot the theme,' she says with a grimace. 'During the summer he did holiday cover at Raycroft Estates, the letting agent for all of the rentals in Brentwood.'

'As Clive Gannet.'

Stilwell's eyebrows go up. 'Yes. How did you know?'

'I worked it out. And then texted Alastair, the person behind the whole thing,' she says ruefully.

'Right. What we can't figure out is how he knew to take a job there – how he could have known you were planning to rent in Brentwood – but we're working on that.'

'I think I know how. Through Anya's phone.'

Stilwell frowns. 'How do you mean?'

'So, I know he put a spyware app on my phone to listen to my calls, probably when he was creeping around at night.' That's how he got Isla's number too, she realizes now. 'I suspect he put the same one on Anya's phone when he was sneaking into her house with the dog-walker's key. If he did, he could listen to her calls whenever he wanted to. He would have heard Eleanor telling Anya back in June that we were moving to Brentwood, when we started viewing houses, and narrowed it down.'

'OK, that fills in a gap, thank you,' Stilwell says, with a pen lid in her mouth, as she notes the new information.

'And once he was working there, he had access to the keys to our house and the alarm code.'

'Yes. Letting agents are very careful with keys generally, making sure not to mix them up or give out the wrong set to the wrong person, but of course, it's the *staff* who manage all of this, and if you've got a bad apple among your staff . . . It wasn't difficult for Vincent – Alastair – to sneak a set of keys and get one cut. We found a whole drawer full of keys at his flat. It looks like he was covering all the bases before he knew which house in Brentwood you'd take. You viewed a few, I think?'

'Yeah, four. Gabe really wanted one there because of the studios out back, and for the safety of a gated complex. So much for the safety,' she adds grimly.

'Indeed. It was easy for Alastair to wander around, acting as though he lived there. Nobody ever really questions why someone with a small dog is walking around a housing estate – it's the most natural thing in the world. It wasn't even his dog. Just one he walked for its real owner, to give him an added air of legitimacy.'

'People trust people with dogs.'

'They do. There's an inherent belief that dog people are good people.'

Julia heaves a sigh. 'I'm such an idiot.'

'Oh look, he had everyone fooled. We spoke to your neighbour, Shirin Hudson – she absolutely believed he lived there, and so did Drew Redking. We trust our neighbours. Especially in nice, safe, luxury gated complexes like Brentwood. If he'd stuck out in any way, seemed like a troublemaker, it would have been different.'

'I hear you. I let my preconceived notions about what criminals look like cloud my judgement.'

'Don't beat yourself up.' Stilwell shrugs. 'Why would you think otherwise?'

That's the thing, Julia realizes now. She *had* thought it was Alastair. She'd confronted him. But he'd had an answer for everything and, looking back, her guilt over accusing him had made her keen to make up for it and even more predisposed to trust him, to let him in. To team up, as Drew would say.

'So that night, Friday night, he pretended his house alarm was going off, left, and then let himself back in when the others were gone?'

'We don't know the precise timings, but yes, he let himself back in at some point, and having texted you pretending to be me, he knew you'd wait there for me, even after the others had left.'

'He'd spiked my wine earlier, I guess?' Julia shudders, remembering how it felt, that dull, heavy sense, that loss of control, that inability to move. Lying on the floor, flat on her face, waiting to die.

'Exactly. Zopiclone.'

'What is that?'

'Sleeping tablets. He crushed them up and put them in the wine when he opened it. You and he were the only ones drinking the red, from what your friend Eleanor has told us, and Alastair didn't actually drink his.'

'Sleeping tablets and wine. Everyone would have thought . . .'

'Yes.'

For a moment, Julia is quiet. Thinking about sliding doors and the late-night call to Eleanor and what would have happened if Eleanor hadn't picked up the phone. Or if Eleanor had stayed in the safety of her own home. *Thank you, Queen*. Julia closes her eyes.

'As if I'd have done anything else!' Eleanor says, two hours later, when Julia thanks her in person. Julia's sitting up again, with two pillows behind her, feeling slightly less nauseous than she did during Stilwell's visit. Now it's Eleanor on the plastic chair. She's wearing a Reiss dress and Gucci boots, hospital visits clearly falling into the non-casual-attire column. At her feet, there's a tote bag filled with a giant Toblerone, a box of Skelligs chocolates, a sharing pack of O'Donnells salt and vinegar, three new paperbacks and a copy of *Red* magazine. *If Carlsberg did hospital visits*, Julia thinks.

'Um, Eleanor, no offence, but you wouldn't have been the first person who sprang to mind as a poker-wielding white knight. You literally made me stay in your house when you heard a creak from your attic,' Julia says, laughing, and the laugh quickly turns to tears.

'Oh, Juju, don't cry.' Eleanor touches her arm. 'I let one friend down long ago. I wasn't going to do it again.'

'We all let her down.'

'I know. And we can't change that, but we *can* be there for each other.' She takes Julia's hand and squeezes it. 'And now we are.'

78

JULIA'S BEEN HOME FOR six short hours when the drama kicks off again. This time in the shape of Isla. She bursts in the door from school and flings herself into Julia's arms. Julia, who is resting on the living-room couch, topples sideways, but Isla is sobbing and seems not to notice.

'Isla! What is it? Tell me!'

Gabe, who's been taking care of Julia, comes rushing in from the kitchen.

'What's going on?'

Julia hugs Isla, peers over her shoulder and mouths 'no idea' to Gabe.

The sobs slow. Her breathing slows. She sits up and wipes her eyes.

'Tell me. I'm worried now. Did something happen at school?'

'My friends back in the States messaged me. It's about Riley.'

Julia freezes.

Gabe puts his hand over his mouth and shakes his head. He was always less sure than she was about keeping the truth from Isla, and Julia sees it written all over his face – he doesn't want this burden of guilt on Isla any more than she does.

'OK, we need to talk this through. It's absolutely horrific. But you couldn't have known this would happen.'

'Mom.' She's sitting up straight, her knee touching Julia's. 'Riley's back in school and she's been telling everyone.'

'OK. But we're here, far away from the gossip, and we'll deal with it.'

'Riley's *bragging*.' Her eyes flash.

'Bragging?'

'About how her mom made up a story so good it forced you to leave town. To leave the country.'

'Made up . . .?'

'Is it true? Did Riley's mom tell you some guy – some adult *man* – turned up at her house and . . . and attacked her? And she had to go to some kind of hospital?'

'Yes.'

'Oh god, Mom, you should have told me. It's not true.'

Julia is confused. 'Which bit's not true?'

'I messaged this boy she'd been texting.' She holds up a hand. 'I know, I know, I shouldn't have done it. But that's all. Nothing else happened. She saw my message and showed her mom and her mom went crazy, said imagine if he wasn't a twelve-year-old, imagine if he was a paedophile, and now he had their address and imagine if he turned up, and then she decided to teach our family a lesson.'

'What. The. Fuck.'

'Mom!' A weak smile. 'I thought we weren't allowed to swear!'

'This is a legit swearing moment. Heather made it up? There was no man?'

'No man. And it's even worse because not only did she do that to you and make us move country, but god, false claims like that just make it harder for everyone. For actual victims.'

Julia knows this and she agrees, but, really, all she can feel right now is intense relief because Riley is OK.

Gabe has a fist to his mouth, his eyes damp with emotion.

'Are you sure?' he asks. 'Riley is OK?'

Isla nods. 'They sent me a video. Riley bragging about the awesome trick her mom pulled on those dumb Sheehy-Birches. I'm so mad.'

Julia squeezes her daughter's hand, but she's not mad. She's just relieved.

'Wait, then, where's she been? Her mom said she was in hospital.'

'In her dad's house. Her mom got sick of dealing with her.' Hand on hip now. 'I did tell you that.' Tears are still slipping down her cheeks. 'I suppose it means we can move back to San Diego . . .'

Julia bites her lip but nods. That's a battle for another day.

'But maybe not until after next Friday,' Isla continues. 'Some of the girls in my class are going to Starbucks in Stillorgan after school and they invited me.'

Julia smiles. 'OK, not until after Friday.'

'And I have a soccer match the weekend after next. Our school team's entered a big cup tournament for the first time, apparently.' She shrugs. 'And the coach said I'm the best goalie they've ever had.'

'We'll let you play the match before we move country.'

Isla smiles now too, looking down at her hands. 'We can think about it after Christmas.'

'Sounds good.'

A whisper now. 'Mom, I'm sorry. I'm so sorry for everything. The way I was with you. I didn't mean it. I didn't—'

Julia cuts her off, pulling her into her arms. 'It's OK. I'm your mother. It's my job.'

After

JULIA QUITS HER JOB. Not the mother-job. The making-people-redundant job. She knows that *somebody* has to do it, but it doesn't have to be her. She's done her time. She's thinking of starting a new business, working for herself again.

But first, Eleanor and Julia have something more important to do. They call to Donna's mother. They apologize for what happened that night, and for not staying in touch. All three of them cry. Then they tell her the news. They've found Andy. Would she like them to ask him to meet? She would, she says. She doesn't want to get her hopes up, she tells them, but it's all there – in her voice, in her eyes, in the clasping and unclasping of her hands. Hope.

Eleanor and Julia call to Andy. They apologize again for what happened to Donna. And all three of them cry. They tell him his mother would love to meet him. They wait, in hope. And he says yes. She might like to meet her grandson, he says. He's nine already. Too much time has been wasted. You can't change the past, but you can change the future. He'll call her himself. And he does.

Julia installs a dating app on her phone. Then she thinks about the couples she's encountered recently – Gabe and Heather, Shirin and Tony, Anya and Chris, Alastair and his ex – and she deletes the app. She doesn't have time anyway, between setting up a new business and attending Isla's soccer matches and hosting Luca's playdates. She and Andy have introduced their nine-year-olds. The boys bonded over *Mario* and *Roblox*, so Julia and Andy arranged a weekly playdate. And she and Andy have fallen into the habit of hanging out during the playdates, even though the boys definitely don't need two adults present. And now Andy's suggested they all go for pizza together, and as Julia surveys her wardrobe, she wonders how she feels about that. Good, she decides, she feels good.

Lynn continues her quest to find out who Anya had been seeing behind Chris's back. Leave it, Chris says; it doesn't matter now. She's gone. Eleanor and Julia agree; so does Lynn's husband, Glyn. But Lynn is determined. She searches and trawls and scrolls through Anya's social media. She quizzes her employees. She gets hold of her date diary. She's like a dog with a bone. And then, deep in the darkest corner of Anya's Instagram, she finds her answer. More precisely, she finds her husband. And Lynn and Glyn are no more.

Tony Hudson is still missing. Shirin still doesn't care. Her theory? He had someone else on the go, as well as Molly. Someone he's quietly shacking up with now. She feels a little bad about the baby-scan fiasco, now that Julia's pointed out the 'Heather Walters' name on it and explained who Heather Walters is. But not *too* bad. Cheating is cheating, after all. And with Hugo moving in, she doesn't have time to worry about Tony ever again.

Tony Hudson's work colleague comes home from Dubai after a call from gardaí; his mobile home in Skerries is nothing more than a pile of rubble. A body has been found inside, authorities tell him. Could he shed any light? Who had a key?

Nobody, he says. Although, there was a key kept under a planter by the bottom step.

Who knows about the key? the police ask.

Quite a few people, it turns out. Even four work colleagues who'd come over to play poker one night. Three had come back regularly, but one had declined. The mobile home was a bit 'grim', he'd said. A far cry from his house in Sicily. Tony Hudson was his name. Had he let himself in, perhaps?

It seems he had, the police say, putting the pieces together now that they know whose body they've found. Tony Hudson had fled to his colleague's mobile home in Skerries, when Shirin kicked him out.

What caused it? wonders Tony's work colleague.

The forensic team have an answer for that. A domestic appliance. A fire. An explosion.

Tony's colleague is worried then. Is he to blame? Something wrong with the wiring? No, nothing to do with the wiring, they reassure him. Strangely enough, the explosion was caused by a faulty coffee machine, they explain. A big, expensive, top-of-the-range machine that Tony had brought to the mobile home himself.

Meanwhile, in San Diego, Heather and Riley keep doing what they're doing – bullying, manipulating, lying, gaslighting – because that's so often how it goes with people like Heather and Riley; they get away with it. At least for a time. But eventually, when they least expect it, karma steps in and they get their comeuppance. Because sometimes life is fair.

Julia and Gabe and Isla and Luca stay in Dublin, but not in Brentwood. They move to an older house in Stillorgan – one with more character and fewer ghosts. And no gates. Gabe has to use a spare room for his art as there's no studio in the garden, but with his Heather dilemma over, he's painting more than ever. He's got his first ever exhibition in an Irish gallery and he's become good pals with Andy. Isla's soccer team are through to the semi-final of the cup and she figures she may as well stay for the year. Or perhaps all six years of secondary school, now that she's made friends. Then she'll see.

Luca finds pizza in Dún Laoghaire that's almost as good as the pizza in San Diego and he's not seeing eyes in the vents of their new house. Once his parents acknowledge that he was right all along, he's happy to stay. And Basil settles very well in this new home, with no more trips to the attic.

The new house is always full of people. Andy and his son. Gabe's new girlfriends, plural, though never concurrent. Isla's first boyfriend and, later, Isla's first girlfriend. Luca's pals from school. Isla's soccer team. Eleanor and her kids. Julia's new friends from yoga. Shirin and Hugo and Drew. Donna's mother. Julia's parents. Her sister, home from Perth, her brother, home from Jakarta.

In their new home, there is no one in the attic, but to Julia's great joy, there is always someone in the house.

Acknowledgements

THANK YOU TO MY amazing editors, Finn Cotton in the UK, Jeramie Orton in the US and Bhavna Chauhan in Canada, who were so easy to work with and so brilliant at shaping the story. Thank you to Tom Chicken, Emily Harvey, Louise Blakemore, Phoebe Llanwarne, Bronwen Davies, Cara Conquest, Lucy Keeler, Catherine Wood, Lucy Beresford-Knox, Becky Short, Jennifer Porter, Rich Shailer, Vivien Thompson, Sarah Day, and all at Transworld and Penguin UK who worked on *Someone in the Attic*.

At Penguin US, thank you to Sara DeLozier, Rebecca Marsh, Christine Choi, Mary Stone, Nicole Celli, Tricia Conley, Tess Espinoza, Diandra Alvarado, Matt Giarratano, Nick Michal, Jason Ramirez, Julianna Lee, Claire Vaccaro, Jane Glaser, Brian Tart, Andrea Schulz, Kate Stark, Patrick Nolan and the entire sales team.

At Doubleday Canada/PRH Canada, thank you to Kristin Cochrane, Amy Black, Val Gow, Kaitlin Smith, Chalista Andadari, Maria Golikova, Kate Panek, Sarah Howland and Robin Thomas.

Big thanks to Jessica Regan, who does a superb job narrating my audiobooks – she narrated my last three, but at the time I was writing the acknowledgments for each book, I didn't know who would be narrating. So this time I'm getting in early – hi, Jessica, and thank you!

ACKNOWLEDGEMENTS

Thank you to my superstar literary agent, Diana Beaumont – none of this would be possible without you. And thank you to my TV and film agent, Leah Middleton – nothing brightens up a day like an email from a TV agent!

Thank you to Professor Alan Smeaton for answering my tech and data questions. When I wrote *Someone in the Attic*, I had a vague idea of what 'getting an IP address' meant. Oh, how wrong I was. Thanks to Alan, my makey-uppy version did not make it into the book. If anyone would like to know how it really works, I can give a TED Talk on it now. (But Alan's would be much, much better, and, of course, any remaining errors are mine.)

Thank you to everyone who put me in touch with their garda contacts and to the gardaí who kindly gave their time to further explain what exactly happens if someone is posting creepy videos that look like they were filmed in your house: Caroline, Mary, Florence, Mike G, John S and Anne-Marie O'F.

Thank you to my very good friend Emily O'Neill, who read a draft to advise on a specific plot point and helped come up with a more accurate solution. Emily, I owe you a big glass of white wine xx.

Thank you, Trina Beakey Wise, for the insider info, yet again.

Thanks to Norah, Laragh and Alice for the tips on rabbit ownership – Basil is named in honour of your lovely Basil.

Thank you to my sisters Nicola, Elaine and Dee for reading early drafts, spotting mistakes, helping me with questions about how to murder people, and saying 'yes' every time I ask if we can have a night out. Thank you, Dad and Eithne, for buying so many copies of my book when it comes out, and also for always being good for a night out!

Thanks to my lovely school-gate author pals and aspiring bon vivants, Amanda Cassidy and Linda O'Sullivan. It has been life-changing to find my local-local gang.

ACKNOWLEDGEMENTS

Thank you to all my writing friends for your ever warm, funny and fun company – I won't name names because I'll forget people, but there was a lot of craic this year at Harrogate, Murder One, Red Line, DNLF and Spike Island, plus some stellar conversations over Brie and rosé around a variety of well-stocked coffee tables.

Thank you to the fabulous community of readers and reviewers on Instagram for your incredible support and your beautiful book photos. Thanks to Sinéad Cuddihy of the Tired Mammy Book Club, to all the lovely Booksta gang I met this year and last year, and to the members of BookPunk for all your kindness. Special shout-out to the Boozy Table 2023 – anyone for one more Campari spritz?

Thank you to my Sion Hill besties for your friendship and cheerleading. I couldn't ask for better pals and I'm not sure I could handle the work-from-home-alone world without our WhatsApp chats and nights out.

Lots and lots of love to Damien, Elissa, Nia, Matthew and, of course, Lola.

And thank you, dear reader, for reading this book.

If you loved *Someone in the Attic*, look out for
Andrea Mara's unputdownable new thriller . . .

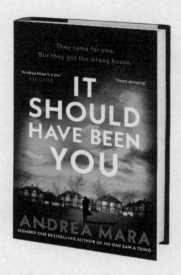

**They came for you. But they
got the wrong house . . .**

Coming soon and available to pre-order now.
Keep reading for an exclusive early extract . . .

Prologue

I HAVE TO KILL my sister.

I can't. I can't do this.

I glance across the kitchen.

I have to. I have no choice.

My face is wet, my throat is bone dry. There's a buzzing inside my head, the sound of abject terror.

'Do it,' my sister says, in a croaky whisper, as if it's that simple, as if killing her is something I can do.

She's my family, my blood, one of the three people I love most in the world.

Tears slide down her face. Greta never cries. She's the strong one, the practical one. And now I have to do something unforgivable.

From outside comes the sound of fireworks. The Oakpark summer party. Our neighbours eating and drinking on the green, oblivious to what's happening in my kitchen.

'I love you so much.' My voice is hoarse, my limbs are loose. 'I'm so sorry.'

The sky lights up with fireworks as she rolls up her sleeve.

My throat contracts with grief.

I lean towards her, Death come to take her. A sob lurches through me.

The syringe feels like nothing. It should feel cold or hot or heavy, something to signify the power it holds, but it doesn't. It's light and nothingy. I glance around the kitchen one more time. How is this happening? Everything looks just as it always does. The scratched wooden table of our childhood, the blue painted cupboards, the knotty hardwood floors.

My hand shakes as I inch the tip of the needle towards my sister's vein. She closes her eyes.

'I'm sorry,' I say again, and push the syringe, flooding her blood with poison.

To my horror, it's instantaneous. As the dusky sky lights pink and gold to the pop of fireworks, Greta slips sideways and slides off the chair. Her prone figure on my kitchen floor. In seconds, it's over.

Ten days is all it took for my world to implode. Ten days, four deaths, one teen in hospital, one in police custody, and my family destroyed.

And all because of a text.

1

Tuesday, ten days earlier | Susan

HAVE YOU EVER DONE something stupid – something unintentional, acting without thinking? You have, I'm sure, we all have. And then afterwards, you pull at your hair and wonder why you didn't slow down and think first? Of course, by then, it's too late. The damage is done.

This is about my mistake.

And it starts with a screenshot. Well, a screenshot accompanied by an uncharacteristically mean message. At least, I like to *think* it was uncharacteristic. Maybe that's just something I tell myself, because I got caught. But when it all kicks off, I'm not thinking at all. I'm cranky and sleep-deprived and ready to do battle with anyone crossing my path. That's a metaphorical path – I'm at home on my couch, under my four-month-old baby, staring at a just out of reach cooling cup of tea. The walls have been closing in over the last few weeks and I'm irritable. Missing my pre-baby structure, the outside world, the old me. And every time that thought bobs to the surface, the guilt sets in. My beautiful Bella. I adore her, of course I do, but still. I miss . . . me. And I'm tired. Have I mentioned the tired? The up-six-times-a-night tired? *Nothing* prepares you for it. And last night was a bad one. And then of course Jon is at work all day (which is fair, he has to go to work) and I'm trying to get Bella to nap and she won't and it's hard. And I'm a little scared too in the last few weeks, just a little, that things will go back to how they were when Bella was born. Back when I didn't cope very well at all.

So yeah, I'm cross and sleep-deprived and ready to do battle and that's when I see the message in the Oakpark WhatsApp group. Oakpark – where we live – is a huge housing estate built in the sixties, with criss-crossing roads and cul-de-sacs and about three hundred members in the neighbourhood messaging group. It's very useful for passing on furniture and borrowing hedge trimmers. It also has occasional open-the-popcorn dramas when something kicks off. I secretly like those moments.

I never planned to cause one.

The message is from Celeste Geary, mistress of pointy comments. Badly parked cars and barking dogs are her pet peeves but this evening, it's about WhatsApp group etiquette. Another resident has shared information about a local business loaning glasses for next week's Oakpark summer party, someone else has thanked them, and I've chimed in with my thanks too. (I'm trapped under a baby, so responding to people on WhatsApp is one of my top three hobbies.) Celeste's missive comes up moments later:

> 'General note: there's no need for multiple people to thank everyone who posts, the group has 300 members, and we all lead busy lives. I appreciate that some are busier than others but please think before you type.'

She's not even the admin of the group, she just takes it upon herself to write posts like this. I read her message again and my cheeks flame. As the second and only other responder, I'm clearly the target. The 'busier than others' part, a dig, no doubt, at my maternity leave, or maybe even my job. I'm a teacher. And nothing annoys people more than the supposedly short hours teachers work. Celeste, something big in a bank, with her frequent travel and airtight schedule, hadn't taken more than a minute's maternity leave when her kids were born. That's according to my sister, Greta, who's lived in Oakpark her whole life. And it's Greta and my other sister, Leesa, I text, with a screenshot of Celeste's message, my cheeks still hot:

> 'omg she's such a smug wagon. I'd love to send her the pics of her husband sleazing over the PR girl at the opening party for Bar Four. Or tell her that her bratty daughter bunks off school to see her boyfriend every chance she gets. And that everyone knows she covered up what her son did to the Fitzpatrick toddler. That would wipe the pass-agg smile off her face. Urgh. I know. I'm awful. I just needed to get that out of my system.'

I throw the phone beside me on the couch, and let out an irritated sigh. Everything is annoying me. This room, where I now spend most of my time. The deep blue walls that looked so good when we first painted them. The velvet ochre couch that cost a small fortune. The cooling cup of tea on the coffee table, mocking me. At this point, the south Dublin water pipes are mostly filled with my cold tea. In the crook of my left arm, Bella nuzzles in, her tiny eyelashes fluttering in sleep. Seven o'clock. Sleep this late is a terrible idea, but god, I can't bring myself to wake her.

Beside me, my phone buzzes and at the same time, I hear the sound of the front door. *Oh, thank god*. Now Jon can take the baby, and I can get a shower or do laundry or any one of the myriad things I've dreamt of doing all day. Imagine dreaming of doing laundry.

My phone buzzes again as Jon comes through to the living room. His eyes crinkle into a smile and he bends to kiss the top of my head, sweat glistening on his forehead from his post-work run. Running is new. He started about six weeks ago and has become completely obsessed. He's already lean and wiry, so I don't think it's a fitness concern, despite what he claims – I have a sneaking suspicion it's a response to Bella's birth. A kind of early mid-life crisis, a sense that he's suddenly adult and old. If you could see him, you'd laugh at that – he's thirty-eight, but with boyish looks and a bouncy energy that make him seem much younger. I get it though. Having Bella has changed both of us.

'How're my girls?'

'OK.' I wriggle forward on the couch until I can stand, trying not to disturb Bella, then pass her into Jon's arms.

'Oh, I was going to shower first and—'

I cut him off. 'No chance, I've been waiting for a shower since this morning.'

He knows better than to argue. That's when my phone begins to ring. Nobody ever rings. Greta, Leesa and I text all day, my friends text, my mother-and-baby group send voice notes, because nobody has time to type. I turn over the phone. Greta's name flashes on screen.

'Hey, what's up?'

'Your message. Delete. *Delete!*'

Greta is the calm one, so to hear her shrieking down the phone unnerves me.

'What? Why?'

'Your message about Celeste. You sent it to the whole Oak-park group. I've been texting you. Delete!'

Fuck. Fumbling, I click into WhatsApp. Oh god. In the pit of my stomach, everything flips. Greta is right. My blood runs cold. I've sent my bitchy message about Celeste to the entire group. *No, no, no . . . please say I'm wrong.* My words stare back at me. I'm not wrong. I've sent it to all three hundred members. Including Celeste.

'Susan, make sure you click "Delete for everyone", not just "Delete for me" or it'll be there forever!' Greta is shouting down the line.

All fingers and thumbs, I hit delete. How many people have seen it? Has Celeste seen it? *Shit. Shit. Shit.*

Greta is still on the line, her voice distant, barely audible through the blood pounding in my ears. Jon is asking what's wrong and Bella is awake and beginning to cry. Before I can process or explain what I've done, I manage to knock my full cup of cold tea all across the living room floor. *Oh for god's sake, can things get any worse?*

As it happens, things are about to get much, much worse.

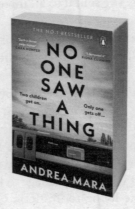